The
Lost
English
Girl

Also by Julia Kelly

The Last Dance of the Debutante

The Last Garden in England

The Whispers of War

The Light Over London

The Lost English Girl

Julia Kelly

G

GALLERY BOOKS

New York   London   Toronto   Sydney   New Delhi

G

Gallery Books
An Imprint of Simon & Schuster, Inc.
1230 Avenue of the Americas
New York, NY 10020

First Gallery Books hardcover edition March 2023

GALLERY BOOKS and colophon are registered trademarks of Simon & Schuster, Inc.

For information about special discounts for bulk purchases, please contact Simon & Schuster Special Sales at 1-866-506-1949 or business@simonandschuster.com.

The Simon & Schuster Speakers Bureau can bring authors to your live event. For more information or to book an event, contact the Simon & Schuster Speakers Bureau at 1-866-248-3049 or visit our website at www.simonspeakers.com.

Interior design by Jaime Putorti

Manufactured in the United States of America

10 9 8 7 6 5 4 3 2 1

Library of Congress Cataloging-in-Publication Data

Names: Kelly, Julia, 1986– author.
Title: The lost English girl / Julia Kelly.
Description: First Gallery Books hardcover edition. | New York : Gallery Books, 2023.
Identifiers: LCCN 2022046196 (print) | LCCN 2022046197 (ebook) |
    ISBN 9781982171704 (hardcover) | ISBN 9781982171728 (ebook)
Subjects: LCSH: World War, 1939–1945—England—Fiction. | World War,
    1939–1945—Evacuation of civilians—Fiction. | World War, 1939–1945—
    Children—Fiction. | Families—Fiction. | Liverpool (England)—Fiction. | LCGFT:
    Historical fiction. | Novels.
Classification: LCC PS3611.E449245 L67 2023 (print) | LCC PS3611.E449245
    (ebook) | DDC 813/.6—dc23/eng/20221019
LC record available at https://lccn.loc.gov/2022046196
LC ebook record available at https://lccn.loc.gov/2022046197

ISBN 978-1-9821-7170-4
ISBN 978-1-9821-7172-8 (ebook)

For Arthur

The
Lost
English
Girl

Viv

January 16, 1935

On the morning of her wedding, Viv Byrne cried.

It should have been simple. All she had to do was keep her head down, walk into the registry office, and say the words that would make her Mrs. Joshua Levinson. Then everything would be okay, just like Joshua promised.

However, sitting in her pearl-gray dress, none of it felt that simple.

Her bedroom door opened, and she met her sister's eyes in the mirror. "Are you all right?" Kate asked.

Viv let her gaze shift to her own reflection. She hardly recognized the eighteen-year-old woman staring back at her with tear tracks streaking down red cheeks. She'd never thought of herself as particularly pretty not like Kate, whose bright smile could illuminate half of Liverpool—but now she felt puffy, dowdy, and tired. Slow tears began to trickle down her face again.

"Oh, Vivie," Kate sighed, closing the door behind her. "Don't cry. Remember, this is a good thing."

Viv nodded, miserable. Yes, this wedding was a good thing—one she wanted—but it wasn't exactly as though she had a choice.

Kate placed her hand on Viv's shoulder. "Just think, soon you'll have your own home. You'll be able to decide who you do your shopping with. You'll be able to choose your laundry day." Her sister leaned in, a mischievous smile on her face. "You'll be able to play the wireless whenever you like."

Viv gave a watery laugh.

"That's my Vivie," murmured Kate. "Now, let's put your hat on."

Her sister brushed Viv's thick, light brown curls and then carefully placed the little gray hat on the crown of her head and pinned it into place.

"There," Kate announced. "You look perfect."

"I don't feel perfect."

Kate clucked her tongue. "Have you been ill?"

Viv shook her head.

"Lucky you. I was sick as a dog with Colin and William," said Kate.

"But not Cora," said Viv, as her sister fished around in her good black leather bag and pulled out a tube of lipstick.

Kate applied red to her Cupid's bow. "Well, Cora's always been a doll."

Viv couldn't help but smile at the thought of her golden-haired niece.

"Maybe I'll start wearing lipstick when I'm married," she said.

Kate capped the tube with a grin. "That's the spirit. Just make it through today, and you'll be free of Mum's rules."

No matter how much her mother disapproved of this wedding, Edith Byrne wouldn't be able to control a married daughter no longer living under her roof.

"Are you hoping for a boy or a girl?" Kate asked.

Viv, who had stood to begin collecting her things, froze with one arm in her navy coat.

"Vivie . . . ?"

Finally, she whispered, "No one's asked me that."

Kate's lips twisted. "We've all made this awful for you, haven't we?"

"Mum and Dad were never going to approve. Mum especially."

Growing up, theirs had been a house of rules. Go to church. Only speak to the people Mum approved of. Never do anything "common."

Viv had always struggled to follow the rules to the T. She went to church every Sunday, but rarely did a service go by without Mum jabbing her in the side to stop her from daydreaming. Viv had started to work at sixteen, but not as a nurse as Kate had done but rather in a postal office, where Viv might meet any manner of girl. She was getting married, but only because she'd fallen pregnant.

"Mum and Dad will soften as soon as they have another grandchild." Kate hugged her. "You're going to make a wonderful mother."

"Thank you," she whispered into her sister's neck.

"Now, are you ready?" Kate asked.

Viv looked around the childhood bedroom the sisters had shared until Kate married. Never again would it be home. She and Joshua would live in the flat above his family's shop, just as soon as the tenants left. She would need to find a new greengrocer, butcher, and baker to do all of her shopping. She wondered whether Joshua would want to keep kosher as his parents did.

Panic clawed at her throat. She should know a detail like that, but she hadn't even *met* her future in-laws.

"Whatever it is you're thinking, stop it," said Kate, taking on a firmer tone than she had with Viv all day. "It won't do you any good."

"You're right. You're right." She lifted her chin and, with a confidence she did not feel, said, "I'm ready."

The sisters made their way down the creaking stairs to the entryway of their parents' house. In the lounge, which was hardly ever used, sat Dad in a somber suit, his hands braced on either knee. Mum, small and stout, perched on the edge of the floral sofa that was her pride and joy. No one wore smiles in this room.

Kate's husband, Sam, peeled off the entryway wall and reached for his wife as soon as Kate passed. Kate leaned into him, and Viv wished that she had someone to do the same.

"Right." Dad rose and crossed the sitting room to join them. "Best have it over and done with."

Mum stood and straightened the hem of her charcoal suit jacket. Viv thought maybe she'd escaped her mother's scrutiny, but Mum's gaze fell on her stomach and then cut away. Then, sure as clockwork, Mum touched a handkerchief to her eyes.

"A daughter of mine married, and not even in white. I never thought after Flora . . ."

Viv clutched her handbag's handle a little harder. Flora, Viv's aunt, was the family cautionary tale. The beloved sister who fell for a Protestant man who up and left as soon as Flora told him she was pregnant, condemning her to a hard life and the family to the weight of a daughter's shame.

"Mum, this is not the day," Kate warned.

"Am I supposed to be happy? He's *Jewish*," said Mum with a sniff.

Sam nudged Kate, prompting his wife to sigh. "Let's just go. We're going to be late."

Viv wished the floor would open up and swallow her whole.

In the back seat of the car Sam had borrowed from a mate at work, Viv hunched her shoulders, doing her best to hold herself away from Mum.

She'd known the rules for as long as she could remember: fornication was a sin, but if she sinned, let it be with a Catholic boy who would have the good sense to marry her or at least had a family who would force him down the aisle. Whatever it took to give Viv and their child the veneer of respectability.

In her mother's eyes, Joshua failed on all points. Not only had he gotten her daughter into trouble, he wasn't Catholic. He was Jewish, and to her mother, that was as bad as being a Protestant.

All through the excruciating drive from Ripon Street to St. George's Hall in the city center, a rising scream lodged in Viv's throat. She wanted to wrench open the car door and run fast and far. Anything to stop the shame and regret.

When Sam parked in front of the massive stone building that housed the Liverpool Register Office, Kate scrambled out and onto the pavement while Mum waited for Dad to open the door for her on the other side.

Finally alone for a moment, Viv gasped for breath. She could do this. She would walk up those steps and come out again a married woman. She wouldn't run because there was no other option.

On the pavement, Viv looked up at the long sweep of steps to the front of St. George's Hall. Through the misty January rain, there was no mistaking the Levinsons huddled by one of the building's massive yellow columns. Mrs. Levinson wore a light blue princess-seamed coat with black leather gloves stretching over hands she kneaded nervously. A younger woman—Joshua's sister, Rebecca—was in a deep, rich red wool military-style coat with brass buttons marching double breasted down the front. Mr. Levinson tugged the brim of his homburg farther down over his brow against the wind that came whistling up the Mersey from the Irish Sea.

And then there was Joshua.

He looked nervous, worrying the brim of his light gray wool hat with his long musician's fingers. His suit, the first thing she'd noticed about him on that bandstand the night they'd met, was beautifully cut, and he'd had a haircut since the day she'd told him she was pregnant and he'd asked her to marry him on the spot. Hope flickered in her. He too had tried to look his best for their wedding.

She started toward the Levinsons, but a hand fell on her right forearm.

"Let your father go first," Mum said.

"I haven't met Mr. and Mrs. Levinson yet," she protested.

"Your mother knows best, Vivian," said Dad.

Pushing down her frustration, she watched Mum take up Dad's arm and approach her new family.

Mr. Levinson put out his gloved hand as her parents approached. "Mr. and Mrs. Byrne."

Mum stared at Mr. Levinson's hand for so long that Dad whispered, "Edith."

With clear reluctance, Mum took Mr. Levinson's hand. If the man noticed her mother's frostiness, he didn't mention it. Instead, he turned to Viv, arms outstretched, and kissed her on both cheeks. "My daughter-in-law."

Joshua made a choked sound from behind him. "Not quite yet, Dad."

"Soon enough," said Mr. Levinson. "My wife, Anne."

"Joshua said you were pretty," said Mrs. Levinson.

Viv blushed. "Thank you."

"This is Joshua's sister, Rebecca," said Mr. Levinson, beaming with pride at the defiant teenage girl who held Viv's eye.

"It's good to meet you, Rebecca," she said.

Rebecca moved closer to her mother.

"I wish to say how happy we are that our two families are joining," said Mr. Levinson.

"Dad," Joshua said softly.

"I know that this may not be what any of us expected for Vivian or Joshua, but a marriage and the arrival of a child is a joyous thing," said Mr. Levinson.

"Hardly," Mum muttered.

"Mum, Joshua and I agreed—"

"You should be married in a church," her mother snapped.

Mrs. Levinson grabbed her daughter's hand as though Rebecca were a buoy.

Joshua cleared his throat. "The clerk will be waiting."

Viv let him pull her up the stairs and to the door ahead of everyone else. At the threshold, she leaned into him and whispered, "Thank you."

Something haunted flickered in his eyes, but then he squeezed her hand, and that was all the reassurance she needed.

Joshua

He couldn't breathe.

He knew that it wasn't his shirt collar. His father had been making them for him since he could remember, and the fit was always perfect.

It was this bloody wedding.

He stood stiffly next to Viv in front of the registrar dressed in a dark ill-fitting suit and tie who droned on about the responsibilities of the marriage they were entering into. Everything in his life was about responsibilities now. Even at nineteen, there was no escaping them.

He'd thought himself burdened before, when Dad had told him that if he didn't plan to attend university he would work in the family business. He would train, assist, and eventually take over the tailoring business that had allowed Mum and Dad to move from the flat over the shop to their family home in Wavertree when he was just five. He nodded and showed up each day to work because what else could he do? The weight of it all pressed down on him, trapping him so that he felt he could hardly move.

The only thing that felt like an escape was music. Joshua's love for the saxophone was rivaled only by the incredible sensation of playing in front of a crowd, all of their eyes fixed on him. He had talent, he had drive, and he had ambition.

He could see how, with another life—another family—everything could have been different. A manager would spot him in an orchestra and pluck him out, giving him a chance to front his own band. After headlining at a famous club, he would record an album. It would be a hit. People around the world would listen to his music. They would want more.

It felt almost inevitable until the moment Viv had caught him outside Dad's shop to tell him she was pregnant.

"Do you have the ring?"

Joshua jerked to attention to find the registrar staring at him expectantly. He dug into his jacket pocket and produced the simple gold band that had cost him nearly all of his savings. Viv held up her hand while he mechanically recited his vows and slid the ring onto the fourth finger of her hand.

He wondered if the unfamiliar gold circle felt as heavy on her hand as it looked.

"I pronounce you man and wife," said the registrar, closing his book with a snap.

It was done. In the eyes of the law, they were husband and wife.

Joshua stole a glance at Viv, her expression unreadable. Was she remembering their first date, after the concert, when he'd walked her to the tearoom? Did she recall the way they'd kissed in the doorway of a closed shop? He could remember every moment.

Was it worth it?

"Joshua, aren't you going to kiss your bride?" asked Dad.

Joshua tried his best to swallow. He should kiss Viv, shouldn't he? That's what husbands did at weddings.

He bent, and Viv turned her face up to his, but at the last moment, he lost his nerve. He brushed her cheek with his lips.

Viv exhaled, and his cheeks burned with shame.

Dad stepped forward, the wide smile on his face showing just how hard he was trying to make the best of this rotten day.

"In our religion, it is custom that the Sheva Brachot are recited during the wedding ceremony," Dad explained to Viv.

"I'm sorry, I don't know what that is," said Viv.

"Dad," said Joshua in a low tone.

Dad ignored him. "It is the Seven Blessings. May I?"

"Is that really necessary? We don't have a cup or wine," Joshua protested.

"Don't speak over your father," Mum admonished.

He snapped his mouth shut.

"*Baruch ata Ado-nai Elo-heinu melech ha'olam, bo'rei p'ri ha'gafen,*" Dad began.

"John, I'm sure they need the room back," said Mrs. Byrne, tugging on Mr. Byrne's arm. "We should go outside."

Dad looked a little stunned at Viv's parents' rudeness, and Joshua was unsure if he felt more embarrassed for his father or his new in-laws.

"Mum," Viv hissed at the interruption before moving to put a hand on Dad's forearm. "Please continue. I would very much like to learn."

"It's all right, Vivian," said Dad graciously. "Perhaps your mother is right. We should give back the room."

They filed out in silence, stopping on the top steps of St. George's Hall. The wind had picked up, grasping at the women's hair and raising the edges of Viv's brother-in-law's scarf knitted in Everton Football Club's blue and white stripes.

"Well, congratulations, Vivie," said Viv's sister, Kate. "And to you, Joshua."

"Thank you," he said.

"Sam and I want to invite all of you to our home to celebrate. It doesn't feel right not to have a wedding breakfast," said Kate.

"That's very thoughtful of you," said Mum before Joshua could decline the invitation. All he wanted to do was escape.

"It's too cold to be rushing all over town," said Mrs. Byrne, tugging up the lapel of her coat.

"Just come for one drink, Mum," Kate urged.

"A wedding breakfast sounds lovely," said Viv, a plea in her eyes. "Don't you think, Joshua?"

Mrs. Byrne glared at her daughter. Then she pointed at Joshua. "I need to talk to you."

Viv clung to his arm a little tighter.

"Don't worry," he said, peeling her hand off him. "I'll just be a moment."

He followed Mrs. Byrne a few steps away. Over the top of the woman's head, he could see Kate move to Viv, the sisters speaking low and swift.

"Now that the wedding is done, I need to know how much," said Mrs. Byrne.

He tore his gaze away from his bride and frowned. "How much?"

"How much will it take for you to go away?"

His stomach fell to his feet. "To go away?"

"You've done your duty. The child will have a father. You've nothing more that you can give my daughter."

"Mrs. Byrne—"

"What kind of life will Vivian have with you?" her mother asked sharply. "You're Jewish. She's Catholic. No matter where you go, people will know why you had to marry. They'll hate her or shun her. I've seen it before with my own sister."

"But we're married."

Mrs. Byrne nodded. "The child will be legitimate, but do you really think you can take care of a wife, let alone a family? Let her father and me take care of her."

"I can't leave her. I made her a promise," he protested weakly. His mother-in-law was right. He had no idea how to be a husband to anyone, let alone to Viv. And a father? Not the foggiest.

But it wasn't just the idea of having a wife and child that terrified him. It was his music. He *knew* that he was destined for so much more than the two-bedroom flat above his father's shop. He was meant to be playing jazz, not worrying about whether a client looked better in single- or double-breasted jackets.

If only he had the chance—just one chance—he could make it as a musician.

His mother-in-law clicked open her handbag and drew out a stack of banknotes. "You're a nineteen-year-old man. What are promises to you?"

He stared at the cash. There was so much money there, more than he had ever imagined holding. What if he sent for Viv after the baby was born? He could set them up in a nice little apartment, maybe in the Bronx, where he'd heard Irish Catholics and Jews lived side by side. Viv could keep house and raise their child while he found work. If he could get a steady gig with a band, he could provide for them and he'd never have to see another jacket pattern again.

He felt Viv come up next to him, the warmth of her body a comfort on the cold day. "Joshua?"

"I need to speak to you alone," he said.

"No," said Mrs. Byrne.

"Mum, what's going on?" asked Viv, her eyes fixed on the banknotes in her mother's hand.

"If we could just have a few minutes," Joshua begged.

"Joshua, what's the matter?" asked his father as the rest of the party joined them.

"Your son is leaving," said Mrs. Byrne.

Viv reared back. "What?"

He grasped her hands. "Your mother has offered us money."

"It isn't an offer," said Mrs. Byrne.

He turned his back to his mother-in-law, desperate to explain to Viv. If only they could step aside. If only he could make her understand.

"Listen, it's enough to buy me a ticket on a ship to New York. I'll find work. I'll find a place to live," he said quickly.

"What about me? What about our child?" asked Viv, her hand cradling her stomach through the gap in her coat.

"I'll send for you after the baby's born. I promise I will." He was practically pleading now.

Viv was already shaking her head. "Think about what you're saying. Moving to America? This is crazy."

"This money—it's my chance, Viv. What I've always wanted. If I can find work with an orchestra—"

"Listen to yourself. If. *If* you can find work. Joshua, you have no idea if that will even be possible."

He took a step back. She didn't believe he could do it. Despite their conversations and the starry-eyed look she'd had when he told her how big his dreams really were, when it came down to it, she didn't think he was good enough.

"We're married. We're going to have a child." Viv's eyes cut to her parents. "You promised me that we would do this together."

"And now I'm promising that I'll send for you. Until then, I'll send money—"

"No," said Mr. Byrne, finally speaking. The sound of the quiet man's voice made Joshua stop short. "If you take our money, you will leave and never come back. You won't write. You won't visit. You will leave my daughter alone."

It was all happening too fast. "I need to think."

He could tell in an instant that he'd made a mistake. A bad one.

Viv staggered back. "You're actually considering it."

He almost took it all back then and there, but his father stepped in. "Joshua, this is ridiculous. You have a wife now and a child coming. You have a good job. You need to be reasonable."

A tailor is never out of work. Can you say the same for a musician?

You should work in an honest profession.

You will grow bored with playing your little songs, and then you will be sorry you gave all of this up.

For years, all of Dad's little comments had chipped away at him, slowly killing his spirit. It was death by a thousand good intentions, and he couldn't endure it any longer.

"This is my chance, Dad. It would take me so long to save enough. . . . It's what I've always wanted to do. You know this."

His father's face turned white. "How can you even think—"

"Enough. Take the money now, or it is gone," said Mrs. Byrne.

In that moment, Joshua hated his mother-in-law as he had never hated someone before.

"Viv," he said, reaching out to wipe away her tears. "This is for the best."

Her lip began to tremble. "Where will I go? How will I raise our child? I can't do this by myself."

He tried to smile. "Don't you see? You don't have to."

"But that is exactly what you're asking me to do. What if you never make enough money to send for me?" she asked.

What if you fail?

Enough.

He screwed up his courage and held out his hand to Mrs. Byrne, who handed the banknotes over with a sense of triumph. They felt heavy in his palm.

"Joshua, please," Viv started.

"This is my life too!" he burst out. "I won't give it up."

Viv took a step back. "If you leave today, I never want to see you again. I don't want your money. I don't want you to visit. I don't want you to write. This child will be my child and mine alone."

He almost lost his nerve then as her words fell like blows. Her child. Not theirs.

"Viv . . ."

She shook her head. "Go. You've done enough. The baby will have your name. That's all I needed from you anyway."

You aren't worth anything else.

Well, if that was how she felt, he wasn't going to stick around and force her to live out this sham of a marriage. He would snatch his freedom and go to New York, just as he'd always wanted.

He began to turn, but his father stepped in front of him.

"Joshua, do not do this," Dad said.

"Let me leave," he muttered.

"Think about what you are doing. Your mother and I—"

"He was always going to leave." They all turned to look at Rebecca, who stood slightly at a remove. She was staring hard at him, as though she could read his most secret thoughts. "He's been talking about it for years. We just haven't been listening."

Mum let out a guttural wail and fell into his father's arms while Mrs. Byrne, wearing her triumph for everyone to see, wrapped an arm around her daughter.

"Come along. It's time to go home," said his mother-in-law.

He watched his bride and her family walk slowly back down the steps of St. George's Hall and climb into the car they'd come in.

He could feel his sister step into place next to him. "She's gone."

"That was her choice," he said.

"Are you certain about that?" asked Rebecca.

Glancing at his sister, he said, "Take care of Mum and Dad."

Rebecca shrugged. "What other choice do I have?"

"I'll be back," he said.

His sister cocked her head to one side. "Will you?"

Even his own sister didn't believe in him. Well, he would go to New York, and he would show them. He'd *prove* that he had talent.

Without another word, he stuffed his hands in his pockets and walked away, the Byrnes' banknotes weighing him down like lead.

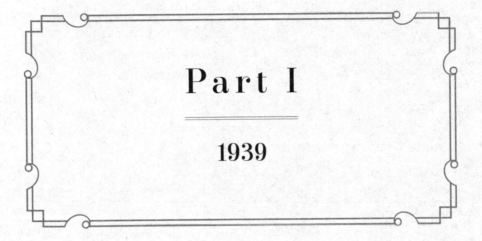

Part I

1939

Viv

August 15, 1939

J ust a moment, Little Bear."

Viv gently pulled Maggie back a step to keep her from repeatedly kicking the wooden baseboard of Mr. Lloyd's shop counter even though she knew persuading a bored four-year-old to do anything she didn't wish to was impossible.

"She'll scuff the wood," said Mrs. Lloyd with disapproval as she weighed out the flour for Viv's order. "And her shoes."

"I'm sorry," said Viv, grabbing hold of her daughter's hand again.

Maggie gave a shriek of disapproval, and Viv automatically let go. A nudge too far in the wrong direction and Maggie would melt down into a tantrum sure to draw even more disapproval from Mrs. Lloyd.

"She's just a little girl," said Mr. Lloyd, peering over the counter to give Maggie an indulgent smile. "I'll bet you've had a long day helping your mummy with the shopping."

Maggie stopped kicking the counter and peered up at the older man with his wire-rimmed spectacles and his wisps of gray hair carefully combed into place over a shining pink scalp.

"Do you have sweeties?" asked Maggie, schooling her face into the picture of innocence that made her look like a dark-haired Shirley Temple.

Mr. Lloyd laughed. "Do you want to choose one yourself, then?"

Maggie jumped up. "Yes, please!"

Viv smiled as the shopkeeper pulled the top off the huge glass jar he kept next to the cash register. Then he stooped to scoop Maggie up so she could pick a boiled sweet just as he used to when Viv had been a little girl. Viv watched her daughter select a green one before unwrapping the twist of clear plastic and popping it in her mouth.

"Most children choose red or purple," observed Mr. Lloyd.

"Maggie likes doing things her own way," she said.

Mrs. Lloyd raised her brow but mercifully remained silent.

"Will you be wanting anything else, Mrs. Levinson?" Mr. Lloyd asked.

Viv pulled out the crumpled list her mother had written in pencil. She didn't need one—she'd been doing her family's shopping since she'd left school at sixteen—but Mum still didn't trust her.

"Just two tins of beans, Mr. Lloyd, if you please," she said.

Mr. Lloyd reached behind the counter to pull down the tins but then frowned. "This one's dinged. I'll just go to the back to fetch you another."

"Oh, please don't put yourself out," she began to protest.

He waved her off. "It's no bother. Back in two ticks."

The older man shuffled off to the stockroom, humming as he went. Viv appreciated his thoughtfulness, but he'd left her with a bigger problem. His wife.

The shopkeeper's wife's hands were already planted on her hips when Viv turned to face her.

"Do you think there'll be another war, then?" Mrs. Lloyd asked.

"I hope not," she said.

Mrs. Lloyd scoffed. "No one hopes for a war. Mr. Lloyd and all of his brothers fought in the last one. He was the only one who came back. Three young men, all dead. It nearly killed their mother."

The story was too familiar. Whole neighborhoods of men had joined up across Liverpool. Brothers and cousins. Uncles and nephews. Fathers and sons. Rich and poor. They'd gone off to fight a war they'd been told would be over by Christmas only to find out how wrong they all were. Troops dug trenches. Battlefields stretched for miles. So many died. So few came home.

"It won't be like that. It can't be," said Viv, even though she'd glanced at the *Liverpool Echo* when she'd passed a newsagent's earlier. The head lines had been the same for days.

Germany was a threat.

Britain would defend herself and her allies.

War was coming.

"And what will you do if it happens?" asked Mrs. Lloyd.

"I've been thinking of volunteering for air raid defense shifts."

Mrs. Lloyd shook her head. "I meant with that one."

Viv followed the other woman's gaze to where Maggie twirled in the middle of the shop, the little blue-and-white-checked summer dress Viv had made her flaring out around her.

"What am I going to do with my daughter?" she asked.

"The government's been taking inventories of children, hasn't it? To evacuate them?"

Her chest tightened even as she stared at Mrs. Lloyd in a combination of horror and shock. How dare she suggest that Viv send Maggie away. How *dare* she.

"Maggie will stay at home with me. Where she belongs," said Viv, fighting to keep her tone level.

Mrs. Lloyd sniffed. "She was born so soon after you were married. It's hard to tell how a woman feels about a child like that."

Every nerve in her fired at the audacity of this woman, yet she managed to bite out, "I love my daughter."

Mrs. Lloyd leaned on the counter. "It must be difficult without your husband around. But then, what can you expect from one of *those* people."

Viv's eyes narrowed. "Exactly what sort of person do you think my husband is, Mrs. Lloyd?"

Mrs. Lloyd shrugged. "Well, a Jew. You can imagine my shock when Mrs. Byrne's daughter took up with a Jew. They're good people, your parents. It must have broken your mother's heart."

Viv took a step forward. She didn't know what she wanted to do— shake the wretched woman? Slap her?—when Mr. Lloyd reemerged with the tin of beans in his hand. He looked from his wife to Viv and hurried to gently edge his way in front of his wife.

"Marjorie, Bill needs you in the back," the shopkeeper said.

Viv thought Mrs. Lloyd might protest, but, after a long moment, the other woman left without a word.

"I'm sorry about that," said Mr. Lloyd as soon as his wife was out of earshot. "Mrs. Lloyd has taken on more time at the shop because my boys are both doing their national service, and we can barely afford to keep Bill in the stockroom let alone hire another clerk who will be gone as soon as war is declared."

Viv smoothed the edge of her light blue cloth coat, trying to swallow down the anger that still sat high in her throat. "Mr. Lloyd, my family has shopped here since before I was born. You and my father were altar boys at Blessed Sacrament together."

Mr. Lloyd fiddled with the edge of one of the large sheets of brown paper he wrapped parcels in. "Mrs. Levinson, please understand. My wife is a good Catholic woman, but I managed to convince her to let you continue to shop here when you were . . ." He waved a hand toward her stomach.

A fierce blush rose on Viv's cheeks. Most of the shopkeepers in her close-knit Catholic neighborhood of Walton had served her, but all of them except Mr. Lloyd had made her feel judged. She couldn't be certain if it was because she had clearly fallen pregnant before her wedding day or because her husband wasn't Catholic. However, considering how many girls she'd gone to school with who married quickly and six months later delivered healthy, squalling babies, she suspected it was the latter.

Maggie tugged on the hem of Viv's tan skirt. "Mummy, I want to go home."

Viv opened her coin purse without looking at Mr. Lloyd. "How much do I owe you?"

She counted out the coins and hurried to put all of her groceries into her net bag. Then she took Maggie by the hand and headed home.

It was a four-block walk to her parents' house where they all lived—the second bed in the room she'd shared with Kate now replaced by Maggie's cot. As soon as they turned onto Ripon Street, Maggie ran ahead. Viv smiled wearily as she watched her daughter dance on their doorstep, no doubt eager to rush in and tell her grandparents about the boiled sweet Mr. Lloyd had given her. If it was a good day, Mum would half listen, her lips tight. If it was a bad day, Viv would do her best to sweep Maggie away before her mother started in on her.

It didn't have to be like this. . . .

Viv juggled her net bag and her handbag, trying to find her front-door key.

"Mummy! Hurry, Mummy!" Maggie jumped from foot to foot.

"Just a moment, Little Bear," she muttered.

The front door swung open. Her mother, shorter than Viv even with her puff of sculpted brown curls, still managed to fill the entryway of the house.

"Maggie, what have I told you about yelling? This is not a schoolground," said Mum.

"I wasn't yelling, Nan," Maggie insisted, throwing her arms around Mum's legs.

Mum stiffened and peeled the little girl off her. "Go upstairs to your room."

Viv was about to protest that as Maggie's mother *she* should be the one telling Maggie what to do and when, but Mum's expression made her pause.

"What is it?" she asked.

"Maggie, go," said Mum, turning the little girl by her shoulders and giving her a little push toward the stairs.

Maggie bounced away without a protest.

As soon as Maggie had crossed the landing, Mum lowered her voice. "Father Monaghan is here. He'd like a word with you."

Dread spread through Viv like dye dripped in water.

"I have to put away the shopping," she said, clutching the net bag. Anything to keep from having to speak to Father Monaghan.

Mum seized the bag and tugged it away from Viv. "He's with your father in the lounge."

Viv carefully removed her straw hat to smooth down her light brown hair in the mirror. It was humid, but her hair still had a little bit of the wave left in it from her nightly pin curls. She wished she had a bit of lipstick to liven up her face, but, even though she was married, she still lived under her parents' roof, where the rules remained the same. No makeup.

As prepared as she was ever going to be, she took a breath, knocked on the lounge door, and pushed it open.

"Viv, there you are," said Dad in his soft voice. He half stood but then seemed to think the better of it.

"I was just at Mr. Lloyd's doing the last of the shopping." She nodded to Father Monaghan, who sat with a cup from the Byrnes' best tea service by his right hand. "Good afternoon, Father."

"Good afternoon, Mrs. Levinson. I hope you're well," he said, his hands spread wide on the arms of what was usually Dad's chair.

"I am. Thank you," she said.

"Your father and I were just speaking about a matter that concerns you. Will you not join us?" Father Monaghan asked, nodding to the seat across from him, as though this were his home.

Viv perched on the edge of the chair and folded her hands, bracing herself.

"I came to speak to your father about the possibility of war . . ." Father Monaghan started.

"I'm aware of the headlines, Father," she said, keeping her voice just on the right side of respectful. Whatever this was about, she wanted the priest out of the house as quickly as possible.

"Then you'll know that there's a very real chance that soon we'll all have to make difficult choices. Sacrifices like Jesus Christ made for all of us," said Father Monaghan.

Viv shifted in her seat at the invocation of the Lord. In her experience, that rarely preceded good news.

"Father Monaghan is worried about Maggie. As are your mother and I," Dad added.

Dad, worried about Maggie? That was unlikely given that worry would have required her father to pay any attention to her daughter. It hurt to see the way he was with Kate's three children, lavishing attention on them whenever they visited, only to ignore Maggie when she tried to tell him a story or invite him to play with her toy tiger, Tig.

"Thank you for your concern, Father, but Maggie will be fine at home with me," she said.

Father Monaghan shook his head solemnly. "I wish that we could all be as certain as you are, Mrs. Levinson, but the truth of the matter is, only God knows what will happen if we go to war."

"I'll take care of my daughter," she said, a hard edge coming into her voice.

"How do you expect to protect a little girl from a bomb, Viv?" Dad asked.

"We will hide in the cellar. Or we'll go to one of the public shelters they're building," she said, as she had done every time this came up.

"You don't know what it's like," Dad said, his gaze hollowing as it always did when he talked about the last war. "You haven't seen the things that I've seen."

Father Monaghan raised a hand to silence them both. "Your father and mother are both concerned for Maggie's safety. Liverpool will be a target. It's a major port, and there's manufacturing here," said Father Monaghan. "I've been speaking with many families with young children across the parish. Naturally, no mother wants to send her children away, but they understand the very grave risks they would take by selfishly keeping their children at home."

Maggie was so young. When Viv hugged her, she couldn't help but feel how delicate her daughter's little body was. Maggie needed to be kept safe, and no one had the instinct to protect her daughter the way that Viv would.

"I've seen the government guidance. Children over five will be evacuated if war comes. Maggie only just turned four last month," she said.

"The church is helping families make provisions for children who are too young for the government scheme. I have already been in contact with several respectable Catholic couples who reside in the countryside and would be happy to take in a bright, cheerful little girl Maggie's age," said Father Monaghan.

She bolted up from her seat. "No!"

"I know this might be distressing," Father Monaghan started.

"I'll not be separated from my daughter."

Since Maggie had come screaming into the world, it had been the two of them. Maggie was her best friend and her reason for living. She was the only thing that made this miserable life living under her parents' roof worth it.

"Your mother thinks that you need to do what's best for the girl," said Dad.

"And what do you think, Dad?" Viv shot back.

Dad's lips thinned. "What your mother says is best."

She shook her head in disgust.

"Mrs. Levinson," said Father Monaghan, his tone stern, "you are letting your own selfishness stand in the way of your daughter's safety."

"It is not selfish to think that a child should be with her mother," she said.

"It is when that may lead to the child's death."

The priest's words froze Viv's blood.

"What if Maggie is killed in a bombing raid when she could have been safe in the countryside?" Father Monaghan pushed.

"There is the risk of air raids everywhere," she whispered, trying to convince herself.

"Is that something you are willing to stake your daughter's life on?" asked Father Monaghan.

Silence stretched in the room, the only sound the faint clink of metal drifting through from the kitchen, where Mum was cooking their evening meal.

Finally, Father Monaghan pushed up out of his chair. "I have parish business to attend to. Mrs. Levinson, think my offer over, but don't take too long. We are only working with good families, and they will be in high demand as foster parents."

Dad saw Father Monaghan out, leaving Viv in the lounge with the door open.

"Father, I must apologize for my daughter's stubborn nature," she could hear Dad saying in the entryway.

"We cannot forget what a difficult thing it must be for a mother to send her child away, Mr. Byrne," said Father Monaghan.

Viv's shoulders relaxed a fraction, but then Father Monaghan added, "You might ask your daughter to think on Isaiah 49:15. 'Can a woman forget her sucking child, that she should not have compassion on the son of her womb? Yea, they may forget, yet will I not forget thee.'"

She stiffened at the implication that the power of a mother's love might fail but God's love never would. Hadn't she already shown that she would do anything for Maggie? Standing on those steps of St. George's Hall, watching her new husband walk away from her, she'd made a choice, putting herself into her parents' hands so that she and her unborn child could have a roof over their heads and money for food. All through her pregnancy, Viv had endured Mum's snipes and jabs. When Maggie was colicky, she alone had soothed her daughter because her mother refused to help. When Maggie grew into a vibrant little girl, Viv had tried to fill her daughter's life with all the love her grandparents didn't show her. Maggie had clothes and food and shelter because Viv had made the best choice she could.

"Please thank Mrs. Byrne for the tea. She always brews a superior pot," she heard Father Monaghan say before the door opened and shut.

Viv moved to the lace curtains that Mum dutifully washed every six months and watched the black-clad figure of the priest retreat down the pavement in the direction of Our Lady of Angels.

No.

She would not be sending her daughter away.

25 August 1939

My darling son,

I know that you are very busy, and I understand if you do not have time to write me back. Living in New York City, you must see so much that you could fill an entire ship's hold with letters.

Normally, I would say that not much changes in Liverpool. However, that is no longer the case. Two more families of refugees joined the synagogue this month alone. We all did our best to welcome them, but they are so very shy, and they wear that horrible haunted look that so many of the people who've arrived from Germany have had. They don't seem to trust anyone, and I cannot blame them. How could you with the things you hear about what is happening in Germany and Austria?

Your father does not believe that Chamberlain's appeasement agreement will hold back Hitler. Still, what can we do but hope? The newspaper headlines and the radio broadcasts all tell us that we are preparing for war without saying that it is inevitable in so many words.

I am very glad that you are safe in New York City. Please stay there, and promise me that you will look after yourself.

With all of my love,
Your mother

Joshua

J oshua and the rest of the packed car jostled gently with the sway of the 1 train as it rumbled up from the Christopher Street–Sheridan Square station just a couple of blocks from his poky little apartment. His saxophone case and garment bag hung from one hand, gently tapping against his leg, but he hardly noticed. His gaze was fixed on his mother's latest letter.

Please stay there, and promise me that you will look after yourself.

He shook his head and eased the letter into his inner jacket pocket. Then he unfolded yesterday's *New York Times* to where he'd left off reading it. Splashed across page four was the headline:

LONDON AMERICANS HEAR SAFETY PLAN
4 Zones Have Been Set Apart to Provide for U. S.
Citizens Unable to Get Home
EXTRA SHIPS CHARTERED
Pressure Is Felt in Scotland—2,000 'Refugees' Are Still
Stranded in Paris

It had been on the wind for weeks. Hitler seemed to be determined to ignore the Munich Agreement that Chamberlain had brokered the year before and brandished like a chump, promising "peace for our time."

"Not bloody likely that," Joshua muttered under his breath, drawing a sharp look from a woman in a straw hat covered in flowers. He offered her a tight smile, pulled out a handkerchief to dab his brow, and then went back to the paper.

Britain looked as though it was marching straight into another war with Germany.

He wanted a drink.

That was the problem with being an expat. No matter how long he lived in New York, Liverpool would always be home.

He'd been so cocksure when, just a few days off the ocean liner in New York, he'd toted his sax to the first audition. He'd given up so much to come here, there was no way he could fail. After a month of trying unsuccessfully to secure a place in a band, however, it had become harder to keep the churn of guilt, homesickness, and relief that always came with thinking about England at bay. More than four years later, there wasn't a night that he didn't lay in bed thinking about how, on the steps of St. George's Hall with gulls screaming overhead and shock creeping onto his family's faces, he'd chosen this life.

He spent most of his nights in the jazz clubs of Fifty-Second Street—Swing Street—where he was in the regular rotation of fill-ins with the house bands at Kelly's Stables, the Famous Door, and the 21 Club. During the day, he had a handful of students. Occasionally his friend Lonnie would call him with studio work. It was enough to eke out a living but not much else.

His life was supposed to be bigger than this, but he'd come to the city and found out what so many before him had discovered. New York didn't give a damn about anyone's dreams.

The train brakes screeched as it pulled into the Fiftieth Street station. The car shuddered to a stop, and passengers began jostling one another as they waited for the doors to open. Joshua folded the newspaper, tucked it under his arm, and stepped into the surge of disembarking passengers.

Once he cleared the station steps, he fell into his regular walk to the Famous Door east down Fiftieth Street before turning north on Sixth and then right on Fifty-Second. He ducked into the club's side door, which was guarded, as always, by Sid, the club's stage manager.

"Hey, English," said Sid around the slim black cigar that always hung out of his lips. The stage manager had set up a fan next to his little pillar desk pointed straight at him, blowing his oiled hair up off his brow in a clump.

"Anyone else in yet?" he asked.

"Root and McKinley," the stage manager grunted. "Looks like Root hasn't dried out since last night. Smells like it too."

The pair of trumpet players were permanent members of the Famous Door house band, unlike Joshua, who was filling in for a sax player who'd fallen off the bandwagon and landed himself in jail for trying to steal a subway train while sauced.

"Thanks," he said, brushing by Sid's desk.

"You're not going to ask why Root's still drunk? See, I think it's that girl Carol—"

"Not my business." Joshua couldn't afford to make anyone sore. Musicians switched venues and bandleaders so often in the city that he never knew who he might end up asking for a job.

Sid frowned. "You seen the headlines this morning?"

"I'm still working on yesterday's paper."

"You think your country's going to try to lick Hitler?" Sid asked.

"I don't know," Joshua said, the tightness back in his chest.

"Good thing you're over here, isn't it?" asked Sid with a smirk.

"I've got to ask Collins for the new arrangements," Joshua said, starting off down the hallway with more purpose this time.

"Collins isn't here yet!" Sid shouted after him.

Joshua put up his hand to thank him but didn't look back.

When he arrived at the dressing room, he found the door ajar. He used his sax case to push it open and found Root with his head on one of the dressing tables. McKinley leaned back in his chair so that two of the legs were off the ground, his fingers dexterously running over the keys of his trumpet as he checked its action.

"English, you're back," said McKinley, dropping the chair legs to the ground. "When's Dorey going to give you a job?"

"You have to ask him," said Joshua, dropping his light gray felt hat onto an empty space in front of the room's long mirror before pulling his suit free from the garment bag. He paused and nodded at Root. "Is he going to be sick?"

McKinley nudged his fellow trumpet player with his shoe. "You dying, Root?"

"Dammit, yes," came the moan in response.

"Too bad you don't play trumpet, English," said McKinley with a shrug. "You could have his job."

Joshua huffed a laugh.

"Fuck you," Root muttered into his arms.

"Don't blame me. You're the idiot who thought it would be a good idea to hug a bottle of bourbon all night," said McKinley.

"What happened?" asked Joshua, pulling the tail of the shirt he'd worn up to the club out of his trousers to swap it for his clean tuxedo shirt.

"Wife left him," said McKinley.

"Josie," Root half sobbed.

"You're married?" Joshua asked.

"Not anymore he ain't," muttered McKinley.

Root lurched up to take a half-hearted swing at his friend.

McKinley dodged with a laugh. "You couldn't hit the wide side of a barn right now."

Root shoved his hands through his unkempt hair. "Why you got to kick a guy when he's down?"

"You really thought that woman was going to stay with you after you left Ohio and told her you'd be back in four weeks?" McKinley asked.

"How long ago was that?" Joshua asked.

"Six years ago," said McKinley.

"I sent money home!" Root insisted.

"Doesn't matter, does it? You weren't there. I'll bet you anything she finally found someone else who is," said McKinley. "At least you didn't have kids."

At least you aren't a total deadbeat.

Joshua fumbled with the clasp of his trousers, rushing to strip them off. He needed to get out of the stuffy, humid dressing room.

He did himself up, tucked in his shirt, and strung his bow tie loose around his neck. Then he headed for the door.

"Where are you going?" McKinley called out.

"To find Dorey and ask him for a job," he said. Again.

"Good luck, English. You're going to need it," said McKinley with a laugh.

Joshua grimaced and tried not to think about how his luck seemed to have run out years ago.

Joshua didn't find Dorey before they were all due onstage. He did, however, corner the band's manager, Collins, just as he was arriving. That gave him enough time to skim over his parts for the new arrangements of "Moonlight Serenade" and "Body and Soul."

The club filled up quickly, the dance floor packed as they played set after set. By the time Joshua and the boys rolled offstage at two in the morning, he was bone-tired.

"We're going to Sonny Fowler's place. What do you say, English?" McKinley clapped a hand on his shoulder. "The music will be hot, and there will be enough bourbon and cocaine to sink a ship. Should be some birds hanging out too. You can charm the panties off them with that 'cheerio' accent of yours."

The prospect of women wasn't particularly tempting, but the thought of quieting his thoughts with cheap booze was. Still, Joshua shook his head.

"Go ahead without me. I need to find Dorey first," he said.

That earned him another slap on the shoulder and a nod. "You know the place if you change your mind."

"Ninth and First Ave," he said.

"That's the one. Good luck," said McKinley.

"Thanks," said Joshua.

He watched the other man amble down the hall singing the opening lines to "Wacky Dust" before turning on his heel to find the bandleader.

Dorey, it turned out, was holed up in the club's office with the owner, Mr. Robbins. The two were kicking back in a pair of armchairs, sharing a pair of cigars and matching glasses of what smelled like brandy.

Joshua rapped on the frame of the open door. "Evening, sir."

"Always so polite, Levinson," said Dorey before turning to Robbins. "You know Joshua Levinson?"

"You play sax with the band?" Robbins asked.

Joshua lifted his instrument case. "Fill-in."

"Levinson's been Randall's replacement while he thinks on his sins in Rikers," said Dorey.

"Ah," said Robbins.

"That's actually what I'm here about, Mr. Dorey. I think I've been playing well with the other guys. I learn arrangements fast. You've been giving me more solos. I was hoping that our arrangement might become more permanent," Joshua said.

Dorey and Robbins glanced at each other. Joshua could feel his palms sweat against the hard leather of the handle of the sax's case.

Finally, Dorey said, "I'd like to help you, Levinson. I really would. The thing is, Randall's been a friend for a long time."

Joshua's heart sank.

"I told him I'd keep his spot open for as long as he needed me to," Dorey continued. "It's what's getting him through while he waits for his trial."

"I understand, sir," said Joshua, trying not to let his frustration show through.

"Why don't I do this?" Dorey asked, leaning forward to ash his cigar. "I'll put in a good word for you with Murray Rabinowitz? He's got a gig with his band at Club Downbeat next month. Maybe he's looking for a sax. And he's a Jew like you."

Joshua nodded without much enthusiasm. He'd tried out for Rabinowitz last year. It hadn't gone anywhere.

Four years he'd been at this, and at every single turn, he got the same answer. He was good, but there was always another musician ahead of him—a friend, cousin, or some guy they'd come up with. Bandleaders wanted to hire the great musicians, but great musicians were a dime a dozen in New York City, especially around Swing Street. That meant they hired who they knew. He might have a reputation as a reliable fill-in, but no one *knew* him. He was "English," a foreigner, and a Jew.

"Thanks, sir," he said, and then nodded his goodbyes to Dorey and Robbins.

When Joshua let himself out onto the street, he found that the night was still hot, but it had rained while he'd been inside, sweeping away the close, humid air that hung heavy over the city most of the summer.

All around him, jazz spilled out of club doors as people half-tight or high laughed and stumbled around him. For a moment, he thought about heading into another club, but the chances of seeing someone he'd been passed over for playing sax was too great. Instead, he settled his sax case under his arm and headed for the 6 train. He was going to Sonny Fowler's, where he was certain he could find a bottle of bourbon with his name on it.

Viv

August 31, 1939

V iv hated Thursdays.

She used to love them back when she worked in the Northern Delivery Office sorting hall because they held the promise of the freedom and hope that accompanied the weekend.

However, when she'd married Joshua, the General Post Office's marriage ban forced her to give up her job, and now Thursdays were laundry day: an arduous affair that she couldn't help but resent.

That morning, she put on an old cotton dress that had once been red but had faded to a muddy rust and pinned and tied up her hair in a printed scarf. She and Mum hauled the tall tin dolly tubs out to the paved back garden and began filling great pots of water to put onto the stove to heat. Maggie sat in a corner of the yard on a chair playing with Tig, her feet kicking in the air as Viv and Mum added the hot water and soap flakes to dolly tubs filled with the family's clothes. Then Viv and Mum stood across from one another, plunging a wooden posser each into their tubs to pump the clothes and agitate the soapy water.

Viv had once made the mistake of suggesting that it might make it more enjoyable to move the wireless from the lounge to the kitchen so they could open the back door and listen while they worked. Mum had sharply reminded her that this was meant to be a chore—not a night out dancing.

After working the posser, she and Mum tipped the contents of the dolly tub to let the dirty water drain and refresh it with new. Viv never managed it without soaking at least part of her apron, skirt, or shoes—sometimes all three. At least it was the tail end of summer now and Viv's hands didn't chap when the water sloughed over them.

Viv worked clothes through the hand-cranked mangle while Mum pulled pins off the clothesline in preparation for hanging them out to dry. She was just bending down to untangle the legs of a pair of her father's trousers when Maggie pulled on her skirt. Viv stood up sharply, sweeping her daughter away from the mangle.

"Maggie, I told you to stay away from that thing!"

Maggie's fat lower lip began to tremble.

Viv dropped the trousers back into the tub and stooped to scoop Maggie up. Popping her daughter on her hip, she smoothed a hand over the little girl's soft hair. "Don't cry, Little Bear."

"You yelled, Mummy," Maggie sobbed into her shoulder, dampening the one part of Viv that wasn't already wet from the laundry.

"I'm sorry, but you can't play around the mangle."

Maggie shoved her little face more firmly into the crook of Viv's neck, and the strings to Viv's heart, which Maggie held so firmly in her fist, yanked.

"You don't want to end up with flat fingers, do you?" Viv asked.

Maggie sniffled and turned her face a little. "Bears don't have flat fingers."

"No, they don't." She took Maggie's hand and popped her thumb into her mouth as though to nibble on it. That earned her a squeal of delight.

"Why don't you go sing Tig a song? I think he'd like that, wouldn't he?" asked Viv with a nod to the stuffed toy tiger.

"Tig! Tig! We're going to sing a song!" Maggie cried out, and went to scoop the toy up into a spin.

Viv smiled, watching her daughter start to sing "Twinkle Twinkle Little Star" while making Tig dance along with her.

When Viv turned around, she found her mother watching with a frown of disapproval.

"You spoil her," Mum announced.

How, she didn't know. Viv didn't regret telling Joshua that she didn't want anything to do with him or his money if he went back on his promise to stay by her side in Liverpool. However, years later, that snap decision made on her ill-fated wedding day had left her with no income at all except for the small allowance her parents provided to buy things like fabric for clothes and the one ruinously expensive pair of shoes a year each she could afford for Maggie and herself. Kate helped keep Maggie in hand-me-downs from her daughter, Cora, but even that bit of help didn't mean they were living like royalty.

"She's happy and healthy, Mum," she said, stooping again to wrestle with her father's trousers.

Her mother cleared her throat and said, "I saw Father Monaghan yesterday."

"For Wednesday mass, I know," Viv said, keeping her eyes on the mangle. She'd gone to midweek services in school because it had been required, but she hadn't been since she left, even though she knew her mother wanted her to. It was the one little act of rebellion she could afford because her father never went either.

"I went back in the afternoon," said Mum. "I wanted to talk to him about Maggie."

Viv's hand stilled on the mangle's handle. "Why?"

"You need to take Father Monaghan's offer and prepare to send Maggie away when the time comes," said Mum.

"*If* the time comes," she said.

"It will, Vivian. Mark my words. You didn't live through the last war. I did." Her mother crossed the yard to her. "Just think how good it will be for Maggie if Father Monaghan can find her a home with a respectable Catholic family."

"If it's such a good idea, why isn't Kate having these same conversations with Father Monaghan?" Viv asked.

"Colin, William, and Cora all have schools that will see them placed. Maggie doesn't," said Mum. "You never know who she might end up with if you don't take Father Monaghan's offer. They could be Protestant."

"Or Jewish," she said archly.

Her mother shot her a look of warning.

"Anyway, it doesn't matter. I don't want to send Maggie away," Viv said.

"This is about choosing Maggie's welfare over what you want, Vivian. That is what it is to be a mother."

Since when had Mum had any interest in Maggie's welfare? And where had Mum's sacrifice been when Viv had been in distress? Where was the forgiveness that was at the heart of so many of Father Monaghan's sermons? Neither of the Byrnes had been willing to forgive that their youngest daughter had been drawn into a moment of temptation.

Viv would never forget the day she told her parents she was pregnant. Her mother had called her a whore and a sinner. Viv had quickly reassured them that the child's father would marry her, and she saw relief pass over Mum's face. Then came the inevitable question of his name. The moment Viv said he was a Levinson, Mum got up, went to the kitchen, and closed the door. Dad had simply stared into space.

In the end there was nothing to be done. Her parents might hate that Joshua was Jewish, but they all knew that Viv needed to be married if she was going to have a child, because the alternative was too grim to contemplate.

"Mum, all I do is think about Maggie's welfare. I won't have you saying any different," Viv said carefully.

With a sniff, Mum turned back to the washing line to start pegging clothes up as the late-morning sun stretched over the backyard and the fresh washing.

Her mother might have backed down, but Viv was old enough to know that this battle was far from over, and the thought of it made her queasy. Mum wielded two powerful weapons: her coldness and her silence. If it was only Viv who suffered, that might have been one thing. However, Mum would ignore Maggie too, a child who had done nothing wrong and didn't understand why she was being punished.

Viv was down to the last few sheets in her wooden tub when there was a clash of a door hitting a wall and shouting in the house.

"What is Kate doing here?" Viv asked, knowing the clatter of her niece and nephews well.

"Why aren't the children in school?" Mum asked.

Their eyes met, and in a flash Viv was pulling at her apron strings and hurrying after her mother through the house.

They met Kate in the entryway, Cora hanging off Kate's left hand while she tried to separate the boys, who seemed in the middle of a scrap.

"Cora!" cried Maggie with delight.

"Colin and William, stop hitting each other!" Kate's voice boomed, and the boys immediately separated, despite scowls. Kate let out a breath. "Cora, go play with your cousin."

As soon as the kids were gone, Kate spun around. "I came as soon as I could."

"What's happened?" asked Viv.

"Has something happened with Sam?" asked Mum, real anguish etched on her face over the thought that something might have happened to her beloved son-in-law.

Kate stared at the two of them. "You mean you don't know?"

"Know what?" Viv asked.

Kate thrust a folded copy of the *Liverpool Echo* at her. "The evacuation. It's starting."

Across the top of page ten read a headline:

CHILDREN ARE TO BE EVACUATED AS A
PRECAUTION—OFFICIAL
Government's Decision to Operate Provisional Plan
3,000,000 People Affected

Viv's hands shook as she skimmed the first paragraph. When she caught the word *schoolchildren*, she couldn't help her sigh of relief. Maggie wouldn't need to be evacuated.

All the selfish happiness evaporated when she saw the devastation on her sister's face. Colin, William, and Cora were all in school. They would be sent away.

She handed the paper over to her mother and gathered Kate up in her arms. "I'm so sorry."

Kate began to sob. "What am I going to do? Sam went to work because we can't afford him losing the shifts, but I couldn't send the children to school. Not when this is happening."

"Of course, dearest," cooed Mum. "You did the right thing. Vivian, put the kettle on for your sister."

Viv bit her lip, wondering if Mum would ever order Kate to do the same for Viv if the circumstances were different. Still, she followed her mother and sister into the kitchen and set about making tea. Outside the window above the sink she could see the children running in and out of the laundry hanging in the yard.

"They're to be sent with their schools, but that might mean the boys and Cora will be split up, and Cora's so young," Kate told their mother.

"They'll all be fine. They're good, sensible children," said Mum.

"Sam has been talking about joining up. I don't know what I'll do if he's gone and so are the children," said Kate, desperation plain in her voice. "Maybe they won't be sent too far. Maybe I can visit them."

Colin, Kate's eldest, popped his head into the room as though to ask for something but then stopped himself when he saw his mother.

"Don't cry, Mummy," he said.

"I'm not, pet," said Kate, giving a great sniff that prompted Viv to hand Kate a handkerchief from her pocket. "I'm not. Now be a good boy and make sure none of the littles fall over running around like that. You don't want anyone with scraped knees, do you?"

Colin leaped up, whatever he'd come inside for forgotten, and raced back out again.

As soon as the cousins resumed playing, Viv said, "All of this might calm down. The government is still speaking to Hitler. All of this worry might be over nothing."

"Oh, Vivie, stop it!" Kate cried out, her hands straining against the handkerchief she clutched. "They're evacuating the cities. Of course we're going to war!"

"They didn't bomb Liverpool in the Great War," Viv argued.

"Girls," their mother bit out.

Kate took a breath. "Sam says that airplanes can fly so much farther now. He thinks we're in every bit of danger the government says we are because of the docks and all the shipping that goes out of Liverpool."

"But—"

"Vivie, I know you don't like hearing this, but you need to," said Kate, her look so pitying that Viv turned to the whistling kettle to compose herself.

They couldn't be going to war.

Sam and all the men she knew couldn't be on the brink of being called up and sent away to fight. Everyone in the neighborhood knew someone who'd lost a brother or a son last time Britain went to war against Germany. Everyone knew a man who'd come back less.

And what about Maggie? She was due to start school next year. Would the war be over by then? What would happen if the government shut down schools?

By the time Viv put milk in the tea and placed the mugs in front of her sister and mother, her breath was shallow. It should not have surprised her then that this was the moment Mum chose to say, "You should take Father Monaghan's offer, Vivian."

"No," said Viv, her voice flat as she took the seat next to Kate.

"Maggie would be cared for by good people—"

"No," Viv repeated, her voice raised.

"What is this all about?" asked Kate, looking between the two of them.

Viv crossed her arms. "Mum and Dad want me to evacuate Maggie, but she's too young. She should be with me."

"You should be reasonable for once in your life and do the right thing," said Mum.

"And you should stop sticking your oar in about something you know nothing about," Viv shot back.

Kate looked shocked, and Mum grew silent and still.

"Mum, I'm sorry," Viv started.

"I am only trying to help my ungrateful daughter," said Mum with a sniff.

Viv stared at the chipped wood of the dining table, feeling two inches tall.

"We can't fight. Not right now when there are so many more important things to think about." Kate turned to Viv and said gently, "Vivie, I think you need to consider that maybe what you want isn't the best thing for your daughter. Tell me about Father Monaghan's offer."

Viv shook her head. It felt as though the room were closing in on her and she couldn't find an escape.

"Father Monaghan will make arrangements for Maggie to evacuate to the countryside to a respectable Catholic family. One who wants her," said Mum, folding her hands across her stomach.

"No," Viv said again, but this time it came out a whisper.

Kate took Viv's hand. "If we're lucky, it won't be for very long."

"How can you even think about . . . ?"

Kate dropped Viv's hand. "How can I think about sending my children away? Is that what you want to know?"

The hard edge to Kate's voice shocked Viv. The pair of them had always gotten along. Mum had made it clear that Kate was her favorite, even before Viv's spectacular fall from grace, but Viv had always felt Kate was on her side, her one ally in a house she never really fit into.

"I'm going to do what's best for my children, Vivie, even if I hate it. I need to make sure they're safe," said Kate.

Viv dropped her head to her hands. She didn't want to believe it. They were safe up here in the north, so far away from London. How could Germany touch them here?

"You've taken such good care of Maggie for four years, but you must see that keeping her with you isn't what is best for her right now," said Kate, her tone softening again.

"I'm best for her. I'm her mother," Viv murmured.

"If we go to war, even you won't be able to keep the Germans at bay," said Kate.

Viv's head was spinning. It was all happening too fast. She couldn't think. She just needed a moment.

"Listen to your sister," said Mum.

"Mum," Kate warned before giving Viv's arm a squeeze. "Just ask yourself, Vivie, will you ever be able to forgive yourself if something happens to Maggie because you didn't want to send her away?"

It was the argument that Father Monaghan had used on her, but something about hearing it from Kate broke her open. She couldn't imagine her daughter living with strangers, but neither could she knowingly keep her in harm's way.

This was impossible. A puzzle that had no good solution.

"I . . . I . . ."

"What if your stubbornness costs Maggie her life?" Kate asked. "After all that you two have been through, could you really take that risk?"

"Kate . . ."

"I hate it too, but it's worth it to make sure the children are safe. You know what you have to do," said her sister.

Kate was right, and Viv knew it deep in her soul, but she couldn't force herself to say the words.

"I can't," she whispered.

"You can, and you will, so long as you live under this roof," said Mum.

"Mum—" Kate started.

"You may send Maggie away and stay here, or you may pack your things."

"That's not fair," said Kate.

"No, Katherine. It's time that she learns there are consequences to her actions," said Mum.

A sour sickness spread through Viv's stomach as she realized that the decision to send Maggie away had never been hers to make. She lived at the pleasure of her parents. She relied on them for a bed and food and money. Everything. If they turned her out of Ripon Street, then where would she be?

She'd hoped, after Maggie had been born, that she might escape. She'd written to Joshua's family to tell them they had a granddaughter because she'd never forgotten Mr. Levinson's kindness on her wedding day. She'd spent her entire pregnancy dreaming that the Levinsons would welcome her and their first grandchild into their home with open arms. However, Joshua's family had never answered her letter.

She didn't blame them—she was the reason their son left Liverpool—but when she realized they weren't going to write, it felt as though her last lifeline had been cut.

"You could stay with me," said Kate, but Viv heard the hesitancy in her sister's words. If Kate helped her, it would be asking Kate to choose between her and their parents. Viv couldn't do that to her sister. Not after everything Kate had done for her during her pregnancy. Not when Kate had held her hand through thirty-six hours of labor and even agreed to post her letter to the Levinsons without criticizing her. Viv had had years of coping with Mum and Dad's coldness, but Kate hadn't. She wouldn't force her sister to push away their parents right when Kate was about to lose her children and her husband.

"I want to know more about this couple Father Monaghan wants to send Maggie to," Viv croaked out.

Mum's features settled into a satisfied smile.

"And I want to be able to visit her," she added, her fingers bunched up in the fabric of her laundry-day dress.

"Very well. I'll see to it that your father gives you train fare to visit," said Mum. "Once."

"I know it's hard, Vivie, but it's for the best," said Kate. "You'll see."

Viv gave her sister the smallest of nods, and then she put her head down on the cool wood of her mother's kitchen table and began to cry.

Joshua

September 1, 1939

Joshua rolled over with a groan, wincing as the sheer force of his hangover smashed into his head. He opened one eye and immediately regretted it. He hadn't closed the blinds when he'd stumbled into bed a few hours earlier, and light streamed into his grubby little bedroom.

His memory of how he'd ended up in this state was hazy. He knew he'd made it to Sonny Fowler's after all, still sore from Dorey's easy rejection of him. He also had a vague memory of planting himself in front of a bottle of King of Kentucky Straight Bourbon.

Joshua groaned again and fell back against the pillows.

It took another few minutes for more rational thought to begin to creep back in. The day before had been Thursday, so that meant it was now Friday. On Fridays he headed uptown to Morningside Heights to teach a Columbia student who thought that learning the sax would make up for the deficiencies in his personality and help him meet girls.

It was tempting to stay in bed, but his need for a paycheck was greater. He pulled himself upright, yanked on the previous night's trousers, and shuffled the short walk to his apartment's kitchen. His head pounded like a jackhammer on concrete, and his mouth was dry from booze and too many cigarettes.

God, he needed a drink.

Instead, he put the kettle on the stove, measured out some coffee from a jar of grounds that he kept on the counter, and prayed that the water would boil fast.

He rubbed his forehead and peered out the window of his ground-floor apartment. Through the slats in the blinds, he could see that a kid hawking editions of that morning's *New York Times* on the corner was doing brisk business.

Joshua pulled up the blinds, opened the window, and stuck his head outside. The humidity hit him square in the face.

"Hey, kid!" he shouted. "What's going on?"

"You haven't heard?" asked the newspaper boy as though he was the world's biggest chump. "Germany invaded Poland."

Shit.

"Give me one of those, will you?" Joshua dug into his trouser pocket and held up a nickel. The kid hurried to Joshua's window and passed him a paper.

There it was, splashed across the front page:

GERMAN ARMY ATTACKS POLAND;
CITIES BOMBED, PORT BLOCKADED

Then, underneath:

BRITISH MOBILIZING

Joshua stared at the paper. It was happening.

"Hey, mister, are you okay?" the kid asked.

Joshua looked up sharply, realizing he was still hanging half out the window. Behind him, the kettle on the stove was starting to whistle.

"Yes. Thank you. I'll be fine," he said.

"You're British?" the kid asked.

"Yes," he said. "Yes, I am."

"Are you going to go back?" the kid asked.

"What?"

"Are you going back to fight? My dad says he'd fight if we go to war."

Every letter his family had written him in the last year had been laced with tension. Rebecca worried that the country would go to war and she'd never be able to go to university. Dad wrote about the whispers at synagogue of horrible things happening in Germany to Jews. Mum, every time, told him how happy she was that he was safe.

Safe when he didn't deserve to be.

"You have customers," Joshua said, jerking his head in the direction of the newspaper boy's stack.

The child scurried back to his newspapers, where three men mulled around, waiting to buy a paper.

"Shit," Joshua muttered. "Shit, shit, shit."

But even as he crashed around, half-distracted while he showered and pulled on clothes to head uptown to his lesson, he couldn't keep his mind off home.

By the time he left Morningside Heights, he knew what he had to do.

Viv

Viv held Maggie's hand tightly as she looked around at the people on the early-morning bus to Liverpool Lime Street station. The children were mostly sleepy-eyed and quiet, while their mothers worried and fretted. A few men dotted the collection of passengers, but evacuation, she was learning, was the purview of women and children.

It's just a precaution, she told herself, even as instinct screamed at her that this felt wrong. What was she thinking sending her daughter away? How could she protect Maggie if she wasn't with her?

Will you ever be able to forgive yourself if something happens to Maggie?

Kate's words echoed in her head as the bus bumped along, bringing her closer to the inevitability that was Maggie's evacuation. The day after the announcement, Germany had invaded Poland. Now the entire nation held its breath, waiting to find out whether Hitler would capitulate to the prime minister's demand that Hitler withdraw by the following day or if they would be at war.

In the end it had been remarkably easy to arrange Maggie's evacuation. Father Monaghan came to the house and told her that Sarah and Matthew Thompson of Wootton Green, a village just outside Solihull in Warwickshire, would care for her girl. Mr. Thompson was an engineer, and Mrs. Thompson tended to their home, Beam Cottage. They hadn't been blessed with their own children, and they were eager to meet Maggie.

The bus came to a shuddering stop on Lime Street, and the driver swung the double metal doors open with a clunk. One by one, mothers and fathers began to stand, hauling young children up onto their hips and taking older ones by the hands to lead them off the trains that would ferry them away to the countryside. Viv turned in her seat to Maggie, who kicked her feet, which were clad in her best shoes, as she played with Tig.

"Time to go, Little Bear," she said.

Maggie looked up at her, her deep brown eyes wide and trusting. Viv's heart broke for the hundredth time that morning.

"Are you ready to go on an adventure?" she asked, forcing cheeriness into her voice while she helped Maggie down from the seat and stooped to take the little tan case she'd packed and unpacked for her daughter three times the night before.

"Will there be sweeties?" Maggie asked.

"There might be if you're a very good girl," she said, settling Maggie's gas mask across her shoulder. It was the miniature of the one that Viv wore over her shoulder, a string laced through the top of the government-issued cardboard box it had come in.

Maggie screwed up her button nose. "I'm a good girl!"

"You are, Little Bear. You are." Viv squeezed her daughter's hand and led her off the bus, Tig hanging just inches above the ground.

Father Monaghan had told them to meet him at the entrance to the North Western Hotel on Lime Street. It was a grand, imposing building, and Viv had always dreamed of one day being able to go there as a guest. Now she hated the Victorian monstrosity that loomed over them.

The *Liverpool Echo* had said that the first trains would leave at eight o'clock for this second day of evacuations, and even with the early hour people already streamed around Viv and Maggie, grim expressions set on their faces. However, it wasn't difficult to find Father Monaghan. An unusually tall, lanky man, he stood out without the help of his stark white collar. When she approached, he removed his hat.

"Mrs. Levinson."

Viv nodded in greeting. It was impossible to look at this man and not remember the time nearly five years ago when she'd sat on the hard wooden bench of the confessional, trembling with fear.

"In the name of the Father, and of the Son, and of the Holy Spirit. Amen. Forgive me, Father, for I have sinned. It has been one week since my last confession. I am unmarried." Her chest squeezed, and tears began leaking from the corners of her eyes. "But I fear that I'm with child."

A long pause stretched between them. Finally, Father Monaghan said, "Surely you know that it is a sin to engage in fornication before taking the sacrament of marriage, my child."

"I—I know, Father."

"Then why did you do it?"

Because Joshua was the first boy who had really listened to her.

Because he'd asked what she wanted out of her life rather than expecting her to stay in Walton and raise a brood of children.

Because he'd made her feel like she was the only girl in the world who mattered.

Because she'd *wanted* to see what sex was like even though she knew she shouldn't.

Stupid girl. Stupid, stupid girl.

"I don't know, Father," she said.

"What you have done is unacceptable. Do you remember what it says in 1 Corinthians? 'Now the body is not for fornication, but for the Lord; and the Lord is for the body,'" Father Monaghan quoted.

A tiny whimper escaped her lips, and she wrapped her arms around her still-flat stomach.

"Please forgive me, Father," she whispered.

The next time she'd seen him in church, Father Monaghan wouldn't even look her way, and she knew. Her life would never be the same.

Now, standing in front of the hotel, Viv rolled her shoulders back.

"Hello, Father! Mummy says that we're going to a place that has cows and horses and sheep and chickens and . . ." Maggie scrunched up her nose, no doubt trying to think of another farm animal.

Father Monaghan looked down from his great height at Maggie. "You'll be living in a village. There will be no livestock."

Maggie looked crestfallen, and Viv hurried to stoop down to her. "I'm sure that Mr. and Mrs. Thompson will be happy to show you the animals in the fields."

"I like animals," said Maggie.

Viv hugged her close. "I know, Little Bear."

When Viv stood again, she noticed a tall, broad nun swathed in black and white hovering a few feet off. Father Monaghan gestured to the woman. "This is Sister Mary Margaret of Blessed Sacrament. She will be escorting Margaret to Wootton Green."

Sister Mary Margaret stepped forward with a warm smile. "Your daughter will be safe with me, Mrs. Levinson." Then the nun leaned down so she was eye level with Maggie. "Hello. What's your name?"

Maggie half hid her face behind Tig, her hand clutching at Viv's skirt.

"It's okay, Maggie," Viv said, placing a hand on her little girl's head. "You can answer the sister."

"I'm Maggie," whispered her daughter.

"Well, then, we have something in common because my name is Sister Mary Margaret," said the nun.

"Do you like sweeties?" Maggie asked.

"I don't eat them very often now"—the nun glanced at Father Monaghan—"but I used to like chocolate limes."

"I like sugar mice the best," said Maggie, immediately becoming animated. "And then jelly babies."

As Maggie continued to rattle off her ranking of sweets, Father Monaghan leaned in and said in a low voice, "Yesterday Sister Mary Margaret escorted four children to North Wales to see them settled into their foster homes. She is very reliable."

He was, Viv realized, trying to be kind.

"Thank you," she said.

"Sister, you should be going," said Father Monaghan.

Sister Mary Margaret rose again to her full, commanding height. "Yes, Father. Would you like to see us off, Mrs. Levinson?"

Tears rose in Viv's eyes. She bit her lip hard, the pain a distraction, and nodded. She would not cry. To Maggie, this was to be an adventure where she would meet animals and have a real garden to play in and didn't have to stay quiet as a mouse for fear of angering her grandmother.

"I would," Viv managed.

The other woman patted Viv's forearm. "I will take good care of your little girl. I promise."

"I will leave you, then," said Father Monaghan. He looked down at Maggie. "God be with you, Margaret, and remember to say your prayers every evening."

Maggie peered up at him, and Viv feared for a moment that her daughter might blurt out that they only sometimes remembered to do bedtime prayers. Instead, Maggie waved to the priest. "Bye-bye!"

Sister Mary Margaret stifled a laugh, and Father Monaghan turned without another word.

"Right," said the nun as soon as he'd gone. "We'd better hurry if we're to make sure this one catches her train. This way."

Viv took Maggie's hand and followed the nun into the station. All around them, the crowd parted for the sister, her long black robes flapping behind her as she forged a path to the ticket gates.

Around them, chaos reigned. Little children cried while older ones half dragged suitcases that were almost too big for them and ferried younger siblings along. Long, orderly rows of schoolchildren walked two by two behind teachers and sisters with clipboards. Great plumes of steam filled the glass roofed station as trains idled in the station, people surging forward to make sure their children were on the right train going in the right destination. Everything felt frantic and deeply sad.

Sister Mary Margaret, however, was determined, and it wasn't long before they stood on the platform of a train due south, first to stations along the way to Birmingham and then down through Coventry before finally ending in London. It was there that the nun halted.

"I'm afraid that this is as far as you go, Mrs. Levinson," said Sister Mary Margaret. "I'll give you a moment."

Viv dropped to her knees, not giving a thought to her stockings, and hugged Maggie to her. The card tag with Maggie's name and information written on it that Viv had looped around her daughter's coat button that morning dug into her cheek. She breathed in, trying to memorize the warm feel of Maggie's soft little body pressed against hers. Even amid the press of bodies and the smell of coal in the station, she could distinguish the unique scent of her daughter. She wanted to bottle up the memory so she'd never forget it.

When Maggie began to squirm in Viv's tight embrace, Viv loosened her arms.

"I have something for you," she said, unclasping the top of her handbag and drawing out a photograph. When Maggie had been nine months old, Kate had taken her to a studio and paid the dear price to have several portraits of Maggie taken. They were almost done when Kate insisted that Viv have one taken holding her daughter.

"You'll regret it later if you don't," said Kate with a knowing smile. "I had one taken with William and with Cora; we didn't have enough money when Colin was born."

Each year since, Viv would wait for a rare day when both Mum and Dad were out of the house. Then she'd dress Maggie and herself up in their best clothes and go into central Liverpool to have their portraits taken at that same photographer's shop.

Now, Viv handed her daughter their most recent portrait, taken back in March. "Do you know what this is?"

"That's me and that's you!" cried Maggie with delight, her chubby fingers pointing them each out.

Viv smiled even while fighting back tears. "That's right. I want you and Tig to keep it safe for me. If you ever miss me, you can look at this photograph and know that I'm looking at it every single night too."

Maggie stared at the photograph. "But where will you be, Mummy?"

The sob she'd tried so hard for the last two days to stifle escaped. She grabbed her daughter and pressed her face into her neck. "Remember, you're going to live with a nice woman named Mrs. Thompson and a nice man named Mr. Thompson. You must mind your manners with them, and do everything they say."

"I don't want to go!" Maggie cried, throwing her arms around Viv's neck.

Viv could feel her daughter's convulsing sobs against her chest, destroying her from the inside out.

"I love you very much, Little Bear," she said, tears streaming down her face even as she tried to smile. "You can tell Mrs. Thompson what to write to me, and she'll put it all in a letter. And I'll send you letters that she can read out to you. You'll like that, won't you?"

Maggie gave her a tiny nod.

Viv hugged her again. "Now, I need you to be very brave and go with Sister Mary Margaret. But I promise that one day we'll be together again."

"Promise?" Maggie asked.

"I promise," Viv said, with the full force of her convictions. "I love you. Never forget that."

A hand lighted on her shoulder.

"I'm sorry, Mrs. Levinson," said Sister Mary Margaret.

Viv nodded up at the nun and then kissed her daughter. "I love you very much, Little Bear."

Then Viv slowly rose and stepped back. The nun took Maggie by the hand, picking up her little suitcase in the other. Viv watched the pair of them climb onto the train, and just like that, they were gone.

The train's whistle blew, and platform attendants began slamming shut carriage doors. Steam billowed out, plunging the platform into a momentary fog. She looked up at the train windows, fear suddenly gripping her. She needed to see Maggie again.

The train's huge pistons slowly began to move. Still searching the windows, she pushed herself down the crowded platform. The train picked up speed, and she struggled to move faster. Then, all of a sudden, there they were. Maggie's little face pressed against the window, waving, while Sister Mary Margaret watched Viv with a sad smile.

All around her, women began to cry out to their children. Viv joined their sorrowful chorus.

"Goodbye! Goodbye, Little Bear!" she cried. "I love you!"

And then the train was gone, taking her little girl with it.

Maggie

Maggie turned her head to the train window and hugged Tig a little closer as Sister Mary Margaret snored next to her.

Maggie felt sad. She remembered her mother crying on the platform, hugging her and telling her to be good. Then her mother had given her one of the photographs she was only allowed to look at but not touch.

She pulled it out of her jacket pocket now. She knew that she was supposed to keep her fingers off the picture, but she reached out and touched her mother's pretty hair.

Yes, Maggie felt sad, but she couldn't quite understand why.

The train shuddered to a stop and woke up Maggie. She rubbed her eyes. Around her, people began to stand and collect their things.

"Are you ready?" asked Sister Mary Margaret.

Maggie nodded.

"Good. Bring your case and come with me."

The case was heavy, and Maggie struggled as Sister Mary Margaret led her through the train car and down to the platform.

The train station was crowded with people, all standing around and talking loudly. Most of what Maggie could see were legs. Legs in stockings. Legs in trousers. She kept her eyes trained on Sister Mary Margaret's long black robe, using two hands to hold up her case.

All at once, she stopped cold.

"Tig!"

The nun glanced back. "Margaret? What's the matter?"

"Tig!" Maggie wailed again, dropping her case.

"What's Tig?" Sister Mary Margaret asked.

"He's . . . He's . . . gone!"

Tears rolled down Maggie's face. She'd lost her toy tiger, even though she'd promised her mother that she would keep him safe.

"Oh, Margaret. Please don't cry," Sister Mary Margaret fretted. "I don't understand."

"What's happened?"

A well-dressed man in a charcoal suit with a matching hat had joined them. He was flanked by a woman wearing a confection of pink and white, her pale hair swept up under a fashionable hat.

"Mr. and Mrs. Thompson?" asked Sister Mary Margaret, her lips twisting in distress.

"Yes," said Mr. Thompson, his expression concerned.

"I'm afraid Margaret is upset. I think she's left her toy on the train," said Sister Mary Margaret.

Maggie wailed louder. Mr. Thompson whispered something to his wife before he slipped away into the crowd that was growing around them.

"Calm down, Margaret," said Sister Mary Margaret. "You're going to make yourself sick."

"I know, we'll go shopping. You can choose a new toy!" said Mrs. Thompson with a cheerful sort of delight, even as she knitted her gloved fingers together.

"I want Tig!" Maggie screamed, stomping her foot and hiccupping.

"She was so good on the journey," said Sister Mary Margaret.

"I'm sure she was," said Mrs. Thompson.

"I say, will you look at that." Mr. Thompson appeared at the edge of the crowd, brandishing a floppy toy tiger. "I think you belong to this little girl."

Maggie opened her eyes. "Tig!"

She opened her arms, hopping up to snatch the tiger from Mr. Thompson and bury her nose in the well-worn fur at the toy's neck.

"Where did you find it?" asked Mrs. Thompson, gazing up at her husband, the hero of the hour.

"It had slipped under a seat. It's a good thing the train was delayed with all the children disembarking, otherwise I might not have had time to find it," he said.

"Margaret," said Sister Mary Margaret, "can you say thank you to Mr. Thompson?"

"Thank you," Maggie whispered.

"I think she's a little shy," said Mrs. Thompson.

"Margaret, I'm Mrs. Thompson, and this is Mr. Thompson. You're going to be living with us for a little while."

Maggie didn't understand. She had a home.

Before she could say anything, Mrs. Thompson bent down and asked, "Do you like ice cream?"

"Strawberry is my favorite," Maggie said softly.

"A very good choice. I like chocolate, and Mr. Thompson likes vanilla best," said Mrs. Thompson. "Why don't we go into Solihull and have an ice cream as a special treat to celebrate you coming to Wootton Green? Would you like that?"

"Could I have two scoops of ice cream?"

The adults all laughed, and Mrs. Thompson said, "I think that if any occasion calls for two scoops of ice cream, it's this one. Don't you, Matthew?"

The man gave Mrs. Thompson an easy smile. "I think so."

They said goodbye to Sister Mary Margaret, and Mrs. Thompson took Maggie by the hand. As they led her away to their car, Maggie had a vague memory that she was supposed to be sad.

She wasn't entirely sure why.

Viv

October 6, 1934

The wall of sound hit Viv the moment she stepped into the Locarno Ballroom's salmon-pink-and-gold foyer. She liked how it felt coursing through her body, shaking her bones and warming the space around her heart.

"I can't believe you've never been to a dance hall, Viv," said Sylvie as they handed over money for their tickets to a harried-looking man behind the glass of the box office booth.

"Mum and Dad don't really approve," she said, gazing around and trying her best to memorize every detail of gold filigree that trimmed the walls and ceilings of the dance hall. It had taken enough persuading to convince her parents that Sylvie and Mary, who sat on either side of her in the sorting room, were nice girls. Then Kate had vouched for the Locarno, promising that it was a respectable place. Viv finally wore them down with the promise that there would be no visits to the pub, no drink, no men. She would be home by ten o'clock, ready to wake up for mass early the next morning. Only then had Mum nodded to Dad and Dad had said yes.

"Mine didn't either at first," said Mary, waving a hand, "but then I pointed out that there are only so many church tea dances a girl can go to before she realizes that she's met nearly every Catholic boy in Walton."

Sylvie laced her arm through Viv's, the slippery rayon sateen of her plum dress whispering against Viv's sky-blue dress that she'd run up on Mum's Singer just for this occasion. "Well, shall we be brave?"

Viv looked at the double doors to their left that pulsed open as laughing patrons flowed in and out of the ballroom, bursts of music following them. She pulled her shoulders back and nodded. "I'm ready."

Sylvie and Mary cheered and surged ahead on their silver-heeled dancing shoes.

A mere two steps into the crowd along the edge of the floor, a man materialized out of nowhere to take Sylvie's hand with nothing more than a "Fancy a dance?"

With a toss of her hair, Sylvie let herself be swept onto the floor.

"Well how do you like that?" Mary said, gazing after their friend. "She's left us behind."

"She's just having a bit of fun," said Viv.

"Ladies!" came a shout from over Viv's shoulder. She and Mary turned at the same time, Viv in confusion and Mary in exasperation, as a short ginger man who looked as though he'd just run a marathon pushed through the crowd to them.

"Kieran, what are you doing here?" Mary demanded, hand on her hip.

"Hello, love," said Kieran, leaning to give Mary a kiss on the cheek.

Mary swatted him away. "Don't call me love."

"Oh, don't be like that."

"I'll be however I want to be, Kieran Cagney. Where were you last Friday?" Mary demanded.

Viv took a step back from the arguing couple, but her path was abruptly cut short by a man's chest. He caught her, one hand at her waist and the other holding her in a ballroom embrace. "Fancy a dance?"

She laughed. "But I nearly knocked you over."

He flashed her a smile. "I'm short, but I'm not *that* short."

"Oh, I didn't mean—"

"I know you didn't," he said, cutting off her stammering apology. "Let's shuffle a bit."

Casting a glance back at Mary, who was deep into an argument with the errant Kieran, she glanced at her partner and gave a nod.

"Good." He maneuvered them onto the dance floor. "What's your name?"

"Vivian Byrne, but everyone calls me Viv," she said.

"I'm Nathan Hoffman," he said, pulling her gently into a spin. "Do you like the band?"

"I do," she said.

"My friend Joshua plays the sax." He jerked his head toward the brass section, which stood to add some punch to the chorus. "He's on the far end."

Viv craned her neck for a better view of this friend. He had on the same somber black dinner jacket that the rest of the orchestra wore, but even at a distance she could see that it fit him better than some of the trumpet players down the line. He stood taller than the saxophonist next to him too, and even from this distance she could see a head of dark hair combed in a deep part.

"What did you say his name was?" she asked.

"Joshua. We grew up together. The Levinsons are tailors, and my family is in wholesale fabric," Nathan said as the song came to the end. "They're heading on break. Come on, I'll introduce you."

"Oh, I don't know—"

"Josh!" shouted Nathan, tugging Viv behind him.

Joshua looked up, his eyes registering first his friend and then landing on Viv. They held hers for a moment—long enough for a blush to creep up from the square neckline of her dress.

He broke his gaze and stuck out his hand to his friend. "Glad you made it," said Joshua, shaking Nathan's hand vigorously.

"And miss the greatest saxophonist Liverpool's ever seen?" asked Nathan.

"He flatters me," said Joshua to Viv. "I challenge you to think of another saxophonist from Liverpool."

"I can't," she admitted.

"Joshua has big plans to go to New York and play," bragged Nathan.

"I'd love to go to America," Viv blurted out, although she'd hardly ever given it a thought.

Joshua looked at her again, something flickering in his dark brown eyes. "Is that right?"

All of a sudden Viv's breath seemed to come a little shorter. She clasped her hands together behind her back, pressing them into her long skirts. He made her nervous, she realized, and perhaps a little unsettled too. It was the way he held her gaze, long and intense, as though he were trying to read what was written on her soul.

Out of the corner of her eye, Viv saw Nathan glance between the two of them and then frown.

"Your break isn't very long, is it, Josh?" Nathan asked.

"Fifteen. They won't give us any more." Joshua nodded toward someone over his shoulder. "Isn't that Esther?"

Nathan whipped around. "Oh no. Where?"

"Just by the stairs," said Joshua.

"I need to go. Viv, we'll dance again later," said Nathan.

Viv and Joshua watched Nathan scurry off.

"Who is Esther?" she asked.

Joshua jumped down from the stage to stand next to her. "His girlfriend."

"Oh," said Viv, drawing out the word.

"They do this. Some bloke asks Esther to dance, so Nathan throws a fit. He goes off and dances with a pretty girl, so Esther blows her top."

"They sound like quite a couple," she said.

"And what about you? Do you have a six-foot boyfriend lurking around here, waiting to pummel me?"

She laughed. "Hardly. I've never had a boyfriend."

"Now, how can that be?" he asked as one of his bandmates walked up and handed him a pint, giving Viv a passing glance.

She tucked her chin, gazing down at her unscuffed dancing shoes. They'd cost her nearly four weeks' wages. Added to the fabric for her dress and the nylon stockings she'd saved just for this evening, the outfit she was wearing was the most expensive she'd ever donned. But she liked the way it made her feel. Beautiful. Alluring. Desirable.

"I suppose I never really met anyone I liked enough."

"And what about dates?" Joshua asked.

Dates. Underwhelming days out with young men who were all very much the same. They'd all left school early just like her, had gone into their fathers' or brothers' or uncles' trades, and enjoyed a pint or four at the pub on Friday and Saturday nights. One day they would buy a house of their own within the same few miles of where their parents and grandparents had always lived. Their greatest ambitions were a car and an annual holiday to Blackpool.

There was nothing wrong with any of it—she wanted some of those things too—but she hated the way that it felt like at eighteen she could see the rest of her life stretched out before her. If one of these men proposed, she'd be forced to resign from the General Post Office. Her life would become about children, laundry, shopping, and Sunday mass with a Saturday evening in the lounge at the local pub from time to time. She couldn't see the excitement. The adventure.

"I want to take you out," said Joshua, bringing her back to the light and froth of the ballroom.

"I'm sorry?" she asked, a little stunned.

"Next Saturday afternoon there's a concert. Would you like to come with me?" he asked.

She hesitated, but then she caught his look of uncertain hope. Her whole body softened into a yes. "All right, then."

His blush and the way he looked down at his shoes when she said yes charmed her.

"Good. Good good good, I'll pick you up at two," he said.

"Oh, no. I'd better meet you there. I have some things to do in town beforehand."

She didn't want to subject Joshua to Mum's scrutiny. It was bad enough that her parents didn't know him, but if they found out he was a musician, she was sure Mum would object and Dad would side with her as he always did.

"All right." He grabbed a scrap of paper and a pencil out of his instrument case and scribbled down the address and time. "Here you are."

"Thank you," she said.

"I'd better get back to it," he said, glancing at his fellow bandmates, who were picking up their instruments and shuffling through their sheet music.

"Oh, just one more thing," Joshua said as he picked up his saxophone and looped the black strap over his neck.

"Yes?" Viv asked.

He shot her a sheepish grin. "What's your name?"

She laughed. "Viv Byrne."

"Joshua Levinson. I'll see you Saturday, Viv Byrne," he said.

She nodded and ducked her chin as Mary glided to a stop next to her. Viv's friend glanced between her and Joshua and back again and then turned to her dance partner.

"I think Viv and I could use a drink," said Mary.

The man bowed his head and slipped away as Mary half dragged Viv away from the stage. "See you Saturday?" Mary asked when they finally stopped.

"He asked me to a concert," she said.

"Viv, you dark horse," hooted Mary with delight. "He's handsome."

Viv's stomach did a little flip. "He is."

"Who is he?"

"His name's Joshua Levinson," she said.

Mary frowned. "Levinson? He's Jewish?"

"We didn't talk long enough for me to ask," she said.

Mary's eyes raked her up and down, and Viv could feel a chill settle over them. "You're braver than I am."

"It's just a date," she said, but she couldn't ignore the flutter of nerves that skittered through her.

3 September 1939

Dear Mum, Dad, and Rebecca,

I've tried three times to write you this letter. Each time I try I can't because I know you're going to hate what I have to tell you. Maybe this time will be better.

Chamberlain's deadline for Germany to withdraw troops came at six o'clock in the morning here. A few of the guys I know from playing around different clubs stayed up to listen. A couple of them are Jews too and have family back in the old country. We hoped that there might be some sort of last-minute reprieve, but we and the rest of the world were disappointed.

Sitting there, listening to the radio, Liverpool felt so far away. New York is great, but it's never been home, and I know that if guys like me don't go back to England to fight, there might not be a home to come to.

I'm joining up—whatever service will take me. I can't sit on the sidelines when I know what's going to happen.

There are things I've done that I'm ashamed of. All I can hope is that, in this, I can make you proud once again.

Your loving son,
Joshua

5 September 1939

Beam Cottage
Wootton Green

Dear Mrs. Levinson,

I am sure that by now you are beside yourself with worry about Margaret. I cannot imagine how difficult it would be to send a child away, especially a little girl as precious as she is. Rest assured that she is safe and well with us.

Mr. Thompson and I took Margaret for ice cream as soon as she arrived. That seemed to cheer her because I am certain she was missing you.

You will be happy to know that she has a pretty bedroom that looks out over the garden, and every night our cat, Misty, curls up to sleep next to her. During the days she is with me or our house-keeper, Mrs. Reed, and we play with the tea set or the dollhouse that are in her playroom. You may be amused to hear that she was disappointed when I told her that our laundry is collected by a woman in the village, for she was very keen that we do laundry at home on Thursdays.

I know that it must be a particular challenge to you that Margaret cannot yet write her own letters or read the ones that you send. However, please know that I will be happy to convey any message that you send.

Margaret is a good girl, and I have no doubt that she will be very happy at Beam Cottage.

Sincerely,
Mrs. Matthew Thompson

7 September 1939

Dear Mrs. Thompson,

Thank you for your kind letter. I cannot tell you how reassuring it is to know that Maggie has arrived in Wootton Green safely. She is a wonderful little girl, very bright and curious. She has been learning her letters with me, and she has most of the alphabet, although sometimes she mixes up E and F. Please remind her that it is important to practice, and I hope that one day soon she may be able to read the letters I write to her.

    In the meantime, could you please read this next part out to her:

Maggie, I'm so sorry that we cannot be together right now. Things are very different at home. Grandad has a new job working at the Littlewoods building welding together wings for airplanes. Your nan knits things like scarves and gloves for soldiers. Although it's still warm now, they'll soon need to be just as toasty as you are when you bundle up in the gloves I made you for Christmas last year.

    I love you very much, Little Bear, and I know that we'll see each other again soon.

Mrs. Thompson, I would very much like to know when I might visit. It would be a relief to see where Maggie is living and to meet you and your husband. Please let me know what date might work best.

    Thank you again for taking care of my little girl.

                Sincerely,
                Vivian Levinson

9 September 1939

Dear Mrs. Thompson,

I thought that Maggie might enjoy some news from the neighborhood. Could you please read this out to her?

My Little Bear, you'll be happy to hear that Moggy, our neighbors' cat, looks as though she will have a litter of kittens this autumn. I know how much you love Moggy, and I know that you will ask if we can keep one of the kittens. I will try my best to see if I can persuade your grandad and nan that it is a good idea.

I hope that you are happy and enjoying your time at Beam Cottage. Remember, you can tell Mrs. Thompson anything that you want to tell me and she'll write it down.

Be a good girl, and I will see you very soon. I love you.

Please give my little girl a kiss for me, and tell her that I will be coming to bring her home as soon as we know it is safe.

Sincerely,
Vivian Levinson

14 September 1939

Dear Mrs. Thompson,

I thought that Maggie might want to know that her aunt Kate sends her love today. My sister, who has also had her three children evacuated, went with me to roll bandages for the war effort. Please tell Maggie that her aunt Kate is thinking of volunteering to become an ambulance driver because Uncle Sam taught her how to drive in his delivery van. Maybe one day Maggie will be able to drive as well.

Please give Maggie a kiss for me, and let me know when I may visit.

Sincerely,
Vivian Levinson

Joshua

September 8, 1939

Joshua staggered down the ship's gangway and pulled his jacket close against the light rain and cool wind coming off the Mersey. His nose filled with the smell of fuel and salt and damp, and a cacophony of voices rose up around him as people greeted their loved ones with hugs and tears. It took him a moment to realize why they sounded so strange: nearly all of them had English accents.

Bloody hell. He'd been away for so long, he'd forgotten what home *sounded* like.

Joshua grasped his case with one hand and his sax in the other, acutely aware that he had no greeting party. He was glad that he'd written to his family to tell them his plans to join up. However, he hadn't told them when his ship was due in. He wasn't ready to face them for the first time since he'd left.

He pushed through the crowds to make for Waterloo Road. His shoulders relaxed a fraction when he saw the Liver Building, familiar as always, rising above the docks with its two huge bird statues watching over city and sea. However, when he turned onto Water Street, wandering his way to St. George's Quarter, things looked different. The hand-painted signs high up on buildings had been redone. Shops had opened and closed. Even the snatches of conversations he overheard were about films, books, and bands he'd never heard of.

Down the road a ways, he spotted a recruitment office. He queued with the other men, a wide range of ages and states of dress. He was, as far as he could tell, the only one carrying a saxophone.

Finally, he was called to the front of the queue.

"Name?" asked a requirement officer without looking up.

"Joshua Levinson."

The man scribbled on his form. "Date of birth."

"Thirteenth of May 1915," he said.

They went through a list of questions including his nationality, schooling, and his religion. Replying "Jewish" had earned him a slight raise of the brows.

"Right, then." For the first time since Joshua had approached him, the recruitment officer looked up. "What branch of service were you hoping for?"

Not the Royal Navy, that was damn sure. Not after spending four days cooped up on an ocean liner, worrying he'd be torpedoed by a U-boat.

"The RAF," he said on impulse.

A recruitment officer glanced him over. "A lot of men want to fly with the RAF. It might not happen."

Joshua inclined his head to show that he understood. The recruiter sighed and noted down his answer.

"What's that?" the man asked, pointing his pencil to Joshua's instrument case.

"A saxophone," he said.

The recruitment officer sat back a little in his chair with a sniff. "You'll be wanting to join that new band, then. The Squadronaires."

It would be so easy to say yes, put him down as a musician, but somehow that didn't feel right. He wanted to fight. He needed to.

"I'd like to be air crew," he said.

The recruitment officer's disapproval melted away, and he gave Joshua a nod. "Good man."

Joshua's orders came eight days after his interview at the recruitment office. He was to report to RAF Padgate and Blackpool for basic training on the twentieth of September.

The instructions gave him plenty of time to go see his family. He didn't. Instead, he went for long walks all the way up the coast, past Formby to Southport. Sometimes he lay on the bed in the cheap room he'd let, smoking cigarettes and reading cheap detective novels he picked up for a shilling at a secondhand bookshop. He took his meals at a café around the corner. He didn't play his sax, and when the twentieth finally came, he went to Lime Street station and stored the instrument in the left-luggage room.

Pocketing his locker key, he eased his way through the mob of passengers and made his way to his assigned train. When he reached his platform, he found himself on the edges of a group of men. They all wore civilian clothes and the same look of nervous excitement. No doubt they'd grown up listening to their fathers' and uncles' stories about the last war, and they were eager to pull on their uniforms, pick up a rifle, and get to the manly business of fighting.

The train's warning whistle screeched, and the men around him jostled to climb aboard. Joshua let himself be swallowed up in the crowd, pushed on board by the inevitable force of the war.

Three cars in, he managed to find himself an empty seat next to a small man.

"Is this one free?" he asked.

The man started, looked at the seat, and then scrunched up against the window as though his slender frame could ever take up enough space to spill over into the empty seat. "It's empty. It's all yours if you want it."

"Thanks," he said, swinging his case up onto the overhead rack and settling down.

Joshua pulled out a newspaper, but as soon as he was settled, his companion jumped in.

"Are you going to RAF Padgate? I heard there are a lot of us on this train. They must have called up dozens. I don't know anyone though. Strange that. Dad said he joined up with half the neighborhood in the last war. But look what that did. Entire roads wiped out," said the man.

Joshua stifled a sigh and looked across the edge of the paper to find that the other man had stuck his hand out to shake.

"Jonathan Gibson, but everyone calls me Johnny."

"Joshua Levinson," he said, reluctantly taking Johnny's hand.

"What are you hoping to be? A pilot? You're not too tall, so you could be a pilot."

Joshua set his newspaper in his lap. "I'll do whatever they need me to do."

"I'm going to be a wireless radio operator, I'm sure. I worked in a radio-repair shop before the war. That's why. I'm sure that's where they're going to assign me," Johnny nattered on.

"You don't want to do something else?" Joshua asked.

Johnny gave him a merry smile. "I've never been good at anything else. Ask my mum. She'd tell you. All I can do is take things apart and put them back together again. I like cars too. What were you before the war?"

Clearly it was going to be a very long train ride.

"I was a musician," he said.

"Playing in one of the dance bands?" asked Johnny, holding one hand up and another to his stomach and wiggling in a mock Charleston in his seat. "Which ballroom?"

"In New York," he said.

Johnny's eyes went wide. "New York City?"

"Yes," said Joshua.

"And you came back to fight?" asked Johnny.

The heroism reflected back in the other man's eyes felt all wrong.

"It's not what you think it is," he said.

"Sounds to me like you came back to England to fight for king and country when you could have stayed away in America. They're not joining the war. Not like the last one," said Johnny.

"It's more complicated than that," said Joshua.

That seemed to give Johnny something to chew over because it was a solid two minutes before he asked, "What do you think basic ground training is going to be like?"

Joshua, who had taken his paper out again, didn't look up. "I don't know."

"My brother joined up in 'thirty-eight. He said that we'll be doing things like learning how to drill and fire guns," said Johnny. "He also said not to expect much of Blackpool. Even if you do get to see it, they only pay us three shillings a day. That doesn't go too far."

"It'll also almost be winter," Joshua pointed out.

"Winter in Blackpool. Wonder what that will be like," Johnny mused.

Probably grim, if Joshua had to guess. Soon it would be dark by four, and the wind coming off the Irish Sea would likely be cold enough to cut through whatever uniforms they were issued. He expected basic training to be a miserable old time, but they were there to serve, not go on holiday.

"You know what my brother also said?" Johnny asked. When Joshua didn't respond, Johnny pressed on in a lowered voice. "He said to watch out for the pilots. He said they can be right bastards."

"Then you'd probably best avoid them," Joshua said.

"But how am I going to do that? They're the ones who fly the planes," said Johnny.

"Good question, Johnny," said Joshua, opening his paper back up again, determined to read it if it killed him before they arrived in Blackpool. "Good question."

20 September 1939

Beam Cottage
Wootton Green

Dear Mrs. Levinson,

Margaret was delighted to receive your many letters, although it is sometimes difficult to encourage her to sit long enough to read all of them out. You do write so many details of your life in Walton, I wonder that you can afford the stamps!

You will be pleased to know that, as always, Margaret is happy and healthy at Beam Cottage. There is a girl, Marion, who is around the same age and lives down the lane, and the two have become fast friends. Margaret attended a tea party at Marion's house yesterday, although it was a bit of a to-do because really none of Margaret's clothes were appropriate. We went to the shops in Solihull, and she picked out the prettiest dress of white with little pink rosettes on it. I also purchased her a new stuffed toy, as her tiger, Tig, is looking rather disreputable!

Sincerely,
Mrs. Matthew Thompson

22 September 1939

Dear Mrs. Thompson,

Thank you for your letter. As you might imagine, I'm desperate for any news of Maggie. I hate to think of all the things I might be missing while she is away.

I'm very sorry that there was nothing suitable for the tea party in the things I sent with her. There was such limited space in her case, I thought that practical jumpers and everyday dresses would be most helpful. Please let me know the cost of the dress, and I will send you the money.

It was kind of you to give Maggie a new toy. However, Tig is very important, as he was a crib present from her aunt Kate, so Maggie has had him since she was a baby. I should hate to think of her without him. She would miss him so much.

Please let me know when might be an appropriate date to visit Wootton Green. I'm very eager to see my daughter.

Sincerely,
Vivian Levinson

24 September 1939

Dear Mrs. Thompson,

Could you please read this out to Maggie?

Little Bear, you'll never guess the surprise I had yesterday! I was getting ready for bed when I opened the cupboard door and saw a strange sight. Moggy had curled up in the bottom of the cupboard, right under my coat. It looks like she's also pulled in one of your old jumpers to sleep on. I wonder if she's making herself a little nest for her kittens.

I love you, Little Bear, and I will see you soon.

Mrs. Thompson, I really must insist on a time and date when I might visit my daughter. You can imagine how much I miss her, and how important it is to me to see where she is living.

Sincerely,
Vivian Levinson

3 October 1939

Beam Cottage
Wootton Green

Dear Mrs. Levinson,

Thank you for your letters. I am sure you will understand that it has been difficult to keep up with correspondence given all the events of the world. I am fortunate in that, although he is too old to be called up, Mr. Thompson is also an engineer and therefore is in a reserved occupation. One can never be too careful.

Margaret has settled in well here at Beam Cottage. Mr. Thompson arranged with a neighbor to have use of a pony he keeps at the local stables. We go out three times a week to ride—don't worry, the pony is very sweet-natured. I have also been teaching Margaret her letters so that she may begin to read before she attends school. She is so settled you would think that she has been living at Beam Cottage all her life!

You mentioned visiting Margaret. I think that is an excellent idea, but I would caution that perhaps we should allow for a little more time to lapse before you do. It is only that Margaret has settled in so well to life here. I should hate to upset her by reminding her of her earlier life in Liverpool.

Sincerely,
Mrs. Matthew Thompson

5 October 1939

Dear Mrs. Thompson,

Thank you for your concern about Maggie settling in to Beam Cottage. However, as her mother I must insist that I be allowed to visit. It was one of the conditions that I discussed with Father Monaghan, our parish priest who worked to place her with you.

I will arrive Tuesday. I take the train to Birmingham and then the bus to Solihull and another to Wootton Green. I hope to arrive by lunch, although I know that all forms of transportation can be unpredictable these days. Either way, please tell Maggie to expect me.

Thank you for your understanding.

Sincerely,
Vivian Levinson

7 October 1939

Beam Cottage
Wootton Green

Dear Mrs. Levinson,

I'm sorry that you felt as though you needed to assert yourself quite so forcefully in your last letter. If you had made it clear that you wished to see your daughter, I would have been happy to suggest a time and a date that might be suitable. However, since you have already set the date of your arrival, I suppose I shall have to make sure that I am available to you.

Sincerely,
Mrs. Matthew Thompson

Viv

October 10, 1939

Viv stepped off the bus in Wootton Green with a sigh of relief. It had been a nightmare traveling down from Liverpool that morning. She'd left early, giving herself what she'd thought was plenty of time because of how difficult the trains could be these days. Reduced service in order to move troops around the country and the rationing of petrol meant that too many people tried to cram onto whichever trains were available and would get them reasonably close to their destination. However, she hadn't been ready for the sheer crush of people packed on the Liverpool to Birmingham line. Then the bus from Solihull just sat there in the depot for forty minutes for no reason before setting off.

When she spotted the village shop, she stopped to ask how she could find the Thompsons' road and was happy to discover that it was only two right turns and a left away from the bus stop.

It was everything to force herself not to run as she sped down the pleasant paved roads. She'd dressed up especially for this visit, wearing the pretty cream dress with navy piping that Maggie always liked seeing her in, as well as her navy coat, knitted lace gloves, and gray hat, all of which she'd worn on her wedding day. She knew that—bar the dress— Maggie wouldn't notice these little touches, but she suspected that Mrs. Thompson would.

Viv made the last left turn onto a sweet lane of small two- and three-story houses of brick and whitewashed render. Each of them had a little door that looked as though Viv, with her diminutive height, might just fit through it with her hat on. In front of several of the homes, painted window boxes framed the doors, and all of them had plaques announcing the house's name.

Viv began scanning the house names. She spotted Beam Cottage midway down the road, standing large and proud among its neighbors—hardly what she'd expected from a cottage at all. It was three stories, with a set of large, symmetrical windows on each of the levels. The front door was painted a welcoming cherry red, and the pavement outside of it had been swept clean.

Viv took a breath and raised her hand to the heavy iron knocker.

Maggie had always loved it when people came to the door of the house in Ripon Street. She would shriek, giggle, and careen down the stairs to try to tug the door open. Every time it happened, Mum would click her tongue and make some snide comment about ill-behaved children, but Viv didn't have the heart to diminish her daughter's joy.

That afternoon, Viv expected to hear the same sounds from the opposite side of the door. Instead, there was silence until, at last, the heavy door swung open, revealing a birdlike blond woman in a cardigan the color of daffodils, a tweed skirt, and pearls.

"Mrs. Thompson?" Viv asked.

"You must be Mrs. Levinson," said the other woman, taking her in from head to toe.

"It's a pleasure to meet you," Viv said.

"How do you do?" Mrs. Thompson said in response, her soft, feminine voice featuring the same tones as the presenters on the BBC's light program that Mum loved so much. "Please do come in."

Viv stepped through the doorway. An intricate black-, orange-, and white-tiled pattern stretched down the length of the entryway broken up only by a long burgundy rug shot through with greens, blues, and creams. There were paintings on the wall—landscapes done in hazy detail that made her feel as though she was looking at them through a fog. A grandfather clock ticked away, its pendulum swinging in a glass-fronted case.

"Shall we sit in the drawing room?" asked Mrs. Thompson in a way that told Viv that it really wasn't a question.

She followed the other woman through a white door and into a room filled with sunlight. It was painted in a soft yellow with a delicate white picture rail running in parallel to an elaborate molded cornice. In the center of the room, a brass-and-glass light fixture hung from a delicate ceiling rose, drawing the eye to it before releasing it to take in the tiled fireplace all done in shades of blue. Even the iron grate was embellished with the figures of two knights standing on either side of what looked like a castle's battlements.

This foreign world with beautiful things that seemed to have no purpose except to be pretty was so far outside of her own family's grasp that it felt laughable. At the center of all of it stood Mrs. Thompson, a woman who appeared just as decorative as her surroundings.

"Please take a seat," said Mrs. Thompson, inviting Viv to the pale-green-and-white-striped sofa opposite her.

Viv grasped the handles of her one good handbag. "I'd like to see Maggie first. I'm sure you understand."

Mrs. Thompson smiled. "You must be worried sick over her. Unfortunately Margaret hasn't come back from her friend Marion's house yet."

This would be her first time seeing her daughter in nearly six weeks, and Maggie wasn't here?

"We weren't certain when you would be arriving because of the poor state of the trains, and Margaret was so excited to visit Marion. You see, they ride together at the stables. Marion's father, Charles, is rather a talented horseman, and he's encouraged his daughter to ride from such an early age. It was his idea that Margaret should give it a try as well, and she turned out to have a natural seat," said Mrs. Thompson.

Viv's lips tightened. She should be the first to know whether Maggie had any particular talent for riding—although how on earth she would have found that out she had no idea. The closest she'd ever come to a horse was the handful of old carts that still made their way through the neighborhood.

"I am sorry if you're disappointed," said Mrs. Thompson, looking a little contrite. "I can only imagine how much you miss Margaret."

"Maggie," she said.

"I beg your pardon?"

"Her name is Maggie."

Mrs. Thompson frowned. "I was under the impression that she was baptized Margaret."

"She was, but all of us call her Maggie," she said.

"I see," said Mrs. Thompson.

Before Viv could say anything else, a tall, athletic man crossed the drawing room threshold.

"Hello, darling. This is Mrs. Levinson," said Mrs. Thompson without rising.

Mr. Thompson strode over to Viv, his hand outstretched before he even reached her. "How do you do? You've raised a fine girl. Margaret is a delight."

"Thank you," she said, taking a moment to study Mr. Thompson. He was a little older than his wife, with brown hair shot through with silver and a dun-colored shawl cardigan with leather patches at the elbows.

"Has Sarah offered you tea?" asked Mr. Thompson.

"She has, but I would like to see *Maggie* first," she said.

"I just telephoned Charles and Joan to tell them it's time to send Margaret home. They were finishing sandwiches after riding. Apparently Margaret did very well," said Mr. Thompson.

Viv could feel the steady creep of worry rising in her chest. "Isn't she a little young to be riding a horse? She's only four."

Mr. Thompson laughed. "I had a pony at three. It's good for children. It teaches them not to be afraid of horses."

"But if you would prefer that Margaret not ride, of course we would follow your wishes," said Mrs. Thompson, glancing between Viv and her husband. "It would be such a shame though. She enjoys riding so much."

"I'm sure that it's fine, if she enjoys it," Viv said cautiously.

Maggie was Viv's daughter, so why did it feel as though she was tiptoeing through this conversation?

Mrs. Thompson's face lit up, and she clapped her hands with delight. "I'm so glad to hear you say so."

Mr. Thompson leaned forward as though straining to hear. "I believe that's the children now."

The doorbell chimed, and they all rose while Mr. Thompson went to the door. There was a scuffling in the front entryway, and Maggie burst through the door trailed by a little blond girl with her hair done in pigtails and an older man.

"Mummy!" Maggie cried as she launched herself at Viv's legs.

Tears stung at the corners of Viv's eyes as her little girl clasped her hard. She'd forgotten how fierce Maggie's hugs could be, as though Viv were a life raft that Maggie needed to cling to. She placed her hand on her daughter's hair, which was French braided with a hair ribbon that matched the blond girl's. She'd never braided Maggie's hair, preferring to leave her soft black curls free.

"My Little Bear," she murmured.

Maggie lifted her face, her eyes open and bright. "Mummy, Mummy, I have a pony!"

"I've heard," she said, glancing to the Thompsons.

"Remember, Margaret, Puffball is Mr. Stourton's pony, but you're allowed to borrow it," said Mr. Thompson.

"Thank you for bringing her back, Charles," said Mrs. Thompson. "You must come play tea party with us again, Marion."

Once the Stourtons were gone, Mr. Thompson said, "Well, I expect you'd like to spend some time with your daughter."

"Yes. I would. Thank you," Viv said. It felt odd asking for permission to visit with one's own child.

Mrs. Thompson's thin lips seemed out of place compared to her earlier ebullience, but still she said, "Margaret, perhaps you'd like to show your mother your dollhouse."

Viv wondered if Mrs. Thompson was deliberately ignoring her request to call Maggie by her nickname, but before she could say anything, Maggie popped up from where she'd nestled herself against Viv's leg on the sofa. "Come, Mummy!"

Viv let herself be pulled out of the beautiful drawing room and up a set of stairs carpeted in a deep, soft gray that sank under her feet. They passed several doors before Maggie pulled her into one.

"This is my playroom," Maggie announced.

Viv sucked in a breath. The entire room was lined with shelves except for the wall where two windows framed in delicate lace curtains let the light spill in. Dozens of books sat on the shelves, but there were dolls, toy drums, balls, all manner of things. In the center of the room, a huge dollhouse stood, its doors open in invitation. The dolls were set up across the house on intricately detailed pieces of miniature furniture. It was exactly the sort of thing Viv had longed for when she had been a child.

"Is this all yours?" she asked.

Maggie nodded. "I like this dolly best," she said, grabbing up a doll who wore a navy skirt suit. The doll maker had taken care to curl the doll's light brown hair into a pageboy and paint a small Cupid's bow smile on its face.

"Why is that?" Viv asked, trying to keep the shake out of her voice.

"She looks like you, Mummy," said Maggie.

Viv gasped out a breath. Even amid all this extravagance that Viv could not in a thousand years provide for her daughter, Maggie still thought of her.

"Where is Tig?" she managed.

"Here!" Maggie tugged at her hand, leading her out of the playroom and into the bedroom next door. It was clearly Maggie's room because the small iron bed was covered with a pink duvet and white eyelet bed skirt that gracefully swept the floor. Sitting on the middle of the bed in pride of place, was Tig.

"Tig likes it here," said Maggie, clambering onto the bed and rumpling the duvet in the process.

"Is that right?" Viv asked.

"Yes. Tig likes Marion too," said Maggie.

Viv sank down on the bed, next to her daughter. She took in all of the things that she would never be able to give her daughter. All she had was a love that the Thompsons would never be able to match—but was that enough?

"Does Tig ever miss home?" she asked.

Maggie fell silent. Finally, she said in a tiny voice, "Yes."

An urge to snatch up her daughter and run from the house surged up in her. To yank the beautiful dress that her daughter wore off and put her into the clothes Viv had sewn herself. To take her back to Ripon Street, even if it meant facing the admonishments of her parents, her sister, and her priest.

It might be torture knowing that Maggie was under another woman's roof, spending her time in a beautiful house with friends Viv had never met before, but the guilt that would crush her if something happened to her daughter was too powerful.

She swatted at the streaks of tears that wetted her cheeks. "I miss you too, Little Bear. But I know that you're safe here, and that is the most important thing. I hope you understand that."

Maggie gave a shallow nod. "Yes, Mummy."

"Good," Viv said, reaching out a hand to smooth down her daughter's hair. "Now, why don't you show me how you play tea party?"

It was nearly five o'clock when Viv finally tore herself away from Maggie. It was tempting to stay, forcing Mrs. Thompson's hand in offering her a guest room for the night, which she was certain the Thompsons had, but she knew that would only prolong the pain of leaving her daughter again.

Mrs. Thompson stuck her head through the door of Maggie's room and said, "Margaret, dear, it's time for your supper."

Maggie looked up at Viv. "We call tea 'supper,' Mummy," her little girl explained.

"Is that right?" Viv asked, although she was well aware that although her family had called the evening meal tea, to a well-to-do couple like the Thompsons it would always be supper.

"Why don't you wash your hands, Margaret?" suggested Mrs. Thompson.

Maggie slid off the chair she'd drawn up to the table they were playing tea party at and went scrambling off to the bathroom.

"Margaret is such a dear child," said Mrs. Thompson fondly.

"She is." Viv hesitated. "I really must insist that you call her Maggie."

Mrs. Thompson's hand flew to her mouth. "Oh, I am sorry. Have I done it again?"

"Yes," she said. "Several times."

"It's a force of habit, and Margaret is so much more elegant, don't you think?" Mrs. Thompson asked.

"I plan on coming down to see Maggie every month," she said, ignoring Mrs. Thompson's last comment.

"Every month? Well, I'm sure Margaret will be delighted," said Mrs. Thompson, her ever-present smile tightening.

"It's important that she sees me and remembers where she is from," she said.

"Well, if it isn't too much of a burden. I know how dear these things can be," said Mrs. Thompson.

Viv's cheeks burned hot with the implication that she might not be able to afford train and bus tickets. In truth, the money her father had given her hadn't covered all of it and she'd had to dip into her own meager savings, but she wasn't about to admit that to Mrs. Thompson.

"I will write to let you know when I'll be coming," she said.

"Very well," said Mrs. Thompson as Maggie bounded back into the room.

Viv dropped to her knees and opened her arms. "I have to go now, Little Bear."

Tears began to shine in Maggie's eyes. "Mummy, no!"

Viv gathered her daughter closer to her, tucking the little girl's head against her breast as she'd held her so often as a baby in those precious moments when it had felt as though they were the only people left in the entire world.

"I will come back soon. We can have another tea party, and maybe you can show me how you can ride your pony," she said.

Maggie sniffled. "Do you promise?"

She wiped one of the little girl's tears away. "I promise, Little Bear."

Viv managed to hold back her tears until she was seated on the bus to Solihull. Then she pulled out her handkerchief and began to weep into it, her sobs attracting the attention of a few of the older women who had boarded with her. Not that she cared. The only thing that mattered was

Joshua

Johnny's brother hadn't been wrong. Pilots could be bastards, but the noncommissioned officers who ran their training were worse.

When they arrived at RAF Padgate, he and Johnny had been billeted in the same barracks with twenty-eight other men, all of whom reported to Corporal Johnson, who was a tall man with a bottlebrush mustache that he pulled on when he was angry. He was, as far as Joshua was concerned, a sadist.

This may have sprung from the fact that Corporal Johnson was a sportsman, having run for England at the British Empire Games.

"You don't know pain until you've raced against the best and felt as though you were going to rupture a lung," shouted Corporal Johnson over the freezing wind that threw sand up into the faces of Joshua and the other recruits as they stood on the edge of a beach at six o'clock in the morning. "Now, three miles at pace, men. Go!"

Joshua, whose physical conditioning in New York mostly consisted of enduring long periods of sitting on uncomfortable chairs at jam sessions after-hours with other musicians, vomited after the second mile.

"Come on." Johnny, who had hung back with Joshua more out of pity than need, tugged on his arm. "Get up or Corporal Johnson will see."

"He's so far ahead, how could he tell?" Joshua gasped out.

that she was leaving the best, most vital part of herself behind in Wootton Green.

She wouldn't survive this war if she couldn't see her daughter. She didn't know how Kate, whose children had been sent off to North Wales for their evacuation, could possibly cope. But her situation with Maggie was different. She would find a way to make sure that she was there each month.

She couldn't rely on Mum and Dad for money. She'd walked out the door that morning with hardly a word from them, almost as though they were perfectly pleased to forget their granddaughter altogether.

No, she would need to find another way, one that didn't leave her beholden to anyone.

As the bus pulled away from the curb, Viv peered out the window at the countryside rolling by and began to think.

"He'll know," said Johnny. "My brother said that only physically fit men get flight crew. Otherwise you'll be stuck on the ground."

Joshua groaned and hauled himself up off the sand.

However, incredibly, things became better. He still hated the early-morning runs and workouts in all kinds of weather, but after a solid three weeks he started to lose some of the nagging soreness that had plagued him since he had arrived on base. And when they weren't being tormented by the likes of Corporal Johnson, he found he was a decent shot and had been able to hone his accuracy faster than some of the other men.

But, it was in the assessments they sat through in anonymous little rooms filled with scarred wooden desks that he shined. His parents had insisted he go to school through eighteen, taking all of his exams. However, when he'd shown little interest in anything but music, Dad had thrown his hands up in disgust.

Now, sitting in front of tests for mathematics, aptitude, and all number of other things, he found that he enjoyed the discipline of the questions. There was a right and a wrong answer, and he seemed to instinctively understand the rules. Almost like music.

"You'll be a navigator," Johnny would announce every time the subject came up.

"I don't know about that," said Joshua, although he secretly thought the same.

"I know it. Maybe we'll be assigned on the same plane. Probably a Blenheim bomber."

"What else are you sure about? Know what Hitler's got planned?" he asked with a grin.

"If I knew that, do you think I'd be here with you? I'd be running the show," said Johnny.

Joshua, despite himself, had come to enjoy the irrepressibly talkative would-be wireless operator's company. Johnny looked out for him in his own little way, and so Joshua had found himself taking it upon himself to do the same. They did PT together, they ate together, they even cleaned the bloody floors together. But every time Johnny tried to ask too many questions about Joshua's life before the war, he shut him down. He would not talk about Liverpool. He did not tell anyone that he had a wife, and he certainly wouldn't admit that he had a child.

But just because Joshua didn't talk didn't mean he didn't think. It usually caught up with him when, at night, his mind began to drift. He no longer had the distraction of late, exhausting nights at the club to keep thoughts of Viv and their child at bay. Now they crept in, unbidden, like specters haunting a forgotten house.

The worst was the shame of admitting to himself that he knew nothing about his child. He knew that Viv had given birth because his sister had written to him. A few months after Viv had been due, Rebecca had waited outside of the Byrne house and spotted Viv with a simple, old pram that looked as though it had carried its fair share of children.

As he'd held the letter in his hand, anger had bubbled up in him, molten as lava. He'd crumpled the letter in his fist and written back to Rebecca, telling her to bloody well stay out it.

Later that night, when he'd drunk half a fifth of bourbon, he'd realized that he didn't even know whether the child was a boy or a girl.

Now he lacked the comfort of liquor, but he could try his best to tire his body out to the point of exhaustion. Anything to make sleep come easier at night.

"And right!" came Corporal Johnson's shout from the front of the pack of men running across the beach for their usual morning training.

Ahead of Joshua, the pack broke to the right, sprinting up a sand dune and over to a bit of marsh. He gritted his teeth. The run was nearly over, but he hated ending on wet, boggy ground. This ugly, bleak place with its wicked wind and unrelenting rain was always wet with mud underfoot.

"Almost done," Johnny gasped out next to him as though reading his mind. "Just think of hot showers and stew in the mess."

"Watch your line!" came a shout from behind them in the clipped, clean accent of the upper classes.

Joshua shot a look back over his shoulder at Moss, the man who'd spoken, managing to keep on balance while pounding up the dune. Johnny wasn't so lucky. Johnny's feet went out from under him, and the little man went crashing down to the ground, rolling to his side and taking Moss down with him.

"You bastard!" roared Moss.

"Hey, hey." Joshua stopped and circled back to them.

Another man with dark hair whom he'd seen around stopped to crouch down next to Moss, so Joshua squatted next to Johnny.

"Are you okay?" Joshua asked.

Johnny's cheeks flamed red. "Fine. I'm fine. Just lost my step in the mud, didn't I?"

"Good," Joshua said before turning to Moss. "What about you?"

"He could have broken my arm!" Moss raged.

"I'm really sorry," Johnny muttered, wiping mud off the side of his face.

"I'm going to be a pilot! He could have ended my entire career!" yelled Moss.

"I didn't mean—"

"It was an innocent mistake that Johnny only made because you were trying to overtake him where it wasn't safe," said Joshua in a low, calm voice that hid his desire to pop Moss in the nose.

"He's right. You should be the one apologizing," said the fourth man.

Moss, both hands braced behind him in the thick mud, glared at the other man. "Nobody asked you, Schwartz."

Moss hauled himself to his feet only to loom over Johnny. "Stay out of my bloody way or I'll see that you're scrubbing out pots in the mess for the rest of the war."

Johnny held up his hands, and Joshua was just about to step forward when Moss muttered, "Fucking yids," and ran off.

Joshua sucked in a sharp breath. It wasn't as if he hadn't been called a "yid" before. Most of the kids in the neighborhood he grew up in were Catholic, and they were fascinated that his family occasionally went to synagogue rather than church and celebrated the high holy days and Passover and not Christmas and Easter. A few kids had tried squaring him up on the pavement or in the park, calling him all manner of hurtful names to try to goad him into a fight. He did fight a few times in scraps that mostly ended in score draws with both boys covered in dirt and sporting black eyes. His mother had hated it, but it had been enough to earn him a modicum of respect, and as he grew older he'd mostly been left alone.

"You too?" Schwartz asked.

He nodded.

Schwartz stuck out his hand. "Adam Schwartz. Always good to meet a member of the tribe."

The tribe. He hadn't thought of himself that way in years. Even before he'd left Liverpool, he'd stopped attending synagogue and stopped keeping kosher. He knew that this turning away from his faith bothered his parents, but he'd taken advantage of their belief that forcing him toward observance would only make him less inclined to return to it one day. Still, here was a man who understood some of who he was and where he had come from.

"Joshua Levinson," he said.

"Are you okay?" Adam asked Johnny, clapping a hand on Johnny's shoulder.

Joshua's friend rubbed the back of his neck. "He hurt my pride more than anything else."

"Come on," said Joshua. "Let's finish this."

All three men began running again, so far behind that they couldn't see the end of the drilling unit until they'd reached the top of the hill. It was when they'd crested that Johnny said, "Did you hear what Moss called you both?"

"Yeah, I heard it," Joshua said.

"He should be reported to the corporal for calling you that," said Johnny.

Joshua looked up and caught Adam's glance.

"You're a good friend, but what will that do? Do you think anyone will care?" asked Adam.

"Even if we did report him, Moss will probably make pilot," said Joshua. "That's what usually happens with bastards like that."

"It's not right," muttered Johnny.

"No, it is not," said Adam as Corporal Johnson came into view, looking mad as hell.

"Shit," cursed Joshua.

"Here we go," muttered Adam.

"It was all of us. You got that?" asked Joshua quickly.

"What?" Johnny asked.

"You're not taking the blame for this," he said.

"Let him yell," agreed Adam. "Don't talk back."

"Once he's done, you'll get that shower you were dreaming about," said Joshua.

The three men put their heads down and sprinted toward their steaming corporal as fast as they could.

Viv

October 15, 1939

Nearly a week after her visit to Beam Cottage, Viv sat with her prayer book open in front of her, gazing absently at the Our Lady of Angels' elaborate altar as Father Monaghan droned on, when the hazy threads of the idea formed in her head.

She could go back to work.

As the congregation dipped their heads in prayer, she examined the idea. All over the high street and in the magazines she flipped through, she saw signs encouraging women to do their bit for the war effort. "Join the WRNS and Free a Man for the Fleet!" one poster shouted at her whenever she walked to the butcher's. "Government Appeal to Women: 20,000 Needed in the A.T.S. Now!" urged a magazine ad. She'd read a story or two about how married women with no children were being welcomed by the war effort. Every little bit of help mattered.

If she could find a job, she could afford the cost of the trip to see Maggie once a month. With money in her pocket, she wouldn't have to endure the shame of Mrs. Thompson's letters telling her that her daughter's clothing wasn't acceptable for whatever outing or party the Thompsons were attending. She could buy her daughter some of the beautiful things Viv had seen in that playroom.

On Monday morning, while Mum was volunteering in the canteen the church had set up for Liverpool's servicemen, Viv boarded the bus to retrace the steps of her old commute to the Northern Delivery Office. Her heart pounded fast in her chest when she disembarked at her old stop, but she took a steadying breath. She would not be turned away.

She pushed through the glass-and-metal front door into a lobby area. A bored-looking woman at the front desk barely glanced up when Viv presented herself.

"This isn't a post office, it's a delivery office," droned the secretary. "To post your letters—"

"I'm here about a job. I'd like to speak to Miss Taylor," said Viv.

The woman shot her an assessing look. "Miss Taylor recently retired. It's Miss Davies who does the hiring now."

Viv's heart sank a little bit. She'd always liked her old boss, and she'd hoped that Miss Taylor might look favorably on her and give her a chance.

Still, she'd come this far. She wasn't going to waste the opportunity.

"Then I'd like to speak with Miss Davies, please," she said.

The secretary raised her brows but picked up the telephone by her right hand, pressed a button, and spun a quarter turn in her chair.

"There's a lady here to see Miss Davies about a job. Yes . . . Yes . . ." The secretary glanced over her shoulder to give Viv a look up and down. "I'd say so, yes. All right, then. Thank you."

The secretary hung up the phone. "She'll be with you in a moment."

Viv took a seat on one of the lobby's hard wooden chairs. It wasn't exactly comfortable, but if she could sit she could hold her handbag on her lap and hide the slight tremble in her hands by clutching its handle.

A good ten minutes passed without any sign of Miss Davies. The secretary answered the phone occasionally, but the girl seemed more interested in a fan magazine spread out on the desk in front of her than anything else. Then, just as Viv had talked herself into approaching the secretary again, the door behind the reception desk opened and the unmistakable figure of her old sorting-office friend Sylvie Davies, all blond curls and Coca-Cola-bottle figure, appeared.

"Well, if it isn't Viv Byrne," said Sylvie with a laugh.

"You're Miss Davies?" she asked.

"In the flesh," Sylvie said.

"What happened to Miss Taylor?" Viv asked.

"She up and left us for the WAAFs, would you believe? Said she'd always dreamed of flying and, with the war on, maybe they could use a woman like her." With a nod to the door, Sylvie said, "Why don't you come back with me and we can talk?"

Viv followed her old friend out of the lobby and down an antiseptic-looking corridor lit with harsh fluorescents. On the walls hung posters reminding the women who worked there that "Loose lips sink ships."

"It's just as glamorous as you'll remember, but we make do," said Sylvie with a laugh. "Why don't we fetch a cup of tea from the canteen and have a proper chat?"

"I'd like that," said Viv.

"You wouldn't believe how much work we've had just in the last few weeks since war's been declared," said Sylvie, pushing through a pair of swinging doors and into the canteen. It was just eleven so there was hardly anyone in, but the familiar scent of cottage pie already hung in the air.

"The government thought they had their ducks in a row, but then they called up all of our boys who weren't already doing their national service and poof! There that went," Sylvie continued. "I can just about manage to keep the sorting office staffed, but it's the deliveries that are really suffering. Some of the old boys who thought they'd ridden their last route are putting their uniforms on again to make sure the post makes it out. And everything's taking twice as long with the censors reading everything out at Littlewoods."

That was good. If the General Post Office needed workers, perhaps a woman with an estranged husband and an evacuated daughter would look a little more appealing.

"Do you still take it with sugar?" Sylvie asked as they approached a woman manning a station with huge urns of tea.

"Just milk these days," she said.

"I still can't drink it unless it's sweet enough to stand a spoon up in it. I just hope sugar won't be rationed. Thanks," said Sylvie as she accepted her cup from the tea lady and pointed to a far table in a corner. "Why don't we sit over there where no one will bother us."

When Viv had worked at the post office, Sylvie and Mary had been her friends, bonded by common experience. They knew what it was like to have papery-dry fingers from going through hundreds of letters on a shift, stuffing each of them into labeled pigeon holes for the postmen to deliver. They would push up out of their chairs at the end of the day, their backs and knees all creaking and cracking as they worked out the stiffness that settled even into joints as young as theirs.

And it had been at a table like this one that Viv had told both Sylvie and Mary that she was going to be married. She'd not told them everything—that she was pregnant and terrified—but she was certain they'd guessed the truth of what she held back.

Now, sitting with her former friend, she tried not to let the thoughts of the life that she once had erode her plans.

"So you'd like a job," said Sylvie, coming right to the point as soon as they were settled.

"Yes." Then, deciding that honesty was the best way moving forward, she added, "I need the money to go visit my daughter. She was evacuated."

Sylvie played a finger over the handle of her teacup. Her nails were painted with a cherry-red lacquer that Viv was certain would not have been acceptable when Miss Taylor had been in charge.

"I heard you had a little girl," said Sylvie

"Who from?" she asked.

Sylvie hesitated and then said, "Mary."

Viv hadn't seen Mary since she'd married a joiner and moved to Everton, but even before that, their friendship had cooled. As soon as Mary had learned that Viv was to become Mrs. Levinson, Mary had stopped waving hello at church or pausing for a chat in the high street. Viv had thought that the loud whispers of "slut" and "whore" would hurt the most, but it had been Mary's betrayal that had really stung.

"I see," Viv said carefully. If Mary had Sylvie's ear, her bid for a job was likely slipping away as they spoke.

"Of course, some of us have longer memories than others. And more forgiving natures. Tell me about your little girl," said Sylvie with a smile.

The sudden ache that always accompanied thinking about Maggie made Viv drop her gaze to her teacup. She wondered if it would ever become easier, this feeling that a part of her had been ripped away.

"Her name is Margaret, but we all call her Maggie. She's beautiful, with dark curls and the longest lashes you've ever seen. When it's cold, her cheeks become so rosy they look like apples. She likes to sing. She's only four, so mostly the songs don't make sense, but she has a pretty voice. Her best friend is a stuffed animal named Tig and . . ." The emotion sitting high in her throat had grown too large to speak around. Instead, she pulled out a handkerchief and carefully folded it to catch her brimming tears.

Sylvie stretched a hand across the table to grab Viv's free hand. "I can only imagine how hard that is."

Viv nodded and sniffed. "You would have thought I would be used to it by now. She went away more than a month ago. I . . . I saw her last week. She's with a couple in a village in the Midlands."

"I'm glad you were able to see her," said Sylvie.

She shook her head. "It was awful. The Thompsons don't have children of their own, so they're doting on her, which I wouldn't mind, but she's living in this beautiful house with her own bedroom and her own playroom. She has new dresses and new toys and they've even got a friend who has a pony who is teaching her how to ride. A four-year-old girl from Walton? Who would have thought of such a thing?"

She looked down as her hands twisted her handkerchief in her lap. "I'm terrified that she won't want to come home when all of this is over."

Or that she might forget me altogether. She couldn't say that out loud because then it might come true, and she didn't think she would be able to survive that.

"I'm living at the mercy of my parents," she said. "I need my own money."

Sylvie studied her for a moment and then tilted her head to the side. "I've always thought it was such a shame that your husband died so young."

Viv started. "My husband?"

"I always worried that sending a card wasn't enough. I should have visited to give my condolences," her friend went on.

"Sylvie, I—"

"Of course, with your daughter evacuated and no husband at home, you would be looking for work. It must be incredibly difficult," Sophie went on. "Fortunately, things have changed a little bit around here in light of the war. We need all the able-bodied women that we can find to deliver the post. Including widows."

Viv's mouth formed an *O* as everything clicked into place. "That's very generous of the General Post Office."

"Isn't it?" Sylvie laughed. "I know they're desperate for posties everywhere in Liverpool. The heads have been moaning about it for weeks now. Do you mind if it isn't here?"

"That might make it easier," she said, knowing that people in Walton would know the story of what happened to Edith and John Byrne's daughter too well.

"Good. Do you fancy yourself on a bicycle?" Sylvia asked.

Viv hadn't ridden a bicycle in years, but that wasn't going to stop her.

"I'm sure the fresh air will do me good," she said.

Sylvie laughed. "Write down your telephone number for me, and I'll ask around. I'll give you a ring as soon as I have news."

"Thank you," Viv breathed as she took the small notebook and pencil Sylvie had produced from her skirt pocket.

"No need to thank me. Just consider it an apology," said Sylvie.

"An apology?" she asked.

"For not making more of an effort to stay in touch."

"It was a difficult situation all around," she said.

Sylvie's eyes grew sad. "Do you remember my younger sister, Ellen?"

Viv had a vague recollection of a younger version of Sylvie meeting them at the gates of the Northern Delivery Office once after work.

"Ellen got into trouble when she was just sixteen. She had a boyfriend—he was at one of the ironworks—and the moment that he realized what happened he was gone. Left her to tell our parents. Well, Mum and Dad sent her away to one of those hospitals to have the baby. It was adopted out, and Ellen hasn't been right since. She cries all the time. She can't keep a job. She hardly makes it out of bed some days. It ruined her life.

"No one helped my sister, but if you keep to your story about being a widow, I promise I'll do everything I can," Sylvie finished.

"Thank you," Viv whispered, overwhelmed by the kindness of the other woman. "Thank you so much."

Sylvie shook her head. "Just work hard, and do right by your little girl. Don't let her forget how much her mother loves her."

18 October 1939

Dear Mum, Dad, and Rebecca,

When I joined up, I thought I was going to be in the air as soon as my basic ground training was done. I've learned since then that there's a lot more to training in the RAF than I'd thought.

My friends in the barracks and I have just received our orders. There's a big division in this initial round between the men who've been slated for ground crew and those who will be flying—not that any of us should assume we're going to see any action in any plane because there's so much training ahead of us we could still wash out. A lot of guys are unhappy with their assignments, but I'm not too broken up about it.

We've been assessed, and those of us who need additional training are being sent on to specialist sites. My friend Johnny, who I've told you about, is going to be a wireless operator, so he'll go on to train at RAF Yatesbury. My friend Adam and I have both been tapped to be navigators, so we're going to train at Cambridge University.

I'm glad Adam's coming with me. He's Jewish too, from Manchester. (Before you ask, Mum, his family attends the South Manchester Synagogue in Fallowfield, so I don't think they would have known your parents.) I wish Johnny could go with us. He needs someone looking after him.

I hope everything is going well with the tailoring business. Rebecca wrote that Mum has dusted off the knitting needles and is making socks for the troops. I know that if I was sent a pair of those in a care package, I'd be happy to have them.

Your loving son,
Joshua

Joshua

October 21, 1939

Joshua knew that he was being a coward, but when he'd been granted forty-eight hours leave before he had to report to Cambridge, he'd panicked. He didn't want to go home, but he couldn't stay on base at RAF Padgate, and Blackpool in the autumn seemed too grim a prospect to stand.

In the end, it was Johnny who'd made the decision for him.

"I'm going home to my mum on the train before I push on to Yatesbury. Do you want to ride up together?" Johnny had asked.

Adam, who'd been sitting with them in the mess hall, had looked at Joshua with those piercing dark brown eyes that seemed to see everything, and said, "You should go with him. See your family."

Joshua had never talked about his family, but maybe it was the way that he so often steered the conversation away from anything to do with his time in Liverpool that Adam knew.

"Is that what you're going to do?" Joshua asked.

Adam nodded. "My wife has been counting down the hours."

Joshua's didn't even know he was in England.

"Yeah, all right," he'd said. "I'll come with you."

However, on the day, as the train edged closer to Liverpool, Joshua began to worry. He'd walked away from his family. He'd hurt them. Carefully considered words written in a letter were one thing. Showing up at his parents' doorstep was something entirely different.

When they pulled into Lime Street station, Joshua jumped down from the train and made a flimsy excuse to Johnny about needing to catch Dad at work. As he walked past the left-luggage room, he felt the weight of the key to the locker where his sax had languished for weeks. He still hadn't played since he arrived in England. The instrument had been the object of every one of his dreams growing up, but back on British soil he could hardly make himself look at it.

It was raining when he left the station, but after the punishing wet of RAF Padgate, he'd hardly noticed. People nodded to him in the street, the uniform he wore bringing him praise and admiration he hadn't yet earned. He walked through St. George's Square, away from the imposing building where he'd been married. He didn't have a direction as he walked past the docks and into Everton. Then, somehow, he found himself on Scotland Road in the heart of Walton.

Viv had told him all about her parents' home. He knew that if he turned off Scotland Road onto Lind Street and then took a left on Goodison Road, he would be there.

She wouldn't talk to him—he had no doubt about that—and he couldn't blame her. Not after what he'd done, naively thinking he could keep his promise to her and chase his dream all at once. She'd known what he hadn't been able to see the truth of at the time: that he would never amount to anything more than a fill-in player.

The light began to go a soft, hazy purple as he stopped on the corner of Goodison Road and Ripon Street. His hands itched for something to do, and he wished—not for the first time since he'd joined the RAF—that he hadn't given up his cigarettes to try to keep up with the boys in basic ground training.

The sound of hard heels on pavement brought his head up. There she was, looking down to fumble for something in her handbag as she rounded the corner across from him.

Without thinking, he darted behind a car parked in the road. Half crouched down, he watched as she looked up at the sky, the first few drops of rain beginning to fall. She pulled her coat collar closer around her neck, touched the scarf covering her light brown hair, and hurried on.

She was still pretty, with a heart-shaped face that came down to a pointed chin. It was her lips that he'd noticed first—brightly painted red and easy with a smile. She'd smiled at him that first night they'd met, and he'd nearly done a double take from his spot on the stage at the Locarno Ballroom.

She wasn't smiling now, but that wasn't the only change. She couldn't be more than twenty-three or twenty-four, but she'd lost some of her fresh-faced glow. Instead, she looked preoccupied, tired.

She pulled a letter out of her handbag and snapped the bag shut. She'd probably post it in the red pillar box he'd passed on the main road. He wanted to know what was in it. A letter to a friend? A lover?

Something bitter and unfair twisted in his chest. They might be married, but he had no right to expect her loyalty. It had been years, and women could divorce their husbands for desertion now.

Only Viv would never do that because she was Catholic.

He watched her round the corner of the road and then disappear from view.

Slowly he stood, his knees cracking in protest. He shouldn't have come here. Somehow he knew that everything would have been easier if he hadn't seen her.

Reluctantly, he slung his kit bag over his shoulder and started the long walk back across the blackout-darkened city in the rain.

Nearly an hour and a half later, Joshua stood in front of a neat redbrick house with white windowsills. It was dark now, and he knew that if this had been normal times there would have been light glowing warm and welcoming in the windows. Instead, the blackout curtains had been drawn to guard against any light escaping and helping Luftwaffe bombers from finding their targets.

He pushed open the small black iron gate that separated the postage-stamp front garden from the pavement, emotion rising heavy in his throat. Still, when he reached the front door, he forced himself to raise his hand and knock before he lost his nerve.

Almost immediately, he heard muffled footfalls.

This was a mistake. What was he doing?

The door swung open, light spilling out into the pitch-black street.

"Dad." His voice cracked.

Dad looked at him from head to toe, taking in everything from his navy uniform cap to his belted tunic down to his polished shoes. Then his father's face crumpled.

Joshua dropped his kit bag and pulled his father into a hug. He squeezed his eyes closed against the rawness around his heart. It had been so long since he'd hugged any of his family.

God, how he'd missed them.

"Mr. Levinson! The blackout!" came a shout over their shoulders.

Joshua's father lifted his head, the shimmer of tears catching the light spilling out of the entryway. "It's my son, Mr. Harris. Joshua has come back home."

"I'm glad to hear that, Mr. Levinson, but as your air raid warden I need you to go inside," called Mr. Harris.

"Come in. Come in," said Joshua's father.

Unable to speak, Joshua nodded and walked over the threshold of the house he'd grown up in for the first time in nearly five years.

"Seth, who was at the door?" called Joshua's mother as she pushed through the door from the kitchen. Her hands flew to her mouth when she saw Joshua.

"Mum," he croaked out.

"Rebecca!" Dad called while Joshua gathered his mother up in his arms and hugged her to him, nearly bringing her feet off the floor.

"You came home. You came home," Mum said over and over again. "You didn't tell us you were coming."

"I didn't know I'd be granted leave," he said, offering her the white lie.

"Rebecca, come see!" shouted his father again.

"I'm coming, I'm coming! I was just finishing up the account—"

When Joshua looked up, he saw his sister, frozen at the top of the stairs. Her face was impassive, her reddened lips drawn into a thin line.

"Rebecca, he's home," wept Mum, tears streaming down her face.

Slowly, Rebecca began to descend the stairs, her gaze never leaving his.

A hollow opened in the pit of his stomach.

"You're back," Rebecca finally said when they were eye to eye, with her stopped two steps up from the bottom.

"Only for a short visit. I have a little bit of leave before going south," he said.

"To Cambridge," she said.

"The Number Two Initial Training Wing, not the university proper. You know I couldn't do that." Not like her. He remembered the day when, at thirteen, she'd put down her knife and fork at the table and announced she wanted to go to university. Their father had thoughtfully blotted his mouth with his napkin and then turned his warm, dark eyes on his youngest child.

"If God wills it, it will be," Dad had said.

Later that night, while they were chatting in Rebecca's room as they always did before bed, she'd scrunched up her nose and said, "If *I* work hard, it will be."

Joshua couldn't argue with her there. Rebecca was pure determination, clever as a cat, and stubborn too.

That's why it shocked him when she said, "Well, apparently neither of us are made for Cambridge. Or any university at that."

"Rebecca," Mum chided her.

"Your sister works in the shop full-time now. She does the accounts and helps with the customers," said Dad. "She's good with the measurements. Alterations too."

Guilt slid through him. Those were all things Joshua was meant to have done.

"She also volunteers with the civil defense, don't you, Rebecca? You're lucky that you didn't come yesterday or she would have been on her shift," said his mother, smiling.

"I'm sorry, Rebecca," he said.

"We're all sorry for something," said Dad, "but we're happy you're here."

"Have you eaten? I'll make you something," said Mum, pushing him toward the kitchen.

Rebecca stayed on the stairs.

His parents kept him occupied for hours, sitting at the kitchen table with Rebecca watching him passively from the other side of the table as he told them stories from New York. Never once did they ask him to explain himself. However, he knew from the way Mum clung to his hand and Dad kept glancing at him as though convinced he might disappear that it would take much more than a visit home to repair the damage he'd done.

It was nearly midnight when Dad declared that it was time for all of them to go to bed.

"Your room's changed a little bit, but I always keep clean sheets on the bed," said Mum as they climbed the stairs.

"I've been gone so long," he said.

On the landing, Mum patted his cheek. "I always knew you would come back."

He dipped his head. "Thanks, Mum."

Inside his old room, Joshua sat on the edge of his bed, staring at the wall that hadn't been repainted since he'd left. It was more cramped than he remembered it now that boxes with labels like "Notions" and "Wadding" lined the wall across from his bed. His childhood bookshelf now held old catalogs and the large bound books of suiting material that Dad used to show clients different fabrics in the shop. Still, the records he'd scrimped and saved to buy were neatly packed in their box next to the gramophone that had been his bar mitzvah present. He pulled out Duke Ellington's *Black and Tan Fantasy* and put it on, keeping the volume low.

He laid back on the bed, letting the music wash over him. He didn't move when the repetitive click and scratch of the record told him that the side had ended. Instead, he listened to the house going to sleep, water groaning through pipes and the final shutting of bedroom doors.

It must have been nearly half past midnight when Joshua finally rose, opened his door, walked down the hall, and knocked. His sister opened the door a few seconds later, as though she'd been waiting for him.

"What do you want?" she asked in a whisper.

"Can I come in?" he asked. It felt strange having to ask. When they were younger, she would leave the door propped open for him so he could tell her about whatever gig he'd just come home from. Her eyes used to light up with his descriptions of the dancers in their dresses, spinning across grand ballroom floors.

Now, Rebecca bit her lip. For a moment he thought she'd say no, but then she opened the door wide.

He took the small creaky chair that he had always sat in when visiting with her. Rebecca remained standing.

"What do you want?" she asked again, voice low to avoid waking their parents but hands on her hips to make her anger plain.

"I'm sorry," he murmured.

"You already said that."

He grasped for the right words, but in the end he spread his hands wide and admitted, "I don't know how to make things right between us."

She gave a snort. "You aren't even trying."

"I am. I really am," he insisted.

Rebecca looked up at the ceiling as though collecting herself. "Were you trying when you were in New York, writing one letter for every four that we sent you? Or perhaps it was when you decided to come home to fight but didn't bother to come see us before joining up."

He winced. That's exactly what he'd done. Seeing his parents' reaction to his homecoming, he knew that he should have gone straight from the boat to Wavertree, but he couldn't make himself do it. Not until he'd shown them . . . what? That he'd been wrong about New York? That he'd been wrong about his talent? That England would always be home and that was worth fighting for?

"You've been in the country for weeks now, Joshua," Rebecca continued.

"I know," he said softly.

"Have you ever wondered what I didn't put in all of those letters I wrote to you?" his sister asked. "Mum cried every day for two weeks when you left. I started going into the shop every day because she couldn't leave her bed. And Dad blamed himself. He thought that he'd pushed you too hard. Hadn't listened to you enough. *Dad*, who never apologizes for anything."

He dropped his head in his hands. "Rebecca, why didn't you tell me any of this in your letters?"

"Because it wouldn't have made a difference, would it? You wouldn't have come back because you didn't want to," she said in a low voice, even in her anger still trying to protect their parents from the difficult things.

He couldn't argue with her. He'd taken the Byrnes' money because he'd been afraid that he was going to lose the one thing he cared most about. He'd been terrified that, as a husband and a father, he would have to give up his music and step into the secure, safe life his parents wanted for him. He'd wanted his freedom, and running away had been the easiest way to get it.

And look where it landed him: adrift.

"What about Viv?" Rebecca asked.

His head jerked up. "What about her?"

"Do you ever think about her or the child?"

Every damn day, but he tried his best not to.

He let out a breath. "I went to her road tonight. I saw her."

"What?" Rebecca asked.

"It was from a distance. I didn't talk to her. She didn't have the child with her."

For a moment, his sister didn't say anything, but then she shook her head. "Do you know Mum and Dad have never met their grandchild. We don't have a name. We don't even know if it's a boy or a girl.

"I've thought about trying to find out for Mum and Dad's sake, but what would that do except make it even more painful for them? They want to see their grandchild so badly. It's so bloody cruel that they can't."

He scrubbed a hand over his face. She was right. It was cruel, and he'd played straight into what the Byrnes wanted: the legitimacy of a marriage without needing to have any interaction with his Jewish family.

"I made a mistake, Rebecca. I'm trying to make it right in my own way," he said.

"By getting yourself shot at," she muttered, sinking onto the edge of the bed.

"Not yet. I have to get through training before that happens," he said with a wry smile that fell flat.

"Why did you come back? You were safe in New York."

He shook his head. "I couldn't stay away. Not knowing that all of you were in the middle of a war."

"If you get yourself killed, I'll kill you myself," said Rebecca.

"That doesn't make any sense."

"I don't care," said his sister stubbornly. "Where's your stupid saxophone? You never went anywhere without it before you left for America."

"It's in Lime Street's left luggage. I didn't know what else to do with it. I haven't been able to play since I arrived back in England," he admitted.

"Are you serious?" his sister yelped.

"Shhh, you'll wake Mum and Dad."

"You broke your parents' hearts because of that stupid instrument. If you don't start playing it again soon, I'll kill you," she hissed.

"Again with the killing," he said.

"I'm serious, Joshua. You're a good musician. You *need* to play," she said.

"Yeah, well, I wish the bandleaders on Swing Street thought the same thing. I never managed to get a full-time gig with a band. It was always piecemeal fill-in work with house bands."

Rebecca rolled her eyes. "You seriously expect me to feel sorry for you? You're doing what you love, and I'm stuck here picking up the pieces. Play the stupid thing for me."

She was right—of course she was. He was letting guilt crush his passion for music. It was what he'd changed his entire life for, turning his back on his family. On Viv. On their child.

"I'll take it to Cambridge with me," he said quietly.

"Good." Rebecca sat back. "Now, I want stories. Have you ever met Billie Holiday?"

A smile tugged at his lips. "Want me to tell you about how I was at Cafe Society the first time she sang 'Strange Fruit'?"

Rebecca sat forward, her hands clasped in her lap the way she'd always done as a kid. "Yes."

"Well, I had a night off when I didn't have a gig booked, so my friend Sonny and I went down to Greenwich Village . . ."

Joshua

Joshua realized he was fussing when he caught himself tugging at his jacket cuff for the fourth time in two minutes. He straightened his shoulders and rolled his neck back and forth.

It was just a date. He'd been on dates before. There was no need to be nervous.

Except that he was. He couldn't explain it, but there was something about Viv Byrne that he liked.

He spotted her, prim and pretty in a long green coat with a buff hat perched on her hair. Immediately he stuck up his arm to wave. "Viv!"

She acknowledged him with a little smile and wave of her hand. He pushed off the building he leaned against, the leather soles of his shoes scraping against the pavement as he hurried to her.

"I'm sorry I'm late," she said. "The bus took longer than I thought it would."

"I should have picked you up," he said.

"Oh, I couldn't have you doing that."

"Why's that?" he teased.

She looked at him as though it was obvious. "I'm Catholic."

Now he understood.

"I'm guessing your parents wouldn't appreciate you going out with a Jewish man."

Viv took him in slowly from the top of his hat to the toe of his shoe. Then she shook her head. "No, they wouldn't."

He was certain that she was going to tell him that she shouldn't be there, and he wasn't going to stop her. She surprised him then when she smiled and asked, "Shall we go inside?"

Joshua's heart skipped when he offered her his arm.

Viv

As the quartet picked up their bows to play the final piece of the concert, Viv stole a glance at Joshua. He tilted the program toward her and ran his finger along the name of the piece: Four Movements for String Quartet by Tchaikovsky.

She smiled when he edged a little closer to lean his arm so that it brushed hers.

Somewhere in the second movement, his hand edged up his knee. She was acutely aware of how close he was now, how she had to fight her fingers twitching from wanting to touch him.

During the third, she gave in and slid her cotton-gloved hand down to her own knee.

In the fourth, he bridged the gap between them and linked their pinky fingers together. A warm sensation filled her chest, but she hardly moved, worried she would fracture this moment and this feeling between them would fall away.

It was only when the hall exploded into applause that Joshua brought his hands up, leaving her strangely bereft.

He offered his arm again as they exited the concert hall. She liked the solidness of him, and the way that, when women glanced at them, she could see the spark of jealousy in their eyes. He was a handsome man, interesting and passionate, and so unlike anyone she'd ever met. All she wanted was more time with him.

As soon as they were outside, she slowed to a stop.

"This has been wonderful," she started to say.

"Do you fancy something to drink? I'm playing later, so I can't stay out too late, but maybe a cup of tea?"

"A cup of tea would be lovely," she said.

"This way," he said, nodding to her right.

After they'd walked a bit, he asked, "What did you think of the music?"

"It was beautiful," she said, unable to admit that her awareness of him had detracted from the pieces. "I recognized some of it from the radio. Did you like it?"

He laughed. "I do, but don't tell my mum. I had some lessons on the violin before I found the saxophone, and I think she'd rather I had stuck to that."

"Why did you change?" she asked.

"Sidney Bechet. I was over at a friend's house, heard one of his records, and that was it for me. I saved up enough to rent a saxophone and started playing. Sidney plays clarinet too, but I like the sound of the sax."

She smiled. "And now you want to become a musician."

"I *am* a musician," he said. "It's the only thing I want to be."

"What else is there?" she asked.

"A tailor. Dad's a tailor. Grandad was a tailor in Manchester."

"That explains your suits, then," she said. "They always look so sharp."

He touched the knot of his tie. "I started working there after school every day when I was fourteen. Now it's my job," he said, sounding distinctly miserable.

"Except when you're playing in the band," said Viv.

"I know I'm good enough to make it. I'm good enough to go to London or Paris or New York. I know that I am," he said, the excitement rising in his voice.

"Then why don't you?" she asked.

The corner of his mouth hitched up. "Trying to be rid of me already?"

"I'm serious. Why don't you go?"

"Money. My parents. The family business. There are a lot of things keeping me here. Anyway, what about you?" he asked.

She glanced up at him, catching his dark eyes watching her. "What about me?"

He waved around in front of them. "You must want more than this."

She opened her mouth, not entirely sure how to respond.

"I don't really know," she finally said.

"Come on. There must be something."

"No one's really asked me before. I'm working for the General Post Office now, but I'll have to quit when I marry."

"So you'll marry and have children?" he asked.

"I suppose," she said slowly. It was what she was expected to do, but laid out for her so simply she couldn't help feeling that it wasn't enough.

"I wouldn't mind seeing a bit of the world," she added.

"Then you should see the world, Viv Byrne. Morocco, Los Angeles, the wilds of Alaska!"

"You're teasing me now," she said with a grin, tugging at the elbow her hand was looped through. He rounded on her. Their gaze met, and something shifted between them.

"Come with me," he said, his voice dropping low.

She let him pull her into the doorway of a closed storefront, sheltering her from the street with his body. The scent of warm wool and bergamot wrapped around her like an embrace.

"What would you say if I told you I was going to kiss you, Viv Byrne?" he asked.

Something about the way he said her name, caressing the words, made her bold. "I'd ask you what took you so long."

He smiled. "Well, then."

She rose up on her toes to meet him. Their lips touched, a spark firing between them. This was nothing like the few stolen kisses she'd shared with fumbling boys who could barely look her in the eye. This was the full, determined kiss of a passionate man. It should have scared her—maybe that was why she clung to the lapels of his jacket as she did—but then her fingers tightened, drawing him closer to her.

A horn honked somewhere down the road. She let go and stumbled back against the shop door. Joshua took a half step back, breathing heavily as he braced one hand against the doorway and shoved the other through his hair. At their feet lay his hat, flipped upside down like a turtle struggling on its back.

"Go out with me again."

"Yes," she said before she could even think about all the reasons that was a bad idea.

Viv

The call came a week later.

Viv was in the kitchen, scrubbing the potatoes that she would peel and mash for the family's tea. The sting of freshly sliced onion for gravy and the scent of the sausages she'd picked up from Mr. Jones, the butcher, earlier that day filled the room. There had been all sorts of rumors about rationing in the first days of the war, but nothing except petrol had officially been put on the list. Still, some things were harder to come by than before, and seeing the fat sausages in their glass case had been too much temptation to pass up.

"I'll see who it is," she said to her mother, who was reading over instructions for tinning beetroot. Kate, who had a small patch of garden, had dropped a sack of them by earlier that day, and Mum was intent on preserving them in case there were shortages that winter.

When Mum didn't look up, Viv wiped her hands on her apron to go answer the telephone, but Dad beat her to it as he always did. The telephone—the only one on their road—had been installed when he'd become a foreman and had been required to be reachable, and it was his one great pride.

"Viv!" her father called. "It's for you."

Viv was out of the kitchen before her mother could ask her who would be calling *her*.

Hurrying to the telephone, she squeezed around her father and picked up the receiver. Dad lingered, so she shifted to give him her back. Cradling the receiver close to her ear, she said, "This is Mrs. Levinson."

"Viv, it's Sylvie," came her old friend's bright tone down the line.

Her breath caught in her throat. "Sylvie."

"Good news for you. A Mr. Rowan at the South East Delivery Office in Wavertree said he'll take you on as a postie—on the condition that you can do the work."

"Oh, that's wonderful," she breathed.

"Be there at the office tomorrow at nine o'clock sharp. I know Mr. Rowan a bit, and he doesn't like to be kept waiting," Sylvie warned.

"I will. Thank you. I can't thank you enough," she said in a rush.

"You just show Mr. Rowan what us old sorting-room girls can do," said Sylvie.

"I will. Thank you," she promised.

The receiver rattled a little from her shaking hands as she put it back on the hook.

"What was that?" Dad asked.

"I have an interview for a position with a delivery office," she said, still not believing it herself.

"But you're a married woman," said Mum from the kitchen door.

"There's a war on, so they're making exceptions. They need all the help they can find," she explained.

"You're a married woman," her Mum repeated with a frown. "Your role is at home."

"With my husband?" she bit out before she could stop herself.

"Vivian," her mother chided her.

"Now that Maggie is away in the countryside, there's nothing to keep me at home," she argued.

"Well, if you think it's nothing tending this house," sniffed her mother.

"That isn't what I mean," she said, trying to soothe her mother without losing her argument. "Even Father Monaghan spoke about everyone doing their bit at church last Sunday."

"You've been rolling bandages," said Dad.

"I want to do more. I'll be helping them find more men who can serve and help our Sam," she said, invoking the name of her brother-in-law. "You must see the recruitment efforts at work, Dad."

"Women have no business welding," said Dad, parroting something she'd heard Mum say when Dad had come home and reported that six women were now working on the line that produced airplane wings at the Littlewoods building.

"But I wouldn't be doing any manufacturing work," she said, seeing her opportunity. "I would be delivering the post. That's all."

"You'd be a postman?" Mum asked. "Who ever heard of such a thing?"

"A postwoman. It's an important job, and respectable too." She turned to her father. "Please, Dad."

Her dad hesitated, and she thought that maybe this time he would speak. This time he might stand up for her—stand up to his wife.

He shook his head, "Your mother needs your help at home."

"I can do both," she said quickly. "It will be like when I was working at the sorting room. Deliveries are in the mornings and afternoons, so I'll still be able to clean and cook tea. And I'll have a bicycle. I can do the shopping at the end of my routes, Mum."

"It isn't right," said Mum.

Viv sucked in a breath. "I'd also thought about joining one of the women's auxiliary services like the ATS. I know they're recruiting and, since Maggie was evacuated, I expect they'll be happy to see me at their door. I've heard they're sending girls out of Liverpool and off to their basic training every day."

She wouldn't join any service that might send her anywhere and prevent her from seeing Maggie, but Mum and Dad didn't know that. To them, she was their difficult daughter, unpredictable and illogical—a source of shame who could be bullied into living a small life trapped in their little house where there was always something to wash, something to cook, something to clean.

She caught the look between her parents.

"You'll continue to help your mother, and you'll go to church as usual," Dad announced, as though this was all his idea.

"Of course," she said, knowing that there would be no Sunday deliveries.

"What will your wages be?" asked Dad.

"I don't know yet," she said.

"You'll hand your wage packet over to your mother like you used to. If you work, you contribute," said Dad.

Viv might hand over her wage packet, but if they thought it would contain everything she made that week, they were sorely mistaken. She knew a few tricks learned from her sorting-office days. A couple of pen strokes and numbers could be made to look like one another. If a few shillings made it from her wage packet into her own coin purse, her parents would never be the wiser.

"Yes, Dad," she said.

"John, I really think . . ."

Dad silenced Mum with a shake of his head. "Father Monaghan says that everyone who can help out should. Let her work. After all, it's just the post."

At her husband's defiance, Mum's lips flattened until they nearly disappeared. Viv thought for sure that she would object. Instead, Mum reached around and yanked at her apron strings to take off the garment. "I'm going upstairs. I have a headache. You may call me when tea is ready."

Mum's anger pulsed off her as she brushed past Viv. Once, Viv might have been afraid of whatever repercussions might be to come. However, she'd lived too constricted to the little life her parents had forced her into. She was determined to break free.

Viv arrived at the South East Delivery Office in Wavertree dressed neat as a pin in a plain gray skirt and white shirt with her old brogues polished to a shine. She knew that postal workers were issued a uniform, but she didn't want to leave anything to chance. She was going to walk out with a job no matter what.

She'd hardly made it two steps toward the door when a rotund man with a graying handlebar mustache walked out to meet her.

"Miss Levinson?" he asked.

"Mrs. Levinson," she clarified, straightening her shoulders.

"That's right. You're the widow. Strange thing, this war," he muttered.

His gaze swept her up and down, assessing her from the tip of her hat to the toes of her shoes. "At least you wore good shoes. You wouldn't believe what some of these women show up in. Right, then. I'm Mr. Rowan. I run things around here. Follow me."

She had to hurry to keep up with Mr. Rowan's long legs as he bypassed the front door to the building and entered through the open door of a garage. There were a few older men and boys in uniform hauling sacks of mail around, but she was surprised at how empty the garage seemed.

"Most of our posties are out on the morning delivery right now," Mr. Rowan said, as though reading her mind. "They arrive early to check and organize their bags before the morning post goes out. Afternoon shift goes out after lunch, so you'll need to always be thinking ahead to the next delivery. We're the only bit of communication some families have with their boys who are off fighting. They're counting on us."

She thought of Kate and how she must be worried sick, waiting for Sam's letters to make it through the army's censors and postal system to the local post office for delivery, wondering what each new letter would bring.

"Now, if I hire you, you'll have a map of your route, and you'll have to check your letters against it, just like the men. Don't expect any special treatment. They keep telling me that women are supposed to pick up jobs from our boys. That includes"—Mr. Rowan turned to a single bicycle standing in a rack as though waiting for her—"riding one of these."

Viv eyed the great red monstrosity before her with a dubious expression. It was a bicycle, yes, but with its black metal rack protruding from the front, fenders, and the red lantern stuck on the front wheel, it bore little resemblance to the neighbor's bicycle she'd learned to ride on at ten.

"Isn't she a beauty?" asked Mr. Rowan, gazing at the bicycle with his fingers hooked in the slashed pockets of his tweed waistcoat.

"She certainly is," she said, unsure of what exactly was meant to be beautiful about the machine but not wanting to offend the man.

"The Federal won't do you wrong. She'll ride like a dream through rain and snow if she has to," he said, sliding his eyes to Viv as though he expected her to flinch at the idea of harsh weather. "Don't think it will be too much for you?"

She nearly laughed. If she could survive the last five years, a little weather wasn't going to scare her off.

"I will be fine," she said.

"Only one way to find out, I suppose," said Mr. Rowan. "You'll have to learn to maintain the bicycle. You can ask some of your fellow posties to show you how. You collect your pay from me on Fridays."

A bell clanged, and they turned to see a uniformed woman riding through the open garage door on her bicycle.

"Miss Sharpe," Mr. Rowan called out as she came to a halt.

"Morning, Mr. Rowan," said Miss Sharpe with a cheeky smile. She climbed off her bike, either not noticing or not caring at the way the men in the garage watched as her calf-length skirt hiked up when she threw her leg over the bicycle's crossbar.

"A new recruit for you. This is Mrs. Levinson," said Mr. Rowan.

Miss Sharpe hitched her bicycle into the rack to keep it from falling over and then surged forward to shake Viv's hand. "I'm Vanessa Sharpe. Pleased to meet you. Don't you worry. We'll have you all trained up in no time."

"Thank you," said Viv with a confused shake of her head. "Does this mean I have the job?"

"If you make it a week, it's yours," he said.

Relief flushed Viv's cheeks. "Thank you, Mr. Rowan. Thank you ever so much."

"Just don't make me regret it," he said. "Miss Sharpe, find her a uniform and show her how to pack a bag. She'll shadow you for the afternoon delivery and the rest of the week. Then we'll give her Bernard's old route and see how she does."

"Yes, Mr. Rowan," said Miss Sharpe with a nod.

They both watched Mr. Rowan walk away, but when Viv turned back, she saw a grin a mile wide across Miss Sharpe's face.

"He's an old grump, but don't worry. Just work hard, and he'll pretend the entire thing was his idea," said Miss Sharpe.

"The entire thing?" she asked.

"Women posties. Welcome to the sisterhood of the South East Delivery Office. And call me Vanessa."

"Vivian, but everyone calls me Viv," she said with a smile.

"Another V. I can tell we're already going to be fast friends. Now, let's find you a uniform. We're not supposed to tailor them, but trust me when I tell you that you'll want to. Horrible baggy things," said Vanessa, plucking at her uniform jacket. "I've taken mine in and added darts, and I still feel like a sack of potatoes."

"They're not the prettiest things, are they?" asked Viv.

Vanessa assessed her, much as Mr. Rowan had. "You're also going to want to raise your skirt a couple of inches. It isn't regulation, but you're short like me, and you want to keep the hem from catching in the gears. Now I'll show you how to put your bag together, then we'll go out for the afternoon delivery."

29 October 1939

My dearest Little Bear,

I wish that you were here with me because I could use one of your very good hugs. The kind where you squeeze me so hard because that's how you know the love is working. Those are the very best hugs.

Remember that I told you I have a new job working as a postwoman? Tomorrow I'm going out on my own for the very first time. I'm a little bit nervous about it because I have been with my friend Vanessa so that she can teach me what to do. I get to ride a bright red bicycle all around a neighborhood called Wavertree and make sure that all the post is delivered in the morning and the afternoon. Vanessa makes deliveries in a different part of Wavertree, but the houses are all a little like ours. There are some bigger ones too that you would like. Some people stop and say hello to Vanessa. There is even a dog named Milo who likes her because she keeps dog biscuits in her jacket pocket. I hope that the people in my new neighborhood will be just as friendly and that I might meet a dog or a cat like Milo. I will be sure to tell you if I do.

Thank you very much for asking Mrs. Thompson to send me the beautiful drawing that you made of your friend Puffball the pony. I will hang it up on the wall of our bedroom so that I can look at it every night when I fall asleep.

I'm going to write to Mr. and Mrs. Thompson and tell them that I would like to come down and see you next month. It will be chilly, but maybe you can show me Puffball.

Keep Tig tucked in at night. I know that he is doing a very good job of looking after you, and we want to be sure he has a good night's sleep so that he can keep watch over you for me.

I love you, my Little Bear, and I cannot wait to see you soon.

With all of my love and hugs and kisses,
Your Mummy

Maggie

And then next year you'll go to school with me," said Marion as she brushed the hair of her pretty blond doll.

Her friend looked up from the brunette doll Marion let her play with. Her friend, who was five to Maggie's four, was already in school, a fact Maggie found very impressive.

"Can we sit next to each other?" asked Maggie.

"You'll be in a different class with babies," Marion announced.

"I'm not a baby," she protested.

"You're not," Marion said, "but you'll be in a class with babies. But don't worry. I'll still be your friend. We can walk to school together."

"I want to walk to school with you," she said.

"Well, it's a long time from now," said Marion with great authority as she went back to brushing her doll's hair. "It's a *year*."

To Maggie, a year sounded like an eternity.

"Margaret," called Mrs. Stourton from downstairs, "Mrs. Thompson will be here any minute now."

Maggie immediately set aside her doll and stood up.

"You don't have to go down," said Marion.

Maggie knew better than that. However, before she could explain that good girls did what they were told, the doorbell rang.

Marion pouted. "Promise we'll play tea party tomorrow."

"We can play tomorrow," she said.

The door to Marion's room opened, and Mrs. Stourton poked her head in and smiled. "Are you ready, Margaret?"

"Yes, Mrs. Stourton," she said.

The girls followed Marion's mother down the carpeted stairs and into the drawing room, where Mrs. Thompson sat on a sofa, a cup of tea in her hand.

"Did you have a good time, Margaret?" asked Mrs. Thompson.

Maggie nodded.

"Margaret wants to come to school with me next year," announced Marion.

A smile broke out over Mrs. Thompson's face. "Well, I'm sure that can be arranged. Come along now. It's time to go home."

Maggie said goodbye to Mrs. Stourton and Marion and then let Mrs. Thompson take her hand while they walked home from Marion's house.

"You like Marion, don't you?" Mrs. Thompson asked.

"Yes," she said.

Mrs. Thompson frowned. "Remember, you must answer questions in full sentences, Margaret. What did you do with Marion?"

Maggie swallowed. "We played tea party with Marion's dolls."

"Marion has many pretty things, doesn't she?" asked Mrs. Thompson.

Maggie nodded.

"Would you like a pretty new doll of your own?" Mrs. Thompson asked.

"Yes, please!" Maggie cried, bouncing next to Mrs. Thompson as they reached Beam Cottage's garden gate.

"Maybe if you're very good, Father Christmas will bring you one," said Mrs. Thompson.

"Marion's favorite doll has blond hair and blue eyes, but I want a doll with brown hair and brown eyes," said Maggie.

"But you already have a doll with brown hair. Don't you want one with blond hair? I have blond hair," said Mrs. Thompson as she let them in through the front door that was never locked.

"Mummy has brown hair and brown eyes," said Maggie.

Mrs. Thompson gave a strangled little cry and looked away. "Sometimes, Margaret, I think you don't enjoy it here one bit."

"I'm sorry!" Maggie cried, throwing her arms around Mrs. Thompson's legs.

Mrs. Thompson hugged her arms around her middle, not touching the child. "Mr. Thompson and I are trying very hard, Margaret. I prayed every day that we might have a little boy or a little girl, and then God answered my prayers when he sent you to me. Thinking that you might not be happy here . . ."

"I am happy," said Maggie in a rush.

"If you want to go back to Liverpool, you can. I can ring up your mother right now and tell her that she should come and collect you."

"I want to stay here," said Maggie, her voice soft and uncertain.

Mrs. Thompson sniffed and dabbed her eyes with a lace-edged handkerchief she produced from her pocket. "Do you really mean that?"

Maggie nodded the way that she knew Mrs. Thompson wanted.

"Well, that's settled, then. You'll stay here, and next year you can go to school with Marion," said Mrs. Thompson, her pretty features brightening once again. "Now, go run upstairs and wash your hands. Your supper is in ten minutes."

Maggie raced up the stairs to the bathroom with the flowered paper on the walls and the porcelain and brass taps. She dutifully washed her hands and dried them on one of the fluffy towels, remembering how Mrs. Thompson had laughed the first time Maggie came out of the bathroom with wet hands because she thought the nice towels were only for guests.

Instead of going downstairs, however, Maggie crept into her room. Tig was waiting on the bed the Thompsons' housekeeper Mrs. Reed had made up that morning. Maggie grabbed Tig and snuggled her nose into the fur of his neck. Then she went to the bedside table and opened the drawer where she kept all of her most prized possessions. A ribbon Marion had given her. A horse figurine that Mr. Thompson had brought home one day. A horse chestnut from a walk she'd taken with her mother the last time Mummy had visited.

Carefully, Maggie slid out the photograph that Mummy had given her. She used to carry it around in her pocket, but one day she'd creased the bottom right corner. Since then she'd kept it in here where she knew nothing bad would happen to it, but she liked to take it out and look at it. To remember.

"Margaret!" Mrs. Thompson called up the stairs.

Maggie bolted up and slipped the photograph back into the bedside table. Then she hugged Tig to her once again and whispered, "I miss you, Mummy," even though no one could hear her.

5 November 1939

Dear Rebecca,

I'm writing you a separate letter even though I know that it's likely Mum will demand you read it out loud. You can if you like, but I think there are some things that you will want to keep to yourself.

It's strange here at Cambridge. Adam tells me that it's like being back at university, but I wouldn't know. What is obvious is that the men here are all intelligent, although I think you'd run circles around some of them.

We're learning everything to do with navigating. I can't say too much or I'll risk the censors blacking out most of this letter, but know that no matter what squadron I end up with, I've been schooled thoroughly. Not only can I now march and salute thanks to basic training, but I can use all the instruments on several models of planes in my sleep. I can also spot a Heinkel He 111 moving at pace on a cloudy day.

We had special classes in Morse code. Even though I won't be a wireless operator, we all need to learn it. It came easier than I thought it would. Maybe all those years staring at sheet music have come to use after all.

I don't know how long they'll keep us here, training until we're given our final assessments. That's when we'll either be sent on to our squadrons or we'll wash out and be reassigned for ground crew. No one who has reached this point wants that.

(Don't read this part to Mum and Dad.)

Other than doom and gloom about who is going to be in the air at the end of all this, most of the men are scheming to try to make it home for Christmas. Adam and I are positive that we won't be granted leave, but I'm hoping that at some point in January I'll be able to come home. Again, don't mention it to Mum and Dad. I don't want to disappoint anyone.

Your loving brother,
Joshua

Viv

Viv learned a lot shadowing Vanessa. First of all, the other woman was the most talkative person she'd ever met. Vanessa said it was because she was the middle child of seven and she had to chatter to get a word in. However, it was Vanessa's cheer that was the most impressive thing about her. Despite having three brothers who'd all been conscripted into the army, she was endlessly optimistic.

"I worry for my brothers every day, but there's no use in being sad about things that haven't happened yet and hopefully never will," Vanessa once said. "Plus, now that they're out of the house, Jessie's moved into Michael's room and I have an entire bedroom to myself. I feel like a princess with all of that space."

Viv, who'd only had her own bedroom when Kate had moved out of the house after marrying Sam, could understand, but the sight of Maggie's empty bed in their shared room still made her miserable. There had been a time when she'd had to tear herself away from watching her daughter sleep, so precious and delicate Maggie had seemed. Now, she woke up each morning and squeezed her eyes shut to delay the awful confirmation that her daughter wasn't there any longer.

The only thing that seemed to distract her was the exhaustion that came with being a postwoman. After changing into her uniform on that first day, she'd pedaled madly after Vanessa on her route on the west side of Wavertree. Viv had rolled up late to each stop, gasping for air while her tutor seemed hardly to break a sweat. Her entire body ached by the time she made the bus journey back to Walton, and her legs felt heavy as lead when she woke up the next day.

It was all worth it—and not just for the pay packet she took home at the end of her first full week. She liked the camaraderie of the delivery office. Betty, an athletic girl with a cheery smile had an ongoing wager with petite-but-surprisingly-strong Peg about who could deliver the most letters between the morning and afternoon deliveries. Vanessa was always done with her shift the earliest because she could ride the fastest, so there was no point in racing her. Each afternoon, after they'd had a bite to eat in the canteen, Rose, a redhead with a vain streak who still managed to be fun, would pull out the silver stopwatch she claimed her father had used to train for footraces two decades ago and time who could pack up their bag the fastest.

What had touched her most, however, was that at the end of Viv's first Saturday on the job, Betty, Peg, and Rose had even been waiting for Vanessa and Viv to return to hand over a small jar of Peg's mother's famous rhubarb jam to celebrate finishing her first week.

After so many years of being half-isolated in the odd limbo of her parents' house, it felt good to be around women who might be friends again.

Monday morning, Viv arrived at the delivery office a few minutes before most of the other postmen and -women stumbled in blurry-eyed to begin packing up their bags. She didn't want to make a mistake her first time alone on her route.

"First day on your own, Viv," Betty called as soon as she walked through the door. "Are you ready?"

She held up the little route map Vanessa had drawn for her when she'd been officially assigned her route. Viv had spent all of Sunday after church studying it, making sure she wouldn't forget on her bicycle that she needed to turn right at Cranborne Road, not left, and that Lawrence Road would be her longest uninterrupted stretch.

"I have it all here," she said.

"Just remember to check and double-check your bag each time you make a delivery. You don't want to have to double back because a letter slid out of place," said Betty.

Viv nodded, and set to work packing her bag with the letters the sorting-room girls had pigeonholed for her.

The garage was full of posties by the time she hauled her full bag on her bicycle. She carefully pulled it off its rack, remembering how often Vanessa had warned her that the Federals had a tendency to fall over the moment one turned away. Then she swung her leg over the crossbar, careful to keep her hemmed skirt well away from the gears and chain, and set off to the cheers of her fellow postwomen while the male posties watched on, bemused.

The sluggish sun was just breaking over the tops of houses as she set out down Wellington Road before turning right onto Lawrence Road. There was a definite chill in the air, with mist making the light from the lampposts stretch out like stars in the dawn. Viv breathed deeply as she pedaled, no longer struggling the way she had just a few days ago. It felt good to be out in the morning before the coal fires that heated homes across the city were lit. The air was fresher now, and if she let her mind drift, she might have almost been able to convince herself that there was no war on, her daughter was safely tucked up in bed, and she hardly had a care in the world.

She turned right onto Spofforth Road, slowed to a stop, and propped her bicycle before grabbing her first batch of letters. Double-checking them, she approached the door of the first squat white house, pushed open the black letterbox flap, and popped the letters inside. They clattered to the floor, and the flap closed with a satisfying bang.

Viv made quick work of the top half of the road. At first it had seemed incredible that anyone received one delivery of their post a day, let alone a morning and an afternoon delivery. However, she'd soon seen how Vanessa worked with precise, efficient movements that helped her cover as much ground as possible.

Viv worked her way down Spofforth Road before turning onto Cadogan Street. The world was waking up around her, and from the houses she visited she could smell the delicious scent of bacon from those lucky enough to find it at the butcher.

"Good morning, lass," called out an older gentleman with a Scottish accent from the door she'd just delivered to as she made her way to the top of Cecil Street.

"Good morning, sir!" she replied, waving a hand.

"You're the new postie, then?" he asked as he stooped over to collect his post and the full milk bottles on his doorstep.

"That's right. I've just started," she said.

"Good for you girls going out to work. It's everything I can do to keep my Violet from joining up herself, but I told her they don't want a fifty-five-year-old woman. They want young blood," he said.

"Perhaps she could be an air raid warden," she said.

He laughed. "Don't give her any ideas. She'll be running the entire civil defense in Wavertree if it will bring our Charlie home sooner."

"Charlie's your son?" she asked.

"Charlie Campbell. You'll look for his letters, won't you?" he asked with a smile.

"I'll make sure they're on the top of the stack, Mr. Campbell," she said.

He gave her a little wave and headed back into the house with his milk bottles.

With a grin, she turned on Salisbury Road. At this rate she'd be able to make it back to the delivery office with plenty of time to have a cup of tea from the canteen and a bite before packing her bag up again for the afternoon delivery.

The houses were slightly larger here, with bow windows looking out onto the road. She could imagine herself raising Maggie in a house like this. The lounge wouldn't be kept only for special visitors or Christmas. Instead, she and Maggie would flop around on well-loved sofas with a stack of books and magazines spread out around them. In this mythic house, there would be no dolly tubs because she would be able to afford to send her laundry out every week. Upstairs they would each have a bedroom and share a shiny new bathroom with a big enamel tub. There would be bookshelves everywhere, and Maggie would have plenty of space for a dollhouse and tea service of her very own. On Saturdays Viv would take her to Wavertree Botanic Gardens or to the Walker Art Gallery.

They could have a happy life altogether in a house like that. Now that she was earning a little, it felt as though one day it might actually be possible.

Dreaming of a future that might be, she hardly paid attention as she grabbed the next stack of letters and let herself in through the short iron garden gate of the corresponding house. She'd just put the letters through the door and turned to leave when the door opened.

"Thank you!" a woman called out.

Viv smiled, turned, and froze. Standing in the doorway, letters in her hand, was Joshua's mother.

The Levinsons *lived* here.

"What are you doing here?" Mrs. Levinson gasped out.

Viv wanted to jump on her Federal and pedal back to the delivery office as quickly as she could, but something about Mrs. Levinson's expression made her stop. It wasn't just shock, it was grief too.

Miserable, Viv said, "I'm your new postie."

Mrs. Levinson's chest expanded as though drawing in breath would give her the strength to continue with the conversation. From behind her, Viv heard a woman call, "Anything from Joshua?"

"How is the child?" Mrs. Levinson asked quickly.

"What?" Viv asked.

"Are they safe? Please tell me they're safe," said Mrs. Levinson in a rush.

"Maggie?" Viv asked.

Mrs. Levinson gasped out a silent cry. "Maggie. That's my granddaughter's name?"

"You know her name," said Viv confused.

"I . . ." Mrs. Levinson shook her head. "How is she?"

"She was evacuated," she said.

The letters slipped from Mrs. Levinson as she covered her face. "I thought she was too young. I worried she was too young."

Viv was stunned by the woman's reaction. She'd written to them when Maggie was just days old, using the address of Mr. Levinson's tailoring shop. She'd told them that they had a granddaughter. That if they wanted to see Maggie, she would bring the child to them. She'd included her address and telephone number, and she'd waited.

She'd heard nothing back.

"I don't understand," Viv started.

"Why do you have the door open, Mum? You're letting all the heat out."

Viv spotted Joshua's sister as she appeared behind her mother. Rebecca had grown taller since Viv's wedding day, and her face had narrowed down to high cheekbones and a sharp jaw. She wore her dark hair—so like Maggie's—in rolls and clipped with a barrette in the back, and her red dress was dotted with small white flowers.

"What are you doing here?" Rebecca demanded, her eyes widening at the sight of Viv.

"Rebecca, stop," said Mrs. Levinson before turning her sad eyes to Viv again. "Tell me about Maggie. What is she like?"

Viv could see now that Mrs. Levinson had changed too. Silver shot through her dark hair and, like her daughter, she was thinner than she had been five years ago. Viv could remember Joshua talking about being a child and watching his mother sew while sitting next to his father. She had such slim fingers, and they would create magical things, he'd told her.

"I don't understand. You want to know about Maggie now? After all this time?" she asked, grasping at the words that didn't make any sense.

Mrs. Levinson clasped her hand to her throat as though trying to hold back all the emotion building there. "She's my granddaughter."

Rebecca stepped around her mother, putting her body between Viv and Mrs. Levinson. "You need to leave."

"Rebecca—"

"No, Mum. She and her family have hurt us enough. Why don't you go back inside? I'll take care of this."

Around Rebecca's slight but imposing frame, Viv could see Mrs. Levinson start to protest. But all at once, the wind seemed to leave her sails. Mrs. Levinson nodded and turned away, head hung down.

As soon as her mother was out of earshot, Rebecca crossed her arms over her chest and fixed Viv with a hard stare. "You have a lot of audacity coming here after everything you did."

"Everything I did?" she asked, incredulous.

"Chasing after my brother. Forcing him to marry you. Did you take one look at him and think that he would be your out?" Rebecca asked with a sneer.

"I didn't chase after your brother." They'd made their mistake together. Stupid, silly children who didn't understand the gravity of the game they were playing. They'd been too caught up in the excitement of someone novel, and too drawn in by simple lust to think straight.

"We made a mistake," Viv said carefully, "but if you think I'm going to regret that, you're wrong. That mistake gave me Maggie."

There was a flash of something vulnerable in Rebecca's eyes, but it was gone before Viv could decide whether it was regret, sadness, or something else.

"You're not welcome here. Don't come back," said Rebecca, bracing a hand on the door as though to close it."

"You're on my postal route," she said.

"Your family paid my brother to disappear, and do you know what? He did. He was a man of his word," said Rebecca.

"Your brother chose to leave. He could have said no to my mother," she argued. "I didn't want any of this to happen either."

"I find that very hard to believe," said Rebecca.

"I live with my parents, who don't want me but refuse to let me leave their house because I'm married in name only and that would bring shame to them. I lost my job when I married your brother, and it took a war for me to find another one. I can't even move on with my life because I'm Catholic."

Divorce was impossible. The repercussions for her family—for her—were unthinkable.

Rebecca's lips twisted, and for a moment Viv thought she might have won the other woman over. Instead, Rebecca lifted her chin. "And what about the man whose life you ruined?"

Viv scoffed. "Ruined? He got what he always wanted, didn't he? He went to New York."

"Yes, well, that's all over now," said Rebecca.

"What do you mean?"

"He left to join the RAF at the start of the war," said Rebecca.

Viv's stomach dropped. If he was serving, it might mean that Joshua would take leave. It might mean that he would come back to Liverpool to visit his family.

She couldn't face seeing him again. He'd gotten his dream. Now she deserved hers: to finally be free of her parents and bring her daughter home to her.

She couldn't keep Salisbury Road on her route. The risk that one day she would run into the man who had so badly betrayed her trust was too great.

Viv pivoted on her heel and made for her Federal.

"Where are you going?" Rebecca shouted.

"To finish my route. I will come back for the afternoon delivery, but after that you won't see me again. I can promise you that," Viv called back.

Viv climbed on her bicycle and pedaled hard, blood roaring in her ears.

Tears she didn't fully understand stung the back of her throat and the bridge of her nose. At the bottom of the road, she made a hard left and skidded to a stop. She slid off the seat, bracing herself on the handlebars as she sucked in deep breaths, and she was certain that if she let go of the Federal's handlebars she might not be able to climb back on her bicycle.

Except that's not what posties did. She couldn't return to the delivery office with a half-full sack of letters. She would finish the rest of the route first and then come back to Salisbury Road, but first she needed a moment to think.

Pulling herself together, she swiped away her tears, grasped the handles of her bicycle, and set off again to finish this hellish route.

Viv rolled up to the delivery office and braked hard, sucking air into her lungs. She'd gone as fast as she could, desperate to return before the other girls. All along her route, she'd thought about what she would do. A few roads from the end, she'd come up with a plan.

As quickly as she could, she put away her bicycle. Then she brushed down her uniform, straightened the hem of her jacket, and walked into the main building of the delivery office.

She found Mr. Rowan in his office. The door was ajar, and Viv could see him bent over a stack of papers. There was a framed photograph on the desk angled in such a way that she could see a woman in a wedding dress, arm in arm with an army officer. Both of them smiled broadly, looking at each other with such love that Viv almost felt jealous of these two people she'd never met before. The photograph was the only thing in the office that seemed personal.

She took a deep breath and knocked on the open door.

Mr. Rowan looked up. "Ah, Mrs. Levinson. How was your first solo delivery?"

She shut the door behind her, blocking out the chatter of the sorting hall. "Actually, that's what I wanted to talk to you about, Mr. Rowan."

He frowned. "Is something the matter?"

"Could I switch routes with one of the other posties?"

"Switch routes? But you've only been on it for one delivery. You haven't even finished an entire day," he said.

She caught herself twisting her hands in front of her and forced her arms down by her sides. "Yes, I know."

"Did something happen on the route? Did a man bother you? I told them at the main office that having girls delivering the post would never work," he muttered.

"No, nothing like that," she said quickly.

His expression grew stern. "This isn't a charitable organization, Mrs. Levinson. If you work for me, I expect you to actually work."

"I want to work."

"And neither is being a postie a chance to visit with your friends. I won't reassign you just because you aren't happy that you don't see your girlhood friends on the route," he said.

Her hands balled up into fists. "It's not that at all."

"Then why should I reassign you?" he asked.

She could lie to him. She could make up some excuse for why the area she'd been assigned wasn't suitable for her, but she was already lying about her husband having died. How many other lies could she tell before they stacked up too high for her to contain them any longer?

"My husband's mother lives on Salisbury Road," she said carefully. "She came out of the door while I was delivering the post, and it was . . . difficult for both of us."

Mr. Rowan's lips pinched, but when he didn't say anything, she pressed on.

"We have never seen eye to eye. I believe she thinks that I took him away from her. I think that my visiting her door twice a day would cause her distress. I'm hoping that I can spare her that—for my late husband's sake."

Mr. Rowan took off his glasses and scrubbed a hand over his face. "It never is easy, is it?"

"I'm very sorry to cause any inconvenience," she said, spreading her hands in front of her.

"Just when you think all the deliveries are covered and everything is finally settled, someone has to throw a spanner into the works," he muttered before lifting his head. "You may miss out that part of your route—"

"Oh, thank you, Mr. Rowan!" she cried.

"*If*"—he gave her a stern look—"you can convince one of your fellow posties to take over that road."

She nodded firmly. She would beg, plead, whatever she needed to do to convince one of the girls that she needed to swap Salisbury Road.

When she returned to the garage, most of the girls were already back.

"Viv, tea break?" asked Vanessa.

"Yes, that would be lovely," she said.

"Are you okay?" asked Vanessa.

Viv realized that Vanessa was looking at her fingers fidgeting with the hem of her jacket. She smoothed the fabric down.

"Perfectly," she said.

As they walked into the canteen, Viv let the chatter wash over her. She would wait for the right moment to ask for a swap when everyone was settled in with a cup of tea.

"I cannot make my set to last more than one day of work," Rose complained, running a protective hand down her red hair as they queued for cups of tea.

"You should try a snood," said Peg, tugging at hers. "It keeps everything neat."

"Oh, I hate those," said Betty as they walked to the canteen.

Rose scrunched up her nose and nodded. "I feel so frumpy when I wear one. What do you do, Viv? Your hair is always neat, and you wear it so long."

"That's because she hasn't had a service in the rain. Just wait. She'll be as much of a drowned rat as the rest of us," said Vanessa.

"Why are you so worried anyway?" asked Betty as they finally reached the head of the queue and retrieved their cups of tea.

"I have a date on Wednesday," said Rose proudly.

Peg laughed. "A date? Is he sixty-four?"

"No," said Rose defensively as they sat down. "He's a soldier based at Burtonwood. We know each other from the neighborhood, but he said that he never had the nerve to ask me before the war broke out."

"He needs an invasion to work up the nerve to talk to you?" asked Betty.

"Shouldn't he be off fighting or something?" asked Peg.

"What fighting?" Betty snorted. "All this fuss about evacuating children and forcing all of us to bring gas masks everywhere, and we haven't even seen an air raid."

Viv dropped her gaze to her lap. All of this fuss and for what? Had she sent her daughter away only to find out that it wasn't necessary?

"My sister, Ruthie, is bringing her boys back. She thought they were fine in Wales. Lots of fresh air and all of that. Turns out that the farmer they were living with wasn't sending them to school at all but was using them as farmhands. I don't think I've ever seen Ruthie so mad. She took all the housekeeping money for the week and went to collect them. She said they might not eat anything but bread for a week, but at least the children would be with her," said Peg.

"Viv, are you okay?" Vanessa asked, putting a hand on Viv's arm.

Viv looked up, realizing that all the other girls were staring at her. She gave a little half laugh and shook her head. "I'm sorry. I was just thinking about my—about my sister Kate's boys and her little girl. She misses them so much."

"I can't even imagine," said Rose.

"Let's talk about something else," said Betty, shooting Peg a dirty look.

"Actually, there was something I wanted to ask all of you. When I was on my route this morning, I had a bit of a fright," she started.

"Stamp on their foot, and then pop them in the nose," said Peg with authority.

She blinked. "What?"

"That's how you deal with men who can be a bit grabby. You can't do anything about the ones who just stare though. There's that one on Rokesmith Avenue who stands at his window, remember, Betty?" asked Peg.

"How could I forget?" Betty asked into the rim of her mug. "He's always staring and sweating every time I come by. If it's dry, I just toss his post over the garden gate."

"You were saying, Viv?" Vanessa prompted with a stern look at the other girls.

"That sounds horrible, but it isn't anything like that. You all know that I'm a widow?" she asked.

The way the other girls all slid looks at one another told her that they'd spoken extensively about this. It might have bothered her if she wasn't already used to her entire neighborhood gossiping about her.

"Well," she continued, "today I was delivering the post, and I realized that my husband's family's on Salisbury Road. On my route."

Vanessa sucked in a breath, while Peg said, "My heavens."

"What happened?" Rose asked breathlessly.

"His mother and sister came out. It was . . ." Awkward? Horrible? "Difficult."

"You poor lamb," cooed Betty.

"I don't think I can stand the thought of seeing them every single day," she admitted. "It's too painful."

"You want to change routes?" asked Vanessa.

She nodded. "I know it's a lot to ask, but maybe someone else could take that road?"

"I'll do it," said Peg. "I keep beating Betty anyway, so I could use a new challenge."

"That's not true! I delivered just as many letters as you did last week," Betty protested.

"But I'm up this week, and that's all that matters," said Peg. "Besides, my route butts up against Viv's. It'll be the easiest thing in the world to nip down to Salisbury Road and do a quick delivery."

Viv let out a long breath. "Thank you. Thank you so much."

Vanessa nudged her with her shoulder. "That's what posties do for each other."

Betty scoffed. "Not the men. Mr. Harlow hardly says hello to me."

"That's because you crashed your bicycle into his in your first week," said Rose.

"It was one little accident. You'd think he would be gentleman enough to live and let live," said Betty.

"Now, can we please go back to important business?" asked Rose. "What am I going to wear on my date?"

Peg rolled her eyes. "That's important business? Really?"

Betty leaned across the table. "But why don't you tell us all about your wardrobe and we'll help you pick something out?"

As the girls began to review Rose's options with as much excitement as their friend had for her date, Vanessa leaned into Viv. "How are you really?"

"I'll be fine," she said.

Vanessa searched her face but then nodded. "Just know that if you need us, we're here."

There were so many things that Viv wanted to trust her with, but her old instincts held her back. She'd seen too often how people could turn when they learned something unsavory about a person. She wasn't ready to trust yet, even if it felt good having a group of girls to turn to.

"Thank you," she said, and settled back to listen to the debate over a black serge skirt or a green woolen dress for Rose's date.

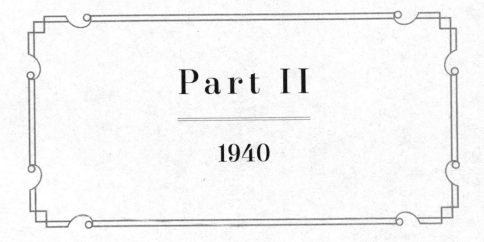

Part II

1940

Viv

April 27, 1940

"Mummy, look!"

Viv leaned on the fence of the paddock, watching her daughter cantering around on her pony, the joy on Maggie's face unmistakable. Viv knew that she should take pleasure in her daughter's enjoyment, but she found she was struggling with jealousy. Not of Maggie, but of the prim woman standing next to her.

Mrs. Thompson was dressed in a tweed skirt and a waxed jacket, a silk scarf tied over her beautifully curled hair. Mrs. Thompson's coral lips were painted perfectly, and her lashes were darkened with mascara, but other than those enhancements, her peaches-and-cream complexion seemed natural.

Viv hated her.

She knew that made her a monster. Mrs. Thompson had done nothing more than be kind to her daughter, but she still couldn't help but resent the woman.

It had started with the letters telling Viv about how many of Maggie's things weren't suitable or were falling apart, as though Viv sent her daughter out in rags. Each visit, Maggie would be wearing a dress Viv had never seen before, and more toys appeared in the elaborate playroom. Then there were the tea parties, trips to the ice cream parlor, and "jaunts" to see Mrs. Thompson's endless stream of friends.

And this bloody horse.

But what Viv really resented was the time. Mrs. Thompson was watching her daughter grow up, and there wasn't a thing Viv could do about it. One visit a month was not enough.

More like every six weeks.

Her job as a postie might have afforded her the money she needed to pay the fares to come see Maggie, but she hadn't anticipated how working shifts would cut into her plans. Twice already she'd had to write to the Thompsons, telling them that she would be working the day she planned to visit. She rescheduled every time, but sometimes that meant going longer between visits than she'd hoped, like at Christmas, when the deluge of presents, cards, and letters into the delivery office meant she hadn't been able to come until December 28. The night she'd had to write that letter to Maggie, Viv had cried herself to sleep.

"Margaret has become quite the country girl," said Mrs. Thompson.

Viv made a noncommittal noise but waved when Maggie rode by again, giggling.

"We took her to one of the local farms to see the lambing. We could hardly tear her away when it was time to come home," said Mrs. Thompson with a laugh. "I can't imagine that there are many lambs in Liverpool."

"Not many, no," said Viv.

"Children thrive so well in the countryside, don't you think? It's all the fresh air and exercise."

"I'm sure," said Viv through gritted teeth.

"Margaret really is such a good girl. We've been reading together every night, and already she's reading from *Babar*. And she's not even five," said Mrs. Thompson with obvious pride.

The breath left Viv's body in a painful whoosh. She'd taught Maggie her letters. She was the one who was supposed to teach Maggie to read and encourage her to grow into the person she was meant to be.

Mrs. Thompson placed a gentle hand on Viv's arm. "It must be very difficult for you, Mrs. Levinson."

Viv lifted her chin. "We're all doing what we think is best for Maggie."

Mrs. Thompson patted her on the arm. "Of course we are."

Finishing another one of her loops around the paddock, Maggie stopped in front of her mother. "Mummy, do you want to feed Puffball?"

Viv's resentment melted away. Here was her daughter, her beautiful, generous, intelligent little girl. She only had so much time with her every month. She was determined to enjoy it.

"Yes, Little Bear. Will you show me how?"

Maggie scrambled down from her pony, using a block to help her reach the ground. Viv held her breath, worrying that her daughter was going to take a tumble off the pony's back.

"Mrs. Thompson, can I please feed Puffball a carrot?" Maggie asked politely.

"Normally I would say that we should ask Mr. Stourton, since he owns Puffball, but I don't think he'll mind just this once. Why don't you take Puffball back to his stall and show Mrs. Levinson how you brush him?"

Viv bristled at the way the woman called her "Mrs. Levinson" rather than "your mother" when talking to Maggie.

Maggie, however, didn't seem to notice. "Come on, Mummy!" she cried, grabbing the pony's reins.

"You'll find a gate over that way," said Mrs. Thompson, gesturing down the muddy side of the paddock.

Viv picked her way along the paddock fence to the gate. Mud squelched under her shoes. It would be a nightmare cleaning this pair, let alone replacing them. She should count herself lucky that clothing hadn't fallen under the rationing restrictions that had come in with the New Year. Only last month, the government had added meat to the list along with butter, bacon, and sugar, sending her mother and every other housewife in Walton into a tizzy. Even her fellow female posties—all of whom still lived at home and helped around the house like she did—griped about the changes.

Viv let herself through the gate and followed her daughter to the stables. At the top of the path, an older man dressed in coveralls, a waxed jacket, gum boots, and a flat cap waved hello to Maggie.

"Miss Levinson, did you have a good ride?" he asked.

"Yes, thank you, Mr. Warner," said Maggie politely. Viv couldn't help but notice the way that Maggie's accent was softening from the lyrical Scouse of Viv and her parents to something less distinctive.

"Hello," said Mr. Warner with a smile. "You must be Miss Levinson's mother."

"Pleased to meet you," she said, putting out her hand.

He laughed and held up his hands, which were streaked with mud. "I wouldn't want to dirty a lady such as yourself. Your daughter tells me you're down from Liverpool for a visit?"

"That's right," she said cautiously.

"Always did like Liverpool. My mother's people were from there. Don't know what she was thinking marrying a farmer out in Warwickshire, but that's life, isn't it?" he said with another laugh.

Viv couldn't help her grin. She liked this man. He was warm and easy, a world away from the polite polish of the Thompsons. "What neighborhood are they from?"

"Out Crosby way. My mum would have liked the little miss here," he said.

"Mr. Warner, we're going to groom Puffball," said Maggie, bouncing on her toes.

"Now that's a very big responsibility for such a little girl," he said with mock seriousness.

"I'm not little!" Maggie cried with delight.

"Silly me," the stable hand said. "Do you think that you can remember all the things that I taught you?"

"Yes!" said Maggie.

"Well, then, why don't you start, and I'll come check on how you're getting along in a few minutes."

Maggie began to tug the pony off to the stables with a look of determination. Viv made to follow her but stopped when Mr. Warner cleared his throat.

"Mrs. Levinson, you'll find some gum boots just inside the door. There's a jacket on the hook too," he said.

Viv gave him a grateful smile, thanked him, and followed her daughter into the stable.

The warm, earthy scent of hay and horse manure hit her in a wave, and she scrunched up her nose. Maggie hardly seemed to notice. Viv grabbed the gum boots and the jacket that Mr. Warner had mentioned, and hurried after her daughter.

When they reached the pony's stall, Viv watched her tiny girl lead the animal in with practiced ease. "Help me, Mummy," Maggie demanded as Viv watched her unbuckle the straps holding the horse's saddle on.

"What should I do?" she asked.

"Lift it up," said Maggie, sounding very grown up.

Viv did as she was told, clumsily helping Maggie unburden the pony of its gear. It was harder work than she'd expected hauling the leather contraptions around, and she soon was sweating. But Maggie looked happy, so she could hardly complain.

"Mummy, you can give Puffball his oats," said Maggie once she was satisfied with the work.

Viv looked around for what might be the horse's feed. "Where are they, Little Bear?"

Maggie scampered out of Puffball's stall, leaving Viv alone with the pony. She eyed it wearily. It wasn't as though she'd never been around a horse before, though she'd never done more than pat one's nose. She certainly couldn't imagine clambering up on one with the fearlessness of her daughter.

Maggie came back with a pail hanging from both of her hands. Her daughter showed her how to feed Puffball and make sure he had enough water. Then they began to rub down and brush the horse.

"You take this brush, and you make little circles," said Maggie.

"How did you learn all of this, Little Bear?" Viv asked.

"Mr. Warner taught me. He says that I am very good with horses," said Maggie.

"You are, aren't you?" Viv paused. "Do you ever think about home?"

Maggie looked confused, and Viv's heart sank.

"I mean Nan and Grandad's house," Viv added.

"I miss Cora," said Maggie.

Viv closed her eyes in relief. "I'm sure your cousin misses you too. She's been in the countryside too, you know."

"Do you think she has a horse to ride?" asked Maggie.

"I don't know." Kate hadn't told her too much about where the children were staying, except to say that it seemed as though it was a respectable farming family. Perhaps they should speak about their children and the pain of separation more, but Viv sometimes worried that if she let herself dwell on it too long, she wouldn't be able to crawl out from underneath the sadness.

"Do you like it here?" Viv asked.

Maggie's smile brightened. "I have Puffball and my dollies and pretty dresses and sometimes on Saturdays I have ice cream."

This was all wrong. It was wrong to be separated from Maggie. It was wrong that the Thompsons were watching her daughter grow up. It was wrong that, very late at night in her most vulnerable moments, she wondered whether Maggie had a better life here than what Viv could ever offer her.

"Do you know what I miss most, Mummy?" Maggie asked.

Viv blinked rapidly even as she forced a smile. "What is that, Little Bear?"

"I miss you."

Viv dropped the currycomb and caught her daughter up in her arms, pressing her face against Maggie's hair. Her shampoo and soap might have changed, but Maggie still had that lovely child smell that couldn't be taken away.

"I miss you too, Little Bear."

"Mummy, don't cry," said Maggie.

She laughed. "Sometimes people cry because they're happy, and I'm so happy to be here with you."

Maggie sniffled as well. "Can I cry because I'm happy too?"

"Of course, Little Bear."

"Margaret?" Mrs. Thompson's call echoed through the barn.

Viv straightened, brushing hay off her skirt. "We're in here."

Mrs. Thompson appeared at the entrance of the pony's stall. "Leave the rest for Mr. Warner. It's time to go."

Maggie slipped her hand into her mother's. "Come on, Mummy. I want to show you my new tea set."

"You run ahead, Margaret. I'd like a word with your mother," said Mrs. Thompson.

The little girl sprinted around them and out of the barn as the two women watched. Then Mrs. Thompson turned to Viv.

"I hope that Margaret wasn't crying," said Mrs. Thompson.

"We were speaking of home," she said.

"Home?"

"Liverpool. Where she's from," Viv said pointedly.

Mrs. Thompson pursed her lips. "I see. I wanted to discuss something rather important with you. I know it might seem a touch early, but there is a very good school in the village where Margaret's friend Marion goes. It would be best to enroll Margaret as soon as possible."

"But Maggie wouldn't start school until autumn," said Viv.

"It can be difficult to secure a spot; however, I've spoke to the head-mistress, and she said—"

"You've already spoken to the headmistress?"

Mrs. Thompson looked a little taken aback by her sharp tone. "Well, yes. It seemed like the only sensible thing to do. I thought there would be no harm in inquiring."

"Maggie might not be here in autumn."

Mrs. Thompson touched a delicate hand to her lips. "You can't be thinking of returning with her to Liverpool? Mr. Thompson reads the paper every morning. German troops are on the march. Look at what's happened in Norway and Denmark."

She knew the other woman was right. For months the papers had called it the "Phoney War." Troops had hardly seen any action on the continent and—although there was fighting on the seas—the threat of air raids that had them all so frightened at the beginning of the war had faded. All the girls at the post office had grumbled every time Mr. Rowan reminded them that they were meant to carry their gas masks on their routes, and even Mum was having a difficult time maintaining her stoical attitude to following every regulation and guideline in the face of rationing.

Then Hitler's troops took Denmark in less than six hours and were battling through Norway. The situation was the grimmest it had been since the war broke out.

"Please don't make any decisions about Maggie's education without speaking to me first," Viv said as evenly as she could.

Mrs. Thompson gave a curt nod. "When can we expect you again?"

"Next month, as always."

"I only asked because Margaret is so disappointed when you write to move the dates of your visits."

"I . . ." How was it that this woman could so effectively slide a knife of guilt between her ribs every time?

Suddenly Mrs. Thompson was all soft solicitousness again. "I'm only worrying for Margaret's sake, Mrs. Levinson," said Mrs. Thompson.

Viv's gaze fell on her daughter, who was petting one of the calico cats that seemed to call the stables home. If this woman thought that a few carefully placed words would shame or bully Viv, she was mistaken. Viv had endured the shame of her parents, her priest, her neighbors. She'd learned to hold her head high and carry on for Maggie.

She wanted more for her daughter, but she'd come to want more for herself too. She didn't know how she would find it, but she was determined.

"Mrs. Thompson, I appreciate all the care you've given Maggie these past months," Viv started.

"Well, I'm only doing what the Church teaches us and—"

"I'm not finished." Viv locked eyes with the other woman. "I've told you before that I call my daughter Maggie, not Margaret. I ask that you do the same."

"Mrs. Levinson, I really don't think—"

"I won't have Maggie forgetting who she is or where she came from no matter when this war ends," she said.

"As you wish."

The way the other woman's mouth twisted as she spoke gave Viv the distinct impression that it was only good manners that made Mrs. Thompson agree.

Viv

May 15, 1940

When Viv walked into the delivery office three weeks later, all anyone could speak about was the Netherlands, Belgium, France, and Luxembourg. The newspapers and radio broadcast on the BBC all reported breathlessly on the Luftwaffe's surprise attacks on Dutch airfields, despite Germany not officially declaring war on the Low Countries. Terrifying reports came in of paratroopers and German troops pressing into the Netherlands with incredible speed.

"But the Netherlands is so close to England," fretted Betty to Rose as they prepared for the morning's delivery. "And France too."

"The Maginot Line should hold them," said Rose.

"The entire German army?" Betty asked.

"Don't worry your pretty heads," said Mr. Archer, an older man who, despite his habit of always calling the girls "pretty" or "lovely," didn't seem offended by the presence of women in the delivery office. "My son's with the Thirty-Third Western Anti-Aircraft Brigade. If a German plane makes its way up here to Liverpool, they'll be ready."

"Oh, I don't even like to think about it," said Betty with a shiver.

"Were you in the last war?" Rose asked the old man as Viv went through her regular checks that everything on her Federal was in working order.

Mr. Archer snapped into a sharp salute. "Lance Corporal Ronald Archer of the Ninth Battalion King's Liverpool Regiment, at your service, miss."

Rose and Betty began to giggle, and Betty said, "You could teach my brothers a thing or two about a salute. Dad says they're too sloppy by half."

Mr. Archer smiled. "I'm sure they'll learn."

"What if you introduced me to one of your brothers?" asked Rose with a twinkle in her eye.

Betty pulled a face. "I'd feel very sorry for you. What if you had better taste in men?"

Rose fluffed her hair. "I have perfectly good taste in men."

"Oh dear," muttered Mr. Archer before resolutely turning his attention back to his bag.

"Viv, what's your 'what if?' this morning?" called Betty.

It was a game they had taken to playing sometimes, asking "What if?" and answering accordingly. The older men thought it was silly, which just prompted the girls to play more often.

"What if we all packed our bags and finished up our routes on time today?" she asked.

"Hear, hear," muttered Mr. Archer.

"Good morning, good morning," Vanessa called out as she rushed in, her uniform slightly askew. Viv raised an eyebrow, and her friend scowled. "I was up late because I had an air raid warden shift last night. And before you say anything, it's not going to wear me down."

Viv held up her hands. "I didn't say anything."

"But you were thinking it," said Vanessa.

Vanessa, always eager to be in the thick of it, had volunteered to become an air raid warden back in February. As far as Viv could tell, it meant spending a lot of time patrolling the streets at night in a tin hat, knocking on doors to threaten people if their blackout curtains were leaking light, but Vanessa assured her that they were training and preparing for every possibility.

"Has anyone seen Peg yet?" asked Betty.

"I'll bet you sixpence that she says her bus is running late again," said Rose.

"Mrs. Levinson?" Viv twisted and saw Mr. Rowan's head sticking out of the door connecting the garage to the main office. "If you would."

"Oooo," the girls all said in unison as soon as Mr. Rowan disappeared.

"Oh, stop it," Viv said with a laugh.

"What have you done?" Vanessa asked, nudging Viv in the side.

"I have no idea."

Viv hurried over to the door Mr. Rowan had popped out of. She found him just inside the hall.

"Mrs. Levinson. You've been doing excellent work with your route."

He cleared his throat once, then twice. Nerves began to jump in Viv's stomach.

"Circumstances have arisen, and we need to make a few changes to several posties' routes," he said.

She let out a breath. "Is that all?"

He rubbed the back of his neck and refused to look her in the eye.

"What's happened? Has the General Post Office requested that we take on more territory?" she asked.

"No, no. Nothing like that," he said with a grimace. "The fact is, Miss O'Sullivan will no longer be working at the delivery office."

"Peg's gone? Why?" she asked in surprise. They'd only just seen each other yesterday. Peg had come back from her route a little later than she usually did, but Viv assumed that the stomach bug she'd been suffering with was to blame.

"I'm going to ask those of you who have routes that touch her area to pick up some of the roads until I can find a replacement for her." He paused. "I also need you to take back the part of your route Miss O'Sullivan took over."

Her stomach fell. He wanted her to take back Salisbury Road and deliver the post to the Levinson household.

"Mr. Rowan, I'm sure I could find someone else to—"

"I never should have allowed it in the first place. Postal routes are meant to be efficient. Taking an entire road out and giving it to another girl makes no sense," he said firmly.

"But Peg did it for months, and she never complained," she protested.

"You'll take on Salisbury Road again, as well as the additional parts of Peg's route until I can find another postie, and that is final."

She stared at him for a long moment, but from the set of his jaw and his crossed arms she doubted she would get anywhere by arguing.

"Fine," she bit out.

"Good," said Mr. Rowan.

He started to retreat to his office.

"Mr. Rowan," she called out, "what really happened to Peg?"

He stopped and seemed to struggle a moment before sighing. "I suppose you are a married woman."

Immediately, she knew. Peg—the sweet, athletic, charming girl who had never once talked about her love life—had gotten into trouble.

"I see. No need to elaborate," she said.

He shot her a grateful look. "Please don't tell the other young ladies. The General Post Office does not look kindly on women who become pregnant out of wedlock, and we certainly wouldn't want some of the girls with more delicate sensibilities to be disturbed by this news."

She fought to repress a laugh at the irony of that, instead schooling her face into what she hoped was a look of somber concern. "I understand."

Besides, she had more important things to worry about, like how she was going to deliver the post to the Levinsons twice a day, each and every day.

After leaving Mr. Rowan's office, Viv finished packing her postal sack slowly but deliberately. A low hum of dread thrummed through her, every instinct telling her to flee to avoid another encounter with the Levinsons.

The feeling stayed with her until she reached Salisbury Road. Her hands trembled as she walked from house to house, dropping letters through their slots. When she reached the Levinsons' front door, she gripped the four envelopes, crinkling the paper in exactly the way Vanessa had taught her not to. She pushed the letters through the slot and stood, ready to run as they dropped to the floor with a faint clatter. There were no footsteps, no twitching of the sitting room curtains. Nothing in the house stirred.

As quick as she could without running, she hurried down the front path to her bicycle.

As she pedaled off, she felt lighter.

Viv finished the rest of her route and the extra roads from Peg's without incident, returning again for the afternoon shift.

Maybe she could make this work. Maybe she'd made more of delivering the post to the Levinsons than she'd needed to. They probably spent most of their time at the shop. Perhaps she and the Levinsons could simply avoid each other.

The following morning, Viv kept her head down while the other girls played the "What if?" game. She rode out, doing her rounds as quickly as possible, and stopped only long enough to have a bite to eat in the canteen.

When it was time to check her bag for the afternoon delivery, Viv tried her hardest not to stop and stare at the Levinsons' letters. However, one had the distinctive "Passed by Censor" stamp in black ink on the front of it, a dead giveaway that it was from a serviceman. In her hand she held something that Joshua had written.

She flicked past it as quickly as she could.

However, as she delivered the post that afternoon, she couldn't help but think of that letter. He'd never written her anything. Their marriage certificate was the first time she'd even seen his penmanship, but what had she expected? She'd told him to stay away.

She wasn't a fool. She'd known when they'd fumbled awkwardly in that car that he wasn't her great love. There had been a spark of attraction—a novelty for both of them—but that was all that held them together. Without the promise of Maggie, they both would have gone their separate ways. Instead, they had a marriage that had been built on nothing but obligation.

She was so distracted that she hardly looked up when Mr. Campbell on Cecil Street bellowed his customary "Hello!" at her as she mounted her bicycle again. She waved and then checked her wristwatch. It was just after half past two, the extra roads Mr. Rowan had assigned her adding a substantial amount of time to her shift. She would be home at least an hour after she should be. She dreaded the thought of explaining to Mum why she would be late preparing their tea for a second day in a row.

What if she no longer lived at home?

She shook her head. That was what women did when they didn't have a husband.

But Viv *did* have a husband.

The realization pulled her up short. If she had managed to fool everyone at the South East Delivery Office into thinking she was a widow, who was to say she couldn't do it again, maybe as a lodger. She would have to pay rent, but any money left over would be hers to keep. No more handing everything over to her mother except what she could skim off the top of her wage packet.

She considered this as she rounded the corner to Salisbury Road. When Joshua left, she'd turned to her parents because it had felt as though she had no other choice. She'd been pregnant with no money, no means. She'd been terrified.

Now she had a job. She had determination. She wasn't quite so scared.

Viv stopped two doors down from the Levinsons' house and chewed her lip as she pulled out the post for the next handful of houses. Maybe she could find a place that would be happy to take her and Maggie. Maybe she could even find a way for them to have a cat, if their landlord allowed it. Maggie would like that very much.

To her right, Viv heard the squeak of hinges. Her breath caught in her throat as Rebecca stepped out of the Levinsons' front door, hands planted on her hips in a way that made her jade utility dress bunch up on the sides.

No. She was not going to be frightened off by Rebecca Levinson, her parents, or the thought of Joshua. She had a job to do.

Viv forced herself to walk up the Levinsons' neighbors' paths, delivering post just as she normally would. Then she stopped outside of the Levinsons' front gate.

"You're back," said Rebecca.

"I never left. I switched part of my route with one of the other girls."

"Miss O'Sullivan, I know. We liked her," said Rebecca.

"I did too." When she looked up, she saw concern in the other woman's eyes and hurried to add, "She's fine. She just can't work any longer."

Rebecca gave a stiff nod. "Do you have our post?"

Viv lifted the letters marked for the Levinsons off the top of her stack. She hesitated, but Rebecca didn't move from the front door.

"I won't bite," said Rebeca with a scoff.

"I don't know about that," she muttered as she opened the gate and walked up with the letters extended.

For a moment, she thought the other woman might snap at her, but instead a smile tugged at Rebecca's lips as she took the post. "I suppose I deserve that. Why are you delivering the post anyway?"

"I need the money."

"The money?" Rebecca laughed, but then stilled. "Oh, you're serious."

"I am," she said.

"There was money enough when your family paid my brother to go away," said Rebecca.

"That wasn't my idea," she said, earning her another scoff. "Dad made enough to get by, but he and Mum used everything they had in savings to pay Joshua."

"So Joshua took all of your family's money?" Rebecca asked.

Viv nodded, expecting Joshua's sister to land a final verbal blow. Instead, Rebecca sighed. "Well, that's my brother to a T."

"What do you mean?"

Rebecca squinted at her. "How well did you know my brother before . . . ?"

"Not well enough, apparently," she said.

"Joshua usually manages to get his own way. He talked his way out of going to synagogue around fourteen. By seventeen he announced that he was going to start playing in bands around town because he was bored at school. There were some arguments, but eventually my parents let him. You can't imagine what my parents might say if I tried to do that.

"Joshua wanted to become a musician. He wanted to move to New York. One way or another, I suspect he would have found a way. But don't think that means I've forgiven you," Rebecca added quickly.

"For giving him a reason to leave? Or for becoming pregnant?" she asked.

Rebecca jerked back. "You and the child were never the problem."

It was Viv's turn to laugh. "Don't pretend that any of you wanted anything to do with me."

She remembered those first weeks all too well. She'd waited, desperately clinging to the hope that the Levinsons would want to see her and the newborn Maggie. That they might take pity on her and lift her up out of the cold isolation of her parents' house despite the choice that Joshua had made and how she'd pushed him away.

Rebecca pursed her lips. "I'll admit, we were shocked when we found out that Joshua had gotten you into trouble—even more so when we learned you were Catholic—but my parents would have welcomed you into the family in a second."

"What are you talking about?"

"They only have one grandchild, you know. It's cruel to keep them away. And what about your daughter? She didn't start a fight with anyone, and yet she's being deprived of her grandmother and grandfather."

Viv was stunned. "I don't understand. After I had Maggie, I wrote your parents. I told them that they had a granddaughter. A beautiful little girl. Margaret Anne."

The fight seemed to go out of Rebecca as her eyes widened. "My mother's name is Anne."

Viv's lungs sucked in shallow breaths. She was beginning to see spots. "You know all of this. It was in the letter."

"There was no letter," Rebecca insisted.

"Yes, there was. I wrote it myself."

She knew that she had. The memory of the pain that her two-day labor caused had faded a bit over time, but everything else was rendered in sharp detail. The way that Mum and Dad had hardly looked at their granddaughter when the midwife had shown Maggie to them. How Kate had come barreling into the house like a guardian angel. How Maggie had refused to latch properly for three days. How even though Viv was bone-tired, she'd asked Kate for writing paper and painstakingly written out a note to her daughter's grandparents. She'd even asked Kate to post it for her.

Kate had done it. Surely she had. Kate was her sister, protective and loving.

Unless . . .

"I'm sorry," Viv said abruptly. "I need to go."

"Wait!" Rebecca called as Viv fled from the Levinsons' house for the second time.

Joshua

Joshua was crossing the college green, collar turned up against the spring rain that had been falling all morning, when he spotted Adam sprinting toward him.

"Levinson!" shouted his friend. "They're here!"

"Finally," he breathed.

Joshua raced after Adam to the building where they'd trained for the past six months in the fine art of being navigators. For a job that was meant to be done up in the air, they'd spent an incredible amount of time in lecture rooms, escaping only for training runs. On those days, they'd go up with a pilot to simulate what it might be like to fly through any number of scenarios. Those were the moments, surrounded by the clouds and the soothing drone of the engine, that made all the training worth it.

"Assignments are in, men. Wait your turn, and you'll all get your orders," said Wing Commander Crusoe, who ran the No. 2 Initial Training Wing.

Wait, Joshua had learned since joining the RAF, could mean five minutes or five days. However, he was pleasantly surprised when he found himself called into a room about a half hour later.

He stood at attention in front of a table of three men including Wing Commander Crusoe while he was told he'd passed. He was now a navigator of the rank of sergeant, courtesy of the RAF's new rule that all air crewmen were to hold, at minimum, that rank. He was to report to the Seventy-Eighth Squadron at RAF Linton-on-Ouse at 1600 hours the following day.

Adam was leaning against the off-white corridor wall just outside, waiting for him. "Did you make it through?"

"Passed," Joshua said.

Adam grinned and pumped his hand. "Congratulations, Levinson. Where are you being stationed?"

"Linton-on-Ouse," he said.

"Never heard of it." Adam turned around to the crowded hall. "Anyone heard of Linton-on-Ouse?"

"Aye!" came a shout. "You're going to North Yorkshire, mate."

"Not me, my friend here," said Adam with a clap on Joshua's back.

Joshua nodded, still a little stunned that after all his work over the past few months it was finally over.

For better or worse, he was on his way to active missions.

The train ride was grueling with delays, long stopovers, and uncomfortable seats, but finally Joshua made it to York the following day.

With stiff legs, he walked out of the train station and spotted a RAF truck and a WAAF waiting by the curb. He pulled at his cap and asked, "Is this truck going to RAF Linton-on-Ouse?"

The woman who wore her own blue cap at a jaunty angle looked him up and down. "You can climb in back with the rest of them, Sergeant."

Joshua nodded and joined three other fliers on the hard benches. One man reading a letter hardly glanced up, while another appeared to be fast asleep with his arms crossed over his chest and a cigarette dangling from his mouth. However, the third man, clean-cut and slim, looked Joshua up and down.

"Pilot?" the man asked.

"Navigator," said Joshua.

The man reached into his pocket, pulled out a silver case, and offered Joshua a cigarette as though they were at a cocktail party.

"No, thanks," said Joshua as the truck's engine rumbled to life and the vehicle jerked backward, waking up their sleeping companion who snorted, looked around, and settled down again.

"Suit yourself. I'm Flight Lieutenant Alan Smythe," said the man with the cigarettes, pulling out a shiny silver lighter.

"Sergeant Joshua Levinson," he responded. He watched Smythe sway with the truck as he lit his cigarette and put both case and lighter away. He'd bet a fiver that Smythe had a second set in gold stashed safely away at home.

"What's in that?" asked Smythe, nodding to Joshua's instrument case.

"A saxophone."

"You play?" Smythe asked, clearly just looking for conversation.

"I do," Joshua said. He'd brought the sax with him to Cambridge under his sister's strict orders. He'd tried his best to play whenever he wasn't on duty, taking his sax out to the fields a little way down from the university where no one would listen in. He'd serenaded some cows who watched him as they chewed. It felt ridiculous, but at least it was keeping his fingers nimble.

"You see they have a girl driving this truck?" asked Smythe. "She's just as likely to run us off the road as she is to get us to base safely."

Joshua had been around enough WAAFs at RAF Padgate and in Cambridge to know that the WAAFs might not be allowed into actual combat, but they could be tougher than a corporal on a morning training run.

"Our driver's doing just fine," Joshua said.

The WAAF proved him right. The men bumped and wove on their seats as she navigated the canvas-sided truck expertly through the tiny, winding streets of the ancient city of York and into the countryside. A couple of times, she had to mash the horn to clear a road—once of giggling girls on bicycles who pointed when they saw the men through the open flap of the truck and once for an errant sheep standing in the way.

The ride wasn't exactly comfortable, but it was spring in Yorkshire, and that meant the air was fresh and clean. Sheep grazed and crops grew lush and green in the fields. In the distance, the sun broke through fluffy clouds. If he hadn't been sitting in the back of a truck, wearing the navy-blue uniform of the RAF with sergeant's chevrons on his sleeve, he could almost have forgotten there was a war on.

The low buzz of two planes' engines pulled him back to reality, and all the men in the back of the truck leaned, trying to catch sight of the planes.

"They're Whitleys," said the man who'd been fast asleep through most of the drive.

"We'll be up in those soon," said Smythe.

The truck pulled up to the gates of the base and drove through. As soon as the WAAF parked, she came around and let down the tailgate. Joshua hauled his kit bag up on his shoulder, grabbed his sax, and hopped down.

Linton-on-Ouse looked just like the other bases he'd seen. Concrete stretched out in front of him, surrounded by fence. There were guard towers and low buildings that would make up offices, briefing rooms, and more. Vast hangars stood with their doors open, and planes sat ready both inside and on the runway. The faint but distinctive scent of fuel drifted on the air.

After months of waiting, he wanted to learn his assignment, meet his flight crew, and see what he would be flying in. But first, he needed to report.

After stowing his gear in the barracks, Joshua found himself standing at attention in front of Squadron Leader Fitzwilliam, a tall, elegant man with a red bottlebrush mustache that made him look like he was more suited for the last war than this one.

"You're on a Blenheim bomber, Sergeant. You'll be flying with Sergeant Gibson," said Fitzwilliam, consulting a clipboard.

"You don't mean Johnny Gibson, do you, sir?" Joshua asked, cracking a smile.

Fitzwilliam looked up, his mustache twitching. "Northern like you. Brilliant. Talks a mile a minute?"

"That's the one. We did basic ground training together at Padgate, sir," he said.

"Well, call it serendipity, Sergeant. Here he is now," said Fitzwilliam, nodding over Joshua's shoulder.

The moment Johnny saw Joshua, his eyes lit up. "Levinson! How the hell are you?"

"Language, Sergeant," warned Fitzwilliam.

"Sorry, sir," said Johnny, quickly saluting. "It's just that Levinson and I go way back. Way, way back. He's been in Cambridge, and I haven't seen him since last autumn."

"Well, you'll be seeing a lot more of each other. He's your new navigator. I'll leave you to introduce him to Russell. Levinson, I hope you fare better than the last man," said the squadron leader before moving on to the next man.

Joshua clapped Johnny on the shoulder. "You're a sight for sore eyes, Johnny. How have you been?"

"Good. Good. Good," said Johnny, bobbing his head with each answer. "I told you I'd end up as a wireless operator and you'd end up as a navigator, didn't I?"

"You did," Joshua said, remembering back to the train ride where they'd first met. "What happened to your last navigator?"

Johnny scratched the back of his head. "The best I can tell, he went on twenty-four-hour leave and came back with a smashed hand, three cracked ribs, and a broken leg. A couple of the guys say he went out looking for a fight, while others say he tangled with a dispatch rider's motorcycle.

"Why don't I show you around and see if we can find Russell? He's our pilot."

Joshua followed Johnny as the smaller man kept up his usual string of chatter. While it might have once bothered Joshua, he found himself sinking into the comforting familiarity of his friend's constant commentary.

"You should have seen Yatesbury, where I trained. Did you know they made us do a church parade every Sunday? Most of the men headed off to the Church of England church, but a handful of us went to the Catholic church nearby.

"Of course, Christmas away from my mum was tough," Johnny continued. "I got forty-eight hours leave in January to go up to Bootle and see her, and I don't think she's ever cried so much as when I had to catch the train back. I swear she nearly flooded the platform with all those tears.

"Did you go back to see your family? No, wait. Not for Christmas. I know you're Jewish. I just thought—"

"I saw them before going to Cambridge," Joshua said.

Johnny let out a whistle. "That long ago? Mum would have killed me if I stayed away that long, but I told her that it might be tougher now that I'm fully trained. Who knows where they'll send us on ops."

"I'm going to try to go home on my first long leave," said Joshua, determined to show his sister and his parents that he was making amends for his absence. "And I've been sending more letters."

He'd found it easier to write home since he'd seen them in October. He still couldn't tell them much about what he was doing day-to-day for fear the censor would strike it out. Instead, he put little things into his letters like what the food in the mess was like and how he'd come to enjoy the morning physical-training runs. He wrote about the sensation of flying—a weightlessness that was strangely grounded by the rumble and roar of the engines—and the breathlessness that always struck him on a landing.

However, there were two things he didn't write about: Viv and their child.

In New York, he'd been able to push down his thoughts and any curiosity about them. However, a part of him had cracked open when he'd seen Viv in October.

He knew that he was building up a single moment of memory into something bigger than it was, but he couldn't help it. He thought about the way she looked up at the sky, her face bathed with the indigo of the falling twilight. Had he read regret in her expression?

"Here's Russell," said Johnny, cutting into his thoughts.

A trim man with his hands knitted behind his back as he stood in a small group of other men, all wearing a flight lieutenant's chevrons on their sleeves, looked up as they approached. His eyes flicked over Johnny and then Joshua before nodding.

"Sergeant Gibson," said Russell.

"I thought you'd want to meet your new navigator, sir," said Johnny.

Russell stuck out his hand. "Flight Lieutenant James Russell. I expected to meet you at our briefing later, but it's good to see you earlier."

"Sergeant Joshua Levinson," he said, shaking the man's hand firmly.

"Levinson and I did our basic training together at Padgate," said Johnny proudly.

"Then you'll know Flight Lieutenant Moss," said Russell with a nod.

Joshua's stomach sank as the other men in Russell's group turned. Next to Smythe, the smoker he'd ridden in with, stood Moss, his face as beet red as the moment he'd shouted at Johnny on the training run back at Padgate.

Next to him, Joshua could feel Johnny suck in a breath.

"We've met," said Joshua shortly.

Moss barked a laugh that was all edges. "Levinson, fancy seeing you here. I always was surprised that you managed to make it through training. Where's your friend Schwartz? I thought your sort liked to stick together."

"Your sort?" asked Joshua, eyes narrowing.

"Jews," said Moss with a sneer.

"Moss," said Russell, stepping into the space between Joshua and Moss, "I suggest you keep your concerns for your own crew."

"I would have thought you'd want to know the kind of man you're flying with, Russell. There's no room for errors on ops," said Moss.

"Quite right," muttered Smythe.

Russell turned to Joshua, cool blue eyes searching him again. "Did you pass your navigator's examination?"

"That's why I'm here," Joshua said, barely holding back his anger at that bastard Moss.

"And is there any reason that I should be worried about going up with you?" asked Russell.

"Levinson's as solid as they come," said Johnny quickly.

"Sergeant Gibson, you'll be free to give your opinion when I ask for it," said Russell, flicking a look at Johnny. "Sergeant Levinson?"

Joshua stood a little taller. "No reason at all, sir."

"Good," said Russell. "Then I trust that we won't need to have this conversation again."

"No, sir," said Joshua.

Smythe looked as though he were about to protest, but Moss snubbed out his cigarette. "Come on. I want to see who they have me flying with."

Joshua watched the pair walk away, the adrenaline rushing through him slowly subsiding and leaving behind dull tiredness. A few of the men in Cambridge had raised quizzical eyebrows when Adam had received a menorah in a care package from his wife, and a couple had even expressed polite interest as they'd lit the candles in their barracks every night of Hanukkah. The other men had had even more questions when Adam had invited the men to a truncated version of the Passover seder some months later. However, in each of those acts of observance, Joshua had participated more out of a craving for familiarity than faith. It had been a long time since he'd been observant.

"The RAF might recruit from Oxbridge for its officer class, but I've rarely found that correlates to good manners," Russell said when Moss and Smythe were well out of earshot.

"Sir," said Joshua with a small smile.

"Do your job, don't end up medicaled out because of a drunken motorcycle ride, and we'll manage just fine, Levinson," said Russell with a nod.

As Russell walked away, Johnny said in a low voice, "He's a bit stiff, but he's good man, Russell. A great pilot too. And I think he's a bit more sympathetic than some."

"How do you mean?" he asked.

Johnny held up his dog tags and showed Joshua where it was printed "Catholic."

"I saw Russell's once," Johnny said. "Wouldn't you know, he's Catholic too."

Viv

For their second date, Joshua picked up Viv from Kate and Sam's house in a car.

Kate, who had helped Viv dress her hair, let out an appreciative sound when she spotted him from the bedroom window. "A car, and he's handsome too. I'll give you that."

"Come away from there. He'll see you," said Viv.

"Better me than Mum," said Kate as a knock sounded on the door below.

Viv stood from her sister's tiny vanity and grabbed her handbag. "It's just a date."

"Which is why he's picking you up here rather than at home?" asked Kate with an arched brow, as Sam opened the door. "You know that Mum and Dad wouldn't approve. And besides, it's two dates, Vivie."

"You wouldn't understand. You've known Sam half your life," Viv said.

"You don't have to date a boy from church, but you need to know that there are consequences to blazing your own trail. Go out with your Joshua and enjoy yourself, but make sure that you're walking into things with your eyes wide open."

"I know what I'm doing," said Viv stubbornly.

She tried to tamp down her excitement as she walked downstairs to meet Joshua. He lit up when he saw her.

"You look beautiful." From behind his back, he produced a small spray of flowers. "For you."

"How lovely, thank you," she said, turning so Kate could help him pin the corsage to her claret wool dress.

They said their goodbyes to Kate and Sam, and Joshua led her out to the Morris. It felt glamorous climbing into a car to be ferried off on a date, and she liked the way he reached for her to tuck her in close to him on the front seat.

He took her to the cinema to see a romance that she didn't pay much attention to. She was too caught up by Joshua. She liked talking to him. He liked things the other young men she knew didn't show any interest in, and he dreamed bigger than anyone she'd ever met. Now those dreams were starting to make her wonder why she'd never done the same.

"What did you think of the film?" he asked as they walked out of the cinema ninety minutes later.

"I don't know," she said. "There wasn't much of a spark."

He grinned. "A spark? Is that what girls call it?"

She blushed. "I just think that I should have been more convinced that he was willing to give everything up for her."

"Do you think we have a spark?" he asked.

She started, surprised by the forward, teasing question but liking the way it made her go liquid inside.

"Maybe," she said.

He laughed and grabbed her hand, pulling her close. She snuggled into his side.

"Do you need to go home?" he asked.

"My parents think I'm helping my sister take care of my niece and nephews tonight," she said.

"Good. I want to show you something."

He drove her through the city, all the way past Bootle and the towns of the coast until they reached Formby Beach. The twilight was falling purple and blue when he parked in a quiet spot.

"It's beautiful out here," she said.

"Mum and Dad took us here before we moved to Wavertree. Now that we live on the other side of the city, I don't get to come out very often."

She turned to him, and her breath caught in her throat. He was beautiful, his thick hair picking up the silver light of the moon. She wanted to reach over and rake her hands through it. To touch him. To feel the low charge of electricity running between them.

"Viv—" he started to say, but she cut him off with a kiss.

He stiffened and then melted against her.

"You're so beautiful," he whispered against her ear when he broke off to kiss a line up her neck.

This wasn't what good girls were supposed to do, but hearing him call her beautiful ignited something in her. She slid her hands under the lapels of his jacket, warmth radiating from his chest through the thick cotton of his shirt.

"Viv," he moaned, but she couldn't stop herself. She wanted to touch him. He made her feel so good, and surely there couldn't be anything wrong with that.

His hands were at her waist, her breasts, her hair, everywhere. As they kissed, he leaned her back on the bench of the car so that his body covered hers. She loved the sensation of it, his hot breath on her neck and the weight of him heavy against her.

"We should slow down," he said, but he didn't sound for one moment as though he believed it.

"I don't want to," she said, ignoring all the voices that screamed in her head that she was supposed to stop. She wasn't even supposed to be on this date, so what did it matter if she didn't stop? She wanted this. She *always* did what she was told. She never had a misstep. Just for once she wanted to do something because it felt good.

Slowing down was the last thing that they should do.

Joshua

If Joshua had been thinking straight, he would have been embarrassed about how fast it was all over, but he was too muddled for that. One moment he was looking out at the sea and then Viv was kissing him, and everything became a blur of skin and sex.

Their breathing had slowed when she finally eased off him, settling her clothes to cover herself. She didn't look at him.

"Are you okay?" he asked.

"I . . . I think so," she said.

Regret flushed through him. "I should have stopped us."

"No, it's my fault. I'm sorry," she said, staring straight ahead.

"I think we should be okay," he said, feeling the wet stain on his trouser leg. At least his brain had been working enough to pull out of her at the last moment. He just had to hope that it was soon enough.

Silence filled the car, the weight of it unmistakable.

"I'll take you out again," he said, his voice flat.

"That would be nice," she said, but there was no enthusiasm there. It was as though what they had done had thrown up a wall between them, and now she was unreachable on the other side.

"Why don't I take you back to your sister's house?" he asked.

Viv bit her lip, her eyes still fixed ahead. "I think that would be a good idea."

Viv

Viv let herself into Kate's house with the key her sister had lent her as quietly as she could. She'd almost made it to Cora's room, where Kate had set up a cot, when Kate's bedroom door opened. Her sister stuck her head out, hair wrapped up in pin curls and a dressing gown held close at her throat.

"How was your date?" Kate asked.

Viv swallowed and nodded. "Good. We went to the cinema."

"You're back late."

"We went for a drive and talked after."

Kate raised a brow. "Talked?"

Viv tried not to think about the shakiness of her legs or the stickiness between her thighs. "Go back to bed. I'll tell you more in the morning."

Kate looked as though she might say something, but instead she gave a curt nod. "All right, then. Good night, Vivie."

Viv began to shuffle to Cora's room, but she didn't miss Kate saying softly, "I hope you know what you're doing," before closing the door behind her.

Viv squeezed her eyes shut. God, she hoped she did too.

Viv

May 16, 1940

Viv's breath came fast as she banged the iron knocker on her sister's front door. She could not stop thinking about Rebecca's claim that the Levinsons had never received her letter. That they'd spent all this time thinking that she'd kept Maggie from them.

The clatter of hard-soled shoes against the entryway boards announced her sister's arrival before Kate swung open the door. Kate's hair, which was tied up in a triangular scarf, frizzed out a little at the sides, and her cheeks were a little red. Viv noticed that Kate wore the blue-and-white-checked apron Viv had made her last Christmas.

"Vivie, come in. You've saved me from the mangle. It's laundry day."

"I need to talk to you," said Viv, pushing into the house.

"My, my, that does sound serious. I'll put a cup of tea on," said Kate.

Viv tried her best to swallow her rising anger as she followed her sister through to her little kitchen.

"I'm glad you're here. The house is too quiet without Sam and the kids rattling around," Kate chattered as she reached for the kettle and turned on the tap. "They say you become used to it, but it's been eight months and I think it's actually become worse as the days have gone by.

"Mrs. Holland must make the kids sit down every Sunday and do their letters because I can't see Colin writing me anything willingly. You know he'd rather be outside. I've heard it's nice countryside in that part of Wales, and Sam knows it a little. He wrote that he went to the seaside around Pwllheli when he was a lad.

"Now"—Kate turned around from the stove after putting the kettle on—"what is it that you wanted to talk about? Is Mum driving you batty again?"

"No, it isn't Mum," she said.

"Well, that is one for the books," Kate said.

"Do you remember the days after I gave birth to Maggie?" Viv asked.

"How could I forget them? My little sister giving me a niece? I couldn't have been happier," said Kate.

Viv swallowed. "I wrote a letter to Joshua's parents, telling them about Maggie. You were going to post it for me. Do you remember?"

Kate turned to pull two stoneware mugs down from a high shelf. "Maybe."

"Did you?" she asked.

"Did I what?" Kate asked, spooning a scant bit of sugar into one of the mugs.

"Did you post the letter to the Levinsons like I asked?"

The teaspoon clattered against the mug. Kate whipped around, stricken. "Vivie, I'm so sorry."

"You promised you'd posted it!"

"You were exhausted and nearly delirious. You'd just given birth," Kate began to protest. "I thought—"

"You thought that you were doing the best for me? Or were you doing what Mum and Dad wanted?"

"I—"

"You're my sister, you're supposed to be on my side!" she shouted.

"You were so upset after Joshua left. I thought that it would only make things worse if the Levinsons didn't want anything to do with you and Maggie," said Kate.

"I wasn't upset. I was *angry*! I was furious at him for leaving, and at Mum for paying him to go away, and at myself for being stupid enough to believe that he would stand by me in the first place." She sobbed. "You were the one person I thought I could trust."

"I'm so sorry, Vivie," Kate said, rushing up to clasp Viv's hands.

"For years I've thought the Levinsons hated me so much that they didn't even want to know their granddaughter. Now I find out they didn't even know about her. How could you, Kate?"

"I thought it was for the best," her sister whispered.

"And what about everything since? All the times that you sided with Mum and Dad, like when they wanted to send Maggie away?"

"Evacuating Maggie was for the best," said Kate. "You know that."

"For who? Mum and Dad, who never wanted her around in the first place? For you, so that you didn't have to think about how you were sending your own children away?"

Kate's head snapped back as though Viv had slapped her. "I sent them away because it was the safest thing to do. You could have made your own choice."

"Because it's so easy to say no to Mum and Dad when I am completely dependent upon them for everything, including the house I live in."

"Oh, stop it!" Kate exploded. "For five years all you have done is mope about how life has been so hard for you."

Viv gasped. "I can't believe you would say that."

"And I can't believe what my intelligent, brave, determined little sister has turned into," said Kate fiercely. "Look at you! You're so afraid of everything. You've done exactly what Mum has said for *years* because it is easier than facing up to your fears."

"I don't have a husband like you, Kate."

"But you do! You have Joshua's name and, whether you think so or not, that's important. You aren't like those girls who get into trouble and are sent away. Your child has his surname. He's on the birth certificate.

"You could have chosen to do so many things, but instead you ran back to Mum and Dad and let them treat you like a housekeeper. *You* chose this life, Vivie. No one else."

Viv gaped at her sister.

"You are one of the toughest people I know. I thought that maybe you'd finally woken up when you stood up to Mum and Dad and went back to work, but nothing else changed," Kate continued.

"So I wasted all of my opportunities and ruined my life because I became pregnant. Is that what you're saying?" she asked.

Kate shook her head emphatically. "I know that it has been hard living in that house, but now you have a chance to change all of that. You can figure this out. For centuries women have lived with less."

Viv's stomach turned as she realized that her sister was echoing back some of the same thoughts she'd had. What if she no longer lived at home? What if she stood up to her mother once and for all and left? What if she made different hard choices?

"The happiest I've ever seen you wasn't when you were with Maggie, Vivie. It was when you were working in the sorting hall," Kate said, her tone softening.

"I love my daughter," she whispered.

"Of course you do. She's your daughter. But is that enough?"

It had never occurred to her before that her life could be about anything but Maggie.

"I thought you were going to earn enough money to have choices that I never had. You were going to live a different life," said Kate.

Wasn't that what she'd managed to do when she'd taken her job as a postie? There was such freedom on her bicycle, doing a job that she had come to love and taking home a wage for it. Sometimes she almost felt guilty because she suspected that she enjoyed the work just as much as she valued the money that paid for her train and bus fare to Wootton Green.

"But everything that I did—"

"Are not the only things that will ever happen to you. I'm sorry that these past years have been difficult, Vivie. I wouldn't wish what happened to you on anyone, and some days I think it's a wonder that you can share a roof with our parents at all."

Viv looked up at her sister as the kettle began to whistle on the stove. "What do I do?"

"Your life is not my life or anyone else's. You're the only one who can figure that out, but I know it starts with you deciding what you want," said Kate, grabbing a tea towel to pull the screaming kettle off the heat.

While her sister poured the tea, Viv stared at the scrubbed floor of Kate's kitchen. Her sister was right. Viv had simply been trying to survive for so long that she'd forgotten to think beyond Maggie and what her daughter might need. But maybe her sister was right in another regard. Viv could figure a way out of this.

When Kate set a mug of tea with a scant bit of milk in it in front of Viv, she looked up. "I need to move out of Mum and Dad's house."

"You do," Kate said with a nod.

"Will anyone want to take in a woman with a child?"

"I don't know, but it can't hurt to ask," she said.

Viv took a sip of tea and then carefully set down her mug again. "I don't forgive you for not sending that letter."

Kate sighed. "I don't know what to say other than I was trying to do what I thought was best."

"Enough people tell me every day what is best for me. Mum, Dad, Father Monaghan—even Mrs. Lloyd at the grocer's gives me plenty of unsolicited advice. I don't need that from you," Viv said.

Kate gave a small nod. "I will try my best not to do it again."

"Just promise me that the next time I tell you that I need your help, you'll do what I ask."

"I promise," Kate said. "Although, may I give you a piece of advice?"

Viv inclined her chin.

"If you decide you want to move out on your own, be ready. Mum will shut you out. Dad will go along with Mum. They might even try to deploy Father Monaghan again."

"I'm sure he'll remind me about the duty of daughters to their parents," Viv said with a grimace.

"I'm serious. You should think long and hard about it because, if you make this decision, a lot of people aren't going to like it," Kate warned.

"Like most of the people I know in Walton? Like everyone from church? That isn't a great loss. They weren't there for me the last time I needed help."

Kate reached across the table to grip her arm. "I mean it. Even though you're Mrs. Joshua Levinson, some people aren't going to believe that you're married, or they'll guess why you got married and why you don't live with your husband. They'll treat you like you're separated or divorced, and we Byrnes aren't posh enough to brush that away."

"You were the one encouraging me to leave. Now you're saying that I shouldn't?"

Kate shook her head. "I'm saying that you should go into this with open eyes. Don't do it because I told you to. Do it because you want to."

"I don't want Maggie growing up the way I did. Always afraid and feeling guilty for every little thing." She wanted her daughter to know she was loved. She wanted her to understand that she was a gift, not a burden.

Kate nodded. "All right, then. Let's come up with a plan."

"You're going to help me?" Viv asked.

"You're my baby sister. Of course I want to help," Kate said.

Viv stood, came around the other side of the table, and hugged her sister. She hadn't forgiven Kate, but for the first time in a very long time she felt as though perhaps she wasn't so very alone after all.

22 May 1940

Dear Joshua,

I don't know how to tell you this, but it doesn't feel right to keep it back from you.

I saw Vivian last week. It isn't the first time that I've seen her. She came to the door back in October, not long after your visit.

She's taken a job delivering the post in Wavertree. Mum said Viv seemed shocked when Mum opened the door and found Viv there. I've thought about it a lot since that day, and I don't think that she realized where we live because she never came here.

After that first time, she must have done something because we had a new postie for a while—a pleasant, chipper girl named Miss O'Sullivan. However, something's happened to her because Viv was at the door again, letters in hand. She told me that the route's come back to her. I don't think she's any happier about it than I am.

I've always resented her over the years because she left Mum and Dad wondering about the grandchild they'd never met. I thought that was such a cruel thing to do, especially since her family was responsible for you leaving Liverpool.

She told me she'd written to our parents right after the birth. She'd addressed a letter to the shop, telling them that she had had a little girl, Margaret Anne Levinson, who she calls Maggie. She said that it didn't feel right, Mum and Dad not knowing. She wanted them to meet their granddaughter.

The letter never made it. I don't know how or why, but for five years she's thought we didn't want anything to do with your daughter, and we've thought she was keeping Maggie away from us.

Viv tells us that Maggie was evacuated to live with a family in a village in Warwickshire. I'm glad for it every time the air raid siren sounds another false alarm, but I think it's breaking Mum's and Dad's hearts a little to know that their granddaughter is so far away.

21 May 1940

Dear Mum, Dad, and Rebecca,

You'll be happy to know that I've settled in on base. I haven't flown my first ops yet, but we've been flying air tests every day. We take the plane up during the day, make sure that everything is running as it should, test all the equipment.

Even though I'm new to the base, Russell and Johnny have been here for long enough that they have a regular plane. Our old girl is D for Dog, but Johnny calls her Dorothy because he says it isn't polite to call a lady a dog. We have our own ekes, or ground crew, who work on Dorothy too. You wouldn't believe what goes into keeping the fleet shipshape.

When we're not in the air, we're in briefings, learning about German planes, or working on our equipment. We also have some time to ourselves. We stay on base unless we're on leave, but there's a NAAFI where we can buy food and something hot to drink. Every so often, someone will rig up a sheet and pull out the film projector so we can watch something. Mostly it's comedies and musicals. A lot of American films, but some of ours too.

I'm glad to hear things are well at the shop. You're right that people will always need clothes, even when there's a war on.

I don't know when I'll next have leave, but as soon as I can cobble together enough time to come up to Liverpool, I will.

Your loving brother and son,
Joshua

I've been thinking for days about whether to write to you about this. You might think it's because I'm angry at Viv. It isn't. Try as I might not to be, I'm still angry at you. If you had stayed, none of this would have happened. We would have known Maggie. I wouldn't have had to watch Mum cry every time she saw a pram in the road, and Dad might not have stayed at the shop working later and later hours but never talking about why when it was so obvious.

You got to run away, Joshua, but you never thought about what that did to us. All of us, including your wife.

I love you because you're my brother. I want you to stay safe, but I also want you to know what I know.

Your sister,
Rebecca

Joshua

J oshua stared at the letter in his hand.

He had a daughter.

A little girl.

Maggie.

Somehow knowing his child's name felt different—more real.

He read through the letter again, and another hard truth dawned on him. His sister had learned his daughter's name before he had. Dammit, his sister had learned he had a *daughter* before he had.

He wanted to crawl out of his skin and hide.

He shoved a hand through his hair. He had a wife he hadn't seen in years, a daughter he'd never met, and what did he have to show for it? A journeyman musician's career with nothing permanent to return to back in New York.

"A quarter of an hour."

Joshua looked up to find Johnny at the foot of his bed, shifting from foot to foot. They'd been briefed that afternoon. They'd be flying out that evening at 19:00 for bombing strikes over German targets advancing through France. They all knew what that meant. Some of the men sitting in the briefing room that afternoon would not be coming back.

Some were tense, laughing a little too loud and practically vibrating with the adrenaline that came with every real ops. Others were somber, choosing to spend their time writing "If I don't return . . ." letters to be posted to loved ones if the worst happened.

In quiet moments, Joshua had taken up the habit of taking out his sax and soothing himself by keying old songs he'd played on Swing Street.

"Right," said Joshua, folding up Rebecca's letter. "Right."

He stood and stretched because he knew that he had hours ahead that would be spent by Russell's side at Dorothy's instrument panel. Then he pulled off his boots, stepped into his flight suit, and laced his boots up again.

Joshua nodded to Johnny, who was pacing around at the door, eyes firmly fixed on the floor. "Let's go."

He and Johnny pushed out of their barracks door, meeting Russell halfway to the tarmac where Dorothy was parked.

"Sergeants," said Russell with a quick nod of respectful profession-alism.

Russell climbed up first, followed by Joshua, and then Johnny, each of them patting the cartoon of Judy Garland from *The Wizard of Oz* that one of the mechanics had painted on the portside of the cockpit. Dorothy was their good luck charm, a reminder that there was no place like home, so that was where they should make their way back each and every time.

Joshua squeezed in next to Russell, who was going through his checks, while Johnny took his place at the wireless radio station. When they were over their target, Joshua would make use of his sliding seat that would allow him to aim the bombs. If they came across any of the Luftwaffe's Bf 109s, Johnny would shimmy up into the gun turret at the aft of the plane and do his best to get them out of trouble while the Spitfires ac-companying them would try to engage the enemy.

The engines roared to life as Russell flipped and twisted his instru-ments for the pre-takeoff sequence. Joshua slipped on the headset that would allow them to communicate over the roar of the engines.

"Let's have a clean flight for Levinson's maiden ops, gentlemen," said Russell into his headset.

Joshua turned to see Johnny give a thumbs-up from his station. Joshua settled back in his chair as best he could and braced himself to fly.

Maggie

"Eat that up, Margaret," said Mrs. Reed, the Thompsons' housekeeper, pointing to the little bit of chicken that was still on Maggie's plate. "There's a war on."

Maggie pulled a face. The chicken still had the skin on it. Her mother knew that she didn't like skin, but Mrs. Reed didn't, and Maggie wasn't about to tell her.

She stabbed the chicken with a fork and popped it into her mouth. She made herself chew it and then swallow, even though she hated the way it felt. It's what good girls did.

"I'm done, Mrs. Reed. May I please be excused from luncheon?" Maggie had learned that, here at Beam Cottage, dinner was luncheon, tea was supper, and the serviette that Maggie put on her lap while eating her meals was a napkin.

The housekeeper made a great show of examining Maggie's plate. Finally, Mrs. Reed said, "All right. Off you go. I've a tea to make."

Maggie bounded up the stairs to her bedroom, but she kept the door open. If Mrs. Thompson was making tea, that meant a guest was coming over and there would be sandwiches and sweets to eat later.

Sometimes at these teas, Mrs. Thompson liked to show Maggie off to the other ladies in the village. Maggie would wear one of her frilly dresses with bows and stiff skirts, and everyone would remark on how pretty and well-behaved she was.

That afternoon, however, the doorbell rang, and no one came upstairs to fetch Maggie. She played in her playroom, waiting to be summoned, but after a little while she grew bored.

She crept out to the top of the stairs, taking a seat on a step that let her just see inside the open drawing room door. She could see a tall man dressed all in black except for a white square at his neck facing the door. He looked like Father Halson, who they saw in church every Sunday, only she didn't recognize him.

"Margaret is adjusting very well, despite a few bumps," she heard Mrs. Thompson say, although she could not see her foster mother. "The things that she would talk about when she first arrived. She actually asked me when laundry day was and who helped me do the washing."

"Sarah," Maggie could hear Mr. Thompson say in the voice he used sometimes when Mrs. Thompson became upset by things he thought were "ridiculous."

"She's from a very different place than Wootton Green. The parishioners there don't have as much," said the priest.

"I read the newspapers, and I thought I understood, but the condition of her underthings was shocking," said Mrs. Thompson. "You could practically see straight through them."

Maggie's cheeks burned.

"We've been consistent, and we've tried not to lose our patience with her little habits," said Mr. Thompson.

"I'm sure you have," said the priest.

"The only problem now really is the mother," said Mrs. Thompson. "She insists on visiting regularly."

"She *is* her mother," said the priest.

"Darling, we've talked about this. Mrs. Levinson has every right to see Margaret when she chooses," said Mr. Thompson.

"You say that, dearest, except every time she comes, Margaret cries and becomes nearly inconsolable. Really, I could understand Mrs. Levinson visiting once to make sure her daughter was settled, but nearly every month is ridiculous. None of the other families hosting evacuated children ever have visits from their parents," Mrs. Thompson finished.

There was a pause before the priest said, "You know that she will have to go back home at some point, Sarah. This war cannot go on forever."

"I think we both need the reminder from time to time," said Mr. Thompson.

"Matthew—"

"Maggie isn't ours," said Mr. Thompson, his voice firm.

Maggie blinked back tears as she quietly picked herself up off the stair and crept quietly up to her bedroom. She closed the door and then sank down on the floor.

She didn't understand why Mrs. Thompson sounded so frustrated with her and why Mr. Thompson didn't want her to stay. She'd been a good girl, just like her mother had told her to be.

She pulled Tig off the bed and cradled him to her chest. As she squeezed the tiger, her breathing began to calm.

Finally, when her sobs stopped shuddering in her chest, she opened her bedside table drawer and pulled out the photograph her mother had given her. She reached out a finger and touched her mother's face. Even though it was only paper, somehow it helped.

Joshua

Joshua leaned back in his chair, tension rushing from his shoulders.

Another clean ops.

They'd had a quiet trip out, flying in formation with the other Blenheims and Spitfires that had taken off from base. It wasn't until they were five miles off their target that they saw any action—a pair of Bf 109 fighters. The Spitfires engaged, ducking and diving in a manic dogfight, but Russell kept their course straight and true.

Joshua dropped the thousand pounds of bombs that they had on board on target. The intelligence had been good and, he'd been able to make out the dark outlines of the factory building that was their target.

"Good work, men," said Russell when Joshua reported that they'd deployed all their bombs. "Let's take her home."

There'd been no relaxing on the flight back. Now that Joshua had flown multiple ops with this crew, he understood that each man was responsible for keeping an eye out for enemy aircraft along with his regular responsibilities. However, he found that the rush of adrenaline that came with this heightened awareness wasn't so very different from being onstage, playing a solo with an entire club watching.

When they neared base, Russell began their descent just as the sun was beginning to show the first rays of light over the horizon. Fiery oranges faded to pink and soft purple, illuminating the British countryside in all her glory.

"Can you think of a prettier sight?" Johnny asked from his station.

"No, I cannot, Sergeant," said Russell.

As soon as they were on the ground and parked, ground crew swarmed the plane. Around them in the growing light, he could see other crews in the squadron talking to mechanics about what had gone wrong or didn't feel right on the flight. Some men worked to refuel, while others went over the condition of the engines.

Out of the corner of his eye, he saw a plane taxi to a stop. A medic team rushed up with a stretcher.

"Shit," Joshua muttered under his breath. His squadron hadn't lost any men or planes yet, but others on base had. He'd heard from the other men that, over the last few missions, the Luftwaffe's Bf 109s seemed to be outmaneuvering them. The German fighters appeared to have figured out that the best way to bring down a Blenheim was to attack from below at the plane's most vulnerable point. Fly too high and Bf 109s could outstrip even a Spitfire, leaving the slower-moving Blenheims exposed. Flying low seemed the solution, but that exposed them to antiaircraft guns, which were also becoming more accurate day by day.

A drop of rain fell on Joshua's nose, and he looked up. The horizon might be clear with the coming sunrise, but the sky overhead was clouded over with gray.

"Just our luck, huh?" shouted Johnny from where he stood back from the plane's wing.

He grunted, careful to climb down from the plane and avoid slipping on the wing that was rapidly becoming slick from the rain.

"All I want is a cup of tea," he said when his feet hit the ground. They served it hot and sweet in the mess, and it was enough to prop a man up until he could eat and drop into bed to sleep for hours.

"I wonder who's cooking today," said Johnny, as behind them Russell shouted down to a mechanic about something to do with the rudder pedals.

"I can never tell the difference," Joshua said.

"That's where you're wrong, my friend. If Florence is in the kitchens, you can look forward to perfection," said Johnny about the pretty red-headed WAAF from Aberdeen who worked the breakfast hour.

"You only say that because you're sweet on her," Joshua said.

"And she gives me extra bacon if I ask nicely," said Johnny. "What a woman."

Joshua rolled his eyes and was about to tell his friend that he didn't care who was working in the kitchens that day so long as they put breakfast in front of him when there was a loud thud behind them. A low, guttural scream pierced the early-morning air.

He whipped around and saw Russell, lying on the ground, his leg bent at an impossible angle.

Dear Mum, Dad, and Rebecca,

I'm sorry I haven't written for a little while. Something has happened here.

I told you about the men I fly with, Russell and my friend Johnny? Well, I'm not flying with them any longer. We were coming back from an ops at dawn. I can't tell you where or what we were doing, but the ops was a success, and so as soon as we were on the ground, we were supposed to hand the plane over to the ground crew, have our breakfast, and then sleep.

It started raining on base. I remember thinking that I needed to be careful climbing down off the wing. I made it onto the ground easy as you like, but Russell, our pilot, wasn't so lucky. One moment he was in the cockpit, and the next he was on the ground with a broken leg. He's usually so careful, but all it takes is one mistake.

A pilot with a broken leg is as good as useless in the air, and Russell is one of our aces on base, so we're sorry to see him grounded.

On the same mission, a bullet tore through the side of one of the bombers in another squadron and hit the navigator. He's laid up with a punctured lung and, being pilotless, now I've been moved over to that crew to replace him. (Johnny has also gone over to another plane in our squadron with a new pilot and navigator.)

I might not mind the change, expect that my new pilot is Flight Lieutenant Moss. You'll remember him because I wrote about tangling with him at training. I can't say that my opinion of him has improved now that I'm flying with him. He seems hell-bent on becoming a war hero rather than just doing his job. That isn't to say that he's sloppy. On the contrary, he runs his checks before flying even more meticulously than Russell did, although I fear that's mostly because if something mechanical were to go wrong and we *had to turn back, he might lose his opportunity to earn his Victoria Cross.*

There is one thing I'm certain of: Moss hates me. I think it's because I'm Jewish, but it's possible it's also because I'm Northern and a musician. I haven't cared enough to ask for clarification. All I am trying to do is keep my head down and wait for another opportunity to open up so I can request a transfer of crew from my squadron leader. There is a chance that he will tell me that the RAF isn't in the business of granting special requests, but it is worth the try not to fly with someone who so clearly doesn't trust me.

Please write to me and let me know how you're faring. Stay safe, and don't be heroes. Leave that to the likes of Flight Lieutenant Moss. . . .

Your loving son and brother,
Joshua

Viv

Viv was fast asleep when the first piercing scream split the air. She jolted upright in bed, her heart hammering against her chest. She knew that sound. There had been plenty of drills with the air raid siren so that people could learn what it sounded like and what to do. However, it was the middle of the night, and that meant this wasn't a drill.

She kicked off the sheets and stuffed her arms into her dressing gown. She'd taken to leaving her hard-soled shoes by her bed because the newspapers said that, if a bomb fell, they were better protection against glass and debris than bedroom slippers.

She flew out of her bedroom door, catching her parents coming out of their room. Her usually immaculate mother's hair was in sponge curlers.

"It's happening! They're coming to kill us all in our beds!" Mum cried.

Dad looked about him, eyes wild.

"The cellar," Viv ordered. "Grab what you need and everyone down to the cellar!"

The three Byrnes scattered. Viv grabbed their gas masks and her handbag, slinging them onto her left arm, and hurried to the lounge to sweep up a stack of library books. Dad rushed by with an old oil lantern. Mum hauled out a bundle of spare bedding that she'd stored in a wooden chest in the hall.

Dad yanked open the cellar door, flicking on the switch to flood the space with a harsh light. At the start of the war, Dad had managed to find a pair of cots and installed a long bench for the family to sit on to keep off the damp cellar floor. Everything had a slightly musty smell about it, but that didn't matter. They were better off than some families who'd be heading to a public shelter.

As Mum and Viv worked to spread bedding out over the two cots and the bench, Dad checked the torches, batteries, first aid kit, and extra oil for the lantern. Finally, as things settled into place, everyone began to slow. Viv's pulse, still heightened from being woken up, hammered as they took their seats on the long bench.

"What do we do now?" she asked.

They all looked at one another, their eyes wide and searching for an answer. They were as prepared as they could be . . . and now what?

"We wait," said Mum firmly.

After a few minutes, Dad looked up at the ceiling. "Do you hear that?"

A low, steady drone—soft at first and then growing stronger—filled Viv's ears. "Planes," she said.

"It isn't a false alarm," said Dad.

Mum began to murmur a prayer. "Heavenly Father, please forgive my sins and guide me in my walk with you. Father, please shield me—"

The first explosion hit—not near but loud enough that Viv flinched at the rumble that vibrated under her feet. Mum let out a cry and began to pray louder.

There was another. And then another.

"They're aiming for the docks. They must be," Dad said with rare authority. The docks, where he'd worked as a young man before moving to factory work, were his domain.

Bombs fell throughout the night—some closer, some farther away. The worst were the ones that exploded close enough that the cellar floor rumbled and tremors reverberated through Viv's body. Mum said the rosary over and over again, and the books Viv had brought down remained unopened. At one point, Viv and Mum both lay down on their cots and Dad stretched out on the bench, but there was no hope for sleep as explosions broke what should have been a silent night.

Viv stared at the ceiling and thought of Maggie. She was glad her daughter wasn't experiencing this. She didn't want Maggie to see her mother frightened of falling bombs and the worry that at any moment it might all end.

No child should have to go through this.

Viv closed her eyes and thought, for the first time since she'd sent Maggie away, that she was happy her daughter was with the Thompsons.

Finally, the all clear sounded. Viv, Mum, and Dad climbed out of the cellar in the late-summer dawn, leaving the bedding for Viv and Mum to deal with later. They switched on the wireless in the sitting room and listened to the report.

Dad had been right. The Luftwaffe had targeted the docks. No one knew yet how many bombs had fallen or how much damage had been sustained.

When Viv left for work that morning, she saw huge plumes of blackened smoke filling the Liverpool skyline. As her bus wound its way through the city, she caught glimpses of the fire brigade battling what looked like a warehouse that was ablaze. Flames danced against the pink sky, and the acrid scent of charred wood hung heavy in the air.

She slumped back against the bus seat. It was a nightmare, her city brutalized in one horrible night. It seemed impossible that this place—the only one she had ever known—had been torn apart by planes and bombs.

When she arrived at the delivery office, the other posties were silent, greeting her only with a nod. Viv looked around. "Where's Vanessa?"

Betty and Rose exchanged a worried look. "She hasn't come in yet."

Viv's stomach sank. Vanessa was always one of the first ones in to the garage.

"Don't worry, she'll turn up," Mr. Archer said, sounding as though he was trying to reassure himself as much as the women.

"Betty, you live in Everton. Did any bombs fall on the neighborhood last night?" Viv asked.

Betty shook her head. "Not in my part, but I'm farther north than Vanessa is."

Viv hated the helpless feeling that had taken root in her. She itched to do something. To find her friend.

"We should play the 'What if?' game," said Rose.

Betty frowned. "I don't think that's such a good idea. . . ."

"No, Rose is right," said Viv. Vanessa could still turn up, and they needed the distraction until that happened. "I'll start. Rose, what if you ruin your last pair of stockings just before a date?"

Rose stopping servicing the gears on her bicycle to gamely pull a face. "Then I wouldn't go out. I can't imagine stepping out without stockings. It would feel wrong."

"Your turn," Viv prompted as she took off her uniform jacket to check over her bicycle.

"Betty, what if you were a man? What service would you want to be in?" asked Rose.

"The Royal Navy," said Betty automatically. "Grandad was a ship-builder, and Dad is one too. The sea runs in the family."

"Why don't you join the WRNS?" asked Rose.

Betty shrugged. "I still help Mum out with the little ones. Being a postie, I can be home in time to give her a hand in the evening."

"They weren't evacuated?" asked Viv quietly.

Betty shook her head. "Too young. They're two-year-old twins. Right, it's my turn now. Viv, what if you have all the money you could ever want?"

"I know," said Rose immediately. "I'd have a wardrobe that even Vivien Leigh would salivate over."

Betty rolled her eyes. "I didn't ask you, Rose. I asked Viv."

"I would buy my own home," Viv said immediately. Since her conversation with Kate in the spring, she'd dreamed of that moment when she could move out of her parents' home, but a house where she and Maggie could live as they wanted to, eating when they chose, singing at the top of their lungs as they danced around the sitting room at all hours? That *was* an even larger dream than she'd dared hope for.

Betty laughed. "That's it? With all the money in the world you'd buy a house? Not a yacht or a palace or something?"

"I think Viv's onto something."

They all turned to see Vanessa, grin on her face, crossing into the garage.

"You're all right!" Rose cried.

"Of course I'm all right," said Vanessa with a laugh.

"We didn't know. You were so late," said Viv.

"The bus never showed up. I had to catch a ride on the back of the grocer's van halfway and walk the rest of it."

As Betty and Rose fussed over Vanessa, Viv quietly stepped back and focused her attention on wiping down her bicycle chain to apply a fresh deposit of grease; her thoughts raced a mile a minute. *What if you have all the money you could ever want?* What if she didn't need all that money but instead had just enough? What would it take to find a home for Maggie and her?

Buying a house was out of the question. She would need her husband's signature for that, and there was no earthly way she was going to go begging to Joshua—never mind the cost of purchasing a house on her own. But she was saving. There were always advertisements in the paper of people looking for a lodger. If she found the right person—a woman, maybe a little older, who missed having children around—she might be able to make it work.

Kate had told her that she'd always thought Viv was tough. Maybe it was time to show herself just how tough she could be.

The night after the first bombing of the Liverpool docks, Viv lay in bed, bone-tired. She wanted to sleep—goodness, how she wanted that—but the anticipation that there might be another air raid that evening kept her body from being able to relax.

Her instincts were right. Again, the air raid siren cut shrill through the night. More German planes were on their way.

The Byrnes all shuffled down to the cellar, a little less manic this time, made up the cots and the bench as best they could, and settled in for another long night.

The explosions started shortly after, again far enough away that they only shook the cellar occasionally.

"I don't know how many more nights I can do this," groaned Mum.

Viv snuck a look at Dad, who simply stared into space. No one knew how long this would go on, but it felt like it was only the beginning. She needed her parents to hold on to something.

Viv racked her brain, wondering what she could say to offer her mother comfort when Mum croaked out, "And what about our Katherine? She's all on her own. What is going to happen to my girl?"

Kate. Her girl. Not Viv, the daughter who was there in the cellar with their mother.

Viv tried to swallow the hurt. "Mum, where are your rosary beads?"

Mum blinked. "My rosary beads. Oh, yes."

Viv nodded encouragingly as her mother pulled out the strand, closed her eyes, and began to murmur the rosary, moving the beads as she went.

A crashing explosion sent all of them jerking up.

Mum wailed, and Dad's shoulders tensed.

"That was much closer than the others," said Viv.

"Vivian, why don't you switch with me so you can sit next to your mother?" Dad suggested. "You can pray together."

Reluctantly, she changed seats with him, leaving Dad perched on a cot, staring up at the ceiling.

Another crash, and a few cans that they'd stacked up on an old metal shelf fell to the floor.

"Why are they doing this?" cried Mum.

"Why would they bomb Walton? It doesn't make sense," muttered Dad.

It did make sense, Viv realized, if they assumed that the Germans didn't want to just destroy the docks. They hoped to destroy Liverpool's very soul: its people.

Another three explosions in quick succession rattled the house, nearly blocking out Mum's screams.

Viv scrambled to snatch up one of the torches and clutched it to her chest. The metal felt cool through the thin cotton of her summer nightgown.

"They're going to kill us all," wailed Mum.

Dad reached across the gap between the bench where he sat and the cot Mum perched on, when a violent explosion threw them all to the dirt floor. The electric light in the cellar went out, and they heard a great crashing and creaking, as though the house above them had been rent in two.

Maggie

A scream frightened Maggie awake. Clutching Tig to her chest, she looked around her darkened bedroom. It took her a moment to realize that the horrible sound wasn't coming from a person or an animal. It was the air raid siren.

Down the hall, a door flew open and crashed against a wall.

"What is happening? Are they going to bomb us?" Mrs. Thompson cried out.

"Not if we go to the Andy," said Mr. Thompson in a stern voice. "Grab the kit."

Maggie's door burst open, and she saw Mr. Thompson outlined against the hall light, his dressing gown open over a pair of striped pajamas.

"Come on, Margaret," he said. "We need to go outside to the garden, just like we talked about. Do you remember?"

She nodded and pulled on the little purple quilted dressing gown Mrs. Thompson had bought for her. On her feet went a pair of matching slippers.

"Hurry up," Mr. Thompson said, impatience lacing his voice.

Maggie opened the drawer of her bedside table and pulled out the photograph of her mother, tucking it into the pocket of her dressing gown. Then she grabbed Tig's paw and slid off the bed.

"I'm ready," she said.

Mr. Thompson stuck out his hand for her to take, his big one dwarfing her little one. They made their way down the stairs, meeting Mrs. Thompson at the French doors off the dining room. Mrs. Thompson clutched a canvas bag to her chest, and two others were on the floor next to her.

"Right, let's go," said Mr. Thompson as he hitched a bag on either shoulder.

Even though it was summer, the night air was cool. Maggie shivered in her robe. They walked across the grass that ran between the flower beds that Mrs. Thompson tended in a long leather apron and a wide-brimmed hat.

At the bottom of the garden stood the Anderson shelter.

Maggie slowed as they reached the three brick steps down to the shelter's door.

Mrs. Thompson noticed first. "Come along, Margaret. It's going to be all right."

"Are there bugs?" asked Maggie.

Mrs. Thompson dropped to her knees. "No, darling. There aren't any bugs."

"Look, Margaret," said Mr. Thompson over the air raid siren. He opened the door, reached in, and the Anderson shelter flooded with light. "I put lights in just like I told you I would."

"The handyman put lights in, dear," said Mrs. Thompson, pushing past her husband with her canvas bag.

"But who rang him and told him what to do?" asked Mr. Thompson.

While her foster parents bickered inside the shelter, Maggie stood frozen outside, Tig clutched to her chest. Finally, Mr. Thompson looked up.

"Why don't you come in, Margaret? We can make the beds and then I'll tell you a story," he said with a smile.

Maggie perked up a little at that, and cautiously she edged down the steps to poke her head into the shelter. Bunk beds lined one side of the space. On the other, there was a small bench and even a little table that swung out from the wall and folded down. Mrs. Thompson had a portable gas ring set out and had put on a kettle for tea. There were three blue-and-white-enameled mugs on the tabletop.

"That's a good girl," said Mrs. Thompson.

Mr. Thompson, who she had never seen make a bed before, struggled to put sheets on the bunk beds' mattresses.

"Matthew, why don't you let me?" Mrs. Thompson tried to step in.

"No, thank you, darling. My assistant and I are getting along swimmingly," he said, making Maggie giggle.

Once the beds were finally made, Mr. Thompson scooped up Maggie and settled her on the top bunk.

"Now, I think it's story time, but you'll need to sleep as soon as I'm done," he said.

"I will," she said, pulling the covers up to her and Tig's noses.

"Once upon a time, in a land far, far away, there was a family of rabbits. This family of rabbits lived in a little house, much like this shelter. It was half underground and half aboveground, and it was a very safe place. . . ."

Maggie fought sleep as best she could, but before long she drifted off.

Viv

This was it. This was the end.

Viv almost laughed at the absurdity of it. She was going to die, not in the arms of a loving husband in their bed with her children around her, but in a cellar next to her parents who saw her as a burden. Would Maggie remember her? Was she old enough to recall the way Viv would sing to her? Would she understand the sacrifices Viv had made for her? How strongly Viv loved her?

Even as dread crept in, Viv shook her head. This was not the end of her story.

"Mum!" she called out. "Are you okay?"

She heard Mum whimper, and then came a faint "I think so."

"Dad?" Viv asked into the darkness.

Her only answer was a groan.

Instinct took over. They needed light.

Viv was still clutching the torch. Fumbling a little, she flicked on the switch. A beam of light cut through the cellar.

Dad was stretched out on the floor. Viv dropped to his side. "What happened?"

"I think I hit my head," he managed as another bomb shook the ground. This one felt, mercifully, a little farther off.

She touched his forehead, where blood seeped between his fingers.

Her stomach twisted, but she pushed the fear away. "It looks as though you hit your head when you were knocked from the bench. What about the rest of you? Do you think you've broken anything?"

He shook his head and moaned.

"Stay right there," she instructed, using the same stern voice she employed when she wanted Maggie to pay attention to her. "I'll patch you up with the first aid kit, but first I need to check the door."

Viv climbed the short set of steps to the cellar door. She felt the door knob in case there was a fire on the other side. Finding it cool, she twisted and opened it wide into the cellar.

She was met by a wall of debris as tall as she was, but there was a gap at the top.

"The house has been hit!" she called down the stairs, coughing on the dust in the air. She wasn't sure how bad the damage was. Shining her torch through the gap in the debris, she could see that at least the corridor wall was standing, but when she shone it in the other direction there was nothing where the other side once stood.

"How bad is it?" asked Dad through a groan.

She took a deep breath. "I think we can dig our way out."

"Dig our way out!" Mum cried.

"Mum, if you come and help me—"

"The fire brigade will come," said Mum with a shaky voice.

"Mum, if we wait and the house collapses on us, we could be buried alive. I need your help."

"I can't. I can't. I'm just— I can't."

Viv gritted her teeth. Dad might have a concussion or worse. Mum was too frightened to be of any use. Viv was going to have to do this herself.

She hurried down the cellar steps and pulled on a pair of Dad's old work gloves.

"What are you doing?" Mum cried.

What you can't.

Back up the cellar steps, Viv began pulling debris off the top of the pile.

It was mostly lath plaster at first, which filled the air with fine dust.

She stopped for a moment, coughing, to yank off her headscarf and wrap it around her face like a mask. That helped a little, and she kept working, yanking away bits of wood, brick, plaster, and metal. There was even stone—although she hadn't the faintest idea why because their house wasn't made of stone.

Finally, when the pile of debris blocking the door was small enough to climb over, she hiked up her dressing gown and carefully stepped into the corridor.

Shining her torch around, she could see why she hadn't been able to see the opposing wall. It was gone, along with the entire right side of the house.

Awed by the sheer destruction of the bomb, she stepped over crunching glass and plaster into what had once been the sitting room. All of her mother's carefully cared for furniture, the fireplace, the wireless, Dad's favorite chair—it was all gone.

"Hey! Hey! There's a light from the Byrnes' house!" came a voice through the darkness. A torch beam flooded her vision, and she held up an arm to block it.

"It's Viv!" she called out.

"You're alive!" called out the voice. Was that Mr. Lloyd, the grocer? "How many alive?"

"All of us, but Dad's hurt. He and Mum are in the cellar now," she called.

Mr. Lloyd blew his whistle, and a group of neighbors came running.

"Is the gas off?" asked Mr. Lloyd.

"Yes."

"Do you think you can make your way out safely?" asked Mr. Lloyd.

"I'm not leaving my parents," she called.

The gentle, kind man cursed in a way she'd never guessed him capable of but then called, "Right! Stay where you are. We need to dig you out. Some of the upstairs is still standing, and we don't know how long it's going to hold."

Viv swallowed hard as a fire truck screamed up the road and stopped in front of the house next door. That was when she looked and realized it was gone. Where once Mr. and Mrs. Hecker had lived, there was nothing but a pile of rubble.

Three horrible thoughts hit her at once.

That could have been her family.

The Heckers could still be in the house, buried under all that rubble.

No one was safe.

The fire brigade and the volunteers collecting in the road moved quickly, splitting off into three teams to help the families two down on either side of them, whose houses had also been partially demolished the way her family home had. Viv hurried back to the cellar, climbing over the debris and down the steps.

"We need to leave," she told her parents.

Dad, who in the torchlight looked pale and wane, nodded wearily.

"He can't be moved," said Mum.

"He needs to walk, and he needs to do it now," said Viv.

"Vivian, your father—"

"The house has been blown apart, Mum. The upstairs could collapse on us at any second. We aren't dead, but we could be if we don't move fast," she said.

Her mother's lower lip trembled and, unbelievably, Viv felt sorry for her. This was a woman whose pride and joy was poured into this house. It was her responsibility, her base. It was where Mum felt safe. And now it was gone.

Still, they had to act fast.

"Help me bring him up the stairs. It will make it easier for the rescue people," said Viv.

They'd just managed to get Dad up when another explosion rocked the neighborhood, making them all stumble.

"Why are they still bombing us?" Mum sobbed.

"Because they want to win this bloody war, and they think killing us one by one will do it. Now grab Dad under the arm," she ordered.

Slowly, they made their way to the cellar stairs. There were shouts close by, and Viv prayed the rescue workers had found a safe way into the house. When they reached the stairs, she took over the full weight of her father, helping him make painstaking progress up to the ground floor.

They were halfway up when the first rescuer's face appeared at the top of the stairs, illuminated like a ghost in a film.

"How many down there?" he called.

"Three. One is a man who has a head injury," she called back.

"Right, we'll get him out first. Don't move. We're coming in."

Down the stairs clattered two middle-aged men who immediately grabbed Dad by the waist. "Up you go, sir."

Viv watched them bring Dad up the stairs, and a third face appeared. "Who's next?"

Mum pushed her way up the steps, past Viv. "I am. I need to be with my husband."

Viv's heart, already fragile and fractured, shattered into a million pieces. She'd always suspected Kate of being Mum's favorite, and she'd been certain of it after she'd fallen pregnant and married Joshua. But she'd soldiered on, happy enough to ignore all the signs of how her mother felt so long as her parents kept her daughter safe and fed. However, after Maggie's evacuation, every interaction with her mother, every slight had chipped away at her a little more until, when Mum had pushed in front of her to get to safety, Viv was unable to ignore it any longer.

Her mother didn't love her.

It hurt a deep, primal sort of hurt, but underneath that there was something else. Freedom.

Viv looked around the cellar. She was never coming back here. Her life in Walton, under her parents' roof, was over.

She stooped to grab her handbag and mounted the cellar steps one last time.

Ripon Street was a study in controlled chaos. A van had rolled up with the Red Cross's symbol on it, and women in starched white uniforms were distributing cups of tea. Someone shoved one into Viv's hands, and she took a sip, surprised at the sweetness of it.

"It's for the shock," said a woman, seeing her expression.

"I thought it was rationed," she said.

"Can you think of a better time for a bit of sweetness?" asked the other woman.

Viv shook her head. No, she could not.

"Do you have a place to go?" asked the Red Cross worker.

"Yes," she said. "I have a place to go for the night."

She would figure out the rest of her life after that.

The destruction across the city was incredible.

All over Liverpool, people awoke to a city that had been changed—horribly.

Viv knew that she and her parents were lucky. Dad had been transported to the hospital for his concussion and his head wound and, after the all clear had sounded, Viv quietly took Mum's arm and walked her to Kate's house.

Kate had opened the door, blurry-eyed and disheveled from her own night in a public shelter, taken one look at the pair of them, and immediately put breakfast on, using up all of her remaining bacon and powdered egg rations in one go.

They managed to coax Mum, who had simply stared at her food, into bed a short while later. Viv and Kate were just pulling up the covers when Mum opened her eyes, looked straight at Viv, and said, "It should have been you."

"Mummy, what are you talking about?" asked Kate.

"It should have been you. You took his seat," said Mum.

Viv pinched the bridge of her nose hard. She had no fight left in her any longer. Not when it came to her mother.

"Viv, what is Mum talking about?" Kate asked.

"Just before the bomb fell, I switched seats with Dad. He asked me to," she said.

Kate stared down at their mother, horror on her face. "Mummy, Viv didn't drop a bomb on your house! The goddamn bloody Germans did!"

"Katherine, you know better than to take the Lord's name in vain," Mum chastised.

"It's my bloody house, and I'll bloody say whatever I want in it!" Kate shouted, going red in the face.

Mum turned to face the wall.

Viv took her seething sister's elbow and steered Kate out of the room. As soon as the door was closed, she said, "It isn't worth it."

"Yes, it is! She has spent the last five years punishing you for something you've paid for over and over again. When does it stop?" Kate asked.

"It's always been like this. You know that."

Kate seemed to deflate. "But I didn't know it was that bad. Why didn't you tell me?"

Viv stared at her sister. "I did tell you, Kate. I told you on my wedding day."

"I—"

"You didn't listen because you have always been the good daughter. It came easily to you," she said.

Kate was the proper wife with a real husband she'd married in a church and children who'd come more than nine months after the wedding. Kate was respectable and could show her face in the community without wondering if someone would snub her. Mum never had to cringe when Kate walked next to her.

Kate had done everything right, and Viv nothing.

Kate hung her head. "I'm so sorry."

Viv squeezed her sister's arm. "Take care of Mum. I'm going to go to work."

Kate's head shot up. "What? You can't deliver the post today."

Viv rolled her shoulders. They ached from bearing Dad's weight, but nothing was going to keep her in the house today. "I can't miss the shift. I need the money."

"Train tickets to see Maggie can't be that expensive," said Kate.

She just gave her sister a soft smile, knowing that she had much bigger plans now.

Viv missed the first delivery, but she'd telephoned ahead to tell Mr. Rowan what had happened, and he'd practically fallen over himself to make sure her shift was covered. She packed her bag before any of the others had returned and headed out early. Everything still felt too raw, and she couldn't stand the thought of answering all of her fellow posties well-meaning questions.

At first, it felt good to be out on her Federal, even if there was no escaping the damage of the previous night. She spent as much time delivering the post as she did weaving around piles of debris, the turns she normally would take cut off.

Because of how Peg's old route connected to hers, Viv didn't hit her own roads until it was nearly one o'clock. The sun was hot overhead, and the heavy material of the uniform she'd scrounged up from the spares back in the delivery office cupboard chafed against her neck. She could feel a train of sweat running between her breasts and another making its way down her back. Once, she lost concentration as she pedaled, nearly pitching her over the handlebars as she swerved to avoid a neighborhood cat.

By the time Viv reached the top of Salisbury Road, she was using the fences and short walls at the front of houses to help herself off her bicycle. Still, she carried on. At each house, she focused on the letters clutched in her hand.

Walk up, post for Mr. and Mrs. McGary, walk back, post for Mr. Sebba, walk back, post for the Mulleys.

When she reached the Levinsons' house, she hardly had to talk herself into lifting the latch on the garden gate and walking up to her husband's family's front door. Neither did she flinch when the curtains of the sitting room twitched, as they sometimes did. Let whoever was home watch her. Let them shake their head and think whatever they thought of her. No one had been brave enough to speak to her since Rebecca's last encounter in the spring, and that afternoon she couldn't find the energy to care.

Carefully, she counted out the five letters and a single postcard and pushed them through the brass letter slot in the front door. A wave of wooziness hit her. The letters clattered to the floor inside as she leaned heavily on the doorjamb. Her head spun. With her other free hand, she tugged at her collar, trying to find some relief.

It didn't help. Her knees began to shake. Bracing herself against the Levinsons' front door, she slid down to the ground to put her head between her knees.

All she needed was a moment, and then she would be on her way.

The door opened behind her, and a woman asked, "Are you all right?"

Viv twisted to look up, immediately pressing her temples to stop her head from swimming. She heard a couple of steps, and Joshua's mother crouched in front of her.

"Vivian?" Mrs. Levinson asked again, concern clear in her eyes.

"I—I'm sorry. My head . . ."

She felt a firm but gentle hand slip under her elbow. "You'd better come inside for a moment."

"I can't. I have the rest of the post to deliver," she tried to protest, but Mrs. Levinson already had her halfway through the door.

"It won't do anyone any good if you collapse in the middle of the road," said Mrs. Levinson.

"I can't leave the postbag outside," said Viv as Mrs. Levinson steered her into the sitting room.

"I'll go fetch it for you, and then I'll make you a cup of tea," said Mrs. Levinson.

Viv sank down into an upholstered armchair Mrs. Levinson had gently pushed her into, her heavy limbs relaxing for the first time all day. She was tired—so very tired—as though a wall of fatigue had hit her all at once. She closed her eyes just for a moment and . . .

Viv awoke with a start and looked around frantically. She sat in front of a fireplace covered by an old-fashioned embroidered fire screen; her hands gripped the arms of an armchair. On either side of the chimney breast there were bookshelves stuffed to the brim—mostly cheap paperback copies with a scattering of large, old leather-bound editions.

The faint ping of metal against porcelain drifted to her. Still groggy, she pushed a hand over her forehead and found that her hair wasn't in its usual neat wave. That was when she remembered what had happened. The bombing. Dad's head injury. The long walk to Kate's. Mum's parting shots. Work. The Levinsons.

Her hands tightened on the arms of the chair and she made to stand up, but she heard the click of shoes on hardwood floor and Mrs. Levin-

son appeared with a tray bearing a teapot, two cups, and a small plate of something that looked like pastries formed into little crescents.

"I'm so sorry—" she began just as Mrs. Levinson said, "I see you're awake."

Mrs. Levinson cleared her throat. "I thought a cup of tea and something to eat might bring some color back to your cheeks."

"You really don't have to," said Viv.

"I want to," said Mrs. Levinson quickly. "That is, it wouldn't be right to send you away without giving you a little something. You seemed faint."

Viv touched her forehead. "I didn't sleep yesterday."

"What happened?" Mrs. Levinson asked, nodding to Viv's hands.

Viv looked down at her fingers, realizing for the first time the backs of them were covered in scratches and bruises.

"A bomb fell on the house next to my parents'," she said.

Mrs. Levinson looked up sharply. "Is everyone—"

She nodded. "We all escaped relatively unscathed," she hesitated, "although Dad hit his head. They took him to hospital because they thought he might have a concussion."

Mrs. Levinson let out a long breath. "I'm very glad to hear you were all well. Was . . . Was anyone else hurt?"

The question hung heavy in the air, but Viv knew what the older woman was asking.

"Maggie is still in the countryside," she said quietly.

The teapot clattered on the tray, and Mrs. Levinson pressed a hand to her chest. "I worried you had brought her back. I know some families did when there were no air raids."

Viv pursed her lips. She'd wanted to bring Maggie back, but to do that would have meant defying her mother's orders and putting their place in her parents' home at risk.

With a trembling hand, Mrs. Levinson passed a cup of tea to her and then held out the plate. "Have you ever had rugelach before?"

Viv shook her head.

"I don't make them often, but I needed something to steady my nerves after the bombings. It's foolish with rationing being what it is, but I couldn't help it."

Viv took one of the pastries and delicately bit into it. Flaky sweetness and the familiar taste of jam exploded in her mouth.

"It's delicious," she said around a bite.

Mrs. Levinson gave her a half smile. "Thank you. I've always enjoyed baking, although it's difficult now."

"I've experimented with the recipes in those pamphlets trying to teach us how to use potato starch in place of flour, but nothing ever seems to come out quite the same," Viv said.

"I'm surprised that you're able to bake with all the work that you do. You must be up with the milkmen," said Mrs. Levinson.

"Sometimes, but when I go home after a day of delivering the post there's still the shopping and cooking to do. I help my mother most days," she explained.

"I see," said Mrs. Levinson before taking a delicate sip of tea.

Viv mirrored her and then put down her cup carefully. She looked around, seeing now the photographs of Joshua and Rebecca proudly displayed on a polished wood sideboard. There was a wireless in a walnut veneer cabinet, and an upright piano was pushed up against the far wall. In some ways, the Levinsons' home wasn't so very different from her parents', but she couldn't shake the sense that this was a room that was lived in and used in a way that her parents' front room wasn't.

"I watch for you every day when I'm not at the shop," said Mrs. Levinson, cutting short Viv's curiosity.

"I've seen the curtain move from time to time," she admitted.

Mrs. Levinson offered her a little smile. "I was never certain whether you knew or not. After you spoke to Rebecca, I worried that she was too harsh."

"She hates me because I'm the reason Joshua went away," she said quietly.

To her surprise, Mrs. Levinson said, "She doesn't hate you. She is angry with her brother because he left and she had to work in the shop. She thinks he's selfish, and she is right.

"Oh, I know that I shouldn't think that about one of my children—my only son no less—but one of the most difficult things about being a parent is realizing that your children have flaws."

"I'm sorry if my telling him that I didn't want to see or hear from him if he took my parents' money meant that he stayed away from you," Viv said quietly.

Mrs. Levinson gave her a sad smile. "Well, I'm certain that didn't help, but it also wasn't what kept him in New York all those years. That was Joshua's choice, and Seth's and my burden to bear."

Viv looked down at her teacup. "I'm ashamed to say, I didn't expect you to be so kind to me."

"Because I'm Jewish?" asked Mrs. Levinson.

Viv's head snapped up, but a protest died on her lips as she saw the sly smile on her mother-in-law's face. "Because I thought you blamed me for everything that happened."

"Well"—Mrs. Levinson cocked her head as she took a sip of tea—"I can't promise that I've always had such a generous attitude. There have been times where I wished he never met you. You see, Jewish law says that Judaism is passed from mother to child. When I found out that my son was going to have a child by a gentile woman, I was devastated. I'd known for a long time that my son's relationship with his religion was far more distant than mine, but I never thought he would . . ." Mrs. Levinson cleared her throat. "It was Rebecca who convinced Seth and me that it was better to have a happy grandchild than no grandchild at all."

"Rebecca did that?" Viv asked.

"I think she hoped it would keep me from pestering her to marry and have children. She wants to go to university," said Mrs. Levinson.

"Joshua told me." Viv took a breath. "Would you like to see a photograph of Maggie?"

The teacup in Mrs. Levinson's hand trembled in its saucer. "Yes, please."

Viv reached into her uniform jacket, pulling out the photograph she'd removed from her handbag when she'd arrived at work. After what she'd seen a bomb do to her parents' house in mere seconds, she wasn't taking any chances.

"This was taken on her fourth birthday. I haven't been able to have one taken since she turned five," she said, handing the photograph over.

Mrs. Levinson stared at the picture, her hand to her lips. "She's beautiful."

"I think she has Joshua's hair," she said. "Mine was never that curly or dark."

"Will you tell me about her?" Mrs. Levinson whispered.

"She's the most affectionate little girl. She wants to give everyone hugs, and if you're having a bad day she seems to know. Right now her favorite things are Tig, her stuffed tiger, and Puffball, the pony she rides in the countryside, but before she left Liverpool she was always chasing after our neighbors' cat. She rarely cries or whines. I think she would be happy singing to herself for hours in her room, but she loves to run and play with her cousins too.

"Sometimes I look at her and I think it's incredible that she could be my child. It's almost as though she was a miracle," said Viv.

"You love her very much," said Mrs. Levinson, eyes brimming.

"So much that sometimes it hurts. I try to show her that, since my parents are not . . . warm. I worry that one day she'll realize that they're different with her than they are with her cousins and that will hurt her."

"A child is a precious thing, no matter what."

"I wish they felt that way."

When Mrs. Levinson pulled out a handkerchief and began to cry softly into it, Viv put down her teacup, ready to reach out for the other woman.

The front door rattled, and Rebecca called out, "I'm home, Mummy!"

"I should leave." Viv rose to her feet hurriedly, but not before Rebecca walked in, shopping hanging from the string bag on her arm.

"What are you doing here?" Rebecca demanded.

"I'm very sorry," she stared to say.

"Why is my mother crying?" Rebecca asked, looking between the two of them.

"I—"

"It's not her fault," said Mrs. Levinson, cutting Viv off.

Rebecca dropped to her mother's side, wrapping her arms around her. "Mummy, if she said something . . ."

"I meant no harm," said Viv, backing toward the door.

"How dare you—"

"Rebecca, stop this!" Her mother's voice cut through the room, bring-ing everyone to a standstill. "Vivian was telling me— She was telling me about my granddaughter." Mrs. Levinson swallowed. "Thank you, Vivian. I hope that I can one day meet her, but learning about her helps in its own way."

Viv nodded. "And thank you for your help today."

Mrs. Levinson rose. "Are you feeling strong enough to continue your deliveries?"

Viv nodded again.

"I will be home two Wednesdays from now. I hope that, if you have enough time, you will stop in for a cup of tea again," said Mrs. Levinson.

"I would love that," said Viv, realizing that it was the truth. The relief that she felt after five years of worrying that the Levinsons blamed her for everything that had happened as her own parents did had weighed heavily on her. And yet here was an olive branch from her mother-in-law. She would be a fool not to take it, even if only for her daughter's sake.

"Thank you," she said.

"No, I should be thanking you," said Mrs. Levinson, handing back the photograph of Maggie. "Rebecca, will you please show Vivian out?"

Rebecca stared at her mother in disbelief, but when Mrs. Levinson lifted her chin, Rebecca relented. "Fine."

They walked to the front door in silence, but when they reached it, Rebecca didn't open it. Instead, she crossed her arms. "Why are you here?"

"I became light-headed while I was on my route. My house was bombed yesterday," she said.

Rebecca slowly uncrossed her arms. "Oh."

"I didn't sleep last night, and I hardly had anything to eat today. Your mother was kind enough to bring me inside for a moment so that I could recover my composure. I promise, it wasn't my intention to come inside, but I'm glad that I did."

"I'm sorry," said Rebecca. "I saw you in the sitting room and I thought . . . I don't know what I thought."

"You thought the worst, and I can't say that I blame you."

Rebecca hesitated. "Did you show Mum a photograph of Maggie?"

"Yes."

"May I see it?"

Viv pulled the photo from her pocket and handed it to Rebecca.

"She looks just like Joshua." Rebecca looked up. "But I think she has your chin."

She snorted. "I don't know whether that's a compliment or not."

Rebecca gave her a little smile and handed the photograph back. "One day, if Dad's home, would you show him?"

"I can do one better," she said, thinking about the negatives stashed in her handbag back at the delivery office. "I'll have some prints made for you. There aren't too many—there really wasn't money for many photographs—but I have a few of Maggie from when she was very little."

Rebecca squeezed her eyes shut. "That's very kind of you. Kinder than I probably deserve."

"You don't have to like me, Rebecca, but I hope that you'll trust me when I tell you that it was never my intention to cut you or your parents out of Maggie's life."

Viv stooped to scoop up her postbag and sling it over her shoulder. The weight of it felt strangely grounding. Then she reached for the door and let herself out into the road to finish her route.

Viv didn't stay with Kate for long. Dad came home the day after the bombing having convinced doctors at the hospital that they needed his bed for other, more injured patients. It hadn't taken much, apparently, because the air raids continued over Liverpool. Kate had no cellar, so the Byrnes trooped to the public shelter two roads over to camp out with what felt like half the neighborhood through the raids. Everyone's nerves were frayed to a few fine threads, and by Monday, Viv couldn't wait to ride her postal route.

Viv had rolled up to the Levinsons' home with cautious curiosity on Monday morning. It wasn't as though one meeting was going to erase five years of hurt and anger, but it had been good to speak to someone about Maggie. However, as she approached the door, she realized that the lights were all off, even during the early-morning hours when so many of their neighbors were cleaning up the breakfast table. She felt a strange tug of disappointment as she gripped the Levinsons' letters in her hand. She'd hoped . . . well, she wasn't sure really. She put the letters through the box and was about to turn when she saw it. A little white paper box tied with a piece of twine. On it, there was a note with her name written across the top in pencil.

She took out the note and unfolded it to read it.

Thank you.

Carefully tucking the note into her jacket pocket, she undid the twine bow and opened the box. Inside there were two of the sweet pastries that Mrs. Levinson had given her when she'd nearly fainted. Viv's lips twisted against the emotion rising in her chest, and she turned and hopped on her Federal again.

All day, the simple gesture of the pastries laid out waiting for her to return stayed with her. Somehow it didn't feel right to accept them without leaving anything behind in return. That night, she sorted through the few things she had in her handbag. She selected a few negatives, and the next day, after her shift at the delivery office was over, she went to the photographer's shop.

While she waited for prints of Maggie's baby photos to be made, Viv set about with her other task. She picked up a newspaper and, armed with a pencil, circled all the rooms for rent she could find.

After her shift ended on Tuesday, she walked the streets of Liverpool, rerouting when she came across a crew of men trying to clear the roads of rubble. Buildings still smoldered and smoked, and there was a distinct tang of acrid dust in the air no matter where she went.

On her fourth visit to a flat, Viv found what she was looking for. Mrs. Shannon, an elderly widow with a small house in Mossley Hill, had transformed her lounge into a bedroom and was letting the top floor of her home. There was enough room upstairs that Viv would have a bedroom and a small sitting room that had been created out of a modest bedroom. When Viv had explained to Mrs. Shannon that her daughter had been evacuated to the country, the older woman had clucked her tongue and suggested that Viv might like to use her grown daughter's old bed when "this dreadful war is over and your daughter is back home." The simple offer had made Viv tear up, and the next day, she went to the post office, withdrew the first week's rent from her savings, and paid Mrs. Shannon.

That evening, Viv sat at Kate's kitchen table and told her family what she'd done.

"You can't live on your own. You're a single woman," said Mum, her mouth twisted up with displeasure.

"I'm married," Viv said calmly.

"Then where is your husband?" asked Mum.

"Shouldn't I ask you the same thing, since you were the one who paid him to stay away?"

Mum threw her napkin down next to her place setting and said, "Reason with her, John."

"It isn't done, Vivian," said Dad.

Viv shrugged. "It's already done. I've paid Mrs. Shannon."

"How can you afford such a thing?" Mum demanded.

Viv simply smiled.

"I can't allow it. Vivian, your mother and I need you at home," said Dad.

"No," Viv said firmly.

"You have a child to think of," said Mum.

"I am thinking of Maggie. Once I can bring her back to Liverpool, she'll have a room of her own and a garden to play in," she said.

Mum rounded on Kate. "Katherine, you talk to your sister."

Kate's brows rose. "Me?"

"You're the only one she listens to," said Mum.

"Oh, I don't think you want me to do that," said Kate.

"Kate," their father warned.

"This isn't Kate's decision. It's mine," said Viv.

"What did I do to deserve such disobedient daughters?" asked Mum, lifting her eyes to the heavens.

"Vivian, you are upsetting your mother," Dad pleaded.

She shrugged. "I've already paid Mrs. Shannon. I am of age. There is nothing you can do to stop me from leaving."

"'Honor thy father and thy mother,'" Mum murmured.

"'And be ye kind to one another, tenderhearted, forgiving one another, even as God for Christ's sake hath forgiven you.'" Kate's voice cut through the din of the kitchen. "All our lives, you've told us to mind our Bible and do what we're taught at church, but you fail to remember Christ's most basic teachings.

"Vivie has done everything you've asked of her. She's cooked and cleaned and cared for you. When she worked, she gave over her wages to you. She did that all while being a good mother to her own daughter, and how did you thank her? By telling her that she was sinful and punishing her for it over and over again. Aren't we meant to forgive?"

"Do not speak to your mother that way, Katherine," said Dad, his voice half pleading as his eyes darted to his wife.

"I have seen what this sort of behavior does to a woman. My sister, Flora—"

"Didn't have to be sent away to that horrible hospital! Your parents could have helped her. They could have kept her home," said Kate.

"That was impossible," said Mum.

"Why? Because your priest disapproved? Because your neighbors would have gossiped about her? How frightened do you think she was when she found out that she was pregnant and the man who got her into trouble was gone? How frightened do you think Vivie was?" Kate raged.

"It's not the same thing," said Mum primly.

"No, it's not, because Joshua, who was just as young and stupid as I was, did the right thing and married me," Viv said, cutting through the argument. "I was lucky, Mum, but you refuse to see that."

"How do you think I felt? Or your father?" Mum shouted, raising her voice for the first time in more years than Viv could remember. "We had to go to church and show our faces knowing that they were whispering behind our backs. You could have chased after any boy in Walton, Vivian, and it could have been forgiven, but you had to choose that man. When your daughter brings that same shame to your door, you'll understand."

Viv's eyes narrowed. "No, she won't, because I cannot imagine doing to her what you did to me."

"Even if you refuse to admit it, Mum, you were wrong," said Kate.

"And, Dad, you just sat there and let her tell you what you should do and think."

"Katherine!" Mum said sharply. "Show your father some respect."

Viv watched in awe as her sister rose from the table, somehow filling the entire room with her righteous anger. "You are *guests* here. If you don't like it, you can leave."

Mum pushed back from the table. "Pack your things, John."

"Edith, where will we go?" asked Dad quietly, even as he scrambled up after his wife.

Viv and Kate were silent, listening to Mum and Dad bang upstairs to retrieve the few things they'd been able to salvage from the fire.

"This is my fight, not yours," said Viv.

"I should have stood up for you years ago. I know you can't forgive me for all of that time, but I will not let you down now," said Kate.

Viv nodded, unable to speak as Kate wrapped her in a hug.

Finally, the front door of Kate's house slammed, leaving silence in its wake.

"Well," said Kate pulling away and swiping at her eyes. "That was certainly an interesting tea."

"I really didn't mean to cause trouble for you," Viv said.

"If you think for one moment that I'm going to sit there and watch them be cruel to my little sister . . ." Kate trailed off, her smile falling. "I will do better."

"I know you will."

"Besides," said Kate with a shaky laugh. "That felt good. Probably too good."

Viv watched her sister drag her chair to a high cabinet, climb up, and open the cabinet door. Kate pulled out a bottle of what looked suspiciously like whiskey, as well as a pair of plain glass tumblers. "Sam thinks I don't know about his hiding spot because I'm too short. As though I don't know every inch of this kitchen."

Kate poured out two fingers of liquor into each glass and then handed Viv one before taking a drink. "Horrible stuff, but it does the job."

Viv took a cautious sip. The moment the whiskey touched the back of her throat, she sputtered. The liquor burned all the way down.

Kate shot her a look. "Are you okay?"

"This is like drinking petrol," she said.

"Like I said. It does the job. And I meant are you *okay*?"

Viv tilted her glass, watching the whiskey swirl around. "I don't know, but for the first time in a long time it feels as though I'm the one who gets to decide that."

Kate nodded and took another sip. "I think that's the best place to be."

Joshua

As soon as the *F-Freddie* plane touched down on the tarmac and rolled to a stop, Moss ripped off his helmet.

"Bullshit. Pure bullshit," the man raged, slamming the instruments' switches and mechanisms with more force than was necessary. He was, Joshua thought, at risk of breaking something, but he knew pointing that out wouldn't be wise.

Joshua exchanged a look with Fortineau, their wireless operator and gunner. Fortineau grimaced, and Joshua's stomach sank a little lower.

He'd fucked up.

He hadn't sent them straight into enemy territory unawares or tried to navigate them into the side of a mountain, but he'd made an error in navigation that had cost them valuable time and fuel. They were flying on a moonless night, through heavy cloud cover above and fog below. They were wretched conditions for a bombing strike, but bomber command had ordered it for reasons that even their squadron leader couldn't explain.

The crew of *F-Freddie* were meant to stay with their squadron, and Joshua had kept them on course until a loud, piercing beep had started up in the cockpit just before Joshua was meant to give Moss a vital heading. Moss's shouting and the ten minutes Joshua had spent scrambling around to figure out which instrument had triggered the warning system had left him flustered. Then Fortineau had received some odd static on the wireless. Moss had sent Joshua back to help. It had taken Joshua another twenty minutes to realize that in his rush he hadn't given Moss the correct heading. Instead of heading out over the Black Sea to bomb a German air base as had been the plan, they were flying due north, away from the rest of the squadron.

Knowing that Moss—a hair trigger in the best of times—was bound to be explosive, Joshua had sucked in his breath and delivered the bad news.

The string of curses that emitted from Moss's mouth left both Joshua and Fortineau staring at the former public schoolboy and Oxford man, but there was never any question they would have to return to Linton-on-Ouse. To rejoin with the rest of the squadron would likely mean running out of fuel. Moss had banked hard to the left, brought the plane around, and carried them home early.

Now, Joshua sat, waiting for Moss to clear out before making a move. As soon as the pilot was clear of the cockpit, Fortineau eased out of his seat and, stooping, clapped Joshua on the shoulder.

"It could have happened to any of us," said the wireless operator.

Joshua gave his crewman a tight smile. "Thanks."

However, when he stood up and eased out of the cockpit, down the wing, and onto the tarmac, he found Moss standing there, his face puce and his forehead sweating.

"You worthless piece of shit," Moss raged, bringing the mechanics and ground crew around him up short. "You fucking useless yid! You blew the entire goddamn ops, you careless bastard!"

Joshua went very still. He'd had hateful words hurled at him before, and he knew that the best way to endure was to allow himself to detach, as though a sheet of glass had dropped between him and the pilot. Still, it was impossible not to feel the precise cut of each word.

"Maybe it's a good idea to take a minute, Flight Lieutenant," said Fortineau, putting an arm on Moss's bicep.

Moss shook him off.

"I told the wing commander that you would be a problem. I told him that I didn't want to fly with you," Moss seethed.

"I made a mistake. I apologize," Joshua said.

Moss stepped into his space until he was nose to nose with Joshua. "Don't you understand? This is life and death. You make one mistake up there, and you could die. Your entire crew could die."

That stoked Joshua's ire. "I was acting on your orders, *sir*. You told me to sort out the instrument warning. You told me to go back and help Fortineau with the wireless problem."

"You think this is my fault?" Moss raged.

Despite his anger, Joshua knew he should have done his primary job. Navigation fell to him, and that had caused the failure of their ops.

"No." Joshua glanced at Fortineau. "I'm going to mess."

He started to turn away when, out of the corner of his eye, he saw Moss clench his fist and draw back his arm. But then again so did Fortineau and two mechanics who jumped on the flight lieutenant, pinning his arms around his back.

"You do not want to do that, sir," said Fortineau, the shorter man's face mashed against Moss's shoulder as he held him back.

"No one wants to be court-martialed," said one of the mechanics. "Not when there's a war to fight."

Those magic words seemed to puncture Moss's fury. Cautiously, the three other men loosened their grip.

Moss rolled his neck and tugged on the opening of his flight suit. "One more mistake, Levinson, and I'm reporting you."

Moss stormed away, and the ground crew picked up their tools and began working on the plane again. All except for one man, small and slight with dark hair held in place with a liberal application of Brylcreem that nearly all of the men on base used.

"Always did hate being called a yid myself. Can't say it's the worst thing I've ever heard, but it isn't the nicest either," said the other man in a thick East London accent.

Joshua snorted. "They have a whole different set of names for us in America."

The other man cocked his head to one side. "Well, isn't that something. People can be bastards no matter where you are."

"They can indeed," Joshua said.

Then he nodded and headed for the crew room to shed his gear and find himself a cup of tea to keep him company while he waited for Johnny and the rest of the squadron to return.

Viv

January 4, 1935

Viv lifted her head off her elbow, where she'd braced it against the bowl of the toilet. This was the sixth day she'd had to rush from her seat in the sorting room. The first time, she'd convinced herself that something she'd eaten over Christmas had upset her stomach. On day three, the first creeping fingers of dread began to grab at her. Now, after nearly a week, she had to admit that she was in trouble.

She used her free hand to swipe at her eyes. She was terrified. She knew that this could happen, but she'd ignored all the warnings she'd heard her entire life and now she was living the consequences.

She touched the little gold cross she'd worn around her neck since her confirmation. She was a fool, an idiot for letting herself be tempted. For being temptation herself.

She hadn't seen Joshua since their second date. All of that lust and excitement she'd felt kissing him had transformed into awkward fumbling, pain, and instant embarrassment. She hadn't wanted to see him again, even if he had tried to call her at Kate's house.

She hauled herself up off the floor and went to wash her hands. She peered into the mirror. There would be no hiding how red her cheeks were, but that would fade with time. This problem, however, would not go away. She needed a plan. She needed to find Joshua.

Viv

Two Wednesdays after her encounter with Mrs. Levinson, Viv finished her route as quick as she could, leaving Salisbury Road until the end. After all the letters were in their slots, she pulled her bicycle inside the Levinsons' gate, where her mother-in-law was waiting for her at the door.

It was a short visit, a little awkward, a little hopeful. Mostly, they spoke about Maggie. Mrs. Levinson was like a sponge, ready to soak up any information about her granddaughter.

"When do you see her next?" asked Mrs. Thompson, as though reading her mind.

Viv set down her teacup. "Two Saturdays from now. I had hoped to get away sooner, but my boss, Mr. Rowan, has us working especially hard because the post is taking longer to make it to the delivery office than usual due to the bombings."

Between working and settling into her new home, Viv had been run off her feet. She needed to sit down and write to Mrs. Thompson to give her new address. She'd also write a note to Maggie about their new home, telling her daughter that they would be sharing the house with a cat named Walter—a fact that was sure to delight Maggie.

"Perhaps next time, I might come with you," said Mrs. Levinson. When Viv didn't immediately respond, the older woman hurried to say, "I'm sorry. That is too much to ask."

Viv reached across the gap between them on the sofa and covered her mother-in-law's hand. "I would like that very much. Perhaps Mr. Levinson would want to join us?"

Mrs. Levinson sniffled a little as she nodded. "Seth would like that very much."

"Will you be able to come on a Saturday?" she asked, remembering the closed signs on the windows of shops owned by Jewish proprietors.

Mrs. Levinson sighed, but not without a smile. "We do not observe the sabbath the way I once did as a girl. Growing up, my family was more orthodox than Seth's, who found that closing the shop on Saturdays was too detrimental to their business. It is kind of you to ask though."

Mrs. Levinson rose and lifted a white box from a side table. "I wonder if you might mind me bringing Maggie this."

Viv took the box from her mother-in-law and set it in her lap to undo the blue nylon ribbon keeping it shut.

When she saw what was inside, she gave a little gasp. Lying in the plain white tissue was a little dress of blue wool—fine enough that it wouldn't scratch a child's skin. It had a Peter Pan collar in white and red buttons marching up the front of it. When Viv turned the hem over, she saw a neat row of perfect stitches.

"It's beautiful," she managed, letting the urge to hold her daughter swell up in her. The grief she felt over her separation from her daughter was like waves, ebbing and flowing but always constant.

"My husband made it. He is very sorry to have missed you today, but his customers keep him at the shop," said Mrs. Levinson.

"I remember his kindness on my wedding day. You were all so kind, while my own mother was awful and Dad stood by and let her do it."

She felt Mrs. Levinson's thin arms wrap around her, resting Viv's head on her breast. Being enveloped in the warmth of this woman only made the ache in Viv's chest even worse because she never would have expected her own mother to do the same thing.

"All parents try so hard to do the right thing by our children. Your mother did something unkind, but she was scared for you. In truth, I was frightened for my son. When he told me that a girl had come to him and told him that he was going to be a father and he would need to marry her, I thought only the worst."

"Joshua said he would marry me immediately. He didn't even hesitate."

Mrs. Levinson set her back gently, touching tears Viv hadn't realized she'd shed. "That is my son. Always jumping before he knows where he will land. I'm glad that he did the right thing."

"Does he ever ask about her?" Viv felt the question form on her lips before she could stop herself from asking it.

"His sister writes to him. She will have told him his daughter's name."

Viv would never understand why he hadn't rushed back on the first leave he could get to interrogate her about their daughter. To try to meet her. She couldn't imagine not wanting to know Maggie.

"You must remember, it's different for him. He walked away from both of you." Mrs. Levinson laughed at her shocked expression. "He is my son, but I will still tell him when he has done something wrong. Maybe one day he can earn your forgiveness."

Viv looked down at the dress in her hands. "Maybe."

But in her heart of hearts, she doubted that if Joshua had to make his choices all over again, he would change a thing about what he'd done.

Joshua

September 15, 1940

It would have been going too far to say that the relationship between the crew of *F-Freddie* had improved, but Joshua was happy to take stony silence over Moss's ire any day. The time alone with his thoughts gave him space to fall a little more in love with flying.

There was a moment each journey when, looking down at the haphazard quilt of fields and hedgerows cut up by roads that was the English countryside, he almost felt giddy. He, Joshua Levinson, was flying. The boy from Wavertree, the tailor's son, had made his life into something bigger than anyone had expected of him. Sure, it wasn't headlining on Swing Street, but the war had derailed a lot of men's plans.

However, the silence also left him unguarded from the other thoughts that sometimes crept in. Thoughts like whether he'd blown his chance of making it into a famous band. Whether he'd given up his daughter and wife and nearly lost his family for nothing. A patchy track record filling in for lushes and teaching spoiled university students how to play the sax.

Joshua shook his head and checked their compass. He couldn't dwell on those thoughts. They would tear him apart.

The moonlit night stretched before *F-Freddie*, the hum of their Blenheim's twin engines mixing with the propellers of the rest of the bombers in their squadron. They'd been in the air for hours, leaving base when it had still been light. The meteorological officer had briefed them to expect a clear easy night— perfect for bombing the German-occupied airfield in Boulogne-sur-Mer, one of the airfields from which the Luftwaffe was launching its relentless assault on London and other cities that newspapers were calling the Blitz. What the chirpy man with wire-framed spectacles and the lilting accent of North Wales failed to mention was that it also made it easier for Bf 109s to spot them.

"Reading?" Moss barked into their headset.

Joshua gave it in clipped, short sentences.

"Better move to the gun, Fortineau," Moss said. "Chances are there will be flacks firing."

Sure enough, the tooth-rattling bang of a German antiaircraft gun cut through the noise of the engines, no doubt hoping to catch a Blenheim flying low.

"Here we go," shouted Fortineau as he climbed into the gun turret. The swiveling gun fixed to the aft of the plane wouldn't be much good against the antiaircraft cannons, but he might be able to get off a few shots at any approaching German fighters.

Automatically, Joshua's brain flipped over from his navigator responsibilities to his bombardier ones as he slid into the flip-down seat at the bomb sight. It was his job to release the bombs cleanly and on target.

"Approached. Ready, Sergeant Levinson?" asked Moss, his eyes sweeping across the cockpit's window.

"Just get me close enough to aim them," he said. If Moss didn't bring them in cleanly with no banked turns, Joshua's chances of hitting anything significant plummeted, but he would do his damnedest. He was determined not to give Moss anything to gripe at him about.

The *ack-ack* of Fortineau's gun rattled through the body of the plane.

"What's going on back there?" Moss asked.

"We have two Bf 109s off our starboard side. They're coming in close to *E-Echo*," reported Fortineau.

"We have to deliver. Can you take them from your position?" asked Moss.

The gun sounded again, along with what sounded like fire from three or four other planes. "Consider it handled, sir."

"Get ready, Levinson," said Moss, holding the plane steady.

Instinct took over as Joshua moved fast, taking wind speed and drift estimates before peering through the backsight spectacles of the bomb site. As soon as the target—a large hangar—was smack in the middle of his sight, he dropped the bombs.

Next to him, he heard Moss curse over the intercom. "Three bogies dead ahead of us."

The rattle of Moss's front guns was drowned out by the explosion of the bombs over the airfield below. Joshua checked his view, even as more fire and smoke billowed toward them.

"Direct hit!" he called out.

"I've got another to port!" shouted Fortineau.

"Got you, you bastard," Moss grunted as the starboard side of a Bf 109 flared and its engine cut out.

One by one, the British bombers around them dropped their payload while doing their best to cut down the German planes. They had the advantage, coming in while so many planes were on the ground, but some of the Luftwaffe fliers had managed to take off.

Joshua's blood surged as Moss and Fortineau did their best to dip, weave, and mow down the enemy.

"Plane down!" Joshua shouted when he caught sight of one of their own plummeting.

"Who was it?" Fortineau asked.

He squinted out, dread creeping up in him as he watched the propellers cut midair. The plane seemed to hang for a moment, the black-and-white Felix the Cat painted on the side grinning at him. He swallowed. "C-Charlie."

McPherson, Hunt, and Shelby.

All of them had just dropped out of the sky and plummeted to the ground.

"Got another!" Moss shouted.

Joshua gritted his teeth and pushed back the sadness that he'd never see those men in the mess again or listen to Hunt, his barrack-mate, wax poetic about the girl he had back home.

"Seems to be clearing, sir!" called Fortineau.

Joshua did a sweep of the sky. Around them, their fellow Blenheims were beginning to bank. The Bf 109s had flown off, mere dots on the night.

"Let's take her home, but keep an eye out," Moss warned.

Joshua quickly rolled through his instrument checks and gave Moss their heading to send them home.

After a stretch of silent flying, Fortineau came over the intercom from his position in the gun turret. "What do you think they'll have for breakfast in the mess?"

"Do you ever think about anything but food?" Joshua asked, making a couple of adjustments as they spoke.

"I want sausages. I dream of sausages," said Fortineau. "Hey, Levinson, have you ever eaten a sausage before?"

Joshua glanced at Moss, who kept his eyes on the skies.

"I don't keep kosher, but I still don't eat pork," Joshua said. He'd tried it once, a little bit of rebellion against his parents' stricter rules of not eating shellfish or pork—a little like smoking cigarettes or sneaking out to play with bands before they accepted that it was better to know where he was at night than not.

Not that that had stopped him from finding his own trouble. Married, walking away from his pregnant wife on the steps of the registry office. He cringed at the thought of it, knowing that he'd left Viv and their little girl.

"I just wondered because—"

Joshua heard the volley of shots, brutal in their speed, and a guttural scream. He wrenched around in his seat and saw Fortineau's hand hanging down from out of the gun turret.

"Fortineau!"

"What—?" Moss started, but Joshua was already shuffling back through the cramped body of the plane as fast as he could. He could see blood already pooled on the floor under Fortineau's motionless hand.

"He's hit!" Joshua shouted as a new volley of bullets tore through the back of the plane, narrowly missing him. He grunted as he pulled their gunner from the turret, cursing his flight suit and parachute pack that slowed him down. Fortineau half slumped out of the gunner's seat, and Joshua saw the brutal outline of a clear shot to the man's head, his lifeless eyes frozen open. Fortineau never had a chance.

"They're ripping her to shreds!" Moss yelled.

Another volley of shots. The Blenheim nearest to them billowed with smoke. Another hit. Another crew that might not make it back to base.

If they didn't figure out how to get out of this they weren't going to make it home either.

"Where the hell is it coming from?" Moss shouted.

Joshua ripped off Fortineau's headset and jammed it on as he pushed up into the turret, now shattered from where the bullet had pierced it. He peered around. There was a flash out of the corner of his eye, and the enemy plane dropped into view.

"There. Up high. Starboard side," Joshua shouted.

"Bastard . . ." Moss muttered into his headset. "I can't get the guns angled without exposing us even more."

More shots—these ones ripping a hole in the side of the plane large enough that Joshua could see the moon. The plane looked like a drunk had attacked it with a can opener.

With a roar, Joshua leaned into the face support, braced himself against the gun, and opened fire. He swept the sky with bullets the way Johnny had told him gunners were trained to do.

The enemy plane started to bank away, but Joshua kept his sights on its portside engine. All of a sudden there was a stream of smoke off the enemy plane. He swept again, aiming high for the glass of the cockpit, shattering it until he could hardly see that there was the shadow of another person inside.

He watched as the German plane's propellers stopped, the plane dipped, and the bastard who killed Fortineau plunged to earth.

"Got him!" Joshua shouted.

"Good shooting, Levinson. Now get up here," Moss ordered.

He did a final sweep. He no longer saw any of the rest of their squadron. Clouds were rolling in, and the dogfight seemed to have separated them.

"What if there's another out there?" Joshua asked.

"In a few minutes, it's not going to matter if anyone's there," said Moss.

The hairs on the back of Joshua's neck stood up. The brash, pompous voice that Moss usually used when speaking to him was gone. It had been replaced with sheer, unadulterated fear.

Joshua wiggled back into the cabin, trying not to look at Fortineau, and took his seat next to Moss again.

"What's the problem?" Joshua asked, jamming his headset back on.

Moss pointed to an instrument that was creeping lower. "The bastard must have hit our fuel tanks. It's a wonder we didn't catch fire, but this isn't any better."

"Can we make it back to base?" Joshua asked.

The grim line of Moss's lips told him no.

"Do we bail out?" Joshua asked.

"I don't particularly want to bail out over occupied France and wait for the Nazis to pick us up after we've just kindly blown up their airstrip, do you?" Moss asked.

"What about over water?" he asked.

"Chances are, if we aren't knocked out on impact and our parachutes don't drag us down, we'll freeze to death waiting to be picked up."

"And we still won't know which side will pick us up," Joshua finished.

This could not be the end. Not when there were so many things in his life he needed to fix. People he needed to apologize to.

"What if I can chart us a path to the nearest base on English soil?" he asked.

When Moss didn't immediately reply, Joshua added, "You are not going to be the last face I see before I die."

Incredibly, Moss laughed. "Agreed, Sergeant. Chart it."

They worked fast, with Moss radioing their position and finding out they were, just as they thought, cut off from the rest of the squadron—or what was left of it. Half a dozen bombers had been lost. Even more were limping home.

"We're over water," Moss announced. "This had better work, Levinson."

"It will," Joshua said, although he had no idea if he was telling the truth or a bald-faced lie.

With the ominous, dark stretch of water below them slowly lightening with the breaking dawn, they didn't talk much except when Joshua called out headings that he hoped would get them to RAF Friston. It was preternaturally calm in the cockpit, but every time Moss called out the fuel levels, the chances of them clearing the Channel looked slimmer.

It wasn't a surprise then when, even as they saw the first rise of land on the horizon, Moss said, "I don't know if we're going to make it."

"We're nearly there," Joshua said, clinging to hope.

"We're bailing out," said Moss, unstrapping himself from his seat with one hand as he held the plane steady.

When he stood up and turned, however, Joshua's eyes widened. On the lower back of his pack, there was a bullet-size rend in the parachute.

"You're not jumping," Joshua said. "Look."

Moss twisted so he could look over his shoulder. "Fuck. How am I not dead?"

"All the fabric must have stopped the bullet," he said.

"It saved my life so I can die in a crashing plane," said Moss, his voice surprisingly wry as he stared at the controls.

"Fortineau," Joshua said sharply.

He scrambled back to his dead crew member and flipped him over. Immediately, his stomach dropped. Fortineau's parachute was ripped to shreds too.

"The backups!" Moss called.

The locker that held the backup supplies was riddled with bullets, but Joshua tore it open anyway. The parachutes were in tatters.

"Nothing," he said as he dropped back into the observer's seat.

Moss fixed him with a look. "You jump. I'll keep her steady."

Joshua snorted. "I'm not leaving you to die here."

Moss furrowed his brow. "You don't like me."

"Yeah, well, just because you're a bastard doesn't mean you should die alone." He peered out the window. "If we get over land, do you think you can put her down?"

Moss stared at him but then shook his head as though banishing a thought. "Maybe. If the landing gear isn't shot to hell."

Joshua gripped the base of his seat as he watched Moss flip and turn his various instruments.

"Fuel is dropping quickly. I don't know if we're going to make it," said Moss.

"Try."

He hadn't prayed in a long time, but Joshua did so as the scene below them went from deep blue water to dark green land.

"The landing gear is stuck. It will only deploy partway," said Moss.

Suddenly both of the propellers slowed and then shuddered to a stop. All Joshua could hear was the wind whistling by them.

"Fuel's run out," said Moss, grunting as he struggled to keep the plane's nose up. "I'll try to glide her down, but be ready to brace."

Joshua leaned over and strapped Moss back into his seat before doing the same with his own seat. Then he braced himself against the wall of now-useless instruments to his side.

The earth rushed up at them faster than he could ever have imagined.

"Brace!" Moss shouted. "Brace!"

The plane slammed into the ground, the stuck landing gear throwing them to starboard. The horrible crunching of metal and glass and the scream of the plane trying to rip itself apart on impact filled his ears. He was thrown against the strapping of his seat, knocking the wind out of him.

When finally they ground to a stop, Joshua lifted his head. Pain shot through his leg and his head. He lifted a hand to his head and drew it back to find blood.

"We're down," he said.

When Moss didn't reply, he twisted painfully to see the pilot sagged forward against his strapping, his head lolling to the side.

"No!" Joshua shouted, falling forward as he unbuckled himself. He stuck his hand against Moss's neck, holding his breath until he found a pulse.

Moss was alive.

The crackle of a flame brought Joshua's head up with a snap. Fear and adrenaline dulled the searing pain in his head, his leg. Even if they had run out of fuel there was enough of this plane that was flammable that it could be a matter of seconds before an explosion.

Moving as fast as he could, Joshua unbuckled Moss. The pilot's weight slumped against his shoulder, and he winced. Still, he levered open the emergency escape next to his station and kicked open the door. There wasn't much space because of the way the plane had landed on her starboard side, but he shimmied out and rotated, yelling at the raw scrape of dirt over the wound on his leg. He did his best to get his hands under Moss's shoulders, careful to keep his head from hitting the ground.

Joshua hauled Moss out from under the plane's wing, cursing as he tried to get them as far away from the plane as he could.

There was a hawthorn hedge a hundred yards off. He'd aim for that. It wouldn't be much match for shrapnel if the plane exploded, but it would be better than nothing.

He yanked and pulled Moss, making it to the rough-hewn wooden gate. He wrenched it open and pulled his pilot around the hedge and sank down next to Moss's limp body.

"You know, you're a heavy bastard—"

The plane exploded behind him, sending Joshua diving over Moss's head while trying to cover his own. A piece of something sharp stabbed him in the side, and he gasped out a breath. The pain that had been pushed away by shock and urgency swelled up, and he blacked out.

15 September 1940

My dearest Little Bear,

Do you remember the story of Goldilocks and the three bears? Well, when you come home to Liverpool, you'll see that we have a new home. I went all over the city looking at places for us to live. Some were too small. Some were too big. But this one is just right.

The house is owned by a nice lady named Mrs. Shannon who says that she cannot wait to meet you. I've told her you're a very good girl who loves to sing and play, and she says that there are other children on the road who were evacuated too who will be happy to be your friends.

But I've saved the best part for last, Little Bear. Mrs. Shannon has a cat! His name is Walter, which I think is a very silly name for a cat, but that's what he's called. Mrs. Shannon says that Walter is very friendly and is good at opening doors. She said that sometimes at night he sleeps on her head like a furry hat!

I cannot wait to see you on my next visit, Little Bear, so I can tell you all about our new house. I'm sure you will love it.

With all of my love and hugs and kisses,
Your Mummy

15 September 1940

Dear Mrs. Thompson,

I am writing to let you know that I have changed addresses. Please post all letters to me to 201 Pitville Avenue, Mossley Hill.

I have written to Maggie to tell her that I have found a new home. What I have not yet told her is that my parents' home, where Maggie and I lived before the war, was bombed. The house was nearly destroyed. Skilled builders are in short supply in Liverpool due to the bombings, and my parents do not know whether what is still standing can be salvaged.

I will not lie to you and tell you that it has been easy being separated from my daughter. However, I will thank you for caring for her. I would never want Maggie to live through what I have been through.

I wanted to let you know that for my next visit, I will be accompanied by my husband's family. As you can imagine, they cannot wait to meet their granddaughter.

Sincerely,
Vivian Levinson

Maggie

Maggie groaned as Mrs. Thompson shook her awake.

"Margaret, that's the air raid siren. We need to go down to the shelter."

Rubbing at her eyes, Maggie let her foster mother pull on her dressing gown and ease her slippers on.

"Are you going to walk this time?" Mrs. Thompson asked.

Maggie shook her head stubbornly, and she felt herself hoisted up and draped over Mrs. Thompson's chest.

"You are becoming too heavy for this, dear," said Mrs. Thompson as they cleared the door of Maggie's room.

"I'll take her," said Mr. Thompson, draping an armful of linens he'd been carrying over the banister and taking the little girl.

Maggie was half asleep as the Thompsons made their way through the house and down to the bottom of the garden. It was colder now, and Maggie buried her nose deeper into Mr. Thompson's warm shoulder. She shifted a little when he laid her on the top bunk, and Mrs. Thompson tucked blankets around her.

Sometime later, Maggie woke with a start, looking around wildly until she remembered where she was. Mr. and Mrs. Thompson always kept a light on in the shelter because Mrs. Thompson didn't like the dark any more than Maggie did, and when Maggie rolled over she could see them asleep next to each other in the bunk under her.

Maggie reached for Tig, only he wasn't there.

She bolted up, and a low buzzing filled the shelter as she stuck her hand into the pocket of the dressing gown. She couldn't find her mother's photograph either.

She'd left her two most prized possessions behind.

Careful as she could, Maggie hitched her leg over the side of the bunk bed and climbed down. Mr. Thompson stirred a little in his sleep, and she froze. He didn't wake up, instead nestling a little closer to Mrs. Thompson and settling into a light snore again.

Maggie crept to the door and pushed it open. The buzzing sound was louder now. She looked up and saw the moon and tiny dots.

Planes.

Her eyes went big, but nevertheless she screwed up her courage and raced into the garden.

Behind her, Mrs. Thompson cried out.

Maggie careened through the house and hit the first of the stairs when she heard Mr. and Mrs. Thompson both screaming for her to leave the house. Huffing and puffing, she pulled herself up to the top of the stairs with the high banister. The planes were deafening now, but she burst into her room. Tig sat alone on her bed.

She snatched up the tiger and pressed her face to his fur. "I'm sorry. I'm here."

An arm swept Maggie up off her feet.

"What are you doing?" Mr. Thompson yelled. "You could be killed!"

"There are so many planes, Matthew!" cried Mrs. Thompson, peering out of Maggie's window.

"My photograph! My photograph of Mummy!" screamed Maggie, reaching for the bedside table drawer.

"We need to go back to the Andy!" shouted Mr. Thompson.

Hot tears streamed down her face, and she pounded her little fists against Mr. Thompsons's back.

"My photograph!" she wailed even as Mr. Thompson flew down the stairs with Mrs. Thompson behind him.

They were nearly clear when an ominous whistle drowned out Maggie's screams. All three of them looked up. Silhouetted against the moonlit sky was a long, dark object headed straight for them.

"Run!" Mr. Thompson screamed, squeezing Maggie tight as he sprinted forward.

There was a great crash as Maggie saw the horrible object cut through the roof of Beam Cottage. All was silent except the sound of Mr. and Mrs. Thompson's gasping breaths in the cold night air.

"The bomb didn't explode," Mrs. Thompson cried.

"They aren't set to explode on impact. They—"

Hot air slammed Maggie square in the face, and she flew from Mr. Thompson's arm as the house behind them blew into a thousand pieces. She hit the ground hard, debris of what had once been Beam Cottage raining down upon her, and then everything went black.

17 September 1940

Dear Mum, Dad, and Rebecca,

I am writing to you from the Queen Victoria Hospital in East Grinstead. I know that will scare you, but the fact that I'm writing just two days after suffering from the plane crash that caused my injuries is a sign that things are better than they might have been.

I can't write much because of the censor, but what I can say is that apparently the volunteers at a local civil defense outpost about a quarter mile away spotted our plane smoking and heard the crash and explosion. They found us in the lane and rushed us to the local surgery, where the doctor patched us up before sending us here for further treatment.

I was knocked unconscious and have gashes on my head and leg, as well as a four-inch piece of shrapnel that was jutting out of my lower back. (Nurse Bishop, who is terrifying, says that the shrapnel wound was nothing compared to what she's seen and to stop whingeing about the pain.) I look a bit like Frankenstein's monster now with stitches across my forehead, but I'm told that the doctor who sewed me up is an ace with the needle, so I will hardly notice once things heal and the redness goes down.

The shrapnel wound hurts every time I breathe, but the doctor seems unconcerned. He tells me that I'll be shipped back to base as soon as they know I'm in the clear, and I'll likely be on ground duties until I'm cleared to fly again by the doctors on base.

I'm told that Moss was in worse shape than I was when we were brought in, having suffered broken bones and serious shrapnel wounds. He did well trying to bring the plane down as cleanly as possible. I haven't seen him since we were admitted.

Don't worry about me. I'm still here. I will let you know as soon as I have moved.

Your loving son and brother,
Joshua

18 September 1940

My idiot brother,

~~My idiot brother,~~

~~How dare you get yourself hurt, and how dare those Germans shoot~~
~~my big brother down? What misguided, stupid idea told you that~~
~~you should join up and~~

Dear Joshua,

I am starting this letter again, but I'm afraid the paper ration means you'll just have to see the struck-out bit above.

   I'm writing to you because Mum is crying too hard, and Dad's hand keeps shaking whenever he tries to pick up the pen.

   I don't really know what to say. I'm happy you're safe and healing. I hate that anyone hurt you.

   Goodness, Joshua. A part of me wishes that you stayed in New York where it's safe. A part of me is incredibly proud of you for enlisting. I don't know how to live with both of those feelings, but I suppose it's what every family is thinking right now. At least you're safe now.

   Promise that you will write to us again to tell us how you're healing.

   Heal quickly, Joshua.

                                    All my love,
                                    Rebecca

Viv

The Luftwaffe is winning this war, mind you, because the RAF was caught sitting on its hands. Let me tell you, if it were up to me . . ."

Viv couldn't help her attention wandering as Mr. Campbell began to describe, in great detail, the way that he would take over RAF Bomber Command to win the Battle of Britain currently raging in the skies and devastating the country's cities.

Everyone seemed to have an opinion about the war these days because it could hardly have felt closer. German planes had dropped so many bombs over Liverpool since the devastating four days of bombings in August, but it was London that everyone was talking about. The Blitz, as the newspapers were calling it, was an unrelenting onslaught. Day and night, the Luftwaffe peppered the capital city with a seemingly unending number of bombs. The harder London was hit, the tenser things became in Liverpool. They all knew what it was to walk down a road one day and the next day find half of the buildings gone.

"Excuse me, Mr. Campbell, but I really must be going," said Viv.

The older man gave a laugh. "I've been talking your ear off and you need to work. You go on, lass."

Viv swung her leg over her bicycle and pedaled the short distance around the corner to the top of Salisbury Road and stopped. Seeing the Levinsons' street sign in bold black and white no longer made her heart jump to her throat. In fact, she was even looking forward to tea with Mrs. Levinson again that afternoon.

She'd written to Mrs. Thompson and told her that Maggie's grandparents would be joining her for her next visit, but she hadn't heard anything back yet. The previous night, she'd slotted coin after coin into a telephone box down the road from Mrs. Shannon's to call the exchange Mrs. Thompson had given her when Maggie had first been evacuated, but the line had rung so long the operator had come back on and asked whether Viv wanted to try again. She'd declined, assuming that the Thompsons had been at one of the endless parties their friends seemed to throw. It would simply be a surprise when Viv turned up on Saturday with Mr. and Mrs. Levinson in tow.

Viv paused to do a check of the letters in her sack.

"Three for the McGarys, six for the Sebbas, one for the Mulleys," she murmured, flicking through the envelopes and postcards.

She looked up and saw Mr. Rowan, red-faced and eyes wild, climbing out from behind the wheel of one of the delivery office's postal vans. Next to him on the bench seat sat Mum, grim-faced as she clutched her handbag.

The post slipped from Viv's hands, scattering across the pavement like snowflakes, and she broke into a sprint, closing the short distance to the delivery van as Mr. Rowan helped her mother down from the passenger's seat.

"Why are you here? What's happened?" she demanded. "Is it Kate?"

Mr. Rowan took off his hat. "Mrs. Levinson, as soon as Mrs. Byrne told me what had happened—"

"What *has* happened?" she asked, her hand shooting out to grip her mother's forearm.

Mum lifted her chin, pain etched on her face. "There was a telegram. One of the neighbors managed to flag down the boy before he went away because he found our bombed-out house. He ran it over this afternoon."

Viv's mouth went completely dry, but she managed to get out, "A telegram?"

Mum slowly opened the top of her handbag. Viv wanted to grab it from her and rip it open, but instead she watched as her mother drew out the slip of paper with trembling hands.

Mum made to hand Viv the telegram, but held it back. "Remember, Vivian, sometimes God works in ways that we do not understand."

Viv ripped the telegram from Mum's hand, clutching it as she read:

BOMB DESTROYED BEAM COTTAGE. ANDERSON SHELTER EMPTY. NO SURVIVORS FOUND.

It had been sent by Charles Stourton, the Thompsons' neighbor.

The world fell silent around Viv. Her limbs went heavy. She forgot how to breathe. This was a dream—a horrible, awful dream.

Only it wasn't.

Viv's knees gave, and she crumpled to the ground with a wail.

"Mrs. Levinson. Mrs. Levinson," she heard Mr. Rowan say, and a hand lit on her back. She couldn't drag her eyes from the telegram. *No survivors found*.

No.

Survivors.

Her daughter. Her beautiful daughter, who she'd sent away, had been killed in the very place she was supposed to be safest.

"How?" she managed to croak out. "Why?"

Mr. Rowan crouched down to kneel beside her, both hands bracing her shoulders now as though to help her stay upright. "If the Germans don't drop all of their bombs over a target, they release them on their flight back. A stray bomb must have fallen."

"She was supposed to be safe," Viv gasped out, looking up at her mother who stood, lips a thin line, her coat, hat, gloves, and handbag all neat and proper as usual. "You promised me that she would be safe if I sent her away. Father Monaghan promised me. *Kate promised me!*" She was yelling now, the betrayal wrenching her apart too intense to contain.

"Vivian—" But whatever Mum was about to say was cut off by the sound of running feet. Viv looked up and saw Rebecca barreling toward them at a dead sprint. Her mother following a few paces behind, her shopping abandoned on the pavement.

"What's happened?" asked Rebecca in a rush, skidding to a stop in front of Viv.

"Miss, please," said Mr. Rowan. "Give Mrs. Levinson some space. She's had a horrible shock."

A shock. That's what people called it when the worst thing that she could imagine happening actually came true. But this wasn't a shock. This felt as though someone had reached in and ripped every vital part of her to shreds.

Viv's eyes skirted over the people surrounding her until they found Mrs. Levinson, huffing and puffing as though she'd just run up. "I'm so sorry," she whispered.

A hand flew to the older woman's mouth. "No."

Viv began to weep.

The elder Mrs. Levinson dropped to her side, wrapping her arms around Viv and holding her close. They both shook, their bodies convulsing with their grief over the child Viv had sent away and the granddaughter Mrs. Levinson had never met.

"I don't understand," she could hear Rebecca say.

"I didn't realize she had a child. If I had . . ." But Mr. Rowan had the good sense not to say anything else. Not that it would have mattered. Maggie was gone.

"Vivian," her mother's voice cut through her grief. "You need to stand up."

Viv lifted her head even as Mrs. Levinson continued to weep against her shoulder.

"You need to stand up," Mum pressed, glancing uneasily at those around them. "You cannot stay on the pavement."

Confused and a little foggy with grief, Viv felt Mrs. Levinson ease away. "Your mother is right. We can't stay here."

"Mrs. Byrne, our house is just down the road," said Rebecca, placing her hand on Mum's shoulder—a gesture of comfort. Mum flinched.

"Vivian, it's time to go to Kate's," said Mum.

"I think perhaps it would be best if we help Vivian inside as soon as we can. My mother too," said Rebecca, her voice rough as though she was fighting tears.

Mum straightened. "Vivian needs her family."

"Mum—"

Her mother cut her off with a shake of her head. "All of this nonsense is over. You need to come home."

Mrs. Levinson took a small step forward. "Mrs. Byrne, you must not remember my daughter and me. I'm—"

"I remember you," said Mum, her words sharp as a knife. "Vivian, it is time to go."

On shaky legs, Viv rose, gripping on to Rebecca's arm when Joshua's sister stepped quickly to her side.

"No."

"Vivian," Mum chided her.

"My daughter is dead. There are more important things than whatever hatred you have for the Levinsons," she said.

"We are not having this conversation here," whispered Mum, her eyes sliding back and forth. It was the second time her mother had checked who was watching, but the first time Viv understood. Her mother had more care about the gossip that might spread about Viv and the Byrnes than she cared to grieve.

Something inside Viv that had been fractured for a long time cracked wide open.

"The Levinsons are good people. Did you know that?" Her voice rose as she swept a hand to point to the two Levinson women who were huddled together, arms around each other. "They are kind and caring, and most important, they *want* to know Maggie."

"Vivian, this is a private matter. It won't do to yell in the street," said Mum nervously.

"My daughter is dead and you're worried about what people will think?" Her voice was so high it was hardly recognizable as her own, fury and disbelief racing through her. "Did you ever love Maggie? Do you even care that she's dead?"

There was a gasp from the crowd, but she didn't care because in that moment she saw her mother lift her chin, determination set in her eyes. Viv held her breath, praying for the answer she wanted. Praying for any sign of affection from her mother.

"A child's death is a tragedy, but it was God's will that Maggie was taken," said Mum.

God's will. She'd heard that thrown out to explain all manner of things, but never had the carelessness with which people used it to explain every tragedy struck her so roundly before.

"Maggie was a little girl. Why would God take away an innocent child?" she asked.

"An innocent child?" her mother scoffed in disbelief.

Viv's eyes narrowed. "An innocent child just like any of the rest of your grandchildren."

"Do not compare my grandchildren to your daughter."

Viv staggered back into Mrs. Levinson, the older woman's arms protectively circling her waist. Out of the corner of her eye, she saw a flash of blue. The sharp crack of a slap rang out in the road. Rebecca stood before Mum, a stunned look on her face and her hand reddening from where it poked out of her blue dress sleeve.

"How dare you?" Mum whispered, a hand pressed to her cheek.

Rebecca clenched her hand into a fist and then spun around to face her mother. "I won't apologize to that woman."

"I would never ask that of you. Come along," said Mrs. Levinson.

Viv's mother-in-law began to gently steer her toward the house on Salisbury Road while Rebecca fumbled for her keys. Mrs. Levinson helped her to the sitting room sofa, but when she tried to straighten, the older woman stumbled, tears clear in her eyes again.

"You sit down too, Mum," said Rebecca.

The sofa sank next to Viv, but she hardly noticed. Instead, she wrapped her arms around herself, trying to protect against the creeping numbness rising in the wake of her ebbing anger.

Maggie was gone. She was never going to see her darling, dear Little Bear again or hear her laugh or sing. She'd never again smell the powdery scent of Maggie's skin, or feel Maggie's soft hair against her face when Maggie climbed into bed with her in the middle of the night. She'd never send her out the door to school, watch her fall in love, see her marry.

Her daughter's life had been stolen from her, and it was all her fault.

It felt too incredible to believe. She *wouldn't* believe it.

A white mug of steaming tea appeared in front of her, and she looked up to see Rebecca standing in front of her.

"I didn't know what else to do," said Rebecca.

"I need to go there," she said suddenly.

"What?" Rebecca asked.

"I need to see Beam Cottage for myself," Viv said. She couldn't believe that Maggie was gone. She couldn't believe that Maggie was dead. It didn't feel possible.

"I could take the train and—"

"I'll telephone Dad at the shop. He'll find a car. He'll take you, if that is what you want."

Viv sucked in a shaky breath and nodded.

Viv sat in the front seat of the delivery van Mr. Levinson had borrowed from a wholesaler he knew, hands clenched into fists.

"Only a few miles now," said Mr. Levinson.

Viv glanced at her father-in-law. He hadn't cried since he'd arrived at the house on Salisbury Road, but she didn't doubt his grief. He stared, hollow and tired, out the windshield, and his fingers clutched the van's wheel so hard that his knuckles turned white. A grandfather mourning a child he would never meet.

This time, when she began to cry, all that came out were long, silent jags of grief.

"I'm sorry," said Mr. Levinson. "Maybe we should stop. You haven't eaten anything."

Viv pressed a hand against her chest, trying desperately to calm her crying, but that only made it worse.

"I—I'm sorry. I'm so sorry," she gasped out, pressing her hands to her cheeks. She could feel salt crusted there. Old tears that had fallen and dried hours ago.

"You don't have to be sorry."

"Mr. Levinson," she said.

"Seth, please," he said, taking a right turn when a roadside marked for Wootton Green appeared. "We are family."

Viv's fists sank deeper into the fabric of her postal uniform.

"I can't believe you are willing to call me family after all the pain my family caused yours."

"That pain was not your responsibility alone," he said.

"Still," she said.

"You are my daughter-in-law and the mother to my granddaughter. Nothing can change that."

She hunched over in her seat, the grief almost too big for her body, as though it were straining to spill out into the world.

"I sent her away," she said, the words coming out like a confession.

"So did many parents," he said.

"But some of them brought their children back. I could have. I could have told the Thompsons that I wanted my daughter back," she said.

Joshua's father was silent as he pulled the car over to the side of the road just beyond the village sign. His seat squeaked in protest as he faced Viv.

"Why did you not fetch Maggie from the countryside?" he asked.

"It was supposed to be safer there. Then I started working for the General Post Office. I thought, if she was away and I worked hard enough, I could create a new life for us that I could bring her back to. There was no one to care for her when I was at work."

"Anne and I would have cared for her, but I suppose you didn't know that."

"No," she said softly.

Maggie would have been safe in Wavertree with the Levinsons. Maggie wouldn't have been in harm's way and—

"Stop." The older man shook his head emphatically. "Whatever you are thinking, it will not help."

"I don't know how to stop," she whispered. "I can't stop thinking about how she might be dead, but I also can't shake this feeling that she's not."

Seth drew in a deep breath. "Vivian, you need to prepare yourself. Seeing the house—or what is left of it—is going to be the most difficult thing that you do on the most difficult day of your life. You will think about everything you have done and all the things you haven't. You will make yourself feel wretched about it, but none of us can read the future.

All we can do is make decisions that we think are right. You did not know what the Germans had planned. None of us did."

Tears filled her eyes once again. "I don't even know if I'll be able to have a funeral."

Seth hesitated and then seemed to decide something. "Do you know what shiva is?"

She shook her head.

"It is custom in Jewish households that have lost someone to observe a period of mourning," he continued. "You mourn at home as a family, but friends, extended family, and members of their congregation will visit to offer you comfort. You say prayers. You grieve.

"When we go back to Wavertree, we will sit shiva for Maggie for seven days. My wife and I would like it very much if you would join us as a member of the family."

"I wouldn't know what to do," she said.

"Our rabbi would be happy to speak with you about what you might expect."

When she didn't reply, he added, "If you are not comfortable with participating in a Jewish tradition, we will understand. If you would like to speak to your priest—"

"No!" she said quickly. "Thank you, but I don't want to speak to a priest."

"There are times when we cannot understand what it is that God has planned for us. Sometimes he challenges us in ways that we do not think we can tolerate or live through. That is the testing of our faith," said Seth.

"I cannot understand why God would take an innocent child's life."

For years she'd hated how Father Monaghan and the Church held sway over her family. She'd been ashamed and angry that the neighbors who'd seen her grow up had turned their backs so easily when she'd married a Jewish man and had his child. However, it was not until that afternoon that she'd ever really questioned her faith.

"I cannot answer that. All I can do is offer you comfort and hope that you will choose to join us," said Seth.

"Thank you," she whispered.

Seth set his hands on the steering wheel again. "Do you still want to do this?"

She squeezed her eyes closed but nodded.

"Then we will go," he said.

The short drive felt as though it took an eternity. Viv couldn't speak, and so she turned her head to the window. She remembered walking down these streets with Maggie dancing merrily beside her. Her daughter was so full of life and energy, it seemed impossible that that light could be snuffed out.

In the dying light of the September evening, Seth took the final turn onto the village lane where Beam Cottage stood.

In the middle of the quiet road was a void. The remains of the cottage were charred black wood and scorched stone. Viv could see past the only remaining front wall all the way into the thrashed garden.

"Is this it?" Seth asked shakily as he pulled the car to a stop in the middle of the road.

Viv fumbled for the door handle and scrambled out of the car.

"Vivian!" called Seth, but she hardly heard him. Her legs were already carrying her through what had once been the door of the proud house but now stood as a mere gap in the remaining fragments of wall.

She stumbled over bits of wood and broken ornaments. The few of Mrs. Thompson's beautiful things that remained were broken or warped by the heat of the explosion. With trembling hands, Viv stooped to pick up a soot-covered hunk of metal. She could just make out the shape of a horse's head that had escaped the fire.

She felt Seth stop next to her. The sculpture slipped from her fingers, crashing to the ground.

A whimper escaped Viv's mouth. She turned into her father-in-law, who wrapped his arms around her, and together they wept.

Viv

January 5, 1935

Viv huddled lower into her coat, trying to shield herself against the freezing wind that whipped through the street. She'd woken up early and snuck out of the house to board the bus to this part of town, not knowing when Joshua would arrive for work. Fortunately, her morning sickness wasn't so bad that day. Maybe it was the cold, or maybe—as she had learned—it was because morning sickness didn't just happen in the mornings. She was nauseous all the time now, although she was lucky that her stomach still looked as flat as it usually did.

That would not last for long.

She spotted his gray hat before she saw him. He was nearly to the Levinsons' shop door when she stepped out into the road.

"Joshua," she called out.

His surprise registered on his face, but then he smiled. "Viv. What are you doing here?"

At least he didn't seem angry. That, she had to believe, was a good start.

"I need to talk to you."

The flicker of fear that flashed across his eyes was unmistakable. He knew.

"I was just going to open up the shop for Dad," he said, gesturing weakly to the door.

"This can't wait."

He hesitated but then nodded. "There's a caff down the road."

They made the two-block walk in silence, nerves jittering through Viv. Her stomach turned at the smell of grease and eggs, but she managed to keep her composure as they pushed into the caff. Joshua pulled out a chair for her at a table in the back and then went to the counter to order them two cups of tea.

Viv wrapped her hands around the warm cup, doing her best to stop the shake in her hands when Joshua finally sat down in front of her.

She opened her mouth to start, but he jumped in. "I'm sorry we never had that date. I . . . . I didn't know if you'd want to see me again after—"

"I'm pregnant."

His eyes went wide like a child's. "How?"

He sounded so baffled, she might have laughed if she didn't feel so much like crying.

"How do you think?" she asked.

"I mean, it was just one time," he said. "I thought I took care of . . ."

"Apparently it wasn't enough," she said.

"But are you sure?"

She nodded.

He scrubbed a hand over his face. "Are you sure it's mine?"

Her eyes narrowed. "What are you saying?"

"No! That is"—he fumbled for the words—"I just can't believe—"

"It's yours. It was my first time, and I haven't done it again."

He slumped back in his chair, looking as amazed as if she'd told him that the birds on the roof of the Liver Building had come to life and were flying up and down the Mersey.

She looked down at her hands wrapped around her cooling mug of tea. "I don't know what to do," she whispered. "I had an aunt, Flora. I've never met her. She got into trouble and was sent away to one of those awful places for unwed mothers. Mum's family never spoke about her again. I only know about her because I overheard Mum talking to Dad about her when a neighborhood girl fell pregnant.

"Joshua, I can't go to one of those hospitals. And the other ways . . . I just can't do it."

He stared at the spot where the table blocked her stomach, as though he expected to see a baby. "Marry me."

He said the words so flatly that she jerked back a little. "What?"

"Marry me. If your parents won't object," he said.

She placed both of her hands on the table, palms down, to steady herself. "They won't be happy."

"Because I'm Jewish."

"Because you're not Catholic," she clarified. Both of her parents would be furious, but she could just about weather that. Her mother would seethe that Viv wouldn't be married in a church. That the neighbors might gossip. That Father Monaghan might think less of the Byrnes. However, when all that settled, it was her parents' disappointment—a lifetime of it—that was going to be more difficult to withstand.

"I will make them understand that this is the only way. Our baby needs to be legitimate. That will matter more," she said with more firmness than she actually felt.

"All right," he said.

"What about your family?" she asked.

He shrugged, but she could see the strain in the fine lines around his eyes. "They'll understand when I speak to them. Mum will probably be thrilled you're pregnant, even if the child won't be Jewish."

"I don't understand."

"Judaism passes along the mother's line," he said.

Viv sank a little lower into her seat. Nothing about this felt right. They were marrying after two dates because of a silly, stupid mistake she'd made in a moment of passion.

They'd made. This child was both of theirs.

"I cannot raise this child by myself, Joshua," she whispered.

He hesitated, but then he reached across the table to take her hand. "You don't have to do this yourself. I'll do the right thing."

She let out a breath. She had no doubt of the hard road she had ahead of her at home, but at least Joshua would stand by her side.

Maybe it would turn out okay after all.

Dear Mum and Dad,

You'll be happy to know that this morning the doctor says I'm improving. I should have a few more days in hospital, and then I will be cleared to return to base. I expect that they'll have me working on something mind-numbingly boring but safe until they can be sure that I can do all the things I need to as a navigator and bombardier.

I'm sorry that I can't promise you that I'll stay out of danger. The reality of this war is that as soon as we're patched up, we're sent out again. So long as we can fight, they need us.

But it isn't just that. The truth is, I'm good at my job. I thought for a long time that the only thing I was good at was playing the saxophone. I was a mediocre tailor—Dad, you know that's true. Every day I looked around the shop and realized that I would never be able to do what you'd done. I don't have the passion or the skill for it. I know this may be hard to hear, but perhaps I should have said it a long time ago.

The way that patterns and draping and stitches all seem easy for you, music is for me. I thought that would be enough. That it would make me into something bigger than Wavertree or Liverpool or even England. I didn't know how to tell you that and how to make you understand, so I did the easy thing and left.

I don't think there is a single day when I haven't thought about the choice I made, but at times I have been able to push the guilt away because I thought I was going to be one of the lucky ones. I was convinced I was going to make it. I thought that was enough to justify how I hurt all of you. How I hurt Viv. I should have told you that I was afraid of being a father, a husband. I didn't want to disappoint you, but I went and did the thing that would hurt you most.

As soon as I am cleared, I'm going to put on my flight suit again and return to ops. I don't want to run and hide from difficult things any longer. I want to do what I know is right.

I hope you can forgive me for now and then.

Your loving son,
Joshua

19 September 1940

Dear Rebecca,

I'm writing you a second letter to go along with the one to Mum and Dad because the luxury of time sitting in a hospital bed with nothing to do but read secondhand books from Red Cross packages means that I have had time to think and realize that there are things I need to say only to you.

You told me that when I left, you had to become everything to Mum and Dad. I don't think I really understood until I had time to sit here and force myself to think about it. I know that I can't undo five years of lost time, but know that I can never tell you how very sorry I am. I never imagined that you wouldn't go to university. I never imagined that your world would be smaller if I left for a bigger one.

I know that I cannot give you back the time that I took from you or that this war has stolen, but I promise you that when all the fighting is over I will do everything I can to make this up to you.

Your loving brother,
Joshua

Joshua

Joshua winced as the stitches on his back stretched uncomfortably as he tried to shift in the hospital bed. In his hand, he held a much-thumbed copy of *Scoop* by Evelyn Waugh. The solider in the bed next to him had recommended it the day before, and he was doing his best to focus on William Boot's exploits in Ishmaelia.

"Is that even a real place?" he muttered, flipping to his page again. Did it really matter? The book broke up the monotony of the ward.

"Sergeant Levinson," came the commanding voice of Nurse Bishop.

He sat up a little straighter, wincing again as one of his injuries pulled against his stitches. "You have a visitor, but don't spend too long. The doctor will be making his rounds in half an hour."

A visitor? Nurse Bishop stepped aside, revealing Moss in a heavy-looking wheelchair pushed by a younger nurse.

Joshua waited until the nurse rolled Moss to a stop by his bedside and Nurse Bishop hurried the younger woman away.

Moss's leg was propped up, his toe sticking out from under the edge of a gray woolen blanket. Joshua could see the heavy plaster cast doctors had used to set it. Moss's hand was barely recognizable wadded in bandages and held steady in a cloth sling. Someone had obviously taken clippers to his hair because it was nearly army-short now.

"You're still here, then," Joshua said.

"I'll be here for a while. They say I need surgery on my hand once the swelling goes down, and then they'll probably send me to a convalescent hospital," said Moss as he lift his bandaged arm.

"How bad is it?" Joshua asked.

"Apparently I smashed it up somewhere between the crash and the explosion. I really don't remember."

A nurse down the ward dropped an empty bedpan with a clatter. Moss turned his head a little, and Joshua could see a row of angry stitches climbing up from beside his right ear across his scalp.

That explained the haircut, Joshua thought.

"The broken leg is almost certainly from the impact of the crash," Moss continued. "Bloody parachute."

"Bloody parachute," Joshua agreed.

They sat in silence for a moment, Moss using his good hand to pick at where the blanket covering his lap had begun to pill.

Finally, Moss lifted his head and asked, "Why did you do it?"

"Do what?" he asked.

"Save me."

Joshua snorted. "You were the one who flew the plane."

"You pulled me free," said Moss. "And before, you could have bailed out."

"You didn't have a working parachute."

"Still . . ."

Joshua stared at him. "I said I wasn't going to leave you alone to die. It doesn't matter how much I dislike you or how much you clearly hate me."

"I don't hate you," said Moss quietly.

That earned him another hollow laugh. "All of those times you've called me a 'yid'? You never wanted to fly with me, and you made it pretty clear how you feel about serving with a Jew."

Moss opened his mouth to reply, but Joshua held up his hand. "In my religion we're taught that you should do everything you can to preserve human life because life is a gift. When it became a question of saving myself and letting you die or maybe being able to save both of us, I wasn't going to leave you."

Moss hung his head. "I don't know if I could have done the same thing."

Anger and disgust swelled up in Joshua, but then he saw the haunted look on Moss's face and pressed his lips together to keep that first flush of rage to himself.

"My sister, Charlotte, married a Jew. He is a solicitor, just like my father. He and Charlotte were introduced at a party, and they fell in love. Charlotte kept it a secret from us until they were engaged, and then she told my parents. My parents said that if she married him, they would never speak to her again," said Moss.

"And you sided with your parents," he said, the similarities with his wife's family not lost on him.

"I never thought she would go through with it, but she did and my parents cut her off. We never saw her again," Moss said.

"And that is why you hate me? Because your sister chose the man she loved rather than your family?"

"She was my best friend," said Moss, his voice cracking.

"Was?" Joshua asked.

Moss gave a weak nod. "She died two years ago. Pneumonia."

Joshua sucked in a breath. "She fell in love. That is all."

"She chose him!" Moss shouted, bringing the ward to silence.

Joshua glanced around them and then lowered his voice. "She wouldn't have had to if you and your parents hadn't made her."

Moss clasped his hand over his mouth, clearly trying to hold back the sobs that shook his shoulders.

"Any apology you make to me is different than the apology you owe her husband and his family. I can't make what you and your parents did right."

And neither did what Joshua did by saving Moss absolve him of what he'd done to his wife and daughter.

Moss straightened, sniffing as he clearly tried to pull his dignity back. "No. No, of course. All the same, I owe you a debt. I'll be recommending you for commendation for bravery. I know that it isn't an apology. It's what you've earned, and I want to see you have it."

Joshua didn't respond, and so Moss signaled for Nurse Bishop to take him away.

Later that morning, Joshua twirled the pencil around his hand and stared hard at his notebook. He'd abandoned *Scoop* and decided that, for once, he was going to try to write a song.

Well, an arrangement at least.

He'd always played other people's arrangements before, never his own. It hadn't really occurred to him to try because he was always running around, trying to book gigs and find a permanent job. However, now that he was forced to slow down and recuperate, he began to get the itch to try.

To his right, a door opened and there was the hurried shuffle of boots on the linoleum tiles that lined the ward. He ignored it, still playing with the melody for "And the Angels Sing," the Benny Goodman hit. There were people coming in and out of the ward all day.

He didn't notice Nurse Bishop until the white skirt of her uniform came into his field of vision. He looked up and saw her standing there, flanked by a young man wearing a telegram company's uniform.

Joshua's blood froze when the boy asked, "Sergeant Joshua Levinson?"

He was acutely aware of every patient's and nurse's eyes on him when he nodded and took the telegram. His mouth went dry as he opened it and saw it was from his sister:

MAGGIE KILLED IN BOMBING. SITTING SHIVA. COME HOME.

Joshua's hand shook as he stared at the thin telegraph paper. His daughter was dead? It didn't make any sense. Hadn't Rebecca told him that Viv had evacuated her to make sure that she wasn't around any bombing?

"When did this come?" he asked the boy, seeing the previous day's date on the top of the telegraph and knowing that meant he'd already missed the first two days of shiva.

"I'm very sorry, sir. There were so many messages yesterday . . ." the boy trailed off.

He nodded stiffly, feeling even more cut off from his family than he had in years. They'd been together, mourning his daughter, and he hadn't even known.

"Can I help?" Nurse Bishop asked in a soft voice, all of her terrifying, ruthless efficiency gone.

He swallowed and looked up at her, lost. "I need to go home. Now."

Viv

People moved softly around the Levinsons' front room, heads bowed as they paid their respects on the fifth day of shiva. Viv sat on a low stool she'd been told was traditional for the family of the deceased, only partially registering the people who passed her by.

On the long drive back from Wootton Green, Seth had explained to her that many of the people who would come through the house for the seven days of mourning would be from their synagogue. Others would come from Manchester, where most of his and his wife's families lived. No doubt, they would wonder about the woman they'd never seen before who was the mother of Seth and Anne's granddaughter. However, each and every one of them stopped and offered Viv a few words of support.

Her father-in-law nodded in greeting to an older man in a well-cut somber suit. Viv absently wondered if he was a fellow tailor or perhaps a customer.

"*HaMakom yenachem etchem b'toch sha'ar avaylei Tzion v'Yerushalayim,*" the man said to Seth and then Anne. Then he moved to Rebecca.

"Mr. Chapin," Viv's sister-in-law said, acknowledging him.

"May God comfort you with the mourners of Zion and Jerusalem," said Mr. Chapin, looking first to Rebecca and then to Viv.

Viv nodded and bit her lip, fighting back the tears that threatened to rise.

As the afternoon stretched on, Viv shifted on her stool. Despite people's curiosity, she found the quiet contemplation of shiva comforting. There was no one to explain herself to, nothing she needed to justify. She was there with the Levinsons by right of being Maggie's mother. That was enough. Still, her body didn't thank her for the hours of sitting straight on the stool. Her legs prickled with pins and needles, and she could feel her back stiffening.

As though reading her thoughts, Rebecca reached over and squeezed Viv's forearm. "Just a little bit longer."

"Thank you," Viv mouthed.

The light softened with the late afternoon and the number of callers was beginning to diminish when the front door opened again. Viv, who had become accustomed to the sound of it opening and shutting, hardly noticed until Rebecca nudged her. She looked up and spotted her sister standing cautiously in the front room's doorway.

Kate, dressed in a black dress with a small black hat perched on her head and a pair of black gloves on her hands, looked about awkwardly, no doubt taking in the seated family members and the covered mirror over the mantel. Then, Viv caught Kate's eye, and she saw her sister's hard intake of breath—half gasp, half sob.

Seth had asked Viv for Kate's address so that he could invite the Byrne family to sit shiva with them. Viv had protested that her family would never come. She couldn't imagine her Catholic mother and father wanting anything to do with a Jewish mourning ritual. She had assumed that Kate would go along with what their parents chose in order to keep the peace since Mum and Dad were now living with her despite their threats to leave in the wake of their disagreement with Viv's decision to move out.

She should have had more faith in her sister.

"Isn't that your sister?" whispered Rebecca.

Viv nodded.

"You should go to her," said Anne.

Viv stood, her knees cracking in protest. She crossed the living room as Kate dabbed her eyes, trying to compose herself.

"You came," Viv said in a low voice.

Kate offered her a watery smile. "How could I not come? Maggie was my niece."

"I didn't know if . . ." She looked around the room, knowing that it must seem as strange to Kate as it had to her just a few days ago. "I didn't know if you would understand."

Kate shook her head. "I saw someone washing their hands with a pitcher of water when they came into the house, so I did the same. I hope that was okay."

She touched her sister's elbow. "It was okay."

Kate glanced around again.

"You can ask questions if you like. I might not be able to answer all of them, but I'm learning so I can try," she said.

"It's very different than a wake," said Kate.

"In some ways. Not in others," she said.

"You have shiva for seven days?" Kate asked.

"Sit shiva. Yes. People come to pay their respects, although they're only meant to speak to us if we speak to them first. Some bring food."

"Why are the mirrors covered?" asked Kate.

Viv had had the same question. "It is supposed to symbolize a lack of self-indulgence from the mourners while they are grieving."

Kate nodded, tearing up again. "I'm so sorry, Vivie."

Something cracked in Viv, and as the tears began to flow again, she wrapped her sister in her arms.

"She was supposed to be safe," Viv sobbed.

"I'm so sorry I told you that you should send her away," Kate choked out. "I was scared for the children. All of them."

"You didn't know."

"I should have listened to you," Kate whispered, her shoulders shaking as they held on to each other, weeping.

Viv wished that she could have stayed in the protective embrace of her sister, but she knew that that wouldn't be possible. She stepped back a little, keeping her arms on Kate's shoulders.

"Would you like to speak to the Levinsons?" Viv asked as she dried her eyes.

Kate hesitated.

"They have been nothing but kind to me," Viv said.

"I would like to give them my condolences, thank you," said Kate.

Viv slipped her hand into her sister's and led her across the room to her in-laws. "Seth, Anne, Rebecca, this is my sister, Kate."

Seth managed a small smile and reached out a hand to take Kate's. "I'm very sorry we are only meeting again under such sad circumstances, but you are most welcome here."

Viv watched Kate, wondering if her sister realized that she was the reason that they were meeting this way. If Kate had sent the letter . . .

But there was no use in thinking about "what if?" the way that the girls in the delivery office did. This was not a game.

"I'm very sorry, Mr. and Mrs. Levinson. Miss Levinson," said Kate. "Please accept my condolences."

"It is very kind of you to come, dear," said Anne, her voice cracking.

"Would you like to join us, Kate?" asked Seth, gesturing to where they sat.

"Oh, I wouldn't want to impose," Kate began to protest.

"It would be no imposition," said Seth. "You are Maggie's aunt. You were special to her, just as she was special to you."

Viv thought for a moment that her sister might protest again, but Kate gave a shallow nod. "I would like that very much."

A friend from the Levinsons' synagogue found another stool, and Kate settled in next to her sister. Viv reached over and squeezed Kate's hand, much like Rebecca had done to her earlier that afternoon. From the stiff way that Kate held herself, Viv could tell that her sister was uncomfortable. Viv didn't care. The Levinsons had embraced her and mourned the granddaughter they had never met. One of her own family could show the grace that the Levinsons had showed her, even if it meant being uncomfortable for a short spell.

"Perhaps you would like to share a memory of your niece," said Seth, leaning forward to address Kate.

"Oh," said Kate, glancing at the two people who had stopped to talk to Anne and were now listening.

Viv squeezed her hand. "Tell them about the time that Maggie and Cora went to the seaside."

That brought a smile to Kate's lips. "Cora is my youngest. She's two years older than Maggie, and Maggie was always running around after her. We took them to the seaside at Southport one summer. Maggie must have been three and Cora was five. Do you remember how cold it was even in July, Vivie?"

"We made Colin and William wear their pullovers, and the girls had cardigans over their swimming costumes," said Viv.

"They still wanted to go in the water though. The boys went racing off and dove into the waves. You should have heard them screaming when they hit the cold. Well," said Kate, "you never can tell Cora what to do, so she went in too, dragging little Maggie along by the hand until she felt how cold it was. The waves were gentle, but you and I were still worried that it might be too much for Maggie, weren't we?" asked Kate.

"We were."

"Cora, who never can stand the rain or snow in the winter, started screaming. We started calling the kids back in, but Cora wouldn't move. And that's when Maggie must have decided that enough was enough. She pushed Cora over, straight into the water.

"Cora came up spluttering and screaming even more. We went splashing in to drag the girls out, and what did Maggie say when you wrapped her up in a towel?" Kate asked.

"'Cousin Cora was being a baby, so I pushed her in for her own good,'" repeated Viv. "When I asked her why, Maggie told me that she wanted Cora to learn that there was nothing to be afraid of."

Kate gave a little laugh. "That's the way she is. Matter of fact as you like, but still sweet as could be."

Viv stilled at her sister using *is* rather than *was*. It was such a little thing, but it reminded her that there would be no more new stories about Maggie to recall. Viv would never send her to her first day of school or help her with her homework. She wouldn't take her to the beach again, or help her study for her exams. There would be no first day of work, no first love, no wedding or christening for Maggie's own children. Maggie would forever be a little girl.

Rebecca must have caught Viv's expression as it crumpled, because she wrapped an arm around Viv and said, "She sounds like she was a wonderful little girl."

"I think you would have found her charming," said Kate quietly.

Viv pressed a hand to her heart, trying to hold back the swell of emotion there. Again, the grief swelled, threatening to split her in two.

The front door opened. There was the splash of water from pitcher to basin. Memories of Maggie flitted through her mind, overwhelming her. She didn't know how much more of this she could take today.

Mrs. Levinson gasped, and without thinking, Viv looked up.

Standing in the front room doorway, devastation across his bandaged and stitched face, stood Joshua Levinson.

Joshua

All the way from East Grinstead, Joshua had held his grief wrapped tightly around himself. Nurse Bishop had snapped to attention as soon as she read Rebecca's telegram. However, it had still taken precious time to work through the hospital's bureaucracy to discharge him, and then there was the matter of contacting his commanding officer and receiving leave. All the while, Joshua sat powerless, consumed by warring feelings of shame, anger, and regret all fighting for supremacy in him. He'd never known his daughter. In New York, he'd told himself that it was for the best—that Viv had made it clear she wanted nothing to do with him—but since he'd been back on British soil it had become harder to keep himself from thinking of the life he might have had. He hadn't *wanted* a child or a wife, but learning Maggie's name had planted a seed that couldn't help but grow.

Joshua had battled with himself on the train, wondering how he was going to face his parents as they sat shiva for a little girl they'd never had a chance to meet all because of him. He'd prepared himself for that. What he hadn't accounted for was that, when he walked into the familiarity of his family's sitting room, Viv and her sister, Kate, would be sitting there too.

It was his mother who at last broke the strained silence.

"You came home," she said, unfolding from her stool, rising on shaky legs.

He took off his uniform cap, passing a hand over his hair as Mum approached, but his eyes stayed fixed on Viv. She looked straight ahead, defiant.

When Mum was a step away, he tore his gaze from Viv and wrapped his mother in a hug despite the sharp protest from his still-healing wounds.

"When we had your letter that your plane had crashed— Oh, look at your stitches— And—"

"It's okay, Mum. I'm here now," he said, as his mother cried into his uniform coat.

When Mum's tears dried, he hugged Dad and Rebecca in turn. From over his sister's shoulder, he could see Viv rise stiffly. Her sister took her hand, tugging on it gently as though to get her attention. Viv shook her head. Hope fluttered in his chest that perhaps this meeting wouldn't be so bad. That she could forgive him.

"Greet your wife, Joshua," said his father quietly.

He took a step forward, but then Viv's eyes flicked up to meet his and all he saw in her gaze was white-hot fire, pure anger, rage.

"Joshua," Mum prompted him softly.

He glanced at Rebecca for support, but his sister's expression was unreadable.

He swallowed and, moving carefully around his mother's rose-patterned sofa, approached his wife. Viv lifted her head as he grew closer, but her expression never changed.

"Viv," he said.

"Joshua," she said.

"I . . ." But he was at a loss for words. He held his hands out wide in front of him. "I'm sorry."

Her eyebrows popped. "You're sorry. That's all you have to say?"

"Could we talk?" he asked, reaching for Viv's elbow. She jerked away before he could touch her.

"I just want to talk."

"Vivie, you don't have to do this," said her sister, stepping forward.

"She absolutely doesn't," said Rebecca.

"Rebecca." Mum's tone was warning.

"It's okay, Mum," said Joshua.

Viv looked between their sisters and then, with a grim set to her mouth, shook her head. "Outside."

She walked out of the room, and he made to follow when his mother caught him by the arm.

"Be gentle with her, Joshua," said Mum. "She's just lost her daughter."

He looked down at his mother's hand bunching the sleeve of his uniform. "I lost a daughter too."

Mum shook her head slowly, sorrowfully. "It is not the same."

His mother's words sliced through him, even as his anger flared up. How dare Mum side with his estranged wife? He was her flesh and blood. Viv was just a girl he'd made a mistake with. One he'd been paying for in guilt for too long.

He caught up with Viv in the small, paved backyard of the house. As soon as the door closed behind him, Viv planted her hands on her hips and fixed him with a hard stare.

"Why are you here, Joshua?"

"Maggie was my daughter too," he said echoing his words to his mother.

She rolled her shoulders back like the fighters he'd seen in New York readying themselves to go twelve rounds in the ring.

"You never once showed any interest in Maggie. You never wrote, telephoned. Nothing."

"You told me to stay away," he said.

He saw her jaw working, her trying to square her anger with him against the truth.

"You turned your back on me," she said.

"I was going to send for you. We could have lived in New York together," he protested.

"Don't pretend as though Maggie and I ever really factored into your decision."

"I promise—"

"You didn't even stop to ask me if that was what I wanted, Joshua. You saw an opportunity to get what you wanted, and you took it," she said.

He opened his mouth and shut it again, the truth of her words silencing him. Finally, he said, "I thought that you would understand. You were so enthusiastic about my music."

"I was an eighteen-year-old girl who was infatuated with a boy she'd only just met!" she yelled.

"And I was a stupid kid too, but I'm trying to do the right thing now," he said.

"The right thing would have been to stand by me, with me, like you promised you would," she bit out.

"I don't know how I can apologize enough for what I did," he said.

"Do you regret it?" she asked.

No. The word almost connecting with his lips, but he held back. He regretted that he hadn't ignored her anger and sent money. He regretted that he'd never met the child that his entire family was now grieving. He regretted that he'd hurt her. But what he couldn't ever regret was that he'd left. He had talent that would have died under the weight of his obligations here. He might not have made it as a famous musician, headlining on Swing Street, but if he'd never left, he never would have known what he was capable of. The regret of that would have eaten him alive.

The seconds ticked by. Finally, Viv held up her hands. "You know what, Joshua? I don't really care."

Viv

Viv had never let herself imagine that she would see her estranged husband again. Sometime during her pregnancy, she'd stopped wondering what could have been, if they might have fallen in love and lived a happy life if only that life had been *together*. Then, when Maggie was around six months old, she'd woken up and realized she hadn't thought about Joshua in days.

Now, with him standing in front of her, she realized that this man held nothing for her. He was a name on a marriage certificate. A tether to a past foolishness. Nothing more.

"I used to be angry with you, every single day, but now I just feel sorry for you," she said slowly. "You will never know our daughter. You'll never get to see her face when she wakes up in the morning, or smell the soft scent of her hair after she's taken a bath. You'll never hear her sing or see her play. You'll never hold her in your arms and comfort her when she's crying.

"You could have been the father to an incredible little girl who would have grown up to be an incredible woman. Our lives could have been different—her life could have been different—and now you will have to live the rest of your life knowing that you gave all of that up."

"You really hate me, don't you?" he asked.

She didn't respond.

"Viv, I'm trying to make amends. As soon as the war broke out, I got myself on a ship. I enlisted. I'm trying in some way to make up for the mistakes that I've made. Doesn't that count for something?"

She tilted her head a little, taking in his face, still handsome despite his healing wounds. It was easy to see why he'd caught her attention at that dance all those years ago, and why it had felt so simple. He'd been a good-looking man who wanted to take her out. He'd been different from all the boys from her neighborhood, which made him a little more interesting, and he'd been interested in her in a way no one else had. Look where that had gotten her.

"Joshua, if you think trying to get yourself killed in a plane is going to earn my forgiveness, you've a lot to learn. Make it through this war for your parents' and Rebecca's sake. They're good people. Better than you deserve."

"I know," he whispered.

"You can tell your mother thank you for letting me sleep here the last few days. I'll be going back to my flat tonight."

He looked confused. "Your flat? Will you be coming back?"

Viv found that bubbling up through her grief was the same determination that had steeled her when she'd told her parents she'd had enough. She was learning to take hold of her life, make her own choices. She certainly was not going to be scared off by this man who had cast such a long shadow over her life.

"There are two more days of shiva, aren't there?" she asked.

"Yes," he said.

"Please tell your parents I will return at eight tomorrow morning."

"Do you want me to leave?" he asked.

"You've always done exactly what you like. Why would you stop now?"

Devastation broke out over his face, and an ugly, petty part of her felt glad for it.

"Viv," he croaked out.

She turned toward the house, but before she went she threw a glance back over her shoulder. "You asked if I hate you. I don't. The truth is, I don't feel *anything* for you—not a thing—and that is exactly what you deserve."

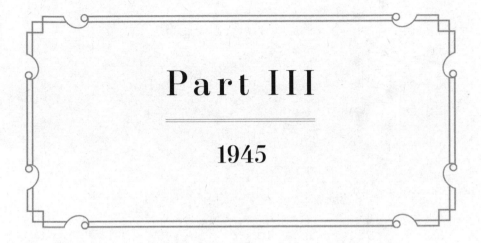

Part III

1945

Viv

L iverpool was drunk on joy.

Viv couldn't help but smile as she edged through the crowd around the bar of the pub near the South East Delivery Office.

"We'll never get a drink at this rate!" shouted Betty above the din of merrymakers and church bells that tolled throughout the city all day.

"Come on!" shouted Vanessa, squeezing past Viv and into a minuscule gap at the polished wood bar. Vanessa jostled a man in an army uniform with a lance corporal's stripe on his arm. He grinned a dopey grin and then, quick as lightning, kissed Vanessa on the cheek.

"Hey!" Viv's arm shot out to stop the man, but Vanessa just laughed.

"I was in France and Germany, and I haven't seen a pretty face in five months," said the man, slurring a little.

"It's fine, Viv. Really," said Vanessa, sending the lance corporal a sweet smile. "Welcome home, soldier."

A whoop arose from the men around them, and even Viv's smile widened into a grin. The war in Europe was over and, although there was still fighting in the Pacific, it felt as though for the first time in years Britain could breathe again.

VE Day they were calling it, and what a victory it was!

"What will you be having, ladies?" asked the barman as the lance corporal made way for Viv and Vanessa.

"Shandy for me!" called Betty from over their shoulders.

"And me," said Rose.

Vanessa glanced at Viv, who nodded.

"Four shandies, please," said Vanessa.

As the barman poured their drinks and Viv twisted to collect money from her fellow posties, Vanessa peered around her.

"So this is what the bar of a pub is like. I've never been in one. Always in the lounge," said Vanessa.

"I imagine there are ten times the people here who are usually in this pub," said Viv, starting to hand back the drinks from the barman.

"The humidity is ruining my hair," Rose complained as soon as she took her drink.

"Then outside we go!" shouted Vanessa with a nod to the door.

The posties made their way outside, gasping for fresh air and sunshine.

"That's better," sighed Rose, tossing her head.

"We should make a toast," said Betty.

"To what?" asked Vanessa.

"To the women of the South East Delivery Office," said Viv.

"And the ones we lost," said Vanessa quietly, leaning into Viv as she took a sip of her shandy.

Viv squeezed her eyes shut but nodded.

"Come on, I want to walk," said Rose.

"You want to flirt," said Betty.

Rose grinned. "Can you blame me? I have an entire war's worth of flirting to make up for."

Betty snorted. "As though the war stopped you."

As their friends set off, bickering as usual, Vanessa and Viv fell into step a few feet back.

"It's hard, isn't it?" asked Vanessa after a moment.

"Yes," said Viv, knowing exactly what her friend meant.

"I wish my brothers were coming home," said Vanessa. "Every time there's a sound at the front door, Mum stops what she's doing. I swear she's listening for them, thinking they're about to burst in."

"I'm sorry they aren't," said Viv, remembering too well both of the horrible days six months apart when Vanessa had learned that two of her brothers had been killed in combat.

Viv had always imagined that the most difficult part of losing someone would be the searing pain that accompanied the news that they were gone. She was wrong. It was the ever-present grief that only receded but never went away.

Not a day went by when Viv didn't think about Maggie. After sitting shiva with the Levinsons, she'd returned to work at the delivery office because she couldn't bear the thought of being alone. Living in Mrs. Shannon's upstairs flat and sharing tea together a few nights a week helped, but even now Viv dreaded the moment when she would retreat to her bedroom. There the silence and grief would press down on her and she'd wonder how she would ever make it to morning. Yet every morning, she woke up and went through the motions of her day again. It was all she knew how to do. The only way to survive.

"What will you do now?" asked Vanessa, bringing herself back to the road where Betty and Rose had stopped to chat with a woman on Rose's route. "Will you stay on at the delivery office?"

"I don't know. I never really let myself imagine it might end," Viv admitted.

"Even after Paris was liberated?" asked Vanessa in disbelief.

Viv offered her a small smile. "It seemed too good to be true."

"You could stay on at the delivery office. Mr. Rowan said that he'll keep women posties so long as the General Post Office allows it," said Vanessa.

"That's quite the change from his attitude before the war."

"We could keep working together. Wouldn't that be fun?" Vanessa asked cheerfully.

Viv couldn't say yes. It wasn't because she didn't like the idea. Far from it. Vanessa had become as good a friend to her as Kate or Rebecca. Her hesitation came from another source.

Three weeks ago, her father-in-law had asked her how she would feel about joining the family business.

Viv couldn't pinpoint the exact moment she'd begun to feel like a true part of the Levinson family because it had been so gradual. After Maggie's death, they'd welcomed her with open arms, extending invitations for tea after her shift on Wednesdays and Shabbat dinner. Soon, Viv realized that she was spending more Fridays at the Levinson family table than she was at Mrs. Shannon's. On the first anniversary of Maggie's death, the Levinsons explained that they would be observing Maggie's yahrzeit to honor her memory. She sat quietly as Seth and Anne lit a candle and said kaddish for Maggie, the rhythmic words mournful yet soothing. The only time Viv absented herself was when Rebecca pulled her aside to tell her Joshua was expected.

She hadn't seen him since Maggie's shiva, and she wanted to keep it that way. It wasn't difficult. As soon as he had healed enough to fly again, the RAF put him back on ops. As far as she could tell, his leave was rarely long enough to make it to Wavertree and back to base, but the few times over the years when he had managed it, she politely made her excuses and stayed away.

It was estrangement by choice and, mercifully, no one commented on it.

If she worked in Seth's shop the way that her father-in-law wanted her to, she would have to admit that becoming part of Joshua's family meant that she might have to see Joshua. That was a possibility she was not yet prepared for, and she didn't know if she ever would be.

"I don't know what I'll do, but I do know that I'm ready not to think about this war any longer," said Viv.

"Amen," said Vanessa, touching her glass to Viv's as the sun streamed down on them.

Joshua

Joshua stared at the "demob" suit hung on the end of his bunk in the barracks at RAF Uxbridge. A few days before, he'd been thanked for his nearly six years of service in the RAF and told that he would soon be returning to civilian life. That morning, his demobilization grant had come through, and he'd queued up in the afternoon to receive his government allocation of a suit, shirts, underclothes, raincoat, hat, and shoes. After so long in uniform, it would be strange casting aside his RAF blues and donning civilian clothes to do . . . what exactly?

After years of being told where and what he should be doing, when he should eat, how much leave he would receive, Joshua was going to be his own master again. It was a strangely uncomfortable thought, and one that left him feeling distinctly adrift.

He probably should go back to New York. He had no idea what he might expect if he turned up to the Famous Door or the 21 Club, saxophone in hand. He'd heard through the grapevine that some of the guys he'd played with had joined the USO and toured around entertaining the troops. However, no matter how much he tried to imagine it, he couldn't see himself fitting back into the New York scene again.

Maybe he would go north to Liverpool and lay low for a while. If VE Day had been any indication, people were desperate for a good time, and one of the ballroom bands was sure to be auditioning musicians as men returned from serving.

If he returned home, however, there was a strong chance that he would run into Viv.

He'd been surprised when, a few months after the disaster of Maggie's shiva, Rebecca had mentioned in a letter that Viv had continued her habit of stopping by for a cuppa with Mum. He'd read the passage twice, wondering whether his sister had meant to warn him. However, there was no censure in Rebecca's words. No anger. It was just a plainly stated fact. Viv, his wife, was now spending time with his family.

He'd prepared himself to see her when he was next home on leave, but the entire four days passed without a glimpse of her. When he asked Mum whether she'd seen Viv recently, Mum had said, "Oh, Viv comes around when she can," but offered no explanation for her absence.

The next visit was the same. And the next.

"Have time for an old friend?"

Joshua looked up and grinned. "Adam Schwartz! How the hell are you?"

"Happier now that I've seen you," said Adam, coming away from the barracks door to clap him on the back.

"A little longer and you would have missed me. I've been demobbed," he said.

"Back to civvy street."

"What about you?" Joshua asked.

"I'm staying in. Everything I've heard from the men liberating Europe . . ." Adam broke off.

They'd all heard the stories filtering back from the troops liberating camps. The people kept just on the edge of life. The massive graves. Jews, Slavs, political dissidents, all manner of people whose lives had been destroyed by the Nazis.

After a moment of silence, Adam cleared his throat. "I requested a transfer to a training unit. I'll be teaching. I'm just up to London for some meetings and to look at flats. My wife will be joining me."

"How about that," Joshua said.

"How's Johnny?" Adam asked, forcing brightness into his smile.

"Last letter I had from him, he was still out in Canada training men there. No word yet when he'll be home," he said.

"When he gets back, we're going to the pub. It doesn't matter where," said Adam.

"Johnny will like the sound of that."

"Hey, are you still squeaking away on the saxophone?" asked Adam.

Joshua nodded. "I've upgraded from playing to cows in a field."

"How so?" Adam asked.

"I'm playing for the boys in the barracks from time to time. I even take requests."

Adam rocked back on his heels. "You sure that's an upgrade?"

He huffed out a laugh. "Probably not. Why do you ask?"

"Do you have plans tonight?" Adam asked, ignoring his question.

Joshua shook his head. "I have a pass off base. I was going to try to find myself a place to live from tomorrow."

"Forget that. Come to the NAAFI with me," said Adam.

He laughed. "It's been nothing but the NAAFI for me for years, mate."

"Come to the NAAFI. There's someone I want you to meet."

Joshua frowned. "Who?"

Adam's smile became sly. "You'll see."

Joshua walked into the NAAFI a few hours later. The shop was set up and manned by a rotation of WAAFs and had tables where servicemen and women could relax with a hot drink. It was a far cry from a pub, but it was all a soldier had when he was on base without leave.

After a sweep of the room, he spotted Adam across the crowd sitting with a man wearing wire-rimmed glasses. As he crossed the room, Adam half stood.

"Joshua, let me introduce you to Flight Lieutenant Hal Greene," said Adam.

Joshua shook Hal's hand, acutely aware that Hal was studying him as Joshua sat down.

"Schwartz tells me that this is your last night with the RAF," said Hal. "That's right."

"In that case, I think you're safe to call me Hal. You're a musician?"

"I was before the war," he said.

"Joshua played in New York City. He was with some of the best bands out there," said Adam.

Hal tilted his head, and Joshua straightened his shoulders a fraction, unable to shake the feeling that he'd walked into an interview.

"Have you kept up with it while serving?" Hal asked.

Joshua crossed his arms. "Why do you want to know?"

Out of the corner of his eye, he saw Adam glance between Hal and himself. "Hal's one of the Squadronaires."

Slowly, Joshua nodded. The Squadronaires were the band the RAF had put together to entertain the troops and boost morale—the same one the recruiter mentioned to him when he first joined up in 1939.

"What do you play?" Joshua asked.

"Trumpet," said Hal, mirroring Joshua's crossed arms. "I'm being de-mobbed soon, and I'm putting something together. A combo. Five-piece. Trumpet, sax, trombone, piano, drums. I'm still looking for a sax. When I mentioned it to Schwartz, he told me about you," said Hal.

"Joshua would be perfect," said Adam.

"Are you offering me a job?" Joshua asked, refusing to let his friend's excitement take him over.

For the first time since he'd sat down, Hal cracked a smile. "I'm offering you an audition if you can hold out for two weeks."

Joshua thought about all the times he'd been here before. Did he really want to take a chance on a man who didn't even know him? He should be boarding a boat and heading for New York, where at least he had some contacts. Or Liverpool, where one of his old bandleaders might still be playing.

Still, he couldn't help but ask, "What's the plan?"

Hal nodded. "I have a relationship with a club in Soho. We'd be due to start a monthlong stand at the end of July. Rehearsals will be for three weeks before that to make sure the chemistry is right, go through some arrangements. That sort of thing.

"We'll use the club to test out some material and then"—Hal's eyes sparkled—"we're heading into the studio."

That caught Joshua's attention. He'd been in a recording studio for session work before, but during those jobs he'd been one of more than a dozen guys. At the end of the session, the band's manager or a record company man would pay him and send him on his merry way. A combo, however, would be something else entirely. With only five instruments featured, he'd stand out. He'd be able to play on solos. His name would be right there on the liner notes. There would be nowhere to hide.

This is what he'd always wanted. This was the step he'd never been able to take in New York.

He took a deep breath. "Tell me where to be and when, and I'll see you then."

Viv

June 30, 1945

On a rare Saturday off from the delivery office, Viv sat reading a novel on the sofa when a knock came on the door separating her flat from Mrs. Shannon's ground-floor rooms.

"Mrs. Levinson, someone's on the telephone for you!" called Mrs. Shannon.

"Thank you, Mrs. Shannon!"

Viv put her book aside and slid her legs out from underneath her. She toed on her slippers. They were starting to show their age, but with the clothing ration in place she needed them to last until the end of the year at least.

She made her way down the squeaking wood stairs. She enjoyed her landlady's company, but Viv still valued her privacy. It was a luxury she hadn't anticipated when she moved out of her parents' home, and she could hardly imagine going back.

In the corridor, she picked up the telephone receiver. "Mrs. Levinson speaking."

"Vivie."

She smiled. "Kate. I would have thought you'd still be up to your elbows in suds at this time of the morning."

Her sister laughed. "I have Will and Colin doing the dishes, if you'd believe it."

"A fifteen-year-old boy and a fourteen year old boy in charge of things that might break? You're braver than I thought," Viv said.

"We'll see if I regret it later," said Kate.

"Give them all my love. Cora too," Viv said.

"You could come around Sunday for family lunch," said Kate, the hope unmistakable in her voice.

"Will Mum and Dad be there?"

Kate sighed. "You know they will, Vivie."

"I'm sorry, Kate. I just can't."

Viv had hardly seen her parents since that horrible day her mother had come to Wavertree. The few times that she'd been forced to be around her parents—usually engineered by Kate, who despite her understanding still seemed desperate for familial harmony—Mum had ignored Viv entirely. Dad had simply stared glassy-eyed into space, not that that was a great change for him.

It all suited her just fine. She'd never forgiven her mother for dismissing Maggie's death as the will of God, and neither of her parents had ever forgiven her for turning her back on the Church. They were at an impasse, and neither party seemed inclined to give way.

"I know, but I have to ask. Have you seen the paper this morning?" asked Kate.

"No."

"Father Monaghan died," said Kate.

"I'm sorry to hear that," said Viv carefully, knowing how important the priest was to her sister.

"There was an obituary this morning. Listen to this." She heard the crackle of newspaper on the other end of the phone, and Kate began to read.

"'Father Brian Monaghan of Our Lady of Angels died of a stroke Tuesday at the age of sixty-four.

"'Born in Manchester and educated at Oscott College, Father Monaghan was a long-serving priest and pillar of the Walton community. Many there will remember him for his compassion and his caring for his parishioners.

"'Visitations, which began yesterday, will continue today, with funeral services to be held on Monday, the second of July at ten o'clock.'"

"Mum must be devastated," said Viv, trying her best to be charitable.

"Yes," said Kate cautiously, drawing out the word. "But that isn't why I called. I'm going to the funeral on Monday. I think you should come with me."

Viv nearly dropped the phone. "Are you joking?"

"I think you should go. You need to say goodbye," said Kate.

"Why would I want to say goodbye to that man? He helped convince me to send my daughter away to her death."

"Because if you still blame Father Monaghan, you still blame yourself."

That stole her words from her.

"It's time to let go, Vivie," said Kate, her voice soft.

"Are you telling me to move on?"

"No, you'll never forget Maggie. But you need to start living again," said Kate.

"I am living. I have my own flat. I work. I have friends," she said.

"You're not happy, Vivie." Kate took a deep breath that sounded like she was steeling herself. "And I don't think it's just Maggie. You haven't been truly happy since before your wedding."

The precision of her sister's words sliced straight to her heart. She'd lived for her daughter, loving her with an intensity that Viv hadn't even known was possible, but since she'd found out she was pregnant all the carefree fun had evaporated from her life. She'd been surviving, not living, until that was all she knew how to do.

"I barely hear you laugh except when you're with my kids," pressed Kate. "You go to work and you go home, but you hardly do anything else. It's like you're sleepwalking."

"There's been a war on—"

"And now that war is over. There's no more excuses," said Kate.

"You think that going to Father Monaghan's funeral will help?" she asked skeptically.

"I think it can't hurt." When Viv didn't say anything, Kate added, "At least come with me to the visitation today. Say goodbye and close that chapter of your life."

Viv pinched the bridge of her nose hard. She didn't want to go. She didn't want anything to do with that man or her old life back in Walton, but she was also tired. So very tired.

"Maggie will always be yours, Vivie. Nothing will ever change that."

"All right. I'll go to the visitation, but you have to promise me that if I decide that it's too much we can leave. And I am not going to pray for that man's soul." She hadn't prayed in years, and she certainly wasn't going to start again for Father Monaghan.

"If all you feel up to is walking up to the church door, that's enough," said Kate.

"If you promise . . ."

"I promise, Vivie. I promise."

Viv tugged at the cuff of her plain black cotton glove and looked up at the imposing facade of the church where she'd spent every Sunday morning growing up. Even through war, Our Lady of Angels hadn't changed one bit. Just down the road was a void where three terraced houses had once stood, destroyed in a second by a bomb. Hospitals, shops, schools—even a prison—had all fallen victim to the Luftwaffe's air raids. Sometimes it felt as though half the city was gone, but Our Lady of Angels endured. The thought disconcerted her.

A few parishioners dressed in black mingled around outside, and Viv scanned the faces for anyone she knew. Anyone who would judge her for being there.

"It's going to be okay," said Kate laying a hand on her arm.

"I don't know if this is such a good idea," she whispered.

"You'll be fine," said Kate, giving her a small smile as she adjusted her black hat. "It's just a church."

She didn't say anything as she fussed with the slim skirt of her black dress. She felt like a fraud, dressed up as a mourner to a man whom she'd in turn respected, feared, and then resented.

"We'll just go in, pay our respects, and then leave. That's all," Kate promised.

Viv swallowed. "Let's get this over with."

Kate held out her hand, and the sisters walked in together.

A low, soft organ piece filled the nave, mixing with the sniffling of a few women clutching handkerchiefs. In front of the soaring altar sat a coffin on a platform skirted with white satin. White lilies spilled out of huge vases on either side of the altar. There was a queue of people waiting to pay their respects down the left aisle of the church, and still others sat in the polished wooden pews. To their right, Viv could see people bend their heads as they signed the book of condolences.

"I'm going to join the queue," Kate said.

Vivian's eyes flicked back to the coffin. Kate began to walk toward it, but she stayed rooted in the spot. She couldn't make her feet move forward. She couldn't pretend.

Kate glanced back and then hurried to her side.

"I'm sorry, I can't," she said in a loud whisper, drawing the attention of a woman at the back of the queue.

Kate squeezed her hand. "Why don't you take a seat? I'll just be a moment."

She watched her sister take her place in the queue. The woman who had been watching them looked Kate up and down and then glanced back at Vivian. Kate scowled, and the woman jerked her head around to look forward again as the queue inched forward.

Viv slid into one of the pews, remembering too well how she'd once found comfort in this light-filled space. She remembered the way that the white columns separating the aisle from the nave glowed at night during Christmas and Easter services, and if she closed her eyes she could still recite from memory the scenes and saints from the stained glass windows that lined the walls. She'd been to weddings, funerals, and christenings here. It had been the center of her family's life, the center of her neighborhood, and the day her daughter had died she'd turned her back on all of it.

As she gazed around the church, however, she began to realize that perhaps her decision to leave hadn't been that abrupt. Her devotion had never been in question until she'd fallen pregnant, but then the wedge of shame had been driven between herself and her faith. Her pregnancy had branded her a sinner in a way that her quick marriage couldn't completely absolve her of, and in her heart of hearts, even she had believed that she'd been somehow tainted. Then Maggie had been born—beautiful, sweet Maggie who had changed everything.

Her daughter had been a darling child, charming and vivacious. Watching her had felt like witnessing a miracle every day. It was in those early moments that Viv had come to understand that a child was a blessing and not a sin.

That was the first fissure between her and the Church, but the cracks broke open and split into chasms when the bomb fell on Beam Cottage and claimed her child's life. On that day, Viv's faith had shattered into a thousand unrepairable pieces.

Suddenly, sitting in the church felt wrong. She cleared her throat and stood, sidestepping down the pew to the right aisle. She would sign the book of condolences for her sister and then wait for her outside.

Viv plucked the fountain pen that stood on a wooden stand at the top of the book and quickly jotted down Kate's name. She would not leave her own. No one needed to know she'd come.

Later, when she thought about it, she wouldn't be able to explain why she decided to thumb through the pages rather than leave. Perhaps she needed a distraction. Maybe she wanted to make sure she didn't draw attention to herself by leaving too swiftly. Whatever the reason, Viv flicked back a few pages in the book.

Most people had left only a name, but some had written messages expressing how the loss of Father Monaghan had touched them. She skimmed through them, paging back absentmindedly. Then she stopped, her eyes going wide. In the middle of one of the pages, there was an entry:

Mr. and Mrs. Matthew Thompson and Miss Margaret Thompson

Viv stumbled back, bumping into a small woman with wiry gray hair and stooped shoulders.

"I—I'm very sorry," she managed.

"That's all right, dear. Visitations are difficult," said the woman, her accent still holding the faint hint of Ireland shared by so many in Liverpool. "Did you know Father Monaghan well?"

"He was my parish priest when I was a girl," she said automatically, her brain still whirring. It could be another Margaret Thompson. The name was not that unusual. But paired with a Mr. and Mrs. Matthew Thompson?

But that was mad. The Thompsons died in a bombing. She'd seen the wreckage herself. No one could have survived what happened to Beam Cottage. She knew that to be true.

But what if it wasn't?

"Are you unwell, dear?" asked the older woman.

"Have you been here long?" Viv asked.

The woman looked alarmed at the urgency in Viv's voice. "All morning and the viewing yesterday evening, and I should. I was Father Monaghan's housekeeper of five years. Mrs. O'Leary."

"Do you know many of the people who have come to pay their respects?"

"Most of them. I wasn't in service as long as Mrs. Summers, who worked for Father Monaghan and the other priests before me, but I took an interest in their parishioners," said Mrs. O'Leary.

"Do you remember a Mr. and Mrs. Matthew Thompson?" she asked.

"Oh, of course. Mrs. Thompson is Father Monaghan's sister."

His sister? He'd sent Maggie off to his sister?

"He never spoke of her," she said, reeling.

"Father Monaghan was a very private man," said Mrs. O'Leary primly.

Viv grasped the other woman's arm. "Do you know where the Thompsons live?"

Mrs. O'Leary gave a start. "No. That is, I don't recall."

Viv forced herself to unclench her hand, and Mrs. O'Leary pulled back.

"Please," begged Viv. "Can you remember anything else about the Thompsons? Anything at all?"

She could tell that the housekeeper didn't entirely trust her, but the way the other woman leaned in told Viv that Mrs. O'Leary thought there was gossip to be shared.

"They came yesterday evening. I was saying hello to the people I recognized. When I realized who they were, I invited them back to the rectory for tea. I don't think the other priests would have minded, but the Thompsons said no. They weren't staying for the funeral, you see. What sister doesn't stay for her own brother's funeral, that's what I want to know," said Mrs. O'Leary with a raised brow.

Viv's heart sank.

"Was there a girl with them? She would have been about ten?" Viv asked, desperate for the answer to be yes but not knowing if she could manage it if it was.

"Oh, yes, Miss Thompson. A very pretty girl, very cheerful. It's funny, you would never have guessed she was their daughter," said Mrs. O'Leary.

"Why do you say that?" Vivian choked out.

"Well, she has such dark hair, and they are both as fair as they come," said Mrs. O'Leary.

"Vivie?"

She turned and saw Kate standing a few steps away. Viv pressed a hand to her stomach, unsure if she was going to scream or be sick.

"I'm sorry. I . . . Thank you," Viv hurried to say before catching Kate by the arm and dragging her out of the church.

"Vivie, what are you doing?" Kate asked in a loud whisper.

"We need to leave."

"Why?"

"I'll tell you outside," she said.

As soon as they pushed through the doors and into the bright light of the summer day, Kate planted her feet, stopping Viv abruptly.

"What on God's green earth is the matter? I know you didn't like the man, but that doesn't mean—"

"I think Maggie is alive," she said, cutting her sister short.

Kate's jaw fell open. "What?"

"There were three names in the book of condolences: Mr. and Mrs. Matthew Thompson and Miss Margaret Thompson."

Kate's brows popped, but then she shook her head. "That doesn't mean—"

"Mrs. Thompson was Father Monaghan's sister. That woman I was speaking to was—"

"The rectory's housekeeper, Mrs. O'Leary. I know. I've seen her at services before. And she told you that Sarah Thompson was Father Monaghan's sister?" asked Kate.

"Well, she didn't say her first name was Sarah, but it's too much of a coincidence not to be her."

Kate planted her hands on her hips and looked to the sky as though deciding how to say whatever it was she had to say next. Finally, she said, "You said you went to the house. You told me what the bomb did to it. The idea that anyone might have been inside and survived . . ."

"But what if they did? What if, after the bombing, they left Beam Cottage behind and took Maggie with them?" she asked in a rush.

"And didn't tell anyone?" asked Kate skeptically.

"Mrs. Thompson was always overstepping her place. She wanted to buy Maggie all new things. She wanted to enroll her in school. Maggie was even beginning to sound like them."

Kate began to shake her head.

Viv clenched her hands into fists. "I'm telling you, Kate, it's Maggie. Don't ask me why, but I can feel it. She's still alive."

And Viv needed to find her. She needed to bring her girl home.

"If she's still alive, then where is she?" asked Kate.

"I . . . I don't know. Mrs. O'Leary said the Thompsons showed up yesterday but left. They weren't going to stay for the funeral. They're gone."

It was so cruel. After nearly five years of believing her daughter was dead, now she had a spark of hope with nothing to go on. No address. No information. She didn't even know if the Thompsons still lived in the same county.

She felt her sister wrap her arms around her. "Oh, Vivie. What are you going to do?"

Viv planted her chin on her sister's shoulder, her eyes looking up at the church looming over them.

"I'm going to find my daughter."

Joshua

July 7, 1945

Joshua tried to ignore the thin film of sweat that made his hand slippery on the handle of his sax case as he approached the studio door. He shouldn't have been nervous. He'd gone on dozens of auditions before the war. He knew he was good, and the fact that he had the chops to have played in clubs across New York City had to count in his favor. However, it had been nearly six years since he'd played for an audience that wasn't made up of his fellow fliers. Nearly six years since he'd made his living with his sax.

Swallowing down his nerves, he pushed open the studio door. Hal sat with a reedy man whose face was pocked with old acne scars. The stranger half perched on a stool, a pair of drumsticks hanging from his long arms as though they were an extension of his body.

"Joshua, good to see you," said Hal, standing up to extend a hand and greet him. "This is Artie Worth."

Joshua shook hands with Artie and looked around the studio. "This is a nice setup."

Hal followed his gaze, as though just seeing it for the first time. "Artie here has good connections."

"I worked as a sound engineer before the war. Played drums on the side," said Artie by way of explanation.

"And you're part of the combo?" Joshua asked.

Hal clapped a hand on Artie's shoulder. "Artie stood in on drums in the Squadronaires for a few months when our regular was ill. We played together in Soho—what? Eight years ago?"

"Nine," said Artie.

Joshua nodded, warming to the idea that Artie had been a fill-in like him.

"Artie's helping me with some of the auditions," said Hal. "Speaking of which, are you ready?"

Joshua nodded curtly.

"Set yourself up, and then let's hear how you can play," said Hal.

Moving methodically, Joshua set his case on a nearby table and clicked open the clasps. He carefully put together the tenor sax, the rhythm of a familiar task reassuring. When finally he was ready, he turned to Hal.

"Go ahead," said the bandleader.

Joshua closed his eyes, breathed deep, and then launched into the opening bars of "Oh, Lady Be Good." He'd always loved the progression of the Gershwin song, and its upbeat bop. He'd played it at Kelly's Stables with Coleman Hawkins's band often enough that, for a short time, it had become something of a signature. However, he hadn't landed a permanent gig with the band, so he'd taken his talents elsewhere just as he'd always done.

This time, however, it felt different. He didn't have a backing band. There were no drums or upright bass to create the spine of the song or comping piano to play off of. It was just him, playing in a studio to two fellow musicians.

When he finished, the last note drifting off, Hal gave him a nod. "Very good."

Joshua lowered his sax, watching as Hal and Artie rose. Hal took a seat in front of the studio's grand piano, and Artie settled down behind the drums. Artie counted off, and suddenly he and Hal were playing.

It was a simple tune—a twelve-bar blues similar to the "St. Louis Blues"—but Joshua hadn't heard it before. He sat back, listening to the beat of the first few bars. Then he lifted his sax to his lips and, with a nod from Hal, began to improvise.

It felt like the old days back in Sonny Fowler's apartment in the Lower

East Side. A bunch of musicians, all getting together to jam, show up, and show off. Those late-night sessions surrounded by half-drunk glasses of bourbon, the air heavy with cigarette smoke, had always felt different from playing with a big band in a club. This was music for musicians, not an audience half listening as they crowded a dance floor, and he loved it in a different way than his paying gigs.

When the song ended, Artie caught the hi-hat and Hal sat, his hands hovering just over the piano. Joshua waited, the last resonant note stretching out to an eternity.

Then Hal smiled.

"If I'd known you could play like that, Levinson, I wouldn't have made you audition," said Hal.

Something like happiness cracked open in Joshua's chest. "I could have told you if you'd asked. You're not too bad on the piano yourself, by the way."

"She was my first love, but the trumpet is my mistress," said Hal with a grin.

"Good playing," said Artie, coming around the drum set.

"Thank you," he said.

"Look, I won't waste your time anymore. We're starting rehearsals tomorrow. It'll be a mix of original compositions and standards you've played before. We're still on track to start the club stand. It looks like September we'll be in the studio," said Hal.

"Are you offering me a job?" he asked,

Hal and Archie exchanged a look, and then Hal said, "If you want the gig, it's yours."

Viv

Viv tapped her short-cut nails on the telephone box's painted wood shelf as the line rang through. Nerves skittered down her back, and she had to remind herself to breathe. She'd spent hours in this telephone box, using every moment she wasn't at work—and nearly all of her spare money—trying to find her daughter.

When the line connected, she straightened.

"Hello?" asked the voice on the other end of the phone. It was a woman, elderly by the sound of it.

"Hello, I'd like to speak to Margaret Thompson," she said.

"This is Mrs. Thompson," said the woman.

Viv's heart sank, but still she recited the speech she'd repeated so many times over the last two weeks.

"Good afternoon. I'm trying to find a Margaret Thompson who was born in Liverpool in 1935."

The woman chuckled. "That wouldn't be me, dear. I was born in Surrey in 1867."

"Thank you for your time."

Viv hung up and then picked up her pencil to cross the woman's name off the long list of names and telephone exchanges she'd already tried. She leaned her head on the cool metal of the telephone receiver.

This was impossible.

As soon as she and her sister had left the visitation for Father Monaghan, Viv had tried to file a missing person's report with the police, but they had looked at her with skepticism when she'd barely been able to give them any information about the Thompsons. Frustrated, her next stop had been the library, where she'd requested every telephone directory they had on hand. She'd written down each instance of the name "Thompson." After she'd called all of those names and found nothing, she'd gone to the Liverpool Central Library to expand her search. Now she was beginning to run out of Margaret, Matthew, and Sarah Thompsons.

Perhaps if she wrote to rectories, or maybe the archdiocese . . .

With a sigh, she pushed open the door of the telephone box and made for Mrs. Shannon's. This should be easy. The Thompsons had come to Our Lady of Angels and signed the book of condolences under their own name. It wasn't the act of people who were hiding, so where were they? Where had they taken her daughter, and how had they disappeared without a word?

Why? was the one question Viv didn't wonder about because the answer was plain to see. The Thompsons didn't have a child but wanted one. Mrs. Thompson treated Maggie like a doll, dressing her up and bringing Maggie around to visit all of her village friends. Viv should have seen it in every little way that Mrs. Thompson undermined her, insisting on calling Maggie Margaret, teaching her daughter to read, making decisions about school without asking Viv first. They were all warning signs that Viv wished she'd seen earlier.

As she rounded the corner to Mrs. Shannon's, however, all of her suspicions faded. Standing at the front door, speaking to her landlady, was her sister-in-law.

"Rebecca!" she shouted, breaking into a run. Her handbag slapped against her hip as it flapped in the wind, and she was certain her curls were flying everywhere, but she didn't care. Rebecca was home.

A huge smile broke out across her sister-in-law's face, and Rebecca dropped the canvas bag she was holding to give Viv a crushing hug.

"It's so good to see you. I didn't know you were back," said Viv.

Rebecca gave her another squeeze and then stepped back, stooping a little to haul her bag back up on her shoulder. "I was only just demobbed and sent home."

"Miss Levinson was just telling me that she was a radar plotter in the WRNS," said Mrs. Shannon, sounding suitably impressed.

"I spent the last four years in a windowless room," said Rebecca with a laugh.

Viv's sister-in-law had joined the WRNS as soon as conscription was announced for women in December 1940. Her reasoning had been that she should choose her service before it was chosen for her, but that hadn't made it any easier to see her go. Viv, who had been exempt because of her work as a postie, had worried about her the entire time, waiting for letters and rare visits home when Rebecca had enough leave to string together a few days in a row. Now seeing her back home and safe felt like a blessing.

"Well, I'll leave you two alone. I'm sure you have many things to talk about," said Mrs. Shannon.

"Thank you," Viv said to her landlady. Then she gestured to Rebecca. "Follow me."

They climbed the stairs, Viv stopped just in the doorway to set down her keys, handbag, and her clutch of papers containing all the Thompsons she could find. Rebecca followed her, looking around as she went.

"It hasn't changed much since I was here last," said Rebecca.

"I don't know if you've heard, but there was a war on," said Viv with a small laugh.

Her sister-in-law gave her a gentle shove. "I like that it hasn't changed. It feels familiar."

"I'll just make some tea," said Viv, doing the automatic calculation of how much was left in her ration.

"Let me help," said Rebecca.

Viv nodded, and they squeezed into the little kitchenette that Mrs. Shannon's sons-in-law had created out of a small back bedroom. It wasn't much, but there was enough room for a sink, two cabinets, a hob, and an oven. A tiny pine table with two chairs fit perfectly in one corner.

"I didn't realize you were coming home," Viv said as she pulled down the tea and mugs.

"I didn't tell anyone because it was pushed back once and I worried it might be pushed again," Rebecca explained, taking a seat at the table.

"You've seen your parents, then?" she asked.

"That's why I'm here." Rebecca reached down next to her and set the canvas bag on the table. "As soon as lunch was over, Mum marched me out of the house with this."

"What is it?" Viv asked, setting the kettle on the little hob to boil.

"Food."

She frowned. "Food?"

"Mum said they haven't seen you in a couple of weeks, and she's worried you aren't eating," said Rebecca, arching a brow. "She also gave me express instructions that you're to come over tomorrow evening. She won't accept no for an answer."

"That's very kind of her, but she shouldn't have done that. This is coming out of your parents' rations," she murmured.

"They're worried about you. Both of them. What's going on, Viv?"

She stared at her friend, seeing the worry etching lines on either side of Rebecca's mouth. They had fallen into an unexpected friendship, two women brought together by tragedy. She owed Rebecca the truth.

"I think Maggie might be alive."

Rebecca's hand flew to her mouth. "What? How?"

She quickly explained her discovery at Father Monaghan's visitation. "The names were right there, Rebecca. Plain as day."

Her sister-in-law chewed on her lip. "It could be another family."

"It must be them," she said, knowing how desperate she must sound but not caring. "The housekeeper described her. I *know* it's her."

Rebecca was quiet for a moment, staring at the linoleum kitchen floor. Then she lifted her head. "If you think that that girl is Maggie, you need to find her. Mum and Dad never met her. If she's still alive . . ."

"Except for work, all I've done these last two weeks is try to find Maggie. I've called every Thompson I could find. I reported her disappearance to the police. I don't know what else to do," she said, letting her frustration bubble over.

Rebecca fixed Viv with a look. "You need to tell Joshua."

She jerked back, nearly rapping her head on one of the kitchen cabinets. "No."

"He has a right to know."

"Since when did you start defending your brother?" she asked.

"I'm not defending him, but Maggie is his too."

"He never showed an interest in her," Viv said stubbornly.

"Don't forget that you were pretty clear that you didn't want anything to do with him if he left for America." Rebecca held her hands up. "I'm not excusing it. I'm stating a fact."

Viv pursed her lips. Her friend was right, but she'd managed to keep Joshua at an arm's length for years. She wasn't ready to invite him into her hope any more than her grief.

"I can't, Rebecca. I don't even know if I'm right yet."

"But you think you are?" asked Rebecca.

Viv nodded.

"Then tell him."

"No."

"What if I tell him? Or my parents? That way you don't have to speak to him," said Rebecca.

Viv hesitated but shook her head. "No, Rebecca. I don't want to hurt them. Just give me a little bit more time."

She would find more numbers to telephone. She would find Maggie.

She watched Rebecca stand and reach into a cabinet to pull down a pair of plates. Her friend opened up the canvas bag she'd brought with her and began pulling out paper boxes of food wrapped in waxed paper. The kitchen filled with the scent of Anne Levinson's cooking. It was like a hug, and it made Viv miss her in-laws even more.

"Here," said Rebecca, holding out a plate.

"You still know your way around the kitchen," said Viv.

"Like I said, some things don't change. But, Viv? I hope more than anything that they will. Find Maggie. Do whatever it takes."

Viv nodded. If there was any chance that her daughter was alive, she would find her. Somehow. Someway.

Joshua

Joshua pushed open the door to his flat, raindrops sliding off his RAF-issued raincoat and onto the floor. He'd left the studio where the Hal Greene Quintet had been rehearsing for what felt like hours and, not wanting to spend money he didn't have yet, took the bus back to Stretham. However, on his walk from his stop to his front door, the heavens had opened and drenched him in a way that felt almost personal.

He set down his sax and hung his raincoat on the door before peeling off his sodden suit, shirt, and socks. Then he went to grab the towel he kept folded neatly on a small chest of drawers. He thought about taking a bath to chase away the distinctly British chill that accompanied rain even in the summer, but the bathroom was down the hall, and he didn't feel like encountering any of the other people who lived in the building.

He toweled off and went to the kitchen, considering the contents of his mostly empty larder. He could blame it on lingering rationing, but the truth was that he was hardly at home, so it didn't make sense to keep much in. Even before rehearsals for the band had started three days ago, he spent most of his time walking the city, simultaneously awestruck by the beauty of London and pained by the devastation that the Blitz and other bombings had done to it. London, like so much of Britain, had been ripped apart by war, and sometimes it was hard to remember that they had won.

A knock on the door pulled him out of his contemplation.

"Who is it?" he called.

"Telephone for you," came his landlord's gruff voice.

Joshua hurried over to his chest of drawers and yanked on a clean shirt and pair of trousers. Then he grabbed his key and clattered downstairs to the telephone, which stood just outside his landlord's flat door.

"Hello?" he asked into the receiver.

"Are you sitting down?"

He grinned. "Rebecca. Are you home?"

"I arrived today," came his sister's curt reply. "Are you sitting down?"

"Sitting down? There's nowhere to sit here," he said, looking around at the sparse entryway. "What's the matter?"

"I saw Viv today," Rebecca said. "She thinks that Maggie might be alive."

Joshua dropped the phone, the mouthpiece of the receiver knocking him painfully across the thighbone before clattering to the carpeted floor.

"Joshua? Joshua?" he heard his sister's tinny voice say on the other end of the line.

He scrambled to scoop the receiver up. "What do you mean Maggie might be alive?"

Quickly, Rebecca told him a story about a dead priest, a signature, a housekeeper. It all washed over him. He could hardly process what he was hearing because one thing kept running through his mind.

My daughter might be alive.

"Viv is driving herself crazy trying to find Maggie," said Rebecca, pulling him out of his fog. "She's calling everyone she can think of who might know anything, but she isn't getting anywhere. I thought . . ."

"Moss," he said, knowing immediately what his sister was getting at.

"He can help, and he owes you." The tightness in his sister's voice told him that she still hadn't forgiven the pilot for how he'd treated Joshua when they'd first flown together.

"I don't know about that," he said, passing a hand over the back of his neck.

"You saved his life," said Rebecca.

He was silent for a moment.

"Do you want to meet your daughter or not?" asked Rebecca.

"It might not be her. That's what Viv said, right?"

Even as he asked the question, he knew that it had to be her. He had to have a second chance. To meet his daughter.

There are some events in every man's life which demarcate a before and after. For him, it was before he learned that he had a daughter and after. Before Maggie, it had been easier to push away the memory of what he'd left behind in Liverpool, his guilt taking on a hazy quality. However, after Rebecca's letter telling him about her, he hadn't been able to ignore the truth any longer. He'd walked away from a child—an innocent who hadn't done anything wrong. The thought had haunted him throughout those first months of knowledge and then, before he could meet her, she had been stolen from him.

Now perhaps he could. If she was alive. If they could find her.

"Viv is convinced that Maggie is alive. This is your opportunity to find out. To do something," said Rebecca.

To do the right thing *and* change his life After Maggie.

"I'll need to know everything she's managed to find out so far," he said.

"You need to talk to her."

"She won't take a call from me. You know that."

"Then come here. She'll hate me for this, but she's coming for tea tomorrow. If you show up when Mum and Dad are here, she'll at least listen to you," said Rebecca.

"Are you certain about that?"

"She won't want to upset Mum and Dad. They're too important to her. Convince her that you can help," said Rebecca, nearly pleading.

He glanced at his watch, a cheap thing he'd picked up in New York when he'd had a rare good month stringing together lessons and studio work. It was half past nine. The likelihood that he could make it back across the river and to the station in time for the last train seemed slim.

"I'll be on the first train to Liverpool tomorrow morning," he said automatically.

"You promise?" Rebecca asked.

He had rehearsals the next day, but surely Hal would understand if Joshua told him that his trip had to do with family.

He said goodbye to his sister and then hung up, immediately placing another call with the switchboard operator. After four rings, Hal Greene picked up.

"Hal, it's Joshua."

"What? You didn't get enough of me at rehearsal?" the bandleader chuckled.

"Something's happened—a family emergency—and I'm going to need to take a couple of days to go up to Liverpool," he said.

Hal paused. "Two days?"

Nerves fluttered in his stomach. "Yes."

"I understand family, Levinson, but I need you back for rehersals this weekend. There's a lot to work on before we start playing at the Hidden Room."

The nineteenth was the following Thursday, and it would be his first gig as a regular in a band—not just a band but a quintet. The stand at the Hidden Room was just the beginning. He wanted in on the recording session Hal had promised him so badly he'd started dreaming of it.

"I'll be back Friday," he promised. "If not Friday, then Saturday."

"All right," said Hal.

"I'll ring you as soon as I know more," he said.

Joshua rang off and tramped up the stairs. With his flat door closed behind him, he went to the kitchen and pulled out a bottle of whiskey, poured out a measure, and drank it down in one gulp.

Viv

===

July 12, 1945

Viv touched her hair for the fourth time on her journey over from Mrs. Shannon's. It was ridiculous to be nervous, but standing in front of her in-laws' door holding a basket of brown bread she felt as jumpy as she had the first time she'd delivered the post to them after learning that the little house on Salisbury Road was their home.

She knew that Rebecca was right. She needed to tell Seth and Anne that she thought there might be a chance Maggie had survived the bombing, but she dreaded what would happen if her theories were wrong. Every year at Maggie's yahrzeit she saw the pain so obvious in both Seth's and Anne's expressions. It was still as raw as the day they received word of the bombing. She couldn't give hope to and then break all over again the hearts of the couple who had welcomed her into their home as a daughter despite all of her own mistakes.

She straightened her shoulders. She could do this.

Viv took a moment to pull herself together and then knocked. She heard heavy footsteps on the other side of the door, and a moment later she found herself standing in front of her husband.

"What are you doing here?" she asked Joshua.

He looked just like he did the last time she saw him, at the shiva, except that this time he was out of his RAF blues and his wounds had healed so that she could hardly see where stitches had once marred his forehead. He pushed back the edges of his brown suit jacket and stuffed his hands into his pockets.

"Hi, Viv," he said.

Viv felt her body deflate. "Rebecca called you, didn't she?"

He gave a nod.

"Do your parents know?"

His mouth tightened, and she knew without him having to say that they did.

"Are they angry?" she whispered.

He shook his head. "No. No, nothing like that. They understand why you didn't say anything. You wanted to be certain."

Viv nodded, not sure of what else to say to this man.

"Don't be cross with Rebecca. Please. She's just trying to do the right thing by everyone," he said.

Viv sighed. "I'm not angry with her." She couldn't imagine being Rebecca, torn between her friend and her brother. Knowing that both had their share of blame to go around.

"Why don't you come in?" Joshua asked, stepping back to let her through.

Viv squeezed tight the handles of her basket, but she forced herself forward, past her husband. She caught the fresh, clean scent of his soap. It was strange realizing that he no longer smelled of the bay-and-bergamot scent she associated so strongly with him.

She found the remaining Levinsons in the front room. Rebecca immediately shot up from the armchair she sat in across from her parents.

"I'm sorry, Viv, but—"

"Is it true?" Anne asked, eyes lit with hope.

Viv clenched her basket even harder. This was exactly why she didn't want to tell the Levinsons until she knew something more.

"I know what I saw at the church, but I haven't been able to make any headway," she admitted.

"Joshua knows someone who might be able to help you find the Thompsons," said Rebecca.

"Joshua, tell her," Seth urged his son.

Viv turned to her husband, and Joshua shrugged. "I don't know if it will work, but there's a bloke I used to fly with in the RAF. He owes me a favor."

"What kind of a favor? And what kind of bloke?" she asked.

"He was injured early during the war and was put on desk duty. He was one of the first to be demobbed, and a couple of the guys I know said that he went back to his job as a civil servant. He's with the new Ministry of National Insurance in Newcastle," he said.

Her stomach flipped. "And you think that this man will be able to find the Thompsons?"

"I think that if anyone is going to be able to do it, he will," he said.

"Think about it, Viv," said Rebecca. "Everyone with a job has to pay into National Insurance. Didn't you say that Mr. Thompson was an engineer of some sort?"

"Yes," she said.

"There you are," said Seth. "If he's made payments, there will be a record."

"When could I speak to this man?" she asked.

"I think it's best if we go to Newcastle and ask in person," Joshua said.

Her brows shot up. "We?"

"This is a conversation that needs to be had face-to-face," he said.

"Why?" she asked.

Joshua hung his head. "Because when we flew together, he didn't know that I had a wife, let alone a daughter."

She felt the collective intake of breath from the rest of the Levinsons.

"Who was this man?" she asked.

"We served together. He was my pilot. There was a crash . . ."

"My dear, Joshua can help you find Maggie. Please let him," said Anne gently.

Ultimately, that was all it took to persuade her because, no matter what she felt about her estranged husband, Viv wanted her daughter more.

"All right," she said.

Joshua looked cautiously optimistic. "All right?"

"We'll talk to your friend together. When can we leave?"

"Whenever you like."

"Now," she said.

"Now?" he repeated.

"Is there a better time to try to find Maggie?" she asked.

"No, of course not," he said, looking a bit sheepish.

"I'll make you something for the train," said Anne, bustling off to the kitchen.

"Why don't I go home and help you pack?" asked Rebecca.

Viv almost protested that she didn't need help—she needed to be alone to think about what had just happened—but she could tell from the way that Rebecca was eyeing her cautiously, her friend was unsure about whether Viv really had forgiven her.

"Come on, then," she said, setting down her basket.

"I'll meet you at the station in an hour and a half," said Joshua.

Viv gave him a nod and walked out without another word.

Viv snapped the latches shut on her battered case that she used to use when she stayed with Kate as an unmarried woman. She'd had it with her the night that she and Joshua had gotten into trouble. The night that had changed everything.

"That's all, then?" asked Rebecca.

"Yes. Thank you for keeping me company," said Viv.

"I suppose you didn't really need help, did you?" asked her sister-in-law, peering around the sparse bedroom.

Viv gave her a little smile. "That's all right."

Rebecca nodded, her fingers making ridges in the quilt that covered the bed. "I really am sorry. I know you told me not to tell Joshua."

Viv sighed. "I wasn't trying to be cruel when I said I didn't want you to tell your family about Maggie."

Her friend shot her a look.

"Maybe I was more worried for your parents than I was for your brother," she admitted.

"He's not a bad man," Rebecca said.

"I know that he's your brother, and I know that you love him, but he promised me that he would stand by me and then left at the first opportunity that presented itself. I don't know how I can ever look past that," she said.

Rebecca grasped her hand. "I'm not asking you to look past it. I think you should always remember that. But people do change.

"He's different, Viv. I don't know how to describe it exactly, but he is."

"Look, I know he fought and that's admirable, but—"

"It isn't about the war. I think it started back in New York. He wasn't happy there. He never really talks about it, but I don't think life turned out for him like he thought it would," said Rebecca.

That would make two of them.

"I don't know what to say," Viv said, pulling out of Rebecca's grasp.

"You don't need to say anything. All I'm asking is that you give him another chance—not as a husband but as a person," said Rebecca.

What her friend was asking seemed impossible, but she kept her skepticism to herself. Instead, she picked up her case.

"I think it's time to go."

Viv spotted Joshua by a bank of telephone booths on one side of the station hall. The door of his booth was half-closed, no doubt to obscure the sound of the trains.

As she walked up, she heard him say, "I appreciate that. I promise I will be there as soon as I can."

She wondered who he was talking to—a girlfriend perhaps?—but shoved that thought aside. She wasn't interested in his life. She didn't need to know anything about him except what his friend could do to help her find Maggie.

Doubt began to creep into her mind as she breathed deep, taking in the musty smell of coal and cigarette smoke. Even if Joshua's friend managed to track down a Sarah and Matthew Thompson and their daughter, Margaret, it was possible that they were entirely different people, just like all the Thompsons she'd seen in the telephone directory. But the coincidence at the viewing was too convenient. They *must* be the same people she had been persuaded to hand her daughter to on the eve of the war.

The door of the telephone booth opened, and Viv turned to Joshua. He had a small case of his own. She wondered if he'd decided to go to Newcastle with or without her.

"Did you have any trouble making your way over here?" he asked.

"No," she said.

"Good. Good, good." He rocked back on his heels as though at a loss for what to say next. When she didn't help him, he added, "We should see if they're letting us on the train yet."

"Fine."

Joshua put a hand to the small of her back to guide her to the ticket barriers. She arched her back away so that his fingers didn't press her best suit to her skin.

They boarded the train, and Joshua found them seats. She wondered whether he'd bought first-class rather than third-class tickets to show off to her.

"Would you like me to put your case up?" he asked.

"Thank you," she said.

He lifted Viv's luggage onto the rack above them, and then followed with his own battered leather case.

"No saxophone?" she asked, knowing she sounded a little arch but not really caring.

He gave her a tight smile. "I left it in London."

"I always imagined you taking it with you everywhere," she said.

"That's actually why I was on the telephone when you walked in. I was telling my bandleader that I'll be away for a few days."

"Oh, I thought—" She stopped herself.

"Did you wonder who I was on the telephone to?" he asked.

Heat pricked at the back of her neck. "That's your business."

He studied her as though wondering whether to believe her. She nearly sighed with relief when he settled into the seat next to her.

"Is there anything else you need?" he asked. "Coffee? Cigarettes?"

"No, thank you," she said.

They sat in silence until the warning whistle sounded and all up and down the platform attendants began shutting compartment doors.

"When are we going to see your friend?" Viv asked.

"He was the first call I made at the station. He'll see us first thing tomorrow morning at his home," he said.

She nodded. "Thank you."

At the scream of the train's warning whistle, she tucked her chin on her gloved hand and peered out the window.

Joshua

They hardly spoke the entire train journey from Liverpool to New-castle. Viv spent most of the trip staring out the window, watching the countryside go by as night fell over Britain. Joshua watched Viv.

He'd been prepared for anger but not suspicion from her. Her resistance to the idea of him helping her had been palpable, and he wondered whether the only reason she'd stayed to listen to him was because she knew how much her walking out would hurt his parents.

Twice now she'd made it clear she didn't want anything to do with him. Once had been when he'd taken her parents' money and run. He shifted in his seat, uncomfortable with embarrassment, at the second: the shiva for Maggie.

He hadn't really been thinking when he'd rushed from the hospital to Liverpool. All he could remember was the unmistakable instinct driving him toward his family to share in their mourning. Then he'd seen Viv, and he'd stupidly thought that the shiva was the right time to try to ask for her forgiveness. She'd been angry at first—that he could have endured—but it was the way that anger had then melted into apathy.

"You asked if I hate you. I don't. The truth is, I don't feel anything for you—not a thing—and that is exactly what you deserve."

Her parting shot had struck him far deeper than she could have known, because she was right. He didn't deserve anything from her: no sympathy, no empathy. Nothing.

He'd left early the following morning, running away from his own childhood home because Viv had been right. He didn't have a right to her grief because he didn't know anything about his daughter. He had no memories of her. Nothing concrete. His daughter had been killed by the very same bombers he was fighting against on every ops, and he struggled to feel anything more profound than the sadness one conjures up when learning about the death of a stranger's child.

Even his parents and Rebecca knew more about Maggie than he did. He had become an outsider in this chapter of his family's history because he'd allowed it.

It was only then that he understood the full impact of the choices he'd made. The regrets he had. What he would do differently if he only had the chance.

And so he watched his wife stare out the window, completely closed off to him, knowing that even if she didn't speak to him the entire trip from Liverpool to Newcastle it would be worth it, because now he did have a chance and he wasn't going to let it go.

When finally the train pulled into Newcastle Central Station, it was dark enough that the city was lit up with the brilliant lights of thousands of houses freed from six years of government-mandated blackout. The train shuddered to a stop, and Viv began to collect her things.

"Right," said Joshua, pulling his hands onto his knees to push upright. "You go ahead, and I'll follow with the bags."

She gave a fractional nod.

They made their way down to the platform and then Viv stopped, looking a little uncertain.

"Moss recommended a hotel not too far from the station," he said, guessing that she was wondering what their next step should be.

"You're certain that he'll help us?" she asked.

"As certain as I can be about anything."

Viv looked at the thinning stream of passengers making their way to the end of the train platform. "About the hotel . . ."

"We'll ask for separate rooms, or you can pretend you've never met me before," he said.

The visible relief on her face almost made him wince. He knew he should have expected it—they'd never been together as man and wife in any real way, and he didn't expect her to want to share a bed with him after a decade apart—but he didn't like the idea that she found being near him repugnant.

"Come on," he said, gesturing to the platform end.

They wound their way out of the iron-and-glass structure and onto Neville Street. Despite the summer month, the breeze was cooling coming up the River Tyne from the North Sea. He saw Viv shiver in her thin-cloth suit jacket and he thought for a moment of offering her his. In the end, he didn't. He didn't want to scare her off any more than he wanted to suffer another flinch or wince.

At the hotel, he held open the door to the lobby and let Viv ahead of him to check in first. He hung back, holding his breath, hoping that the clerk who glanced curiously between the two of them wouldn't tell them that there were no vacancies or—worse—that there was only one room left. Instead, the man plucked the key to number twelve off the hanging board behind him and gave it to Viv.

Key in hand, she turned to him and reached for her case, which he'd carried for her from the station. "Thank you."

"You're welcome," he said, letting go and stepping back to give her the space she seemed to crave.

"I will meet you in the lobby at half past eight tomorrow morning," she said.

He nodded, waiting to see if she would say more. Instead, she lifted her case and slowly mounted the stairs to the upper floor.

"Sir?"

Joshua jerked, realizing that he had been left gazing after his wife.

"Can I help you?" asked the clerk.

"Yes. One room, please. Checkout tomorrow."

"The same as the lady?" asked the clerk, his brow slightly raised.

"Where do I sign the register?" he asked, ignoring the question.

"Right here, sir," said the clerk, turning the book for him.

He signed his name right below Viv's, two Levinsons in separate rooms.

Viv

July 13, 1945

Viv looked in the mirror that hung on the wall across from her hotel room door and touched her straw hat to adjust it slightly. She didn't know what one was supposed to wear when visiting a man who might be able to help them find whether their long-lost daughter was still alive, so she'd dressed in the navy summer suit she'd worn the day before, switching out her blouse for another simple cream shirt.

Her armor in place, she took one final check of her appearance and then descended the two flights of steps to the hotel lobby. Joshua was just where she'd left him the night before, except now he paced the short distance between two potted ferns, his hands shoved into the pockets of his brown suit and a frown etched onto his brow. She recognized the nervous energy pushing around him. It had been what prevented her from sleeping much and had her turning on the light at five that morning.

"Good morning," she said as she approached.

Joshua pulled his hands out of his pockets, looking a little sheepish for having been caught pacing. "Good morning. You look very nice."

The compliment threw her, leaving her uncertain what to say. This was uncharted territory for her.

Ultimately, Joshua saved her from having to speak by gesturing to the door. "Shall we be on our way?"

Newcastle had come alive in the morning light. The road in front of the hotel was already filled with delivery lorries, although the continuing petrol ration meant that there were fewer passenger cars than she would have expected to see before the war. People streamed around them, everyone simply going about their day. None of them knew how important this day was. That today she might find her daughter.

"Do you know where we're going?" she asked.

"I took a look at a map in the lobby while I was waiting for you," said Joshua.

"I could have been down earlier," she fired back, immediately stung by all the imagined implications of his response.

He gave a little sigh. "That wasn't meant to be an insult, Viv, I promise. And it wouldn't have mattered if we'd met earlier. Moss said nine."

Viv lifted her chin but let the argument die there. Fighting with Joshua wouldn't bring her any closer to Maggie any faster.

They walked a good fifteen minutes before Joshua had them take a right turn into a municipal building. They gave their names at the front desk, and the secretary there telephoned up to a higher floor.

After a moment, the woman smiled and said, "Second floor. Mr. Moss's secretary will meet you at the lift."

They crossed the lobby of the building and gave the floor to the lift attendant. Viv realized halfway through the ride that she was clutching her handbag to her stomach like a shield. She forced her arms down, trying to relax, but still she could feel her hands sweating in her gloves.

When they reached their floor, a woman in a light blue skirt and jacket paired with a plain white shirt greeted them. "Mr. Levinson?" the woman asked.

Joshua stepped forward. "Yes."

"Mr. Moss is waiting for you in his office. This way, please," said the secretary.

Halfway down a starkly lit corridor, a wooden door stood open and the woman led them inside.

"Mr. Levinson is here to see you, sir," said the secretary.

Mr. Moss, a ruddy-faced man with narrow shoulders, rose from behind the big wooden desk framed by tall windows looking out over the

Tyne Bridge. He looked curiously between the two of them and then stuck out his hand. "Levinson, come in, come in."

Joshua took Moss's extended hand. "Thank you for seeing us on such short notice."

"It's my pleasure. I was glad for your call," said Mr. Moss.

Viv cleared her throat, and Joshua started. "Moss, this is my wife. Vivian."

Mr. Moss almost managed to hide his surprise as he extended his hand to Viv. "Mrs. Levinson, how do you do? Please, do take a seat."

She took one of the leather armchairs that sat opposite Moss's desk.

"Now, Levinson's told me that you're looking for someone. Is that right?" asked Moss, folding his hands in front of him.

"Yes," said Viv, shooting a look at Joshua before continuing. "We're trying to find our daughter."

Mr. Moss coughed. "Your daughter?"

"Maggie—Margaret—was evacuated in 'thirty-nine from Liverpool," she said. "It was a private evacuation arranged through my church. She went to stay with a couple called the Thompsons in Wootton Green."

"Your church?" asked Mr. Moss, glancing at Joshua. "But I thought . . . ?"

"Viv isn't Jewish," Joshua explained.

"I see," said Mr. Moss, leaning back in his chair.

"In September 1940, I received a telegram. A German bomber let loose a load of bombs over Solihull and some of the surrounding villages on the way back from a failed mission. The Thompsons' house was destroyed. There was no one found in the Anderson shelter. Everyone believed the Thompsons were killed by the bomb and Maggie along with them. However, I have reason to believe that they may still be alive."

She told him everything about the funeral and what Mrs. O'Leary had told her. Her search and the frustration of trying to find a needle in a haystack of records and telephone directories. She knew that her voice became desperate, but she couldn't stop until it was all out there.

"I see," said Mr. Moss again. "And now you've come to me."

"If there is anything you can do to help . . ." Viv trailed off.

The man looked from Viv to Joshua and then nodded. "The war was chaotic, as you might expect, and many records were lost, but if this Mr. Thompson is paying his National Insurance, as he should be, we'll have record of him."

"What if he changed his name?" Viv asked, articulating a fear she'd been worrying about since she pulled her first telephone directory. What if all of those Thompsons amounted to nothing because there was no more Matthew Thompson?

"Well, that would prove to be more of a challenge. All one needs to do to change one's name is make a declaration and have it published in the *London Gazette,* as that's one of the government's papers of record. Going through the *Gazette* is an arduous process, and that's assuming that everything is on the up and up," said Mr. Moss.

Dread spread through her.

"And if they didn't do things on the up and up?" she asked.

There was a sparkle in Mr. Moss's eye. "They might get away with a casual name change for some time, but eventually everything comes back to this department. Everyone must have a National Insurance number. If you work, you must pay in. And if you change your name, you must inform the Ministry of National Insurance. So, you see, Mrs. Levinson, I'm fairly certain that I'll be able to help you."

It was what she had prayed for on the train ride over and most of the previous night. A lifeline that might lead her back to her daughter.

"Thank you," she breathed.

"Now," said Mr. Moss drawing a paper toward him and lifting the pen from its place on his desk set, "what is your daughter's full name?"

"Margaret Anne Levinson," she replied.

"And her birth date?" he asked.

"The twenty-first of July 1935," she said.

"And what about the two foster parents?" he asked.

"Matthew and Sarah Thompson. I don't know their birth dates."

"Do you have a guess as to how old they might be?" Mr. Moss asked.

"I'd say that Mr. Thompson is probably in his midfifties. His wife is probably about five years younger than him," she said.

"What did the Thompsons do for work?" Mr. Moss asked.

"Mr. Thompson was some sort of engineer," she said, recalling the brief conversations she'd had with the man. "Mrs. Thompson was at home."

Mr. Moss nodded as he wrote. "I will make a few phone calls and see if I can have this request expedited."

"How long do you think it will take?" Joshua asked.

"It could be a day; it could be a week," Mr. Moss said.

A week. She'd called Mr. Rowan to tell him that she wouldn't be in for her shift that morning. She'd been vague in mentioning a family emergency, but she knew that anything longer than a couple of days would require an explanation. She would telephone him again as soon as they returned to their hotel and beg for more time off. She doubted he would deny her request, but that still left her without as many shifts at the General Post Office as she normally would have.

She'd figure it out. Whether she dove into her savings or had to ask Kate and Sam to lend her a bit of money, finding Maggie was so much more important.

"We're staying at the hotel you suggested," said Joshua. "Rooms twelve and fourteen."

This time, Mr. Moss schooled his features fast enough to hide whatever his reaction was to a married couple taking two hotel rooms. "I'll be in touch as soon as I have any information."

Viv nodded a thank-you and started to stand, but Joshua gave a tight smile. "If you'll excuse me a moment."

Mr. Moss gave a discreet nod in the direction of the toilets.

As soon as Joshua was out of the room, the civil servant turned to Viv. "I hope that you won't think me out of turn for asking, Mrs. Levinson, but I flew with your husband during the war. Men who had wives back home usually spoke about them."

She looked down and realized she was fiddling with the clasp on her handbag. "We've been estranged for many years."

"I see," he said. "Then you probably don't know that your husband is the reason that I'm sitting in front of you today."

She looked up sharply. "What?"

"We were stationed together at RAF Linton-on-Ouse. Levinson's original pilot was grounded, so he was reassigned to my plane. We were shot at over France when on an operation, and we managed to limp back over the English Channel only to be forced to try to put her down with dodgy landing gear as soon as we were over English soil. The crash knocked me out on impact and, from what I understand, your husband dragged me to safety just before the entire thing exploded. He earned himself some shrapnel scars for his efforts."

That must have been why he had stitches when he'd appeared at the shiva. She was so wrapped up in her own grief, she'd hardly given them any thought at the time.

"I had no idea," she said.

"I've sometimes wondered why he did it. I was a different man then—a much angrier one. I said some terrible things to him and one of his friends when we were in training about them being Jewish. I didn't treat anyone particularly well then, but Levinson bore the brunt of it." He cleared his throat. "Anyway, I have many regrets in this life, and that is one of them."

"Have you asked for his forgiveness?" she asked.

"I did, right after it happened. I told him that if I can ever do anything to even begin to repay him for saving my life, I will happily do it. This is the first time he's ever asked me for anything.

"The way I see it, it isn't his responsibility to forgive me. It's my responsibility to try to atone and one day, if I'm very lucky, he may find it in his heart to accept that." Mr. Moss gave a laugh. "At least that is what my priest says."

Joshua walked back into the room, and Viv stood. "Thank you, Mr. Moss."

The man dipped his chin. "I hope you find your daughter, Mrs. Levinson. I will certainly do my bit here."

Joshua

Joshua and Viv walked back to their hotel in silence. He wanted to ask what she and Moss had spoken about while he was out of the room, but he sensed that this was not the time to push her. They were teetering on such thin ice, any little misstep could send them plunging into the depths once again.

"What will you do for the rest of the day?" he finally asked when they reached the front of the hotel.

"I don't know."

He nearly suggested that she spend the day exploring the city with him, but he stopped himself. It was too much too fast.

"When do you think Mr. Moss will call?" she asked.

He shrugged. "I don't know."

When she lifted her big brown eyes, he saw all the fear, worry, and desperation of a mother who was trying her very best to simply hold on.

"Moss will call the hotel as soon as he knows something," he tried to reassure her. "We won't miss him."

Joshua wouldn't let her down.

Not this time.

*   *   *

At six o'clock that evening, Joshua opened the door to his hotel room and went two rooms down the corridor to his wife's room. After saying good-bye to Viv that morning, he'd thought that he might go for a walk around the city but he couldn't seem to make himself walk away from the hotel. Instead, he went to his room and tried to read. He laid down at some point and tried to nap. He went down the hall and took a bath. Anything to make sure he would be near if Moss called.

Finally, after no word all day, he decided that he needed to eat. If he had to hazard a guess, he would say that Viv did too.

He lifted his hand and knocked on the door of room twelve. After a long moment, Viv answered it. She had changed into a pale green dress with white buttons down the front. It set off her light brown waves and rosy cheeks.

"Evening," he said. "You look lovely."

This time when he complimented her, she touched her hair and looked away but said, "Thank you."

He chose to consider that progress, a slight unfreezing of the glacier that stood between them.

"I thought you might like to find a bite to eat," he said.

The way she bit down on her lip told him that she was hungry, but still she shook her head. "I don't want to leave the hotel."

"The pub next door does food. I thought we might ask the front desk clerk to run over and let us know if Moss telephones," he said.

She hesitated again, and he thought she might say no, but instead she said, "Let me find my handbag."

He waited outside her door while she collected her things, and when she opened the door again, he offered her his arm. After a moment's consideration, she took it and allowed him to lead her down the stairs.

After a brief word to the hotel clerk, they settled into the lounge of the pub next door. They pulled out their ration books and ordered pies that were sure to be heavier on vegetables than meat, as well as a lager for Viv and a pint of ale for Joshua. Finally there was nothing left to do but talk.

"You're no longer living with your parents?" he asked.

"No. I took a flat a few years ago."

That must have cost her dearly—accommodations weren't cheap for a man starting out, and it would be even more difficult on a woman's diminished wages to put together the rent—but he could sense she was proud of what she'd done.

"You were a postie during the war, right?" he asked.

"I still am. Or at least I was when I left Liverpool. I'm not sure how long my boss will hold my job for me. Has Rebecca been talking about me?"

"Just the basic facts. You can trust her, you know," he said.

"I know that. Your sister has become a good friend," she said.

"Why didn't you want her to tell me about Maggie? Would it really have been so bad for me to know?" he asked.

"It was actually Anne and Seth I was more concerned for. I thought I could spare them a lot of pain if it turns out that I'm wrong and Maggie is . . . that Maggie isn't with us any longer," she said, her voice catching a little.

"You care for my parents very much, don't you?" he asked.

"They've been incredibly kind to me. I don't see my own much anymore," she said.

He remembered her mother and her father all too well. Mrs. Byrne was a strong-willed, stubborn woman who had stood at their wedding looking like she was walking straight to the gallows. Mr. Byrne had been the epitome of a weak man, hiding behind his wife's determination because no doubt it was easier than standing up to her.

Viv took a sip of her drink. "Rebecca said that you managed to make a go of it in New York before the war."

Heat crept up the back of his neck. "My sister's flattering me. She always was my biggest fan growing up."

"How so?"

"I arrived in New York and immediately realized that there were hundreds of talented musicians just like me who had the same idea. Too many men were all looking for the same spots. I bounced around, played a lot of different places with a lot of different people. I never found a permanent spot, and I ended up having to cobble together a living with lessons and spot work," he admitted.

She tilted her head a little. "But you still became a musician."

"Yes, but—"

"Not everyone becomes famous, do they?"

She said it so simply, almost as though it was obvious. Perhaps it should have been. He should have realized before he left for New York that he'd be walking into auditions with some of the best in the business. To stand out, he would have needed more than talent. He would have needed connections that a boy from thousands of miles away simply didn't have.

"Rebecca said you have a band you're playing with in London now," Viv said, pulling him back to the Newcastle pub and his pint of ale.

"A combo. It's a smaller group than the orchestras and bands I used to play with in Liverpool and New York. We have a gig at the end of the month, and then we'll be recording our first record. The music is something else. It's stripped down but warm. Nothing you'd hear in a ballroom—"

He cut himself off abruptly, realizing that he had been rambling. She didn't care about his music.

Viv took another sip of her drink. Finally, she said, "Mr. Moss mentioned that you didn't get along when you flew together."

"Did he?" he asked, surprised at his old pilot's candor.

"He also seems to feel that he owes you a debt," she said.

"He doesn't owe me anything," he said, tugging at his collar before realizing what he was doing and forcing his hand down.

"You saved his life," said Viv.

"I did what anyone would do," he said.

"After he was awful to you," she said.

Joshua looked away. "It wasn't anything I hadn't heard before."

"When was the last time you saw him?" she asked.

"In hospital after our crash."

"That was before the shiva?" she asked.

He cleared his throat. "Yes. Afterward, I was grounded on desk duty while I healed, but then I was up in the air again after three weeks. Moss never flew again."

He took a drink. The air was thick with unsaid things. With words that he needed to express before he lost his nerve.

"Being grounded gives a man a lot of time to think. Viv, I wanted to say—"

"Please don't," she said.

"You don't know what I'm about to say next."

"Whatever it is, if you're using that tone I'm certain I won't like it."

He swallowed. "I'm sorry. That's all I wanted to say. I know that isn't enough—I don't know if it ever will be—but I am.

"I was selfish. I was too focused on what I wanted, and I thought that taking your parents' money and going to New York was my only chance. I had to take it."

"You could have said no," she said, her voice brittle.

He dropped his gaze to his hands wrapped around his pint of ale. "And you could have come with me. I was serious about that."

She snorted. "No, you weren't."

"I was," he insisted.

She leaned forward across the table. "Are you really trying to tell me that you wanted to cart around a wife and a child? While you were trying to make it as a musician in a foreign country?"

"I could have done it," he insisted.

"But would you have *wanted* to? I wanted a husband, Joshua. Someone who would be by my side like my sister's husband is for her. That was never going to be us.

"We never should have been in that registry office in the first place. I never should have gone out with you the first time, let alone a second."

"So this is my fault?" he asked, his hackles rising.

She shook her head. "No, but I've spent a lot of years carrying the full weight of blame and the burden for what happened to us."

"I had burdens too," he protested.

"Like what?" she scoffed.

"My family—"

"Would have taken you back in a heartbeat if you'd simply asked. Did they make it difficult for you when you came back to England?" she asked.

"Rebecca wasn't exactly happy," he started to say, but then stopped himself. It sounded ridiculous when he said it out loud. No matter how he looked at it, his parents had welcomed him back into their home with hardly a stern word.

"They forgave you for everything. Even marrying me," she said with a shake of her head. "I know that a Catholic girl from Walton probably isn't what your mother hoped for in her heart of hearts, but she's never made me feel anything except welcome.

"I didn't have that from my family. I got pregnant, and even though we married, I lost friends. People I've known for years will still barely speak to me when I go back to Walton to visit Kate. I don't speak to my own parents any longer. So do not sit here and tell me that your burdens were the same as mine."

"I couldn't stay in Liverpool. I knew I had talent." He realized it sounded like he was begging now, but he didn't care. He needed her to understand—to absolve—just a little bit.

"No one is doubting that, Joshua, but was it worth it?" she asked.

He swallowed hard. This wasn't how he'd expected this meal to go. He felt as though his conscience was being raked over and left exposed for all to see.

"There is one thing that I will never regret, and that is having Maggie," Viv continued, steel in her eyes. "I can honestly thank you for that. But I've also had a lot of years to think, Joshua. You talk about being grounded giving you time to think? Going it alone meant that I had many nights to think as well. At some point, I realized that I don't need you any more than I want to forgive you."

"Viv . . ."

"Thank you for showing up to the wedding. Having your name has made some things easier. And thank you for Maggie. She is the best thing that has ever happened to me. But that is all I will thank you for.

"Once Mr. Moss calls, we go our separate ways. I raised my daughter on my own. I'll find her that way too."

Viv pushed back from the table, throwing her napkin down next to her seat. "I'm finished here. Don't bother checking at the front desk whether there are any messages. I'll do it myself."

Joshua sat back in his chair with a long sigh as his wife walked out of the pub lounge, leaving him behind just as he'd done to her all those years ago.

Viv

Back in her room, Viv couldn't settle.

She hated that a simple conversation with Joshua about the past could rile her up so badly. She wanted to believe that he couldn't affect her any longer. That he was solidly a part of her past that would shrink to the background again once all of this was over. Once she had her daughter back. However, the reality was proving to be much more complicated than that.

She shouldn't have asked if he regretted his decisions. Sitting there, waiting for him to say yes and hearing nothing but excuses about his talent and his dreams, hurt more than she'd known it would.

With a huff, Viv checked the time on the clock. It was just before ten. She glanced at the telephone on the bedside table. She wanted to speak to a familiar voice. Someone who knew her almost as well as she knew herself.

Her first thought went to Kate, but her sister was bound to be spending the last few minutes awake with Sam before he went in for his early delivery shift. That left only one other option.

Viv reached for the telephone and picked up the receiver.

"Yes, madam?" asked the front desk clerk.

"Switchboard, please," she said.

There was a brief pause and the line connected with the switchboard. "Number, please?" asked the operator.

"I'd like to place a call to Liverpool," she said, trying not to think about how much the call was going to cost her.

"Hold the line, please," said the operator.

There was a pause on the line, and then the operator for the Liverpool exchange repeated the question. Viv gave the exchange.

"Hold the line, please," the second operator droned.

The line connected on the fourth ring.

"Hello?"

"Rebecca, it's me," Viv said.

"Viv, is there any news? Is Joshua with you?"

"No, no news yet. Mr. Moss couldn't be sure when he would be able to find us details but he promised to try."

Rebecca sucked in a breath. "I'm sorry."

"We're just waiting at the hotel for word now. He's supposed to telephone as soon as he has anything."

"That must be costing you a fortune. Do you need money?" asked Rebecca.

She did a quick calculation of the money in her post office savings bank book. She could last the weekend if she only ate out one meal a day. After that, she wasn't certain what she would do. Mrs. Shannon would be understanding if Viv told her that she needed to pay the rent late, but she was already working six days a week. She didn't know how she would be able to find the extra money she was spending in Newcastle.

But none of that mattered, she realized, if this search returned Maggie to her.

"I'll be fine," she said with a confidence she didn't feel.

"Is Joshua with you?" Rebecca asked again.

"He has his own room. We had a bite to eat, but I left early."

"What did he do?" asked Rebecca in a tone that showed her friend fully expected her brother was in the wrong.

"He started talking about the past."

"Oh, is that all?" Rebecca's tone was distinctly sarcastic.

"I told him that I can't forgive him for our wedding day and everything that happened after," she said.

"That's your prerogative, Viv," said Rebecca after a short pause.

"It isn't just me," she stumbled to explain. "It's you and your parents—"

"That's very sweet of you to think of us, but my parents forgave him a long time ago," said Rebecca.

"And you?" she asked.

"My brother is a person. He made mistakes—catastrophic mistakes—but he's never pretended to be perfect. I know that he loves me, no matter what, and that is the most important thing."

Viv thought back to all of her own disagreements with Kate over the years. At the time, she hadn't been sure she could forgive Kate for not posting her letter to the Levinsons after Maggie's birth, but eventually that anger had faded. Her sister had made mistakes. She had forgiven her.

She could not extend the same grace to her husband.

"Now, none of this means I'm going to tell you that you should trust my brother until he earns your trust," said Rebecca. "Don't forgive him if you don't really mean it, Viv, because taking it back would be cruel."

"This must be difficult for you," Viv said quietly.

Rebecca laughed. "What? My best friend being the estranged wife of my brother? Not at all."

"Your best friend?" Viv asked, choking around a watery laugh.

"Don't cry on me."

"And to think that I once was just the girl who your brother got into trouble with," Viv said.

Rebecca chuckled. "Well, on your wedding day, I was sixteen, angry, and determined to hate you for my brother's sake, but look how things can change."

"All I had to do was deliver your post," she said.

"All you had to do was be nice to my mother. What good girl can't help but like someone who is nice to their mother?" asked Rebecca.

"Thank you," Viv whispered.

"I worry about you, Viv," said Rebecca with a sigh.

"Worry about me?"

"You and Joshua—"

"Nothing will happen. I can promise you that," Viv said with conviction.

"I only wondered. It's been so long . . ."

"No," Viv said with a shake of her head.

"Have you ever thought of a divorce?" asked Rebecca.

"I'm Catholic," Viv said.

"I know, I just thought with you not going to church anymore . . ."

No longer attending Sunday service was one thing, but divorce was something entirely different. Perhaps to her friend who wasn't Catholic it seemed strange, but Viv couldn't fully leave behind all the teachings that had shaped her from childhood.

"What about an annulment?" Rebecca asked.

"I wouldn't even know where to start," Viv admitted. Annulments were long, difficult processes—not that it really mattered. The Byrnes didn't have their marriages annulled.

"Don't you want to meet someone one day?" asked Rebecca.

"What I want is my daughter," she said.

"Then you'll find your daughter. I have no doubt about it," said Rebecca with all the conviction Viv, in her vulnerability, was finding it difficult to conjure up. "You are going to find her, Viv. I can feel it."

Viv finally drifted off around four o'clock in the morning only to be jerked awake by a horn blaring in the road. With limbs like lead, she forced herself out of bed and down the corridor to bathe. She pulled on her green-and-white dress again and combed through her hair. She didn't know what she was going to do with herself that day. She'd finished the novel she'd packed, and she should probably go to the WHSmith to buy another. However, she was beginning to feel the pinch of her impromptu trip and the wages she was losing.

She was just finishing her lipstick when there was a knock on the door. She capped the cosmetic and went to answer it.

Joshua stood in the hallway, holding a piece of paper between his fingers. "I have it."

Viv ushered him in, her heart rattling against her chest.

"Moss telephoned first thing. Apparently he called in a favor and whoever found it rang him at home over breakfast," said Joshua by explanation.

"Where is she?" Viv asked.

"South Devon."

"South Devon?" It was nearly as far south as one could go in Britain and still be on land. "Why Devon?"

"I have no idea," he said cheerfully.

She held out her hand. "May I please look?"

"I want to come with you," he said, not handing over the paper.

"No." She didn't need to think about her reaction. She knew that was a bad idea.

"I've already shown that I can help. I can do more."

"No," she repeated, reaching for the paper.

"I'll carry bags. I'll read the maps. I'll find us a place to stay," he said.

"I can do all of those things on my own." She'd been fending for herself for years, she didn't need him to come riding in like Prince Charming now.

"I can also help pay," he said.

Viv hated that, for a moment, that almost swayed her.

"In fact, I can pay for all of it. Our train tickets, rooms, meals," he pressed, no doubt having read her weakness.

"I've never asked you for money. Why would I start now? Besides, can you even afford it?"

"I've hardly spent any of my RAF wages, and I was paid for rehearsals. Please, Viv. I meant my apology yesterday, ham-handed as it might have been. I promise you that I'm not a bad man, but you wouldn't know that. How could you? We haven't spent any time together."

Viv searched his face for any malice or sarcasm in his words. Instead, all she found was open earnestness. Still, she knew she couldn't let herself trust him.

"Finding my daughter is not the time for a happy family reunion," she said.

"No, but she's my daughter too. I know you won't believe this, but I want to meet Maggie. I want to be a part of her life. I know that I missed out on the first ten years of her life, and I don't want to miss out on any more."

This was all too much. She didn't want to travel with him, but more than that, she didn't want him to see her at what could be the most joyous or worst moment of her life. To raise her hopes to these heights and dash them again. . . .

"I don't—"

"Please let me be the father Maggie deserves."

She pressed her hand to her forehead as guilt and mistrust and sadness battled in her gut. She didn't want him there, but could she really deny her daughter the chance to meet her father if that's what she wanted? Maggie had never really shown any interest in Joshua, but that had been when she was four. She would be ten in a few short days. She'd know more about the world. She would have friends who had a mother and a father, and she might wonder why she didn't have the same. Could Viv in good faith keep her daughter from her father if she wanted to know him?

She let out a long sigh. "I speak to her first. She's still a child, and she doesn't know who you are."

Maggie might not even really remember Viv—a thought that cut her deeper than anything Joshua could ever do to her.

Joshua looked up sharply. "You mean . . . ?"

"That might be her address on that piece of paper, but if it isn't, I'm not going to stop searching. The moment you start to complain that you're bored or you don't want to be on the road any longer, you can go back to London."

"I won't," he promised.

She could remind him how much he'd adhered to his promises in the past, but she held back. Maybe it was time to give Joshua the chance to show that he meant what he said.

Viv cringed as Joshua paid both of their hotel bills, each with an extra night added on that they hadn't anticipated. She was certain that she was going to regret allowing him to come along in the search for Maggie, but she couldn't deny that money helped.

They made for the train station, Joshua lugging both of their cases, and bought two tickets to Devon via London.

"Do you need anything?" he asked as they turned from the ticket counter. "A cup of tea? A book? A paper?"

"No, thank you," she said, not wanting to be in his debt any more than she would be taking this trip.

Despite her protests, Joshua went to the newsstand to purchase a copy of *The Journal* and a Ngaio Marsh paperback.

"They're for me, but I can't read them both at the same time," he said.

He held the paperback out until finally she took it.

They took their seats on the train to Birmingham, and Viv tried to push down the nerves that clawed at her as they left Newcastle. She watched the countryside rush by, wondering what it would be like to see her daughter for the first time in five years. She wanted so badly to hug Maggie, to wrap her arms around her. Maggie would be taller—she knew that—but it was hard to imagine. All she could picture in her head was her little girl, just as she was the last time she'd been down to Wootton Green to see her.

When they reached Birmingham, they alighted to change trains.

"Sandwich?" Joshua asked.

Viv pursed her lips and shook her head.

"You have to eat something," he said.

"I'll eat at tea," she said.

Joshua gave a quick nod and then excused himself. When he came back a few minutes later, he had two sandwiches wrapped in waxed paper in one hand and two paper cups of tea in the other.

"It won't do Maggie any good if you waste away before you even have the chance to find her," he said.

Reluctantly, Viv accepted the refreshments and followed him to their next train.

She lasted until they reached Warwick and then unwrapped her sandwich, taking a first bite of cress and a thin slice of cheese.

Joshua gave her a smile but didn't say anything.

For that, she was grateful.

Joshua

July 14, 1945

Joshua stepped down from the bus that had wound through the small streets of Totnes and turned to offer Viv a hand. He knew she was reluctant to have him there, but she didn't shrink away from him violently the way she had when she walked into his parents' home a few days ago.

"We're nearly there," he said, having read the map that was now tucked into his left jacket pocket. "Apparently it's just two rights and a left."

"Good."

He couldn't help but notice the shake in her voice.

As they made the first right, he said, "There's a chance that Moss's information might be wrong."

"I know that," she said quietly.

"But if it isn't the right place, we'll figure out what is. If she's alive, we'll find her," he continued.

She shot him a look in the late-afternoon light. "Don't you have rehearsals to be getting back to?"

Oh, didn't he. He'd telephoned Hal that morning from the hotel in Newcastle, waking up the jazz musician.

"Levinson, do you know what time it is?" his bandleader had asked.

"It's just after eight," he said.

"I was up until three at a jam session," Hal groaned.

"I thought RAF men were used to early call times," he said.

"We're demobbed," Hal reminded him. "Anyway, what are you calling about?"

"Things are complicated here. I may need more time," he said.

Hal grunted on the other end of the phone and then yawned. "I'm sorry. You can have until Monday, but I really do need you back then. 'This Lonely Love' needs work, and I've been working on new arrangements for 'What Happened Once.'"

Joshua hesitated. "Okay. I'll be back Monday," he promised, even though he wasn't confident that would be true.

"See you at rehearsal," Hal said. "And, Levinson? Don't miss it. This job won't hold."

Joshua had sat in his hotel room, his bandleader's warning ringing in his ear, until the switchboard operator came back on the line and asked him if he wanted to place another call. That had snapped him out of it, and he'd put the telephone down and dressed.

He knew that the longer he continued on this journey with Viv, the closer he came to jeopardizing his career. He couldn't give up his chance for a place in the band —not when he'd come this far and fought so hard to finally make a regular player's spot.

As they turned onto Lower Collins Road he tried to push the thought from his mind. He needed to focus on the search. That was the most important thing right now.

"Don't worry about rehearsals. Now, we're looking for number fifty-seven," he said.

Viv craned her neck to look down the road.

"There," she announced, pointing to a large double-fronted house painted white and set back from the road. There was a low stone wall in front of it, and a fruit tree grew in the front garden, shading some of the windows from the summer sun.

He gave a low whistle. "Not bad."

"The Thompsons' house in Wootton Green was a long way from Walton," she said grimly.

"Are you ready?" he asked.

Viv peered up at the house for a long moment and then gave a nod.

Viv

===

Viv's hands shook as she opened the garden gate to 57 Lower Collins Road, but nonetheless she marched up the path and rang the doorbell.

A dog barked somewhere in the house, and there was the sound of a woman's muffled shout. Vivian and Joshua exchanged a look, but before either could say anything the door swung open to reveal a small brunette girl in a teal dress with a pink ribbon tied around her hair. Cradled in her arm was a porcelain-faced doll.

"Maggie?" Viv whispered.

"Hello!" the girl trilled.

She felt Joshua step forward in line with her. "You wouldn't happen to be called Maggie, would you?"

A dark-haired woman wearing a floral apron appeared behind the girl. The woman's frown deepened as she looked between the two of them. "Who are you?"

Viv shook her head. "I'm sorry, we're looking for a little girl—"

The woman pushed the girl behind her.

"We don't mean any harm. It's just, is her name Margaret? Or Maggie?" Viv asked, her eyes fixed on the girl who poked her head out from behind the woman's legs.

"No, her name is Clemmie. Now what is this all about?" asked the woman.

Viv sagged against Joshua's left arm. This wasn't her daughter. Moss's information was wrong.

Joshua glanced at Viv. "Are you by chance related to the Thompsons?"

"The Thompsons?" the woman asked.

"Yes, we were told that they live here. We're looking for them," he said.

Now that Viv had time to study the girl, she could see that her first impression had been all wrong. Clemmie's eyes were rounder that Maggie's, and her lips were far less pronounced. Her hair also lacked her daughter's beautiful curls, although she'd wondered whether Maggie's fine baby hair would straighten out when she became older the way that Viv's had.

"The Thompsons don't live here any longer," said the woman. "They sold us this house about six months ago. They charged us a fair bit for it too. More than it's worth, I say, but my husband had his heart set on it. He grew up around here."

"Did they have a daughter? She would have been ten this month," said Viv.

"I never met them. The house was shown through an agent, and my husband signed the paperwork at a solicitor's office."

An idea sparked in Viv's mind, and she asked in a rush, "Did the Thompsons leave a forwarding address?"

The woman shook her head. "They didn't leave anything behind. Not even the curtain rods in the sitting room, and they were bolted down."

Hope dashed, she started to turn down the path. Behind her, she heard Joshua say, "Thank you, madam. We're sorry to have bothered you."

Maggie wasn't there, and now they would have to start all over again.

"We'll find her," said Joshua as the woman closed the front door behind them with a resolute bang.

"Excuse me," a man called out. He had a small dog on a smart blue lead and matching collar, who was straining to chase after a wood pigeon. "Are you looking for the Thompsons?"

"Yes, do you know where they might be?" asked Joshua.

The man wrapped his hand around the lead, pulling the animal closer to him to let them out of the garden gate.

"I'm afraid that you're a bit late. They moved away at the start of this year," said the man.

"You wouldn't know where they went, would you? It's vital that we find them," Viv said.

"They're in Harberton now, a little village just southwest of here. Little Margaret still comes up to take piano lessons with my daughter, Kayleigh," said the older man.

That had to be her. She *knew* that this Margaret was her daughter.

"Her parents, are they Matthew and Sarah?" asked Joshua.

"That's right," said the older man. "You'll find them at the Old Bakery, just off Vicarage Ball."

Viv could have kissed the dog walker. Instead, she breathed, "Thank you. Thank you very much."

"I hope you find what you're looking for," said the man, giving a gentle tug on the dog's lead.

As the man shuffled off, Viv turned to Joshua. "That *must* be her. We need to go to Harberton."

"Hold on," he said, pulling the map out of his jacket pocket. He spread it across the low stone wall.

She scanned the map, jabbing her finger when she found a tiny "Harberton" printed in black across the map. "There!"

"Let's find a bus," he said.

What she wouldn't have given for a car in that moment. However, bus it would have to be. They retraced their steps and stopped in a corner shop to ask for directions. The shopkeeper told them to board the bus on the other side of the road. It was all Viv could do to keep herself from dancing from foot to foot until it pulled up.

"We're almost there," Joshua kept murmuring as she squirmed in her seat.

Viv shot a look at Joshua's leg, which was jiggling quickly next to hers.

He stilled, but repeated, "We're almost there."

When finally the bus reached Harberton, they rolled by a sign for Vicarage Ball. As soon as the bus stopped, Viv was off like a shot, moving as fast as her low-heeled shoes would take her.

"Look out for the Old Bakery," she called.

"It must be here somewhere," he muttered.

"There! On the right!" She jabbed a finger at the black sign with white lettering that read "The Old Bakery."

She broke out into a run. This was right. She could *feel* it.

"Viv!" Joshua called, but she was already through the iron arch that stood framed by a brick wall. Down the garden path she went, hardly noticing the profusion of roses on either side of her. With a trembling hand, she pressed the shining brass doorbell.

Joshua panted as she caught up to her. "You know, we really should be careful—"

The door swung open, and Viv found herself standing in front of the pretty, petite figure of Sarah Thompson.

"No!" Mrs. Thompson cried, trying the close the door but Viv was too fast. She stuck her arm out, her palm landing flat against the hard wood.

"Mrs. Thompson, we've been looking for you," Viv said, her voice unnaturally calm.

"No, no, no, you're not supposed to be here," Mrs. Thompson continued to push against the door.

"This is her?" asked Joshua behind her.

"Where is Maggie? Where is my daughter?" Viv demanded, giving the door a shove so it bounced out of Mrs. Thompson's hands and smacked against the entryway wall.

All the fight seemed to go out of the other woman. "She's not here."

Dread filled Viv. Something *had* happened to Maggie the night of the bombing. Something horrible and—

"Mr. Thompson went in the car to collect her from her riding lessons," said Mrs. Thompson.

All of the breath left Viv's lungs in a whoosh. "Then she's not . . ."

"She's fine," said Mrs. Thompson, even as tears collected in the corners of her eyes and threatened to spill out over the finely milled powder covering her creamy skin. "Actually she's more than fine. She's a beautiful, healthy, happy girl."

There was something about the way the other woman said it—something almost possessive—that snapped Viv back from relieved to furious. "We'll wait for her inside, then."

Mrs. Thompson gave a pathetic nod and finally made way.

Viv brushed past the other woman into the entryway. It was decorated differently than Beam Cottage had been. Where that property had been all dark antique wood and oil paintings of horses and hunting, this was all light and air. A still life of flowers overspilling their vase hung on a white wall across from a gold-framed mirror. The furniture was now delicate, highly polished cherry that hardly looked as though it could withstand the accidental bump of a toe, let alone a growing child careening around corners.

With Joshua following right behind her, Viv took the first door off the entryway, guessing correctly that it would be the drawing room. It was, like the entryway, a beautiful, feminine room, all tasteful pastels and light pouring in from the rose-framed windows outside.

Viv walked herself straight to one of a pair of carved wood and upholstered chairs placed on the opposite side of a coffee table from a sofa and dropped down into it. Then she fixed Mrs. Thompson with a hard stare.

"I want to know what you were thinking keeping Maggie from me for five years," Viv continued. "I want to know *everything*."

Mrs. Thompson fished one of those lace-edged handkerchiefs Viv had first hated in Wootton Green out of the left cuff of her white blouse and began to cry softly into it.

"We thought you were dead," sobbed the other woman.

"Dead?" she asked with a half laugh. A part of her had felt dead these past years. For months she'd moved through the world only because she'd had to. She had a flat to pay for, and she'd needed her job for that. Her fellow posties—even the men—had treated her delicately, giving her a wide berth in all things. Kate called in on her at Mrs. Shannon's. Rebecca had come to drag her out for meals with the Levinsons when they felt Viv was looking too wan on her route.

Slowly, it had become easier—not the grief but the living. She could make it through a day without feeling as though the weight of her sorrow could crush her, but she never forgot what she carried with her. She could see a child walking down the road with its mother and not need to stop for weeping until she was in the privacy of her own flat.

However, it never entirely went away.

"I wrote a letter," Mrs. Thompson said meekly.

"What letter?" Viv asked.

"I told you that the house had been hit by a bomb and that we left," said Mrs. Thompson. "When I never heard back from you, I assumed that you didn't want to be contacted."

"Where did you send this letter?" she asked.

"The address you gave me. The one you wrote all of your letters from when Margaret was first settling in," said Mrs. Thompson.

"My parents' house. That house was bombed. I wrote to *you.*"

"Well, that explains it, then," said Mrs. Thompson hurriedly. "The post must have been lost."

"That explains nothing. You took my daughter and you ran," she said.

"We did not!" cried Mrs. Thompson.

"A bomb destroyed Beam Cottage, and you decided that it was your chance to leave with her. Do you know who told me what had happened? Your old neighbor who you were supposed to be such good friends with. He sent a telegram because he thought all of you were dead," Viv said.

"Why would you walk away from your home and let people believe that you'd been killed if you didn't intend to disappear?" asked Joshua.

Mrs. Thompson squeezed her lips into a tight line.

"Here's what I think happened," said Viv. "The bomb hit the house and you saw your opportunity to take Maggie. You didn't tell anyone what you were doing except for your brother, Father Monaghan."

Mrs. Thompson went pale at the name of her deceased brother.

"Yes, we know about your connection. I saw your name in the book of condolences at his viewing," she continued.

Mrs. Thompson turned her face away, and Viv could have sworn she heard the other woman mutter, "We never should have gone. Matthew was right."

"Father Monaghan was how you found out about Maggie, isn't it? You wanted a daughter for your own, and your brother delivered one to you under the pretense of an evacuation," she said.

"My brother was a good man and an excellent priest. He knew that Margaret needed to be raised in a respectable Catholic home," said Mrs. Thompson, showing the first bit of fierceness since Viv had walked through her door.

"If your brother was such a good man, why didn't he tell me that my daughter was still alive when he found out?" Viv spat.

"We thought you were dead," insisted Mrs. Thompson.

"The house was destroyed, but Father Monaghan would know that my mother and father were still alive. They never stopped going to church. He could have told them . . ." A thought struck Viv. "You told him in confession."

Mrs. Thompson hung her head.

"Why does it matter if she told him in confession?" asked Joshua.

"Because a priest can't break the sanctity of confession. It's a sacrament," she said, hating that she fundamentally understood why Father Monaghan had not told her about her daughter. The power of belief and the strength of canon law were bonds too strong to break.

"I was doing what I thought was best for Margaret," said Mrs. Thompson.

"You are not her mother. You are not the one who gets to make that decision," Viv said, her rage pulsing against her slipping self-control.

"Look at this house!" Mrs. Thompson swept an arm around her. "Look at all the things we've been able to give Margaret. She goes to the best school for girls in the county. She has piano and riding lessons. She has beautiful clothes. Even with rationing on, she never wants for food. She is happy and safe and healthy here. With *us*."

"She was all of those things with me," Viv spat out.

Mrs. Thompson gave a small laugh. "Can you honestly tell me that you can provide those things for Margaret?"

"*I* am her mother. I'm the one who carried her and gave birth to her. I fed her and I clothed her and I sheltered her. I raised her and taught her what was right and wrong in the world. I love her so much that it physically hurts. *That* is what matters.

"You took my daughter without a single thought for what that would mean for her or for me."

"No! That's not true!" Mrs. Thompson insisted, but she was cut off by the opening of a door.

"Darling, we're home!" called out Mr. Thompson.

Viv rose to her feet slowly as Mrs. Thompson sprung up and took a step toward the door. However, before the older woman could reach the door, it flung open with a "Mother! Mother!"

Viv and Mrs. Thompson cried out simultaneously, and a split second later Maggie stopped short two steps into the drawing room, her eyes darting from woman to woman.

You are so tall, Viv thought, drinking in the sight of her daughter. She was dressed in jodhpurs and a neat little black riding jacket, her boots still on her feet. Maggie's curly hair had softened and grown out over the years. Viv's little girl looked like a young woman.

"Maggie—" Her voice cracked. "Do you remember me?"

For an excruciating moment, her daughter said nothing. Then she whispered, "Mummy?"

"Oh!" Viv cried, rushing forward to throw her arms around Maggie. It was indescribable, the feeling of holding her child in her arms once again. Her faith had been shaken to its very foundation these last ten years, but burying her nose in her daughter's hair once again and smelling the faint scent that was entirely Maggie's made her want to sing out.

After a moment, Viv realized that Maggie wasn't moving. The girl hadn't put her arms around her like she used to, clinging to Viv's neck.

Viv loosened her arms a fraction and leaned back to peer at Maggie's face. She saw nothing there. No light of joy, no tears of happiness. Instead, her daughter looked confused.

"Maggie, aren't you happy to see me?" she asked, only fleetingly aware of the other people in the room.

Maggie opened her mouth as though to respond, but then snapped it shut and ran out of the room.

Joshua

Joshua watched his wife's heart break in front of him as their daughter pulled away and fled the room.

"Maggie!" Viv cried.

Viv started to go after their daughter, but Joshua grabbed her arm. "Let her go. Give her time." When still Viv struggled, he added, "Think of the shock this must be for her."

He thought that she might snap that he wouldn't know the first thing about what Maggie needed, but instead her shoulders slumped and she nodded.

Waves of disappointment coursed off Viv so powerful he could practically see them. Yet Joshua felt strangely . . . detached.

What was wrong with him?

He'd just seen his daughter for the first time, and all he could conjure up was sympathy for his estranged wife. He'd been certain that as soon as he saw Maggie he would somehow *know* that she was his. There would be some intrinsic bond between them. However, she looked just like a little girl with her mother's eyes and his coloring.

There was a shuffling at the door to the drawing room, and he saw a middle-aged man in a tweed jacket filling the doorway. The man's eyes widened before settling into a resigned line. "Mrs. Levinson."

"Matthew," gasped out Mrs. Thompson, rushing to the man who Joshua now knew to be her husband. "They came to the door and forced their way into the house."

"Margaret just ran past me. I take it that she has seen you," said Mr. Thompson to Viv, his arm automatically wrapping protectively around his wife.

"Yes," said Viv.

"Why don't we all take a seat?" suggested Mr. Thompson as though they were houseguests rather than parents coming to retrieve their missing daughter.

"No, I'll be taking my daughter and leaving," said Viv, starting to make for the drawing room door.

"I wouldn't do that if I were you," said Mr. Thompson. "From what I saw, Margaret is upset. Give her a few minutes to calm down and you'll find her the most reasonable ten-year-old in the world."

Joshua watched Viv's eyes go devastated again. Anger flickered in him. She should be the one to know that about her daughter. Not this stranger.

"She isn't ten yet," Viv murmured.

"She will be in a week," said Mrs. Thompson defiantly. "We have a party planned for her. All of her friends from school will be there. There will even be a cake. We've been planning for it for weeks, saving ration coupons. She is looking forward to it more than anything else in the world."

The dam on Joshua's anger broke. "Stop it! Stop it right now!"

Mrs. Thompson gasped as though he'd slapped her. "How dare you speak to me like that in my own home. Matthew—"

"You let Viv think for *years* that her daughter was dead. Can't you understand the pain that you've put her through? And now you're trying to twist the knife even more by guilting her?" he gritted out.

"Matthew, how can you let him speak to me that way?" Mrs. Thompson pushed. "I want these people out of my house."

Mr. Thompson sighed and took off his glasses to knead the bridge of his nose. "Be reasonable, Sarah. It's over."

"Do not tell me to be reasonable! After all that I've done for you—for this family—these last five years." Mrs. Thompson turned to her husband, her fingers wrapping around the lapels of his jacket. "You cannot tell me that you haven't loved every moment of being a father to that child."

Mr. Thompson lifted his eyes to meet Joshua's gaze. "She is the most wonderful little girl. It's been a privilege to care for her."

"Why did you do it?" Viv asked, staring straight at Mr. Thompson.

"Matthew, don't . . ." his wife warned.

"I need to know," said Viv.

Mr. Thompson glanced at his wife, and Joshua knew instinctively that Mr. Thompson was a weak man. He'd seen it before—in Viv's own parents. But while Mrs. Byrne had always struck him as the one tugging her husband around by the nose, Mrs. Thompson appeared to be a different sort. Pretty, flattering, capricious, difficult. He suspected that she had all sorts of ways of wearing her husband down until he did what she wanted him to do.

"When the bomb fell on Beam Cottage, everything was chaos," Mr. Thompson said. "Margaret had run back inside for Tig, and we barely made it out. We were knocked back, and we weren't thinking straight. I grabbed Sarah and Margaret and we fled.

"I used to leave my car by the railroad station so that I could commute into work. I didn't realize that no one would think to look for it in the aftermath. I swear. We took it and drove to Totnes. I went to boarding school not too far away and knew it from childhood. All I could think about was taking Margaret out of harm's way. Totnes is such a small town, it was the safest place I could think of.

"After we were settled, we took a house. I tried to telephone, but your exchange wasn't connecting. We tried to send a letter, but it was returned undeliverable because of bomb damage. We learned your house had been destroyed. We thought you were dead. It wasn't until Sarah spoke to her brother that we learned that you and your parents had survived.

"By then we'd sent word to our old friends in Wootton Green about where we were. We told ourselves that you would come looking for her, and that would be enough, but you never came."

"I did look for her. I went to Beam Cottage the day that I got word. There was nothing there," said Viv, her voice cracking. "I thought she was dead."

Mr. Thompson spread his hands out in front of him. "I'm sorry. I don't know what else to say."

"That's all?" Joshua asked in disbelief. "You're sorry? You should have done more. You knew that Viv was alive, but you did *nothing*. How can you live with yourselves?"

The Thompsons were silent.

Joshua shook his head. "You stole five years of Viv's life with her daughter from her. You let Maggie think she was dead."

"I beg your pardon, but who are you?" asked Mrs. Thompson, turning on him.

"I'm Maggie's father."

Mr. Thompson glanced at his wife. "We were told there wasn't a father."

"Of course there was a father. I'm married. I never pretended to be anything else," said Viv.

"But we thought . . ." The way that Mrs. Thompson trailed off told him everything he needed to know. They'd assumed Viv had been lying about her marriage. They'd guessed that he was a do-no-good who had gotten her into trouble and then ran off when she needed him most.

And wasn't that exactly what he was?

"Where is Maggie's room?" asked Viv, pulling her shoulders back.

"I really don't think that's a good idea. The girl is upset," Mrs. Thompson tried to stall.

"I want to see my daughter," Viv insisted.

"Up the stairs and the second door to your right," said Mr. Thompson.

"Matthew!" cried his wife.

"Sarah, it's over," he said.

"But they're going to take her!" Mrs. Thompson burst into wracking sobs.

Mr. Thompson wrapped his arms around his wife, but the set of his jaw remained grim. "We knew this could happen, darling. It's time for Margaret to go home."

Maggie

Maggie sat on her bed, cradling Tig against her. The toy tiger was several shades darker with dirt than when she'd first arrived with the Thompsons and all of his limbs were beginning to look threadbare, but she refused to let anyone wash him. She was too worried that he might fall apart and she would lose her best friend.

She shoved her face into the toy's matted fur, trying to understand what had just happened in the drawing room below her.

Her mother was still alive.

Her mother.

Alive.

She remembered only flashes of her life before the Thompsons. However, she remembered her mother's visits to Beam Cottage well. Her mother would come in like a ray of sunshine, smiling and happy. Maggie would show her drawings, her dolls, her dresses. She would go horseback riding on her pony, Puffball, and when her mother would leave, Maggie would sit in her room and wait, wondering when she would see her again.

All of that had ended when the bomb fell and Mr. and Mrs. Thompson had taken her in the car and driven all night. They'd stayed in an inn and then eventually moved into a house. That was where Mrs. Thompson had sat Maggie down and told her that her mother couldn't care for her anymore. Maggie was to call Mrs. Thompson "mother" and Mr. Thompson "father," and they would be a family.

No one called her Maggie after that day.

As she'd grown up, Maggie had come to understand what the Thompsons were being kind not saying out loud, the way that some people said that her school friend Jacqueline's father was "with the angels now," and it was the only thing that made sense. Her mother had died.

Now, Maggie sat on her bed, clinging to Tig, and not understanding at all how her mother could be alive because, if that was the case, why had she not come for her sooner?

Viv

Viv bounded up the stairs, desperate to reach her daughter. She could put behind her all the horrible things the Thompsons had thought about her to justify what they'd done as long as she could hold Maggie again. That would be enough for now.

When she reached the second door on the landing that Mr. Thompson had told her about, however, she hesitated. She didn't know what had been more horrifying to witness: the blank look on her daughter's face before Maggie had recognized her or the way that Maggie had spun around and run from her.

She took a deep breath. She could do this. Maggie was hers. They could find their way back to each other.

She lifted her hand to knock lightly before pushing open the door. Just as in Wootton Green, Maggie's room was a pink-and-white confection topped with eyelet and frills and, sitting in the middle of the bed with her boots still on, was her daughter.

Maggie unfolded herself to look up at Viv, revealing the ratty figure of Tig clutched in her arms.

"I see you still have our old friend," said Viv, forcing down her rising tears. She would not cry and make her daughter any more confused than she already was. She would be calm and warm, the mummy Maggie remembered. She could do that for her daughter.

When Maggie didn't say anything, Viv asked, "Would you mind if I came in and said hello to Tig?"

Her daughter gave an almost imperceptible nod, and Viv slowly approached the bed. Gingerly, she sat down on top of the down duvet, sinking into the deep, plush feathers.

"I remember when Auntie Kate and Uncle Sam gave you Tig. You were so small that he was bigger than you," she said.

Maggie stroked a hand over the toy's head. "Some of the girls at school say that only babies still play with toys."

"I don't think that's true. Do you?"

"No," Maggie said, holding on to the vowel in a way that betrayed her hesitation. "But I hide him when they come over to play."

Viv's heart broke for her daughter in a new way. Maggie was on the edge of a new stage of life—somewhere between being a little girl and a young woman. She would face so many tests, so many questions about the kind of person she would become. Viv wanted to be there with her, every step of the way, to guide her in a way her parents had never helped her.

"Well, Tig can be our secret if you like, but I for one still think he's a wonderful companion," she said.

Maggie nodded but stared straight at the patch of carpet in front of her.

"Maggie," she started slowly, "I know it must be a shock to see me."

That got her daughter to lift her head. "I thought you were dead."

Viv swallowed hard. "I'm so sorry," she whispered.

"Where were you?" Maggie asked.

"I . . ." How did she explain this to a child? "I didn't know where you were for a time. If I had, I would have been there in a flash. You know that, don't you?"

Maggie nodded, but she could see how skeptical her daughter looked.

They sat in silence, Viv trying her best to figure out a way to explain to her daughter everything that had happened. She wanted to tell her everything all at once and nothing at the same time. To give her every reason in the world why she'd made the choices she had and yet explain none of them because it was too difficult, too embarrassing, too horrible.

Finally, she asked, "Do you understand what it means now that I've found you again?"

Maggie shook her head.

"It means that I'm going to take you home."

Maggie started, looking up at her with wide eyes.

"We'll take the train back to Liverpool, but we won't go back to Ripon Street where we used to live. It was destroyed in a bombing, like Beam Cottage was," she explained.

"Will we live with Nan and Grandad again?" Maggie asked.

She shook her head. "We live in a flat above a nice woman named Mrs. Shannon now. She has seven granddaughters and four grandsons, and I'm sure she'll be very excited to meet you. Would that be okay?"

Maggie furrowed her brow. "We don't live with Nan and Grandad?"

"We don't, no. Do you wish that we did?" Even though she might be estranged from her parents, she wasn't going to push that on her daughter. Enough people had made decisions for Viv about who was or wasn't in her life that she vowed she wouldn't do the same.

Still, she would be lying if she didn't admit to feeling relieved when Maggie hesitated and then shook her head. No child should have to tolerate Mum and Dad's coldness, and she could kick herself for putting her daughter through any of that.

"There is one other thing that I need to tell you about, Maggie," she said, taking her daughter's hand. "That man downstairs? His name is Joshua Levinson. He's your father."

"My father?" Maggie asked, scrunching up her nose.

"We were married before you were born, but he wasn't around when you were younger because he lived in a different country. He's a jazz musician," she said.

For the first time since Viv walked into the room, Maggie brightened. "Does he play the piano?"

"No, the saxophone."

"Do you think he would play with me?"

Viv bit her lip, trying to tamp down her jealousy. She wouldn't resent Joshua for Maggie showing more interest in him than in her. Maggie was a child.

"I'm sure he would if you asked him to," Viv said. "Now, why don't you help me gather your things and then we'll go downstairs and you can meet him properly? We're going home."

Viv helped her daughter pack things she'd never seen before into a case Viv hadn't bought her.

Mr. Thompson knocked once to ask how they were getting on. Viv tried to pretend that she couldn't hear the hitch in his voice. She didn't want to feel sorry for this man or his wretched wife. Not when they'd done the things they'd done.

Finally, Viv took Maggie by the hand and led her downstairs, Tig clutched in Maggie's other hand. They went into the drawing room, where they found Joshua sitting with the Thompsons in silence.

"Are you ready for your adventure?" asked Mr. Thompson, putting on a brave face as Mrs. Thompson dissolved again into tears.

Maggie, looking a little lost, peered up at Viv. Viv's stomach twisted. She'd imagined so many different scenarios, everything from sweeping in to take a grateful Maggie off to barging into the Thompsons' house with a battalion of police officers behind her. However, she'd never envisioned herself feeling sorry for the people who had taken her daughter away.

She could never forgive them for what they'd done. They'd spirited Maggie away and then kept them apart because they'd assumed they knew better. However, she was smart enough to see how well Maggie had been loved here. Her daughter had been cared for and even spoiled a bit, and that was more than some children received from the world. They had kept Maggie safe from a bombing, educated her, and loved her. A part of her heart would always be grudgingly, strangely grateful to them.

"Oh, Margaret," Mrs. Thompson sobbed, throwing her arms around Maggie. "Whatever are we going to do without you?"

Viv watched Maggie cling to the woman she called mother.

Finally, Mrs. Thompson set Maggie away from her and rose. It was the first time Viv had ever seen the always flawless woman look shattered, with smudged lipstick and running mascara.

"Please, can we at least write to her?" Mrs. Thompson asked.

The *no* was on the tip of Viv's tongue, but then she looked down at Maggie, who was peering up at her, hope so clear in her eyes.

"If Maggie wants to write to you, you can respond," she allowed, even though it cost her.

"Thank you," whispered Mrs. Thompson.

"Thank you," echoed her husband.

Mr. Thompson crouched down to Maggie and pulled her into a short hug. "You will always have a place in our hearts, Margaret. Remember that," he said.

"Thank you, Father," murmured Maggie.

Viv's eyes flashed to Joshua. He looked dazed hearing his daughter call another man "Father." When she caught his gaze, she gave him a soft smile, hoping that it conveyed all of her understanding for the hurt he must be feeling.

"Come on, Maggie. We need to catch the bus to go to the train station," she said, putting our her hand to hold.

"I could drive you to Totnes," offered Mr. Thompson.

Viv shook her head. "We'll say goodbye here. It will be easier to have done with it."

The older man nodded and cleared his throat. "Right. Right."

With her shoulders square to the door, Viv put one foot in front of the other to begin the long journey back home with her daughter by her side.

Joshua

It was too late to start out the previous evening after leaving the Thompsons, so Joshua found them two rooms over a pub in Totnes. Maggie stayed in Viv's room on a cot the publican had been happy to provide, and Joshua stayed across the way.

"I'll knock at six, and we can find something for tea," Viv said to him as soon as Maggie was safely in her room. Then she closed the door, leaving him on the other side feeling once again apart.

Immediately, worry gripped him. Something had happened when Mrs. Thompson had looked at him, disbelieving that he could be Maggie's father. He'd felt a protectiveness over the child he'd only just met for the first time in his life. But it had taken hearing Maggie call another man "Father" to really solidify his feelings. It was wrong—all wrong—and he wanted more than anything to fix it. He wanted his daughter to know him, to turn to him when she was distressed. To laugh with him when she was happy.

As he sat in his room, finally *feeling* like a father even if he knew nothing about how to be one, he realized that he couldn't imagine leaving his daughter now.

*   *   *

The following morning, Joshua rose long before the church bells began to ring out over Totnes, calling people to Sunday service. Viv knocked on his door at the agreed-upon time, and he helped carry all of their cases down to the little desk that served as the pub's reception.

While he paid, he heard Maggie ask Viv, "Will we be going to church?"

Out of the corner of his eye, he saw his wife kneel down in front of their daughter. "Not today, but if you want to go to church I'll take you."

Maggie frowned at that. "Mother says that we must always go to church unless we're ill."

It was impossible to ignore the pain that lanced over Viv's face when their daughter called another woman "Mother."

"That was very true when you were living with Mr. and Mrs. Thompson, but now that we're going home you'll be able to choose what you wish to do," said Viv.

Maggie hugged the stuffed toy he'd heard her call Tig a little tighter to her.

"Right, that's all paid. Now we can start our trip," he announced, putting on a smile.

Viv straightened, and Maggie nodded.

"Why don't you help with the door?" he suggested to Maggie, picking up all three of their cases.

He hung back as Maggie obediently went ahead to hold open the door. The distance between them afforded him the opportunity to lean over to Viv and ask, "Are you all right?"

Viv sniffed and pulled up her chin. "I have my daughter back. Of course I'm all right."

He thought it best to ignore the shake in her voice.

Safely ensconced in the first-class carriage of their second train home, Joshua couldn't help stealing glances at his daughter. This trip was bleeding him for every shilling he had, but he couldn't make himself upset about it. The most important thing was taking Maggie home, and if first-class could afford them a bit more comfort all around, that is what his daughter would have.

His daughter. It was still such a strange, foreign thing. He'd gone so many years knowing he had a child but not having even the most basic details about her. Now that he'd met her, he didn't understand how he could have stayed away. Even now, he wanted to run up and down the aisles of the train compartment, shouting to everyone who could hear that this was his daughter. His family.

His gaze flicked over to Viv. There was a deep furrow in her brow as she watched Maggie stare out the window, much as Viv had done during their train journey to Devon. He wanted to be able to reach out and place a reassuring hand on her arm, but he didn't know what her reaction would be, so he didn't dare.

He hated the awkwardness between them. He hated feeling as though he were standing on the outside, looking in at his own family.

He had to fix this. He knew that his attention should be on the band he was supposed to return to the following day, but he found it impossible to think about London and the Hal Greene Quintet right now. Viv and Maggie were what mattered.

As the train pulled into Lime Street station, the dread that had been rising in his throat since Wolverhampton nearly choked Joshua. The station was the end. The place where he would have to say goodbye to his daughter the day after meeting her. However, he had one last trick up his sleeve, and he was certain he would use it.

They alighted from the train, Viv taking Maggie by the hand, and walked to the end of the platform. It was surprisingly crowded for a Sunday night train, but he didn't mind. It delayed their parting for a little while longer and meant Joshua could imagine that they were like the other families he saw walking past them, children and their parents at ease with one another.

Finally, near the information desk, Viv stopped and turned to him. "We should say goodbye."

He bit the inside of his cheek but nodded. "How will you make your way home?"

"We'll take the bus from outside the station." Viv gave their daughter a warm smile. "You'll be able to see your brand-new bedroom. You'll like that, won't you? A room all your own?"

Maggie looked up at her, still seeming a little shy and perhaps wary of everything that was happening to her. He couldn't blame her.

He smiled at his daughter. "Did you know that your nan Anne and grandad Seth have a piano?"

Immediately, Maggie's face lit up. "They do?"

"I don't know how long it's been since anyone played it, but I'm sure they would be honored if you would." He glanced up at Viv. "If that's okay with your mother."

Maggie started, turning her face up to Viv with an expression of such open longing Joshua knew that Viv would be powerless against it.

Viv nodded. "We can go tomorrow. I know they'll be desperate to meet you, and if you ask politely, I'm sure they'll let you play."

For the first time since they'd bundled Maggie onto the bus and driven away from the Thompsons' home, Maggie smiled. Joshua caught his breath. *This* was what it was like, then, knowing that he had made his child happy. It felt better than any solo he'd ever played. It might even feel better than flying.

Over the top of their daughter's head, he caught Viv's eye, and his estranged wife stunned him all over again by mouthing, "Thank you."

"We'll telephone your grandparents first thing tomorrow and find out when they want us to come," said Viv.

He knew Mum and Dad would want them there now if they could have their way, but he sensed Viv needed some time alone with their daughter to recover from the last two days.

There would be time the next day for all of them to learn what being a family to this little girl would be like.

Viv

July 15, 1945

"And this is your room," said Viv, opening the door to the little room off the kitchen that she'd kept for Maggie. She'd taken the flat in Mrs. Shannon's home because of the landlady, the neighborhood around them, and this room. It had been such a stretch when she'd first moved to give her daughter her own bedroom, but it had been a point that she'd stubbornly held to.

However, now, standing in the doorway, all she saw was how it was lacking. She hadn't had a chance to decorate it for Maggie before that horrible day when she thought she'd lost her daughter, and over the years it had become something of a box room with a single bed that Rebecca or one of her postie friends stayed in if they didn't want to brave the buses home at night. Compared to what the Thompsons had been able to provide Maggie . . .

She shook her head. The Thompsons might have had affluence Viv would likely never see in her lifetime, but they weren't Maggie's parents. She was.

"I'll see what I can find in the way of fabric to make you some new curtains and a new bedspread," she promised, not entirely sure if her ration book would stretch to it but wanting to give her daughter something that could be her own in this flat.

"Why don't you unpack your things and then we can have tea?" Viv suggested.

Maggie nodded, set her case down on the bed, and flipped open the clasps. Viv waited for something—anything—from her daughter, but Maggie had been virtually silent since the train station except for a polite hello to a delighted Mrs. Shannon. Maggie was so self-contained, so quiet, Viv wondered where the exuberant little girl she'd put on an evacuation train had gone.

Quietly Viv backed up, half closed the door behind her, and made the short trip to the kitchen. However, standing in front of the half-empty larder shelves, tears began to fall, blurring her vision. They were a family again, so why did she feel so wretched?

She pulled her plain cotton handkerchief out of her pocket and swiped at her eyes. Then she shut the larder door and slipped out of the flat to Mrs. Shannon's telephone downstairs.

Kate picked up after only two rings, and her first question was, "Did you find her?"

Viv burst into tears.

"Oh, Vivie. Oh, I'm so sorry. I worried that you might get your hopes up," Kate cooed down the line.

"I found her, Kate. I found her," she managed between sobs.

"But that's wonderful news!" Kate cried.

"She's upstairs in the flat right now. I gave her the second bedroom, but I left her to unpack because . . . because . . ."

"Tell me what's the matter," said Kate in that encouraging, firm way that older sisters have.

"She won't speak. It's as though she's looking right through me. She's so *different*," she said, feeling like she was betraying her daughter just talking about her but unable to stop herself.

"She's nearly ten now," said Kate gently.

"I know I'm being ridiculous, but something isn't right. I— I don't think she wants to be here," she whispered.

"You're her mother. She wants to be with you," said Kate.

"I don't know."

"Have you talked to her yet?" asked Kate.

"Of course I've talked to her."

"No, have you talked to her about what happened? About why she was evacuated?"

"She's only nine," she said.

"Nine-year-olds are far more perceptive than you might think." There was a long pause before Kate said, "I haven't told you about what happened when Cora came home, have I?"

"What do you mean?" she asked.

"Cora was a nightmare for a good two weeks after returning from North Wales," Kate said.

"But she was so sweet when I saw her," Viv protested.

Kate gave a laugh. "With everyone else, yes. Not with me. She was a terror, screaming at me at every little thing I did. Nothing was good enough. The food I made her was disgusting. Her clothes itched. She didn't want to go back to school."

"I didn't know. Why didn't you say something?" she asked.

"It felt a little rich complaining about my daughter returning when we thought that you'd lost yours," said Kate.

"What did you do?" Viv asked.

"It was Colin who finally told me what was the matter. Cora thought I'd sent her away because I didn't love her anymore. He said that she used to sit on the floor of their bedroom in their foster house and cry. For the first month in Wales, she wouldn't speak to anyone, until finally she began to come out of her shell. She adjusted, but it took time.

"It ripped my heart out hearing that, but Colin was right. He and William were nine and eight when they were evacuated. They understood a little bit of what was happening. Cora was six. She got it into her head that I didn't want her, and that's why she was taken away." Kate's voice broke. "I don't think I'll ever forgive myself for that.

"I sat her down, and I talked to her. I did my best to explain why she was evacuated. I told her that I loved her—that her dad loved her—that we never wanted to be separated again. Then she began to talk to me.

"She said that she had a friend in the village who was also an evacuee.

They went to school together, but after six months their mother came to collect her and her brothers. She said that she sat at the window for weeks, waiting for me to come down the garden path to take them all home."

"Oh, Kate. I'm so sorry."

"I don't think that there's a family in this country who sent their little ones away who isn't struggling to figure out how to be a family again. Talk to Maggie. Tell her that you aren't going anywhere, and she isn't either. Remind her that you love her, and try to explain that you did what you did because of that love. It might take time, but you'll find your way back to each other," said Kate.

"You're right," said Viv, sniffling.

"Of course I am. I'm your big sister, aren't I?" Kate laughed. "Now when can I see my niece? I don't want to frighten her off."

"I'm taking her to see the Levinsons tomorrow morning. I'm sure they wouldn't mind you joining us," she said, pushing aside the thought that the following day was Monday and that meant at some point she was going to need to telephone Mr. Rowan and hope she still had a job.

Cautiously, she added, "Joshua was there when I found her."

The sharp intake of breath on the other end of the line was unmistakable. "Joshua?"

"He had a friend who was able to find the Thompsons. He . . . he was helpful."

"You aren't thinking about taking him back, are you, Vivie?" asked Kate, the censure all too clear in her voice.

"No," said Viv firmly. "That part of our lives is over. But he is Maggie's father."

"I never thought I'd live to see the day when you would go soft on that man," said Kate.

Viv couldn't quite articulate when things had shifted, but she hadn't missed the way that Joshua kept stealing glances at their daughter. Neither had she missed the devastation on his face when Mrs. Thompson had asked who he was.

"I'll ring you tomorrow and let you know when you can meet us," Viv said.

"Thank you, Vivie. And remember, just give her time."

Viv hung up the phone and steeled herself to climb the stairs to cook for her daughter.

The Levinsons' door flew open as soon as Viv opened up the garden gate to the house on Salisbury Road with Maggie in tow. Anne raced out, followed swiftly by Seth and Rebecca.

"Oh, look at you!" Anne cried before stopping, her hands covering her mouth.

Maggie's grip tightened on Viv's hand, and Viv felt her daughter move closer to her. Viv placed her hand on Maggie's shoulder and leaned down.

"Maggie, this is your nan Anne. She's been wanting to meet you for a very long time." She looked up and smiled at Seth. "And this is your grandad Seth and your aunt Rebecca."

"Hello," said Maggie, her voice meek as a mouse.

"It's very nice to finally meet you, Maggie," said Anne, her eyes shining.

Rebecca smiled. "Maggie, your father tells me that you're quite the piano player."

Viv looked up and saw Joshua leaning against the doorframe, his arms crossed over his chest and an easy smile spreading over his face as he watched his family with his daughter.

"Would you like to try our piano?" asked Seth.

"Yes, please," said Maggie, a little louder this time.

"Why don't you let Rebecca and your father show you while I make the tea," said Anne.

As they walked toward the house, Seth hooked Viv's hand through his arm. "She looks well."

"She does. She's a little quiet," she warned.

"I'm sure that this is all more overwhelming for her than any of us can guess. We'll try not to be too excited all at once," he said.

"Thank you."

"And what about you?" asked her father-in-law.

She let herself sag a little into his side. "I'm okay."

"You have us to lean on. Remember that," he said.

She reached up to squeeze his hand.

"Kate wanted to see Maggie. I told her that she could come by," she said.

"Your sister is always welcome in our home," he said.

They settled in the front room, Maggie happily installed at the piano with her father sitting next to her, Rebecca doing her best to sing along to the songs Maggie played. Anne passed around cups of tea, hardly taking her eyes off her granddaughter, and Seth watched on with a satisfied smile.

After a half hour, there was a knock on the door. Viv rose. "That will be Kate."

She went to the door and opened it, but rather than her sister, she found her mother and father on the Levinsons' doorstep.

"Mum, Dad, what are you doing here?" she asked.

"We'd like to see our granddaughter," said Mum, holding her handbag up like armor.

"Kate told us about Maggie," explained Dad.

"You should have brought her to us first, Vivian," said Mum.

Viv kept her arms braced against the door, not giving them a path inside. "You *never* showed any interest in Maggie when we lived with you."

"That isn't true," insisted Mum.

"You hardly spoke to her except to scold her," she said.

"She was unruly," said Mum.

"She was just a little girl."

"Where is she?" Mum asked, craning her neck.

"You told me that it was God's will that she was taken from me, Mum. You didn't care about her," she said.

"Don't tell me that I didn't care. I'm not so hard-hearted as that," said Mum.

"Viv?"

She felt Joshua come up behind her.

"You," said her mother.

Viv turned in time to see Joshua assess her parents and then square his body to them, creating another barrier between them and everyone in the Levinson household.

"You're not supposed to be here," said Mum.

"Nonetheless, I am," said Joshua.

"Joshua helped me find Maggie and bring her back to Liverpool. This is his parents' house. He has every right to be here," she said.

There was a yelp from the road, and Viv saw Kate nearly trip out of the front seat of Sam's delivery truck. "Mum, Dad! What are you doing? I am so sorry, Vivie. Mum was over when you called, and I started crying. I was just so happy."

"It's okay. I understand," Viv said.

"Where is the girl?" Mum insisted.

"She is with her grandparents," said Joshua.

"Vivian, you cannot seriously be thinking about letting these people—"

"Letting these people what, Mum? Be happy that they have finally met their granddaughter for the first time?"

"Joshua?"

They turned to find that Anne, Seth, and Rebecca had all joined them in the entryway.

"Mr. and Mrs. Byrne, please join us. We have enough tea to go around," said Anne, an unmistakable stiffness in her voice despite her polite offer.

"Thank you, Anne, but no," said Viv. "My parents are leaving because I don't believe they're here out of love for Maggie or out of the goodness of their hearts. There is something else they want," said Viv.

Mum's eyes narrowed. "Now that the girl is back, it's time for you to come home."

"I already have a home," said Viv.

"Living by yourself? Whoever heard of such a thing. And how are you expecting to work and care for a child at the same time?" Mum shot back. "The girl should be at home with us. She'll attend church again and—"

"So that's what this is about," Viv cut her mother off with a laugh.

"Vivie," Kate started.

"No, Kate. I need to make myself very clear so that Mum and Dad understand me once and for all. I will work. I will raise my daughter. I will protect her from people who are unkind to her, even if those people are members of her own family. I will not criticize her so much that she's afraid of putting a foot wrong. I will not bring her up in a household that cares more about what the parish priest and the neighbors think than what is best for her family.

"Outside of Kate, the Levinsons have been more like family to me these last five years than you have. If you want a relationship with my daughter or with me, you can show me that you've earned that. Until then, I will respectfully say goodbye," said Viv.

She turned, pushing beyond Joshua and the Levinsons.

In the front room, she found her daughter sitting on the piano bench, staring at the keys. She sat down next to Maggie.

"Did you hear all of that?" she asked.

"Yes," said Maggie.

"I'm sorry. Sometimes things can be difficult between adults." Viv looked down at her daughter, her heart pinching at Maggie's tight lips. She thought about what Kate had said about Cora, and she knew that she needed to talk to her daughter.

"Maggie, are you unhappy that you're back home?" Viv asked, articulating the one thing she was most afraid of.

Maggie burst into tears.

"Oh, Little Bear," Viv soothed as she pulled her daughter into a hug, letting Maggie's tears soak the front of her blouse. "Oh, Little Bear, I'm so sorry."

"Why didn't you look for me?" Maggie wailed.

"I didn't know," whispered Viv, emotion high in her throat. "I thought you were gone."

"I was waiting for you. I waited for you to come back and take me home," Maggie sobbed.

"I didn't know," said Viv. "I thought that the bomb . . . It was the worst feeling in the world."

"Then why did you send me away?" Maggie asked through her tears.

She hung her head. "I wish I hadn't."

"Then why did you?" Maggie insisted, pushing at Viv's deepest wound.

"I thought that if you were evacuated and you went to live with the Thompsons, you wouldn't be hurt. I didn't send you away because you were bad or because I didn't love you. I *promise* you that.

"I love you with all of my heart, Maggie. When you were a little girl, it was just the two of us. We lived with your nan and grandad, but it was really just us. We did everything together. I took you everywhere with me because you were so precious to me."

Viv took a deep breath, wondering how best to explain what she had to say to a child. "Things were difficult because your father and I didn't live together."

"Why not?" Maggie asked.

"Because he was a long ways away in America. That meant that it was just you and me from the very start." One day, when Maggie was a little older, she would tell her the whole story of her and Joshua. She owed her daughter that.

"Will he live with us now?" Maggie asked.

Viv shook her head. "Your father has a job in London, but I'm sure he will come see you as often as he can. That sounds nice, doesn't it? You and I will live together in our little flat, and you can come see Nan Anne and Grandad Seth as much as you like."

Maggie looked up at her. "Can I see Cora?"

Viv smiled. "You remember your cousin?"

Maggie nodded.

"I'm sure Cora would be delighted to see you. Auntie Kate and Uncle Sam are here. Do you remember them?"

Another nod.

Viv slipped an arm around her daughter's shoulders. "Why don't you say hello, and then I'm sure Nan Anne and Grandad Seth wouldn't mind you playing the piano again."

When Maggie leaned into her hug, Viv felt for the first time since boarding the train from Totnes that things might be on the right path.

"Go on now," she said, releasing Maggie, who went running from the room, a little of that childhood enthusiasm she remembered restored.

When she looked up, she saw Joshua standing in the doorway, watching the two of them.

"I do want to see her," he said. "I really do."

Viv examined him, still wary of him despite all they'd been through to find Maggie. "Then I hope you keep your word because I don't know if I can forgive you if you break her heart."

Joshua

July 16, 1945

Later Monday afternoon, after Viv and Maggie left and his childhood home finally settled into a pleasant calm, Joshua kissed his mother's cheek, picked up his hat and case, and made his way to the train station.

He hadn't meant to listen in on Viv speaking to their daughter, but her words wouldn't stop ringing through his mind.

"Your father has a job in London, but I'm sure he will come see you as often as he can."

He knew that she was being kind, opening the door to Joshua being in Maggie's and her lives, but as he watched his daughter and his wife on that piano bench he'd never felt more alone and adrift. He couldn't continue his life as he'd been living it. He needed to make a decision.

The train to London pulled into King's Cross late that evening. By the time he crossed the city and collapsed into his bed, he was exhausted. When he hauled himself up the following morning to bathe and shave, he felt as though he'd hardly slept. With heavy legs, he pocketed a few shillings and went to the telephone box down the road from his flat to keep his landlord from overhearing.

Viv's landlady answered his call, and he tried not to mind as he pumped coins into the telephone for a good five minutes before Viv came on the line.

"Hello?" her voice filled his ear.

"Viv, it's Joshua."

"Yes?"

He thought there was more warmth in her voice than when she'd clapped eyes on him for the first time in years a week ago. Had they been through enough though?

"How is Maggie?" he asked.

"She's settling in slowly. I telephoned my boss this morning and asked to put back my return a little longer. I couldn't just leave her," Viv admitted.

"No," he agreed, understanding the instinct.

"We're going back to your parents' house so she can play the piano in a few hours. Will we see you there?" she asked.

"Ah, no," he said, rubbing the back of his neck. "I'm in London."

"Oh. Of course. You were supposed to be back yesterday, weren't you?" she asked, immediately distant.

"I want to be there, I really do, but there are some things I need to do here," he said.

He could hear Viv's sigh.

"What do you want me to tell Maggie if she asks after you?" she asked.

If, not *when.* As though he needed any more reminders that if he went away that day, he couldn't be certain that his own daughter would miss him.

"Tell her that I will see her as soon as I can. I promise."

"Joshua—"

"I *promise,* but there are some things I need to do here," he said.

He could feel the tension on the line.

"Don't do this to her, Joshua. If you're going to be in her life, be there. If not, don't leave her dangling by a thread, hoping that you might choose to be there," Viv finally said.

He deserved it, every little last bit of her disbelief.

"I'm not going to let her down. I'm not," he said, forcing as much conviction as he could into his words.

"You'll forgive me for not believing it until I see it." And then she hung up the phone.

Joshua stared at the receiver and then carefully replaced it. Then he pushed out of the telephone booth and retreated to his flat.

Just after three, Joshua pushed into the studio, the hat in his hand wet from the rain that had been pelting London all afternoon. Hal and Artie were chatting with Jimmy, the pianist. Tommy, who played trombone, was fiddling with the valves on his horn. Another man Joshua had never seen before was stooping over an instrument case. He swallowed hard when the stranger straightened and pulled out a saxophone.

Artie was the first person to notice him. The taciturn drummer jerked his head in Joshua's direction, bringing Hal's gaze up. The bandleader's lips thinned, but he pushed away from the piano and walked over.

"Joshua, good to see you," Hal said, sticking out his hand.

"Hi, Hal," he said.

"You don't have your sax," Hal said.

"Looks like you don't need it," he said, gesturing to the new sax player.

Hal glanced over his shoulder. "When you didn't show or call yesterday, I decided we couldn't take any chances. Keith stepped in."

"Is he any good?" Joshua asked, nodding to the stranger.

"He's good," said Hal.

Joshua took a deep breath. He'd already chosen one path, and it had led him here. Now it was time to try a different path and see where his life would lead.

"I'm sorry I didn't call. That was unprofessional. However, there was a good reason for it," he said.

"I'll be glad to hear it," said Hal.

"My estranged wife discovered that our daughter, who she thought had died in an air raid, was still alive. We needed to go find her. That's where I've been."

Hal unfolded his arms slowly. "That's quite a story."

"It's the truth. I'd say you can ask Adam, but I never talked to him about it. It isn't something I'm proud of, but I wasn't around after I married Viv."

"Marriage can be a hard thing," said Hal as though he knew that fact too well.

Joshua shook his head. "No, this is my fault."

"Can you fix it?" Hal asked.

"I don't know." All he knew was that he needed to try.

"Keith was just helping out. He knew that you were supposed to come back," said Hal, softening. "He can stand in for the first week at the Hidden Door while you sort things out. The job is still yours if you want it."

Old instincts tugged at him. He'd earned this chance after all those years of near misses. Yes, even though the desire to stay in London and play with Hal's quintet was powerful, as he looked around the rehearsal space, he realized that what he really wanted was to know his daughter. To play the piano with her. To watch her grow up.

He didn't have a plan, but he knew that the Hal Greene Quintet, their stand at the Hidden Door club, and their recording session weren't for him. Not right now.

"Thanks, but I need to go home to Liverpool," he said.

Hal gave a sharp nod. "I don't know many musicians who would turn down this chance, but I respect you all the more for it. If circumstances ever change, call me. I can always use a good sax player."

"Thank you," said Joshua.

Back out on the road, he looked up at the sky. The clouds had broken, and the sun was shining again.

Viv

July 21, 1945

Viv stood at the hob, a half apron wrapped around her waist. Maggie sat at the kitchen table, a book they'd borrowed from Kate's children in front of her. Viv smiled as she watched her daughter turn the pages, marveling at how grown up Maggie was reading chapter books.

It was Maggie's birthday, and so Viv was doing her best to cook a special breakfast for her with what her ration book could buy. That, she realized, was one of the simple joys that being reunited with her daughter had brought her. Time together.

The week had been far from perfect. Viv had felt the inevitable jolt of jealousy when Maggie had asked whether she could write to Mr. and Mrs. Thompson. However, when she saw the hopefulness behind her daughter's eyes, she relented. The Thompsons had been Maggie's foster parents for nearly six years. Viv could rage and scream and risk snapping the delicate bond she was beginning to forge with her daughter, or she could admit that the couple would always be a part of Maggie's childhood in ways that Viv would never like or understand.

Then there was the matter of her job. After Joshua telephoned, she'd taken Maggie to her in-laws and then gone to the South East Delivery Office to see Mr. Rowan. He'd sat quietly while she explained the situation, and then he'd tried to find a way that he could make her shifts as a postie work. However, after an hour of back-and-forth, they'd both agreed that it was impossible. The early mornings wouldn't work with a child's school schedule, and Viv was unwilling to have her daughter wake up each morning and find her gone.

The following day, Viv had taken Maggie with her to the South East Delivery Office to introduce her daughter to Vanessa, Betty, Rose, and Mr. Rowan and to say goodbye. Then she'd gone to Seth's shop and asked him if his offer of a job still stood. He'd said yes immediately.

Viv gazed at her daughter. It still felt like a wonder that Maggie was sitting there quietly at the kitchen table. Viv was determined not to let a day go by without being grateful for the second chance she'd been given. "Little Bear, time to wash your hands," she said.

Maggie scrunched up her nose. "You can't call me Little Bear anymore, Mummy. It's a baby name."

She planted a hand on one hip. "Then what should I call you?"

Her daughter cocked her head to one side, deep in thought. Finally, she said, "Just Maggie, I think."

"Just Maggie it is, then," Viv said with a smile.

There was a knocking on the door to the flat. "Maybe Mrs. Shannon decided to join us after all. Could you answer it?"

Maggie set down her book and hopped up from her chair. The sound of her shoes pounding on the floor made Viv grin, but still she shouted, "No running, Maggie!"

She could hear her daughter slow and then make her way down the stairs. Viv lifted the edge of one of the precious real eggs she'd managed to find at the shop the day before to check whether it was done. Compared to the horrible tinned egg powder the government tried to convince all of Britain was a good substitute for fresh, it would feel like a feast.

Two pairs of feet sounded on the stairs, announcing their guest's arrival.

"Mrs. Shannon, I'm glad you—"

She turned and saw it wasn't Mrs. Shannon trailing after her daughter but Joshua.

"Daddy's here!" sang out Maggie.

"Hello, Viv," said Joshua.

Viv put down the spatula and wiped her hands on her apron. "Joshua. I thought you were in London."

He'd called twice that week. They'd barely spoken—he'd spent all of his time on Maggie, as he should. After the second call, Maggie had bounded up the stairs, Tig in hand, and reported that her "daddy" told her that he had a birthday present for her. Viv assumed that it would arrive in the post, sent from London because he couldn't get away from his life there.

This is how it will be, Viv had thought to herself, reconciled to reality. By the end of their trip to find Maggie, Viv had no doubt that Joshua was interested in their daughter even if she'd been reluctant to believe it at first. She'd wondered for a mild moment whether he would stay in Liverpool, making up for lost time. She'd surprised herself by not disliking the idea as much as she once might have because how could anyone, having met Maggie, not fall in love with her?

It had surprised her just as much how disappointed she'd been to find that, just one day after arriving in Liverpool, he was already back in London.

Now here he was, standing in her kitchen.

"I came back from London yesterday night, but it was late enough that I didn't want to disturb you both," he said.

"I don't understand. You're supposed to be in rehearsals," she said.

He shook his head. "I quit the band."

"What? Why?"

"I didn't see how I could keep on in London while you were both here," he said.

Viv's eyes widened.

"I know I've made mistakes, but I want to do this the right way," he said. "I needed to go back to London because I had to wrap some things up. I closed up my flat, and I spoke to my bandleader in person. It's a small world, and reputation matters. I wanted to quit the right way. But I'm back."

"What about the club you'd be playing at. The record. Isn't that what you wanted?" Viv asked.

"I thought it was, and it still is, but I found something more important." He put a gentle hand on Maggie's shoulder. "I want a second chance."

She wanted to believe it—she really did—but that old suspicion reared its head again. "Maggie, could you go play in your room?"

"What about breakfast?" asked Maggie.

"Oh!" Viv swiftly scooped the eggs out of the pan and deposited one on the plate in front of Maggie. Then she shoved it into her daughter's hands. "You can eat in your room. I need to speak to your father."

Maggie merrily gathered up her plate and her book and flounced out.

"She seems to be cheering up, doesn't she?" he asked with an amused smile.

"What do you mean by a second chance?" Viv asked, ignoring his question.

Joshua's expression grew serious again. "I really did mean it when I said that I was sorry, Viv. I am willing to spend a lifetime apologizing.

"We were so young when we married. I was scared. I ran. I don't know what else to say except that, when it happened, I genuinely thought I was doing the best thing for both of us. I understand now how selfish that was."

"We never should have had to marry," she said quietly. "We hardly knew each other."

He smiled softly. "Two dates. Do you regret it?"

She'd asked herself that so many times over the years. What had happened to her and the choices she had made had showed her the absolute best in people like Kate and the Levinsons, just as it had shown her the worst of others like her parents. It had caused her pain and misery. It had brought her the greatest joy.

There was no saying what her life would have been without those two dates, without a foolish decision in a car parked on a quiet beach, without a wedding that had started and ended in tears.

Slowly, she shook her head. "If it hadn't happened, Maggie wouldn't exist. Having her back, it's like the sun coming out again after the winter."

"I hate that I don't know what that is like, but I want to. I'd like to be a part of her life, and not just every once in a while when I can make it up to Liverpool. I want to see her as much as I can. If that's okay with you."

She knew that the decision wasn't really hers to make. "You'll have to ask Maggie, but I expect she would love that."

"Can I admit, I don't really know where to start?" he asked, looking a little sheepish.

"Start with music. You two have that in common. The rest will come," she said.

His gaze caught hers. "And what about you?"

"What about me?"

"We never really had a chance to get to know each other before we married. We could—"

"No." The word was out of her mouth faster than she could think it, but she knew the moment that she said it, it was the right decision.

"No?" he asked with a little laugh.

"Don't ask me something that we might both be embarrassed by," she said.

"We are husband and wife," he pointed out.

She popped a hand on her hip. "And what if we weren't? Are you telling me that you actually want to be with me? Not because we're already married and it's what people think we should do. Do you want to be with *me*?"

When he didn't answer immediately, she knew she was right.

"We were too young, Joshua, and we didn't have a choice. Now we do. I want Maggie to be happy. That is the most important thing," she said.

"And that means nothing could happen between the two of us?" he asked.

"If we fought or fell apart . . . it wouldn't be fair to her."

He seemed to think about it for a moment. "People will talk."

She burst out laughing. "People have been talking about me for years. I used to care, but do you know what matters more than that? My daughter. Everything else is irrelevant. It's better to be happy with the life I'm living with her than be worried about what other people are thinking.

"For four years, I was Maggie's mother. Then I sent her away. Now I'm trying my best to figure out how to be a mother to a ten-year-old who's acquired a taste for riding horses and lace-collared dresses. You'll have to do the same, but you'll also have to learn how to be a father faster than most."

Joshua rubbed a hand over his face. "I don't know what I'm doing."

"Neither do I," said Viv cheerfully. "We'll find our way together."

The thought of doing this with someone else by her side—with Joshua—heartened her. Maggie was already calling him Daddy and clearly didn't mind the idea of him being around. Maybe he could be the father that Viv had never thought he had any interest in being.

She wanted him to prove all of the past versions of her wrong.

"Would you like to stay for breakfast?" she asked.

"Is it a birthday breakfast?"

"It is," she said.

"Good," he said, drawing something out of his jacket pocket. "I have something for Maggie."

"A present?" Maggie asked through the door.

"I thought you were in your room," said Viv, pushing open the door to find her daughter sitting on the corridor floor with a half-eaten egg on her plate.

"It sounded like you were going to have a serious conversation, and no one ever lets me listen to serious conversations," said Maggie.

She laughed. "All right, then. Why don't you sit down and we'll finish breakfast?"

Viv managed to make three plates out of the remaining breakfast, and she settled down between Joshua and Maggie to eat.

Before she began, however, Joshua slid the small present across the table to Maggie. "Here."

Maggie tore off the brown paper wrapping and held up a little box. She opened it and pulled out a long, flat beige object.

"What is it?" Maggie asked with a frown.

"It's a reed. I thought you might want to give the saxophone a go. I know someone who will get me a secondhand instrument. You can try it out and tell me what you think," he said.

"Thank you!" cried Maggie, throwing her arms around Joshua's neck.

"So there will be two of you now?" Viv asked with mock exasperation.

"There can never be enough musicians in a family," he said. "I looked up one of my old bandleaders. He wants me to come on as lead sax. We're playing at the Locarno on Wednesday."

The place where they'd met. The ballroom where it all started.

Viv began to laugh. For the first time in a long time, her heart felt full.

Viv

July 1952

"Has it come?" Joshua asked, taking off his hat as soon as he walked through the door and depositing it on his usual hook in the entryway.

"Yes. She's in the kitchen, waiting for you. She didn't want to open it before you arrived," said Viv, accepting a kiss on the cheek from her husband.

To most looking in, theirs would seem like a strange arrangement. All these years, Viv and Joshua had remained married, despite the fact that he lived on his own in a flat near the city center and she had the house. One night the previous year, while waiting up for Maggie to come back from her first dance with school friends, Joshua had floated the idea of an annulment or a divorce over tumblers of whiskey. Viv, to her surprise, didn't balk at the idea as she once might have. More than a decade away from the Church had softened some of her feelings. However, when they really thought about it, there was no one in either of their lives to make a divorce necessary, and their marriage worked in its own way.

For Viv's part, she'd learned to love her independence. She'd been brokenhearted when Mrs. Shannon had died four years ago; however, her kind landlady had one last surprise in store for her. She'd left Viv the house and all its contents. It had taken nearly a year of construction and almost all of Viv's savings but, with the help of some friends of Sam's, they'd managed to convert it back into a house once again. Finally Viv had the home she had always dreamed of with enough room to share with Maggie and their cat, Milly. Her life looked like the dream she'd conjured up for herself while riding her Federal around the streets of Wavertree at the start of the war.

"Dad?" Maggie called from the kitchen.

"She's nervous," Viv warned in a low voice. "I almost didn't go into your dad's shop today to stay home with her."

"She doesn't have anything to be nervous about," Joshua said, but she could tell from the way that he hurried through to the kitchen that he was just as on edge as their daughter.

Viv followed Joshua into the kitchen and found Maggie sitting at the kitchen table with an envelope in front of her.

"Are you ready, dearest?" Viv asked, passing a hand over her daughter's short, curled hair, which was cut to make her look like Elizabeth Taylor.

"Yes. I think so," said Maggie sucking in a breath.

"Just remember, no matter whether you passed or not, you worked hard," said Joshua, hugging their daughter.

"Thanks, Dad," said Maggie quietly.

Viv watched as her daughter took a deep breath and then tore open the envelope to pull her A level results free. The new testing system had only been introduced the year before, but it had already become recognized as the gold standard for judging whether eager, ambitious young students like Maggie would be suitable for university admissions.

As Maggie unfolded the paper, Viv held her breath.

A grin broke out over her daughter's face. "All passes."

Viv let out a cheer, and she rushed to hug her daughter. "My brilliant girl!"

Maggie started laughing as Joshua swept her up and spun her around. "Your aunt Rebecca will be so proud!"

"She's been talking about you going to Liverpool for years now," said Viv with a laugh.

Rebecca had hung up her WRNS uniform and entered the University of Liverpool the following autumn. After getting her PhD, she was invited to join the faculty as a lecturer in mathematics. She'd been lobbying for her niece to attend since she'd caught wind that Maggie had developed a greater interest in her studies than she had in music.

"Congratulations, darling," said Viv, hugging her daughter.

"Thanks, Mum," said Maggie.

Viv gave Maggie an extra squeeze and then went to pull the pie they'd have for tea out of the oven.

After they'd eaten, Maggie's friend Sheila picked her up to go to the cinema, leaving Viv and Joshua to do the washing up. Viv was elbow-deep in suds with Joshua drying when he asked, "Are you okay?"

Viv glanced at him. "Why wouldn't I be okay?"

He shrugged. "She's leaving. I know how much you hate the thought of that."

Viv stopped scrubbing. "You're right. I don't like the thought of her leaving."

"She could live here when she's at university."

She shook her head. "She wants to strike out on her own and take a room with her friends. I know if I don't let her go, she'll only resent me for it."

Joshua's hand fell on her shoulder, and she rested her cheek on it for a moment before straightening.

"She always was going to grow up. There was a time when I thought I wouldn't get to see that."

"Me too," murmured Joshua.

She smiled softly, knowing that in so many ways she'd been luckier than she'd ever imagined she would be.

For her, that was enough.

Author's Note

The idea for *The Lost English Girl* came from one of those old family legends that are fascinating but scant on details.

When I was twenty-one, I spent seven months studying abroad at the University of Manchester in the northwest of England. I chose that location specifically because of its proximity to Liverpool, my mother's hometown and the place where many of my family members still live. I was welcomed with open arms and a good story, as is my Scouser family's way, but no one opened her home to me in quite the same way as my aunt Anne.

Of all of my mother's three sisters, Anne seemed to me the keeper of the family photographs, stories, and perhaps a few secrets. It was through her that I learned bits and pieces of my mother's cousin's story.

This cousin had a last name traditionally associated with Ashkenazi Jewish families, which stood out from the rest of my Irish Catholic family. The story I was told was that his Catholic mother, my great-aunt, had "gotten into trouble" in a time when being pregnant and unmarried could mean unthinkable hardship for both a woman and her child. The socially acceptable options for a working-class girl like her at the time were limited: go off to a hospital or home for unmarried women and give the baby up for adoption, or marry the child's father before the birth to legitimize the child. In this case, my great-aunt and her child's Jewish father were forced by their families to marry and then separated on their wedding day. We believe that the reason behind the separation was because, in that era, a marriage between a Catholic girl and a Jewish boy would have been taboo. Family legend says that the child's father went off to America, while my great-aunt stayed in Liverpool, living with her own mother and raising my mother's cousin on her own.

I wanted to know more. Were the young couple in love? What did their families think about each other? What was it like for my great-aunt raising a child essentially on her own, knowing that people must have understood she'd only married a man outside of her religion to legitimize their child? What was her husband and his family's side of the story?

Years later, I began to write a short story about a woman who marries the father of her child and is separated from him on their wedding day. Being a novelist, that short story soon stretched to fifty pages and then eventually became the book you've just read.

Religion in Liverpool

In building out the characters of Viv and Joshua and their families, I became interested in the relationship between Catholic, Jewish, and other religious communities in Liverpool during the interwar and wartime periods.

For centuries, Liverpool has been a vibrant port city that has seen the settlement of many different groups of people, giving it its unique identity today. During the early twentieth century, Liverpool had a very large Irish Catholic population, an identity that it still maintains, although to a lesser degree today. Liverpool's Jewish community, which has its roots in the 1700s, is also one of the oldest in Britain. In researching this book, I found that in the 1930s and 1940s Catholic and Jewish families would likely have lived side by side rather than in strongly delineated communities of a single religion. That meant there were opportunities for people from different religious backgrounds to mix and interact.

Dr. Tony Kushner, professor of the history of Jewish/non-Jewish relations at Southampton University, was incredibly generous with his time in giving me a grounding as to what the experience of the Jewish community in Liverpool during the interwar years might have been, as well as the individual experience. Additionally, speaking to Dr. Tereza Ward about her work on intermarriage and how Joshua's family might have viewed his wedding to a Catholic woman was invaluable.

Evacuations during World War II

A number of my mother's siblings were children evacuated from Liverpool on the eve of World War II. Operation Pied Piper, which began on September 1, 1939, officially relocated to the countryside approximately 1.5 million children and vulnerable people from urban centers in London, Liverpool, and other cities that the government deemed at high risk of aerial attack. This precaution proved to be prudent. Liverpool suffered many nights of bombing, including the August 1940 bombings described in *The Lost English Girl*; the Christmas Blitz of 1940, when 365 people were killed; and the May Blitz from May 1 to May 7, 1941, which left nearly three thousand casualties and leveled entire sections of the city. The Liverpool Central Library has an excellent collection of harrowing photographs and eyewitness accounts of the bombings and their aftermath.

There were further evacuations during the war, but Operation Pied Piper is indelible on the British memory because of the sheer scale of it and the unforgettable images of small children wearing name tags on their coats and carrying tiny suitcases as their parents put them on evacuation trains in the care of teachers, nuns, or other adults. These images were evoked in 2022 as people fled the Russian invasion of Ukraine, in some cases making the impossible choice to send their children on without them so they could remain and fight.

By all accounts, the children in Britain who were evacuated during World War II had a mixed bag of experiences in their foster homes. In Julie Summers's book *When the Children Came Home: Stories of Wartime Evacuees*, she draws on interviews and recollections from many people who were sent from their homes as children. To some city-raised children, their new rural homes were strange places that never felt fully comfortable. Others, however, discovered a lifelong love of the British countryside during their evacuations. The families fostering some children were warm and welcoming, while it's also possible to find stories of abuse or neglect.

The Thompsons and what they did in taking Maggie after the bombing of Beam Cottage is pure fiction. However, again, family lore provided some of the early structure for that story line. My mother's eldest siblings were evacuated during the war and sent to live with families in North Wales, as were many other Liverpudlian children. The story goes that, toward the end of the war, the childless older couple fostering my aunt telephoned my grandmother and asked if they could adopt my aunt. My grandmother was having none of it, and my aunt returned home.

Returning Home

The Lost English Girl didn't always end the way that it does now. In the first draft, the discovery of Maggie occurred much closer to the ending. (The timeline of the search and discovery chapters of the book were also set in 1961, which would have made Maggie a young woman rather than a little girl when she is reunited with her mother—an interesting but very different scenario.) In edits, I decided to reunite Maggie and Viv just after the war and give some chapters over to what happened when they returned to Liverpool.

I was surprised to find that the meat of Summers's book deals more with the psychological impact the evacuation had on children and their families than it did on the mechanics of Operation Pied Piper and subsequent waves of evacuation during the war. Before reading it, I hadn't thought about what being sent away from home because of a huge world event like a war would mean for children during some of their most impressionable years. Some children felt that they had been abandoned, and many parents and children alike struggled with their separation— sometimes for the rest of their lives.

The reunification of families could also be incredibly difficult. Some children returned after being evacuated to other parts of England or even as far as Canada or Australia and found their parents almost strangers. Given that the war in Europe stretched from September 1939 to

May 1945, a child who was five—the minimum age for the government evacuation program—might have returned home at eleven and far more mature than when they'd left. A child of twelve would be eighteen and eligible for conscription on VE Day.

Some families who struggled were able to overcome the very deep rifts that the evacuation caused, while others could not work their way past anger, rejection, and disappointment.

When writing novels set during World War II, I often ask myself what I would have done if presented with the same conundrums as my characters. It was impossible to write this book without wondering what it would have been like to send a child away the way that Viv and millions of other families did. Not being a mother myself and never having been presented with this choice, I can't be certain. However, I can say that I think many men and women were forced to make the best of incredibly painful situations with the little knowledge they had, and I hope that books like *The Lost English Girl* leave readers with a greater empathy and understanding of the lives of those who have come before us.

Acknowledgments

It would not have been possible to write this book without the support and generosity of many people. In particular, I want to thank Dr. Tony Kushner and Dr. Tereza Ward, who took time away from their own research to answer questions that arose in the researching of this book. Thank you to Marla Daniels for all her valuable insight and feedback while sensitivity reading this book. (It was a joy working with you again, Marla!) Thank you also to the staff at the search room at the Liverpool Central Library and the London Library.

Thank you to Dr. Mary Shannon, Alexis Anne, and Lindsay Emory for their support while writing this book, and Susan Seligman for providing an early read—and her husband for checking the Hebrew!

Thank you to Emily Sylvan Kim, the best agent an author could ask for, and my wonderful editor, Hannah Braaten. I am incredibly grateful to everyone at Gallery Books who worked on this book, including Jennifer Bergstrom, Aimée Bell, Jennifer Long, Sally Marvin, Mackenzie Hickey, Jessica Roth, Gaitana Jaramillo, Emily Arzeno, Caroline Pallotta, Lisa Litwack, John Vairo, Pamela Grant, Brigid Black, Christine Masters, Jaime Putorti, Paul O'Halloran, Fiona Sharp, and Andrew Nguyễn. Thank you also to Kristin Dwyer and Jessica Brock from Leo PR, and Danielle Noe from Ward Consulting Co.

Thank you to all of my readers who made it possible for *The Lost*

English Girl to be my first book written as a full-time author, but in particular, the faithful viewers of Ask an Author with Julia Kelly.

Mum, Dad, Justine, and Mark, you have been wonderful and supportive, cheerleading for me every step of the way. I cannot thank you enough.

And finally, my greatest thanks to my partner, Arthur, who was by my side for every word of this book, happily providing countless cups of tea, hugs, and pep talks. I cannot imagine how I would have made it through this crazy, exciting first year of full-time writing without all of your love and support.